OF FLAMES & FATE

Claire Butler

Page Turner Publishing

Copyright © [2026] by Claire Butler

All rights reserved.

No portion of this book may be reproduced or transmitted in any form or by any means, electronic or mechanical, including photocopying, recording, or information storage and retrieval systems, without written permission from the publisher or author, except for the use of brief quotations in a book review.

For permissions contact Claire Butler.

https://www.clairebutlerauthor.com/

This is a work of fiction. Names, characters, places, and incidents either are the products of the authors imagination or are used fictitiously. Any resemblance to actual persons, living or dead, places, businesses, companies, events, or locales is entirely coincidental.

Cover by 100Covers

Editing by Phoenix Rising Literary Services

CONTENTS

Dedication	VI
Content Warning	VII
Note To The Reader	VIII
Goddesses and Gods of Merovia	IX
1. PROLOGUE	1
2. CHAPTER ONE	9
3. CHAPTER TWO	31
4. CHAPTER THREE	44
5. CHAPTER FOUR	62
6. CHAPTER FIVE	77
7. CHAPTER SIX	102
8. CHAPTER SEVEN	115
9. CHAPTER EIGHT	128
10. CHAPTER NINE	144
11. CHAPTER TEN	161

12.	CHAPTER ELEVEN	180
13.	CHAPTER TWELVE	199
14.	CHAPTER THIRTEEN	217
15.	CHAPTER FOURTEEN	229
16.	CHAPTER FIFTEEN	250
17.	CHAPTER SIXTEEN	268
18.	CHAPTER SEVENTEEN	285
19.	CHAPTER EIGHTEEN	296
20.	CHAPTER NINETEEN	317
21.	CHAPTER TWENTY	337
22.	CHAPTER TWENTY-ONE	359
23.	CHAPTER TWENTY-TWO	377
24.	CHAPTER TWENTY-THREE	394
25.	CHAPTER TWENTY-FOUR	414
26.	CHAPTER TWENTY-FIVE	435
27.	CHAPTER TWENTY-SIX	451
28.	CHAPTER TWENTY-SEVEN	473
29.	CHAPTER TWENTY-EIGHT	489
30.	EPILOGUE	506
	Review Request and Bonus Scenes	512
	Also By Claire Butler	514

About The Author	515
Acknowledgments	516

For all the best friends who caught feelings.
This one is for you.

CONTENT WARNING

Please note: This book contains explicit content and elements that may be triggering to some. It includes trauma, violence, reference to human sacrifice, reference to child abuse (physical), reference to slavery, explicit sexual scenes, strong language, drug use, grief, and death. It is not intended for anyone under the age of 16. For a full list of triggers, please visit www.clairebutlerauthor.com

Note to the Reader

The Divine Tapestry books takes place in a Middle Eastern inspired world. The landscape, the food, and other elements were inspired by various places and cultures that I have been fortunate enough to travel to and fall in love with. Having said that, Merovia is a fantasy world and this is a work of fiction. It is my sincere hope that nothing in this book is offensive to people from the Middle East. I have tried to ensure that this is avoided, however, if it does occur, please know that it was not intentional on my part.

x Claire

GODDESSES AND GODS OF MEROVIA

Water Goddess: The deity who holds power over the essence of water in all its forms.

Sun God: The deity who commands the sun and light. Artists often depict him wearing a fiery crown that symbolizes the sun's rays.

Moon God: The deity who governs the moon and lunar forces. He is sometimes shown holding the lunar phases on a string.

Goddess of Endings and Beginnings: The deity who embodies the cycle of endings and beginnings. She often holds a silver hourglass of sand.

God of Justice and Kingship: The deity of justice, kingship and cosmic order. He upholds the principles of fairness and righteousness. He is depicted as holding a balanced scale in one hand and a crown in the other.

God of Beauty and Fertility: The deity who grants the birth of children. He is known for his admiration and collection of beautiful women. He is sometimes shown holding a mirror in one hand and a rose in the other.

God of Fire and Ash: The deity who wields fire. He receives the sacrifices that are cast into the fire and is responsible for bringing them to the gods. He is represented by holding a staff of flame.

God of Earth and Salt: The deity who shapes the earth. He receives the lesser sacrifices that are buried and is responsible for bringing them to the gods. He is typically portrayed holding a fist full of soil in one hand and a fist full of salt in the other.

God of War and Valor: The deity embodying strength, courage, honor and the spirit of battle. He is often depicted as holding a shamshir or spear.

Lesser Gods: Gods who were human once.

Higher Gods: Gods who have always been celestial beings.

PROLOGUE

TEN YEARS AGO

ISA

Isa carried her lifeless body in his arms as he walked out into the desert, far enough away from the city to ensure that he wouldn't be seen, not even from the palace windows. He cradled her close to his chest. She was wrapped in soft white linen sheets, a death shroud. He couldn't see her face, but even in death, he knew she would be beautiful. A beautiful, cold, empty shell where mere hours ago there had been warmth and life and love. He knew that nothing really remained of her anymore, just skin and bones, but he still held her with tenderness. The instinct to protect and care for her had not dissipated just because her heart had stopped beating.

Above him, a riot of stars sparkled against the silk of midnight. The silver moon hung high in the sky, illuminating the sand dunes in shades of dark purple and blue. The night air was cool, though the sand beneath his feet still pulsed with warmth from the day. Isa had waited for the sun to melt from the sky before he stole Tahlia's body away from where the healers had left it in preparation for burial. She would not want to be buried here in the Kingdom of the High Mountains. Nor would Isa let the God of Earth and Salt claim her. She did not belong to him. She did not belong to anyone. She never had.

Goddesses cannot be claimed, only worshiped. He had said those words to Tahlia once. Her expression had been a blend of wonder and fear, as if she didn't know how to respond to such bold words. Isa could hear her voice clearly now as he had then, as if the memory were whispering to him in the wind, *I am not a goddess.*

But she was.

Since childhood, she had been chosen by the God of Beauty and Fertility to be sacrificed and ascend to divinity. She had fled her fate and hid from the eyes of the gods for years. Until one day, she prayed and begged them to save her king's life. In doing so, she revealed herself to them. The gods do not forgive nor do they forget. They hunted her. It wasn't enough that she had managed to outwit and trap the God of Beauty and Fertility. The gods came for her anyway. They took the air from her lungs, the beat from her heart, the blood from her veins. They stole her away from him.

In his first inhale after Tahlia's soul left her body, Isa made a decision. A small part of him continued to debate it quietly in the recesses of his mind but he ignored the voice of dissent. Nothing could stop him now. He had come too far to turn back. He cast his eyes up to the night sky and shivered as he walked. Not because the air was cold, but because it felt like thousands of celestial bodies were watching him, bearing witness to what he was about to do. Perhaps his actions stirred memories amongst the stars of their mortal existence before they joined the constellations.

Isa carefully laid Tahlia's body down on the sand. It shifted beneath her, as though inviting her into its fold. A delicate breeze stirred the particles across the dark dunes. He retrieved a small vial of oil from his kurta and poured its contents over her. Then he took out two firestones and knelt close to her body before he struck them. The spark ignited the oil-soaked cloth, and the flames quickly spread from head to toe. Isa stood, his body suddenly feeling heavier than it had a moment ago.

Around him, the desert was quiet and still, almost complicit, as he watched her burn. As if it were a secret they shared. Like he was the last soul remaining on earth. It was one of the desert's tricks. When he was young, on the threshold of manhood, Isa had wanted nothing more than to be a warrior. For the Naiab, those who wished to be warriors had to endure a trial. They would be cast out into the Idris Desert for eight days with nothing and no one to help them survive, forced to face their darkest fears, their truest selves. Those who survived told the same tale. They would speak of how the desert had played tricks on them, sending them visions and divinations. During his trial, Isa had been so delirious with heat-sickness that he had almost come to believe he was the last remaining soul on earth. The emptiness and isolation of the desert consumed him. But then he saw her face.

Tahlia.

"What have you done?"

The sharp female voice cut through his memories. It was as familiar to him as his own but still Isa could not bring himself to turn away from the burning flames. Even as the Water Goddess came to stand beside him, he maintained a watchful vigilance. He didn't need to see her face to know what it would convey: judgment. The favorite pastime of the gods. He knew she would not approve of what he'd done. Her eyes, portals to the boundless depths of the ocean, would be churning like stormy seas. Her features would be pulled tight like the sky before lightning cracked.

"I can't just let her die. She can't just ... not exist." Isa's words were both broken and fortified, defending the choice he'd made with every fragile thread of strength he had left. "Forever is too long."

"That was not your decision to make. She never wanted to be one of us."

The debate in the recesses of his mind grew louder now that it had found an ally to give it voice. It didn't matter though. What was done was done. The flames crackled and the sky was illuminated with drifting embers.

"She might condemn me for it," Isa agreed, bracing himself against the thought as if it were capable of cutting him to the bone. "I can live with that."

"So, it seems, must she."

If it worked.

The God of Fire and Ash may not accept her like this. Tahlia hadn't been sacrificed by a priest amidst prayers and a ritual. There had been a delay between her breath leaving her body and her bones being burned. Even if the God of Fire and Ash accepted her, the other gods may reject her ascension to divinity out of spite. If it didn't work, Tahlia would be lost forever. Her remains becoming one with the desert sands, absorbed into the earth and sky as if she had never existed.

At the very least, the God of Beauty and Fertility could not claim her. Isa reached for the brass vial around his neck, where Tahlia imprisoned the god who had hunted her. Its presence against Isa's chest was reassuring. As long as he lived, he would be warden to Tahlia's enemy and ensure that the god never escaped. It was all he could do to keep Tahlia safe, in death or divinity, as he had tried to do in life.

But he had failed her.

"What will you do now?" The Water Goddess's question held an undertow of sadness.

He knew she wanted him to return home to the Citadel. To the sanctuary his people shared with her. As a Naiab warrior, Isa had served the Water Goddess faithfully. She, in turn, had grown fond of him. She had even deigned to share some of the secrets of the spirit world with him. It was the Water Goddess who had told him about the beautiful woman he had seen in his visions. Who she was. Who hunted her. It was the Water Goddess who had told him how to trap a god.

"I promised Tahlia." Isa choked on her name. It sounded wrong to say it aloud now that she was no longer alive to hear it. It felt like a growth in his throat, blasphemy on his lips. "I promised that, should anything happen to her, I would pledge myself to Kala, the heir to the Black Sands."

In an ironic twist of fate, upon murdering the King of the Black Sands, Tahlia had claimed his kingdom for herself. But she knew that despite killing her mortal enemies and trapping the god who hunted her, the other gods would never permit her to live. So she had named an heir. Kala. A young girl from the Thaka who had served as a spy to King Henri and been adopted into his household. In the short time they had spent together, Tahlia and Kala had forged a close bond. Isa suspected Tahlia saw pieces of herself in the girl. Someone who had been abandoned by her family. Who had no choice but to fight for her survival. Someone who would never give up, who deserved all the beautiful things the world had to offer.

The Water Goddess turned on Isa in an instant, her eyes flashing with a gale's sudden intensity. "You cannot go back there."

Back to the Kingdom of the Black Sands. No one knew why the sand was different in that kingdom compared to the rest of Merovia. People assumed it had always been that way. A natural phenomenon. Except Isa suspected that it wasn't. He knew that the black sand held a dark secret. The Water Goddess knew it too. If Isa had learned anything living alongside the Water Goddess, it was that there was very little she did not know, and everything had a history.

He studied her now, his expression carved from curiosity. "Why?"

"You know why."

"The black sand."

The Water Goddess gave a subtle nod of confirmation.

"What is it?" he pressed.

Poison. Of that, he was sure. It had infected him the moment he stepped on its dark surface. He had tried to use his sand magic to wield it and move amongst it, but each grain felt as though it was a weight pulling him down to the bottom of the ocean. Each molecule held opposing magnetic forces that raged to tear him apart. The people of the Black Sands were seemingly unaffected by its power but Isa was not one of them. He was Naiab.

When Isa survived his trial, the Water Goddess had granted him sand magic, as she did for all Naiab warriors. He could dissolve into sand completely, only to transform back into a man at will. He could travel great distances amongst the dunes and fashion weapons from sand with half a thought. The granules circulated beneath his skin, encapsulated within water laced with the goddess's power in the form of turquoise tattoos. When he set foot on the black sand, however, the dark particles crawled inside him, taking root in his soul and turning his tattoos the color of ink.

The raging seas in her orbs calmed a little as the Water Goddess considered her answer. "A curse."

"A curse on the land?"

"Partly." Her clipped tone indicated she was unwilling to reveal more, but she leveled him with a penetrating stare. "You cannot return."

Isa knew the Water Goddess did not issue the warning lightly. In any other circumstances he would heed her words, but he had promised Tahlia he would serve her heir. Kala was still a child. She would need him if she was going to rule the Black Sands as queen.

The prospect of returning to the Kingdom of the Black Sands, of letting its obsidian poison seep beneath his skin, filled him with dread. In the short time he was there, he had fought every single second to maintain control over himself and not give in to the dark urges that were seeping into his soul. He had barely managed it. The relief he had felt upon leaving the kingdom was instant. The moment he crossed back into the Idris Desert, the black sand had drained from his system and his tattoos had returned to their normal turquoise shade. His emotions had steadied and he felt like himself again. That was after mere days in the Kingdom of the Black Sands. If he returned now, he wouldn't be able to leave for years. Isa didn't know how he was going to endure it or who he would become because of it. All he knew was that he had made a promise.

"I have no choice. I swore an oath to Tahlia and now I will swear one to Kala. My life belongs to her."

A weight settled on his heart as they both returned their attention to the embers dancing in the midnight sky.

"Then I can't save you," the goddess replied. "Either of you."

CHAPTER ONE

TEN YEARS LATER

KALA

"Kafei." The merchant greeted her as he swept into the great hall, his strides confident, a cheerful smile stretching across his ruddy cheeks.

"Stay where you are," she ordered.

He immediately stopped, her sharp voice slicing through his composure momentarily before he quickly recovered to spread his arms wide in greeting. The gesture was strange considering he was a guest inside her palace.

"You asked to see me, Kafei."

Kala sat expressionless on the dais in her throne room. The seat was large enough that she could almost lie down on it. Its cushion was embroidered with a complex pattern of silk thread but the structure itself was carved out of dark wood. Her friend Zaynab had designed it for her. Kala had chosen everything in the palace, from the tapestries that hung on the walls to the mosaic tiles that lined the floors. It had taken years, but eventually, there was no trace left of the kings who had come before her. Unlike them, she didn't need to sit on a golden throne to convey her wealth and power. There were far more effective ways to earn the respect of her people and intimidate her enemies.

Kala's back was perfectly straight but her long legs extended out to the side casually. Around her shoulders, her olive python slithered slowly, adjusting its position in response to the coiled tension it sensed in its master. She could feel the snake's muscles constrict as it shifted along her skin, its movements smooth and sure. It was strangely comforting to feel its weight pressing down on her, like a heavy woolen blanket around her neck. The merchant, though, was clearly not comforted by its slow, slick movement. Though he kept the jovial smile plastered on his face, his eyes watched the python carefully, sensing the threat of a rousing predator.

"Would you say you are an ambitious man, Murat?"

The merchant laughed indulgently, as if she were a child who had asked a curious question that everyone else knew the answer to.

"I am a successful businessman, Kafei. I run one of the largest trade caravans in your kingdom."

The largest, in fact. Even if she hadn't read all of his trading ledgers, his wealth would be obvious from the clothes he wore. They were opulent to the point of obscene, and each of his fingers were adorned with thick golden rings. Kala's informants had told her that his home was sizable, large enough to keep a wife and eleven children. He also had mistresses in every city he traded in and more children than anyone could count.

"My land has kept you rich." Kala observed as she ran her fingers down her tight braids, feeling the smoothness of copper beads interwoven within the strands.

Unlike the other kingdoms of Merovia, Kala's kingdom relied on trade to survive. The Black Sands provided unique agricultural conditions where certain plants and herbs that couldn't be grown anywhere else flourished. Craftsmen transformed the black sand into various unique wares such as obsidian glass, ebony ceramics, and onyx building materials. Both the vegetation and wares were rare enough that their demand was high and their price was profitable.

"You can imagine my confusion, then, when I noticed you have paid less tax this quarter than the quarter before."

A hairline crack appeared in Murat's cheerful expression but he quickly smoothed it over with condescending charm. "Your Master of Coin would be able to explain such matters to you, Kafei. Though I would think you'd have far more important issues to concern yourself with, such as your upcoming birthday festival."

Kala returned a brittle look. "On the contrary, I consider people stealing from me to be a very important issue, worthy of my personal attention."

"Stealing?" Murat's ruddy cheeks deepened slightly as he scoffed, his meaty hands coming together to clasp each other for support. "I would never dare steal from you."

Kala stood up suddenly, the movement elegant but strong, and Murat had the good sense to flinch.

"Then explain to me why you have not paid the tax you owe me."

Murat gaped like a fish, grasping for excuses. "Business ebbs and flows. One moment the market is saturated with money and the next it's in drought. Competition springs up from foreign lands, driving prices down."

"You are lying to me."

"Pirates!" Murat blustered. "There are pirates on the road. They come out of nowhere and harass us, killing my men and taking my goods!"

"Pirates." Kala quirked a cynical brow. "In the desert."

"They have cost me a lot this quarter."

Murat glanced around nervously, as if he had spilled a secret. He stilled when his gaze locked on Isa. The Naiab warrior stood across the throne room in the shadow of a marble pillar, his muscular arms crossed in front of his broad chest, his eyes watching the scene unfold as he waited in tepid silence. Murat looked shocked to see him there. The merchant should have known better.

Since the day Kala became Queen of the Black Sands, Isa had rarely left her side. No matter if she was learning to read and write, or practicing with a shamshir, or wandering the streets of her city, Isa was always with her. He watched over her and protected her but somehow, she never felt stifled by his constant presence. He always made sure to give her space, even when they were in the same room.

Kala stepped down from the dais, her movements luring the merchant's attention back to her.

"Kafei." Murat approached her, no doubt to try to grab her hand and press the back of it to his forehead in a sign of respect and fealty.

"Stay where you are."

Murat froze at her command. As she approached him, the python glided between her shoulder blades and coiled around her right arm. She extended her arm out, providing the snake with a branch to perch on, though her muscles strained beneath its weight.

"Have you met Cemal?" Kala asked innocently.

She was close enough now to see that Murat had started sweating. She could tell he wanted to retreat a step, to put distance between himself and the python, but his pride would not allow him to cower.

"Cemal is an exceptional judge of character. I trained him from a hatchling to detect deceit in people. You see, pythons have heat-sensing pits near their jaws." Kala traced a finger along the underside of the snake's smooth head. "These pits allow them to detect the body heat of warm-blooded prey."

The python slowly reared up from her arm, flattening its body, as its beady eyes peered at the merchant. Murat went rigid with fear.

"When a person lies, their body heat increases. Cemal can detect this and is trained to strike."

The python hissed and Murat released a whimper. Beads of moisture collected on his brow only to slide down his face.

"Please, Kafei. I swear to you."

"Swear to me that you will pay the tax you owe me." Her words cracked like a whip.

"Yes." He nodded eagerly.

"That you will never again try to cheat me."

He sniveled in agreement.

"This is your only warning, Murat. You are nothing without me. Everything you have, I can take away from you. Understand? If you defy me, you will not survive me."

Murat bobbed his head vigorously. It seemed he had lost the ability to speak, as well as his condescending charm.

"Good. Go. And know that I will be watching you."

The merchant stumbled backwards on shaky legs and then bowed low before fleeing the throne room. Kala turned her head to Isa as he stepped out from the shadow, his expression hard as stone. His focus remained on the door that Murat had fled through, as if he were fighting the urge to go after him and slit his throat.

"If he fails to pay by the end of the week, you can kill him." Kala strolled back to the dais and carefully uncoiled Cemal from her body, draping the python over her throne. When she turned back to Isa, her expression was curious. "Pirates?"

"Drunken rumors, nothing more," he said dismissively.

Her informants hadn't told her of such rumors but she didn't question him further. She knew Isa kept many secrets from her. Their relationship had been built on the things they refused to speak about. Tahlia's death. The fact that Isa had burned her body and offered her to the God of Fire and Ash in an attempt to force her ascension to divinity. The way his turquoise tattoos had changed to the color of ink the moment they arrived in the Kingdom of the Black Sands. Kala had accepted long ago that there were some things they would never talk about, but she also knew that he would never keep something from her that could harm her. So she allowed him his secrets, because there was no one in the world she trusted more than Isa.

After Tahlia died, Kala's world had changed overnight. She left everything and everyone she cared about to travel to her new kingdom and become Queen of the Black Sands. She was still a child, though she didn't feel like one at the time. Isa became her guardian, keeping his promise to Tahlia to serve her heir. Alone in a strange kingdom, Isa was the only person Kala knew. She drew comfort from his daily presence. Even though they never spoke of it, their shared love and grief for Tahlia bonded them. Through Tahlia, they were tethered, bound to a shared fate neither of them asked for.

"Murat was right about one thing." Isa shifted his weight between his feet. "You should be planning your birthday festival."

Kala rolled her eyes. She usually didn't make a fuss about her birthday but this year was special. She was approaching her twenty-first year, and she had been waiting for this birthday for a decade, imagining what her life would be like. What *he* would be like.

"Majid is planning it for me," Kala replied.

"Of course he is."

Majid planned all her official events and oversaw every festival in the city. The love of festivals was deeply ingrained in Merovian culture. There were festivals for almost everything, from the changing of the seasons to winning the favor of the gods and goddesses.

Kala began counting on her fingers. "A hundred musicians, thousands of barrels of wine, enough food to feed a small army, and two dozen courtesans for my private courtyard party. The festival will run through the city streets, the people will enjoy themselves, and I will be a year older."

"And Ele?" Isa probed.

"He writes that he will be here." Kala tried to keep her expression neutral, her voice casual.

It was pointless, really. Isa knew her better than anyone. He wouldn't be fooled by her nonchalance for one second.

"He's a man now." Isa's words were heavy with implication.

Kala averted her gaze, as if she didn't know what he was trying to say. Except she knew exactly what he was trying to say. As children, she and Ele had been best friends. Inseparable. In hindsight, leaving him to become Queen of the Black Sands was the hardest thing she had ever done. She hadn't known it at the time. She was young, so she gave no thought to how lonely she would be living in a foreign kingdom. Nor did she know that it would take several years before she would see her friend again.

When they parted, Ele had promised that he would visit her often, but time passed so quickly and the distance between them was not insignificant. They would make plans to see each other and then inevitably something would delay them. Ele had devoted himself to become a soldier in King Henri's army, and King Henri would frequently entrust him to carry out duties and responsibilities across his vast kingdom. Ele would never turn down an order from his king. His loyalty to King Henri would always be his first priority. Kala had considered traveling to Ele but she couldn't risk leaving her kingdom ungoverned. The only person she trusted completely was Isa and he would never let her travel without his protection.

They had only managed to see each other once, when Ele had traveled to her kingdom five years ago. At first, their reunion had been awkward. As a boy of sixteen, Kala had hardly recognized him. He was tall and lanky. His face had changed. He also seemed to have lost some of his sweetness. It surprised her. In his letters, he was still the same Ele but in person he was different. It had taken a few days to feel comfortable enough to joke and laugh with him. Her idea to sneak up to the rooftop of the palace and smoke balgarum had not helped the situation. She had heard that the plant, which could only grow in her kingdom, reduced inhibitions and stimulated a recreational high. Instead, it had given them both a stomachache. Eventually, though, they had found their old rhythm with each other. Or perhaps found a new one. But by then, it was time for Ele to return home.

Kala wasn't sure what to expect now that several more years had passed. Isa was right. Ele would be a man now. She could only imagine what he looked like. Tall and lean and muscular. Perhaps his face was more angular or his smile had changed.

Henri had recently appointed Ele as Captain of the Guard. It was not a surprise, given that he was known throughout the kingdoms as one of the best warriors Merovia had ever seen. He'd achieved what he always dreamed of, his life's purpose had been realized. So had she. She had grown into a powerful queen and under her reign, her kingdom had prospered. But Kala couldn't help but wonder who they were outside of their grand achievements. Were they still just Ele and Kala? Best friends? She wasn't sure.

When they were kids, Ele had promised to tell her a secret on her twenty-first birthday, something he hadn't even revealed to his king. Kala had held on to that promise all these years because it meant that she would see him again. She almost didn't care what the secret was, as long as he was here to tell it to her.

ELE

Ele strode up and down the lines of sparring partners, assessing every detail from their footwork to their thrusts. It was the middle of the day and the soldiers had been at it for two hours now, with the desert sun beating down on them like a fiery furnace. Their bodies were soaked with sweat, their skin flushed crimson. It took more than skill with weapons to become a soldier in Merovia. It required endurance. The desert was unforgiving, the Sun God relentless in his punishment. Ele had seen the most talented warriors collapse amidst the roasting heat. This was why he trained his soldiers in the middle of the day, when the heat was at its peak. It forged them, like steel put to the fire, so that they could fight under any conditions.

Today's training session included a mix of experienced soldiers and fresh recruits. Ele had been careful to pair them up accordingly so that none of the novices lost a limb. He remembered what it was like when he first joined the army. Despite his years of private training with a sword-master, at fifteen years old, he didn't have the muscle or the experience to stand a chance against the older soldiers. He regularly limped off the training field with broken bones and cuts that were deep enough to require stitches.

Most of the novices had their aspirations beaten out of them so badly that they left the army within the month. The Captain at the time saw it as weeding out the weak. Proof that they did not have what it took to become a soldier of Merovia. Steel was beaten into a sword, the Captain would say, and they clearly were not made of metal. Ele disagreed. There was a difference between hardening someone and abusing them. Even metal could be mistreated. Ele had refused to let the experienced soldiers win, though. Each injury had made him even more determined to become the best soldier in King Henri's army.

Now, he was Captain of the Guard.

"Keep your arm up. Your right side is exposed," Ele called out as he passed the pairings. "Watch your grip."

The shamshir fell from a recruit's hand, landing in the sand between him and his opponent. He sheepishly collected it and wiped his sweaty palm on his kurta before adjusting his hold. Ele continued pacing along the line until he paused in front of two novices.

"Stop! Everyone stop. Gather around. Not you two." Ele strode over to the pair who were looking aghast at being singled out. "What's your name?"

"Halil," the boy replied, his voice unsteady. He looked to be in his late years of adolescence and his sparring partner was not much older.

The soldiers formed a wide circle around them, relieved to have a moment's break from training to catch their breath.

Ele waved his hand at the two novices. "Go ahead and spar."

The boys looked at each other, unsure, and then begrudgingly complied. They parried and thrusted, trying to demonstrate the skills they had learned over the past few weeks. Ele knew what that felt like. To be desperate to impress others.

"Stop," he commanded and the boys halted. "Halil is focusing too much on the offense, trying to land a strike. He is forgetting to defend himself. Against any other component, he would have been hit by now. The aim is to kill your opponent but it's also not to die in the process. Sinan, swap in."

An older, brawny soldier stepped forward, his expression unimpressed. Halil shrank a little as his sparring partner gladly retreated into the crowd. Sinan took a stance opposite Halil and raised his shamshir, preparing to engage. Halil gripped his blade tighter and shifted anxiously between his feet.

"Begin," Ele ordered.

Sinan was quick, his movements strong and precise. Halil barely had time to raise his blade before it met crushing steel. The vibrations visibly sang through his lean frame. To his credit, Halil didn't lose his grip. He lost everything else, though. In one move, Sinan had spun the boy around and pressed the edge of his blade to his throat. Halil froze in terror, his Adam's apple bobbing nervously in his throat.

"Defend yourselves," Ele reminded the soldiers. "Live to fight another fight. Return to your pairings."

Ele began to walk away when the sound of a sharp cry and breaking bone made him pivot. Halil was clutching his nose with both hands as blood gushed through his fingers, dripping onto his kurta. His eyes were watering, and he was whimpering through the pain, though Ele could see that he was trying hard to bear it in silence.

"Who did this?" Ele demanded.

He speared Sinan with a dangerous glare, but the man had already moved several paces away. It couldn't have been him. Ele turned his attention to the nearby soldiers, and they each averted their gaze one by one, hoping not to catch his eye.

"Only a coward would not own his actions," Ele growled.

"It was me." A soldier stepped forward, widening his stance and broadening his chest in open challenge.

Ele should have known. Zaid. He and his two friends, who were now flanking either side of him, had always worked as a pack to terrorize the new recruits. Young, female, wounded–they didn't care. Anyone who they considered weaker than them was fair game. They were experienced soldiers, efficient at killing the enemy, but they also derived sick pleasure from tormenting their own comrades. As a young soldier, Ele had fallen victim to their abuse on more than one occasion. He still bore the scars.

"You assaulted a fellow soldier."

Zaid shrugged, unapologetic. "You told him to defend himself. He didn't. Lesson learned."

"The lesson was finished."

"He was armed. He could have blocked me. Really, he's lucky I didn't run him through. We're training warriors here, Captain, not weaklings. Not everyone gets a free pass."

There it was. The narrative that had dogged him for years and continued to nip at his heels even now. The belief that he had only risen through the ranks because he was favored by the king. His appointment to Captain of the Guard was recent. It had surprised Ele as much as anyone else. At twenty-one years of age, he was the youngest Captain of the Guard in the history of Merovia. But when King Henri announced his decision, he had spoken clearly of all the reasons why Ele had been his choice.

There wasn't a soldier in the kingdom that Ele couldn't best. From hand-to-hand combat to any weapon an opponent might choose, Ele had mastered them all. His fighting skills were renowned throughout Merovia. The people whispered about him in the meyhanes, saying that he must be god-touched. He was too fast. Too strong. Too talented. His skills were a gift from the God of War and Valor, they said. Henri hadn't mentioned any of those rumors, instead he spoke of the many missions Ele had led to victory.

Ele had not been born to privilege. As a child of the streets, one night Ele had tried to pickpocket a drunken prince as he tumbled out of a pleasure house. Instead of killing him, Henri had made him one of his spies. Hence, gathering information and stealing secrets came naturally to Ele. There wasn't much that happened in this country that he didn't know about. Ele had uncovered traitorous plots and thwarted uprisings. He had protected his king at all costs. These were the reasons why Henri appointed him as Captain of the Guard.

It didn't matter, though. The announcement had caused disgruntlement amongst the more experienced soldiers, many of whom had been waiting for the old Captain to retire in anticipation for their chance to rise. They felt cheated. Resentful. Since Ele's appointment, they had taken every opportunity to undermine him, whilst also being careful not to outright defy him. They would never give him enough reason to discharge them. Or kill them. They would simply make his life as Captain difficult and never accept that he earned his place above them. On the one hand, Ele could understand their bitterness. But it wasn't his decision, it was Henri's, and Ele would never refuse anything his king asked of him. He had accepted the appointment with outward humility and buried exhilaration. Right now, though, it was being thrown in his face like sand.

"You're right." Ele forced a tight smile to his face. "I am training warriors here. You three and me, right now. Let's fight." He turned to the crowd and raised his voice, "Everyone, make a circle."

The soldiers gathered and Halil fell back into line with them, still holding his spouting nose. Ele unsheathed his shamshir and twirled it by the handle, warming his muscles and letting the steel slice through the dry air. Zaid stepped forward, his features turning deadly at the chance to take Ele down. His two friends spread out to either side of him, cautiously approaching Ele as they would a wild beast. Ele knew that they were hoping to get behind him, perhaps take advantage of a blind spot, but they would never get close.

"I'm waiting," Ele taunted.

They advanced in a synchronized attack and the world around him fell away. There was no audience of soldiers watching him. There was only the slow beat of his heart and the swift movements of his body. His mind emptied of thought and reason. He was muscle, sinew, and steel. He sensed their blades, their intentions, and anticipated their blows. He dodged them with ruthless efficiency and delivered near-lethal strikes in a mad shower of steel. It was over in a matter of seconds. Blood had been drawn and splattered across the ground. Deep gashes ripped through their bodies, parting muscle from skin. It was only Ele's self-control that allowed them to live, though the scars would cheer him in the future whenever he saw them.

Releasing a frustrated roar, Zaid lunged again, and Ele delivered a formidable punch to his face using the handle of his shamshir. Zaid's cheekbone shattered and he stumbled backward as if he couldn't quite believe he'd been hit. The man was a mess. The flesh of his upper bicep had been ripped open and blood was rushing down his arm, while his cheek was jutted at an unnatural angle. Ele could see Zaid's eyes darken in reckless resolve to advance again.

"My next strike will be lethal, so choose wisely," Ele warned. "I have given you enough free passes for today."

Zaid hesitated and one of his friends tugged on his arm, encouraging him to stand down. Violent murder raged in his eyes but Zaid didn't take another step. Satisfied, Ele allowed himself to take in his surroundings again. His gaze fell on each of the soldiers in the crowd. Some were staring at him with open admiration and respect, whilst others glowered at him with hatred and envy.

"We train together as one fighting unit, but we do not attack each other outside the confines of the training grounds. We are King Henri's soldiers. We act with honor at all times. If anyone breaches this, they will answer to me." He let his words linger in the air for a moment, marinating in the tense silence. "Return to your pairings."

The soldiers dispersed to resume sparring. Ele watched as Zaid and his friends made to leave the training grounds, most likely to seek out a healer.

"Where are you going? I haven't dismissed you. Pair off. I'm not training weaklings here."

Ele hid a smug smile from his face as they resentfully returned to training. He knew they couldn't fight in their condition and he hoped their sparring partners would take full advantage of it.

"Eventful training session, little shadow."

Ele turned to find King Malik standing a short distance behind him. He was wearing a deep purple kurta lined with gold thread and several silver necklaces hung around his neck. His eyes were lined with kohl and his ears were pierced with diamonds. Ele flashed him a crooked smile. Malik had coined the nickname little shadow when Ele was still a child, and King Henri had sent him to spy on the former regent to see where his loyalties lay. Ele couldn't have predicted that Malik would fall in love with Henri, his loyalty solidified with a public vow and a stolen heart.

"Just showing the recruits how it's done," Ele replied.

Malik smirked. "Your king would like a word."

Malik inclined his head, and Ele followed the direction to see King Henri waiting beyond the training grounds, beneath the shade of the high palace wall. Henri was clearly trying to be discreet and Ele was grateful for it. If Henri approached him directly in front of his men, it would only fuel the unrest among some of the soldiers. Still, Ele knew that some of the men would be watching them regardless and using the king's presence as evidence of nepotism. There was nothing he could do about that, though. He was more curious to find out what matter could not wait for a few hours until training was over.

Malik and Ele strode over to Henri, doing their best to maintain an easy demeanor. Even though a decade had passed since Henri had fought rival kings and conquered the majority of Merovia, he still had the presence of a formidable warrior. Ele knew Henri and Malik trained together regularly to ensure that their bodies didn't turn soft, that they could dispatch their enemies if they needed to. When Henri had first arrived in this foreign kingdom, it was Malik who had taught him how to fight in the harsh desert conditions. Malik had always been an impressive warrior. It was difficult to say who was the most skilled between them.

"How are the new recruits?" Henri asked as they approached.

"Young and green but eager to prove themselves. Is everything all right?" Ele's brows tightened in concern.

"Are you still leaving for the Black Sands tomorrow?"

"Yes," Ele responded warily.

Henri knew very well that he was leaving to travel to the Kingdom of the Black Sands tomorrow for Kala's twenty-first birthday festival. Ele had been impatiently waiting for this event for what felt like his whole life.

"Before you go, I need you to do something for me."

Ele's heart sank. "Henri, I can't miss her birthday. It's important to Kala. It's important to me."

"You won't miss it," Malik interjected, ever the diplomat. "The assignment is time sensitive, that's all."

So was Kala's birthday.

Ele sighed, fully aware that he would never turn down any order given by his king. "What is it?"

Malik exchanged a look with Henri that set Ele's nerves on edge. "We recently received information that the priests from the Old City have resumed the practice of human sacrifice."

Ele's brows drew together in abject horror. The Old City was a holy city known for its devotion to the gods and goddesses of Merovia. The priests of the Old City believed that if they dedicated their lives to the gods and served them diligently, they might be called upon in death to ascend to the spiritual world as divines. There were many gods and goddesses to appease, and therefore, many rituals to complete.

Historically, these rituals had included human sacrifice. Through the priests, the gods chose their sacrifices and these chosen ones were taken to live in a Hara, which was a temple with a boarding house. The chosen ones were given the mark of the divine and then sacrificed to the God of Fire and Ash by being burned alive. Once chosen, no one refused. They were honored to be chosen and willingly surrendered their lives. Some even begged the gods to choose them, desperate to experience existence as a divine. Men, women, and children had regularly been sacrificed. Until King Henri outlawed the practice.

At first, the people of the Old City had been outraged, and the priests had called endless curses down upon Henri, inviting the gods to unleash their wrath in revenge. But amidst the people's righteous indignation, the gods were curiously silent. Henri had allowed the priests to continue all their other rituals, and they had responded by increasing their other offerings and sacrifices of animals. Ele had hoped that over time, they would forget about the old ways. Clearly, they had not.

Over the years, Ele had heard whispers that the priests were growing bolder in their efforts to reclaim their position of power among the people and their favor with the gods. But he hadn't realized they had resumed practicing human sacrifice.

"What do we know?" Ele's tone turned somber.

"Not a lot, unfortunately," Malik replied. "They carry out the sacrifices in secret. Only the most senior priests are privy to the times and location. Despite our spies' best efforts, they haven't been able to obtain the details in time to intervene."

Henri met Ele's stare with hardened eyes. "I need you to go to the Old City, find out when and where they are holding the next human sacrifice, and make sure it doesn't happen. Every priest involved is committing high treason."

Making their actions punishable by death. He was being sent to kill them. Ele glanced up at the cloudless blue sky as he considered his options. It was concerning that even Henri's spies had not been able to infiltrate this group of religious zealots. Ele had no hope of traveling to the Old City and finding the details of the next sacrifice in time to stop them *and* attend Kala's birthday festival. It would take at least a month to watch the priests' daily movements, find a way inside their ranks, and gain their trust enough to be told the particulars of their next ritual. He simply didn't have the time.

"There is one person who might know this information." Ele rubbed the stubble on his chin, already regretting what he would have to do.

"Good. I'll leave it in your capable hands, Captain." Henri gave him a curt nod of confidence that Ele didn't share.

Malik clapped Ele on the shoulder and gave it an encouraging squeeze. "Give Kala our love when you see her. Let her know we miss her and think of her often."

"You could come with me, you know," Ele suggested, not for the first time. "She would welcome you both."

"Another time." Henri pulled Ele in for a hug. "Be safe. Take whatever men you need."

Ele shot a look at Malik over Henri's shoulder. Malik simply pressed his lips together, the words hanging unspoken between them. Ele didn't think Henri would ever travel to the Kingdom of the Black Sands. Because the last time he had seen the Naiab warrior, who was now Kala's guardian, Henri had tried to kill him.

CHAPTER TWO

KALA

Kala loosened her headscarf as she stepped inside the shade of the sandstone building. The school was one of her favorite places to visit. She'd had it built several years ago so that even the poorest children in the kingdom could get an education. Unlike all the other buildings in the city, which were solid square structures with flat roofs, this building was an oval shape. Her friend Zaynab had designed it that way, at Kala's request, to replicate the sand dunes but also to mirror feminine symbols of strength and fertility. Inside, several classrooms ran along the outer perimeter, and in the middle was a lush oasis where the children could play. The elliptical shape of the building ensured that one half of the area would always be in the shade as the sun shifted across the sky.

The teachers of the school taught everything from reading and writing to art and weaving. They also provided the children with three meals throughout the day before sending them home to their families. Kala's steps were silent as she paused in the doorway of a classroom and peered inside. She did not want to disrupt the lesson. Dalieh continued instructing her class as if she were unaware of her queen's presence.

Looking at the children eagerly hanging on to their teacher's every word, Kala felt her heartstrings pull taut. In truth, she became emotional every time she visited the school. As a child, she had lived in the Thaka, the poorest area of King Henri's kingdom. Her life had been a daily struggle to avoid predators, survive violence, and find enough water and food to sustain her to see another sunrise. Education was the last thing on her mind, but that hadn't stopped her from envying those who had more than her. Clean clothes. Food to eat. A safe place to sleep. And a mind that knew the secrets of the world. She always thought she was smart, that she could learn if someone taught her, but she never had the opportunity until she became Queen of the Black Sands.

Isa had watched over her as she attended every lesson with private tutors. She still remembered his proud smile when she handed him the first letter she ever wrote. It was to Ele, of course. When she told Isa she wanted to build a school, he had promptly called for stonemasons to attend the palace so that she could commission it. Isa had always supported her in whatever she wished to do as queen.

Now Isa hovered behind her, guarding her back. It was unnecessary. She had never faced an attack while walking amongst her people. She was beloved. There was no need to take a dozen guards as a precaution when walking the streets of her city. Still,

Isa insisted on escorting her everywhere. Old wounds, it seemed, never healed.

"Today we are going to look at a map of Merovia," Dalieh announced.

The children squirmed excitedly in their seats as she unfurled a large cloth map and pegged it to a cord that was strung across the wall. A small smile tugged at Kala's lips as she viewed the map. Once upon a time, she had been unable to read maps but now she had the map of Merovia memorized.

"Can anyone tell me where we are on this map?" Dalieh asked the class.

"The Black Sands," one of the children said.

Dalieh reached up to point to a part of the map that was shaded black. "That's right. And what kingdom lies to our southern border?"

The children shifted and squinted at the writing on the map.

"The Salt Plains," one of them shouted. "King Malik's kingdom!"

"Correct. And who can tell me what kingdom lies in the heart of Merovia?" Dalieh indicated to the middle of the map.

"The Idris Desert. Where the Naiab live," a girl answered.

"That's not a kingdom. They don't have a king," a boy protested.

"Neither do we," the girl shot back.

"That's right. We have a queen," Dalieh replied.

"The Naiab have a goddess," the boy continued, keen to demonstrate his knowledge. "My father says no one dares to travel to the Citadel because the Water Goddess does not welcome strangers. The people who live there are said to be god-touched. The Naiab are giants who have command over the sands."

"Oh, I don't know about giants," Kala said as she stepped into the room. The children spun around in their seats, their eyes widening in an instant as they looked past her to behold Isa. Kala glanced over her shoulder at him, a cheeky grin dancing on her lips. "He's large but he's not a giant."

Gasps and murmurs filled the room. To her delight, Isa shifted uncomfortably and averted his gaze in mild irritation.

"Are you really a Naiab warrior?"

"Do you have sand magic?"

"Look at his tattoos! They're moving!"

"Children." Dalieh clapped her hands together. "Eyes on the map, please."

The children reluctantly turned around. Kala flicked her gaze back to Isa to find him scowling at her. She swallowed a laugh.

"Can anyone tell me who rules the rest of Merovia?" Dalieh moved her hand from the north-eastern corner of the map all the way down until it hit the ocean.

"King Henri," a child called out.

"That's correct. A decade ago, Merovia looked very different from this map. It was divided into five kingdoms and five kings ruled our country. Every year, they held a summit in the Old City where the kings could challenge each other or be challenged by anyone from the ruling family. They had to fight to the death to keep their throne."

The children gasped in horror.

"What happened?" A boy asked as the children leaned forward eagerly.

"One year at the summit, King Henri, our first foreign king, defeated a fellow king and took his lands. King Malik also defeated a king and claimed the Salt Plains for himself. Then they joined forces with the Naiab and declared war on the king of what used to be called the High Mountains." Dalieh pointed to a mountain range on the map. "A great war took place there, one that would change the face of Merovia. Because it occurred in a mountainous valley, we remember it as The Valley of a Thousand Heroes. Your queen was one such hero. She fought in the war."

The children turned to her, their expressions filled with surprise and wonder.

"What was it like?" One of the boys asked.

Unease slithered beneath Kala's skin. She tried not to think about the war or what happened after it. Her role in saving Merovia had helped to legitimize her as Queen of the Black Sands, but she had absolutely no desire to brag about it.

"Violent," she blurted out the word and then immediately felt foolish. It sounded like a gross oversimplification but it was true. "And senseless. I hope you never have to see one."

"Is that how you became our queen?" A young girl stood up from her seat. "You fought in the war?"

"No." Kala could hear the tremble in her own voice but she tried to keep an easy smile on her face. "I was named heir by the queen who came before me."

"There was another queen?" A boy frowned, confused.

Kala didn't dare look over her shoulder at Isa. The knowledge that Tahlia had been forgotten so easily was heartbreaking.

"Of course there was!" the little girl retorted. "My mother told me she was beloved by the gods. One day she even called on the Water Goddess to make it rain!"

"You lie!"

"I do not!"

"Children." Dalieh clapped her hands again. "Who wants to come forward and study this map?"

The children's hands shot into the air.

"One at a time, then."

The children filed into an orderly line. Dalieh made her way past them until she was standing in front of Kala at the back of the classroom. She took Kala's hand and bowed as she pressed the back of it to her forehead before releasing it again. Before the war, only nobles would request blessings from their king in such a manner, but now that there was equality among the people, anyone who dared could perform the act. It was also a sign of respect and recognition of rulership.

"The children are overly excited today." Dalieh's expression was apologetic. She glanced past Kala, extending her contrition to Isa. "They have never seen a Naiab warrior before."

Years ago, when Kala and Isa first arrived in the Kingdom of the Black Sands, a dozen Naiab warriors had been waiting for them. They were Isa's men, but they had been charged by Tahlia to keep her kingdom safe while she and Isa traveled to join the war.

They had expected Tahlia to return and were aggrieved to learn of her death. Isa had informed them of his pledge to Kala and given them a choice: stay in the Kingdom of the Black Sands under his command or return to the Citadel.

Some had stayed whilst others left. But the ones who stayed did not stay for long. Over the years, each one of them had left Isa's side until he was the only Naiab warrior who remained. Isa never informed Kala when they resigned their positions, she simply noticed one day that they were no longer around. Yet another secret he kept from her. Kala could only imagine how painful it must have been for him each time one of his men left to return home to the Citadel.

"Was there a reason for your visit today, Kafei?" Dalieh asked.

Kala shook her head, trying to clear her thoughts. "No. I just wanted to see the school. Do you have everything you need?"

"More than enough."

"Good. I won't disrupt you further." Kala turned to leave.

"We are always glad to see you. We are so grateful. For everything."

Kala glanced back at Dalieh, her words conveying gratitude for more than a building and school supplies. Kala had been a child when the war horn sounded in the Kingdom of the High Mountains. She had lacked the good sense to be frightened or to find a safe place to hide until the fighting was over. She had thought she was grown, but in truth, she was reckless. Living life on the precipice of poverty made one numb to the prospect of death. Death had been her constant companion, more friend than foe.

When she looked back on those days, she admired the little girl who had fought so bravely and naïvely. She had no idea that her life was about to change forever. She wouldn't have been able to comprehend all the things the war would cost her.

ELE

Ele strolled the streets of the Thaka, careful to keep his stride casual but his senses sharp. He hadn't tried to disguise himself, there was no point, and he didn't have time to waste. He wanted to be seen. The sooner he could lure her out, the sooner he would get his answer. If she didn't know the location of the next human sacrifice, Ele was screwed. There was no way he could carry out the mission in time to make it to Kala's birthday festival.

He kept walking at a leisurely pace, eyeing each door he passed as though he were weighing his options for the evening's entertainment. In some ways, the Thaka had evolved since he was a child, yet in other ways it remained the same. Ele still remembered the first time he walked these streets as a boy. Henri had sent him on a mission to find a young girl by the name of Kala. Henri had wanted to recruit her to be his eyes and ears in the Thaka. He thought that by making Ele her contact, she would feel more comfortable and accept his offer. The gold coins in Ele's pocket would certainly convince her as well. When Ele entered the Thaka, an eerily familiar feeling had washed over him. He almost felt like he was back home.

A decade ago, the buildings in the Thaka district were derelict, their mud-brick walls crumbling. Where the buildings had disintegrated into dust, there were cramped huts. Hundreds of people lived in those spaces, crowded together in squalor, poverty, and desperation. Most of them had been born in the Thaka and would die there, never knowing anything beyond the basic need to survive.

During the day, the streets of the Thaka used to be empty and silent. One could be forgiven for assuming the area had been abandoned. Except the air was pungent with sewerage, rot, and decay. At night, the Thaka came alive. All manner of addiction and depravity could be found on its streets once the Sun God turned a blind eye. Years ago, it had even been the perfect hunting ground to kidnap people to force into slavery. But when Henri learned of the Thaka and the mistreatment of the people by their former king, he had sought to help them.

Now the buildings of the Thaka stood with sturdy walls. The huts had been removed and there was sanitation and clean water. But change had only run skin deep. The people of the Thaka welcomed an improvement in their living conditions but were stubbornly resistant to changing their way of life. It was all they had ever known. The body shops and underground markets were thriving enterprises. For generations, the Thaka had operated under its own rules and hierarchy. The people recognized Henri as King of Merovia but he had no authority in the Thaka. They tolerated his soldiers patrolling the streets but it didn't stop them from carrying on with business. The soldiers were easily evaded.

"Captain of the Guard," a lilting female voice taunted.

Ele breathed an internal sigh of relief but kept his features neutral as Sabine slinked out of a nondescript door and cut across the street to stand directly in his path. Her dark hair was twisted into a long braid that fell over her shoulder, and her hazel eyes sparkled as if she knew all his secrets. In truth, she probably did.

Sabine was wearing long, dark pants with a simple beige kurta and a leather belt cinched at her slender waist. A scythe blade was tucked inside it at the front, and Ele would wager she had another tucked in at her back. Scythe blades were her weapon of choice and she was deadly with them. He had seen her slice clean through an enemy in close combat and throw the scythe across an impressive distance to carve into the throat of a rival.

"Somehow your new title makes you even more handsome." Sabine's hands traveled from his torso up his chest, exploring the hard planes of his body unashamedly. "Are you here for business or pleasure?"

"Business. Which is none of yours." Ele side-stepped her and kept walking.

"Everything that happens in the Thaka is my business," she called after him and quickly caught up to his stride. "You're not even trying to be discreet, walking out in the open like this. So obviously trying to get my attention. It reeks of desperation."

"If I wanted your attention, it would be easy enough to get. But I don't. Now leave me alone, I don't have time for this." Ele glanced around determinedly, as if he were looking for something. Or someone.

"You're sexy when you're mean," she purred. "Tell me, why are you really here?"

Ele gritted his teeth in forced irritation. "I'm looking for Qasim."

Her features instantly morphed into angry disgust. "Don't insult me."

"As I said, this doesn't concern you."

"Qasim doesn't know half the shit that goes on in the Thaka."

"I'm not after information about the Thaka."

"There is nothing that goes on in Merovia that I don't know about."

"You wouldn't know about this." He kept his tone level but the jibe was clearly implied.

"That's twice now you've insulted me. Fine." Sabine stepped in front of him, causing him to abruptly halt. She placed a hand firmly against his chest. "Let's make a bet. If I don't know the information you're after, I will owe you a favor. If I do know the information you're after, you will owe me a favor. Agreed?"

In one swift move, Ele grasped her arm, twisted it and forced her into a backstreet. As he released her, he shoved her up against the wall, caging her body between his own, before they disappeared into the shadows. It was so dark he could barely see the outline of her face. However, her breathy gasp, the fact that she didn't pull a blade to his throat, and the way she pushed her body back against his, told him that she welcomed the thrill. Her warm breath on his face meant that her lips hovered only inches away, tempting his.

Ele allowed himself a second to enjoy the feel of her breasts flush against his chest, her fingers grasping at the waistband of his pants, pulling his hips into hers, lining him up against her entrance. For years, they had flirted with each other, each one taunting the other, both lured by the temptation of their forbidden pairing; the soldier and the criminal. Sabine was undeniably beautiful, but there was something else that Ele found alluring about her. Something he couldn't quite name or describe. Months ago, Ele had given in to temptation and kissed her. It had been hot and frenzied, like a tightly wound spring that had burst free. He had stopped himself before it went too far but he would be lying if he said he didn't think about that kiss. Particularly when his hand was fisted around his cock.

"What do you know about the location of a religious ritual in the Old City that only the high priests are privy to?"

"Does the Captain have a kink for human sacrifice?"

Ele's heart jumped. She knew. "Tell me."

Sabine made a noise as if she were considering it. He pressed himself into her under the pretense of intimidation while he tried not to enjoy the sensation of her body against his own or the hitch of breath that escaped her lips. Sabine was a bad idea for so many reasons. She was high up in the hierarchy of the Thaka, her family having risen to become one of the deadliest cartels in the kingdom. He used her for information when he needed to but it was always a transaction. He would agree to look the other way on certain things, and she would give him what he needed to protect his king and his people. It was a delicate arrangement. Ele was no fool. He knew how easy it would be to fall into her depraved world and get tangled so deep he wouldn't be able to pull himself back out again. He had a reputation to maintain and his loyalty would always be to his king. As long as they used each other strictly for business, no one would get hurt.

"We had a deal," he reminded her.

"I don't know," she admitted reluctantly. "But I can find out."

Damn it. He didn't have time for this.

"You'd better find out. In fact, I'm calling in my favor. You're coming with me."

CHAPTER THREE

ISA

Isa waited patiently as he leaned against a wall, watching the back door of a small house across the way. He had followed the merchant Murat and his caravan across the border into the Kingdom of the Salt Plains. An hour ago, he had watched the trader enter this house, stationing a few of his men outside for protection. The men looked unfamiliar to Isa. Most likely, Murat had hired them after his recent conversation with the queen and the threat that now loomed over his head. The knowledge made Isa smirk. He was glad the man took Kala's threats seriously. Isa had never known her to back down from her word once given. She was a queen to be feared and loved in equal measure.

The men paced idly outside the door, bored, their vigilance dull and complacent. No doubt the house belonged to one of Murat's mistresses. Isa hoped it wouldn't take long for the trader to emerge again. He hated being away from Kala and was keen to get this business done.

Isa flicked his gaze up and down the street but it was quiet. Even when people passed by, they paid no attention to him. A small mercy, given that it was the middle of the afternoon and there was nowhere for him to hide. Despite wearing a floor-length hooded traveler's cloak that partially disguised his features, Isa knew he stood out. He was larger than the average man in every way possible. Standing over six feet tall was usually enough to draw curious glances, but then his body was also marked with tattoos that swirled beneath his skin. Only the Naiab had such tattoos, though theirs were turquoise whereas Isa's were black.

The poison prowled in his bloodstream, tainting his thoughts and feeding his darkest impulses. When he first returned to the Kingdom of the Black Sands, he knew he would have to find a way to manage the effects of the obsidian venom. Each minute he remained in the kingdom was a battle to stay in control of himself. If he didn't find a way to counter the influence of the black sand, he knew he would soon evolve into a depraved monster.

So Isa had ensured he left the kingdom every few weeks, even if it was only to spend a few hours in the Idris Desert, to release the hold that the black sand had on his soul. The moment he crossed into another land, the black sand drained from his system, and his tattoos would return to their normal turquoise color. His emotions would calm and his thoughts became rational. But the moment he crossed back into the Kingdom of the Black Sands, he felt the curse seep into his senses and his tattoos returned to murky ink.

He continued that way for years, leaving the kingdom as often as he could without raising suspicion to temporarily drain the black sand from his system. It worked. Until one day it didn't. One day, as he crossed into the Idris Desert, his tattoos did not change. They remained as dark as night, as thick as oil. It was like the poison had taken permanent hold of him, and there was no longer a way to rid himself of its curse, not even temporarily.

Since then, the dark urges had grown infinitely stronger. His emotions were in a constant heightened state. His mood swings were vicious, oscillating from brutal violence to insatiable lust to an irrepressible craving for power. The toxic sickness pooled in his gut, morphing his insides, coating his bones. It had terrified him to realize it was only a matter of time before he gave in to the depraved urges.

So he gave in.

There were rules, of course. Conditions that needed to be met. Justifications for the lives he took and the blood he spilled. Though he could never really justify the sadistic pleasure he felt as he drew out his victim's agony. It was like the ripple of an orgasm, the infinite high of a drug. Isa tried to keep his activities discreet. Where possible, he would carry them out beyond the borders of the Black Sands. The release he felt, if only for a few moments, was enough to take the edge off the dark creature inside him. He could fight the compulsions if he knew that soon he would be able to unleash his inner demon.

Today was that day.

At dusk, the back door to the small house opened and Murat stepped outside looking smugly satisfied. His men promptly stood to attention, sharpening their awareness of the surroundings. Honestly, Isa wasn't sure where the merchant had recruited such piss poor men from. They should have noticed a large, cloaked man lurking across the way hours ago.

Murat stepped out into the street and his men clustered around him in a defensive ring. Isa swiftly dissolved into sand. In a haze of particles and wind, flesh and bone, he cut down the men one by one. Isa moved like a storm, morphing from solid flesh to whirling sand, conjuring a blade from the granules as sharp as any forged steel. The men never stood a chance. Murat looked around at his men, now slaughtered at his feet, aghast. The trader's cheeks were flushed and his eyes were wide with terror.

Isa stood naked in front of him, his broad chest heaving from exertion. The black sand was heavier than normal sand, which made it difficult to command. It burned like molten lead beneath his skin and controlling it depleted his strength at a rapid rate. Every time he transformed, the process was punishing. It was why he rarely used sand magic anymore. The cost was excruciating.

"Sand wielder," Murat breathed.

"Were these men meant to stop me?"

"No! Of course not. I have nothing to hide. Nothing," Murat pleaded.

"I'm not interested in what you're hiding." Isa took a menacing step towards him, his arms hanging heavy at his sides. "I'm interested in what you owe."

"I'm going to pay the taxes, I swear. That's why I'm here, to collect the coin. I just need a little more time."

"It's been weeks. The queen gave me leave to kill you after one week."

The merchant blanched. "Such a large amount takes time to procure."

"Wrong answer."

"Wait! I can give you these." He tugged the bejeweled rings from his plump fingers. "Take them, in good faith. We could even come to an arrangement, you and I. If you help me pacify the queen, I could make you a wealthy man."

Isa sneered at him in disgust. "I don't want your riches."

"We both know that's not true," Murat said, suddenly growing bold. "Your people—"

Isa seized his throat in a death grip and lifted him off his feet. The rings fell from his hands as Murat gurgled, gasping for air. His meaty fingers desperately clawed at Isa's wrist, trying to pry them from his throat, but they were useless against him.

"What did you say about my people?" Isa squeezed until the capillaries in the merchant's eyes burst.

Murat couldn't answer even if he wanted to. Isa slowly lowered him to the ground before loosening his grip on his throat just enough to let him splutter out a few words.

"Nothing. I would never say anything."

"Except you did."

The slice was neat but the mess that followed was not. Entrails spilled out of the wound carved across Murat's belly. The organs sizzled as they hit the hot sand. Normally, Isa's retributions were not so quick. He would usually take his time, enjoy every minute of it, and ensure that the darker parts of himself were well fed. But this was not the place or the time. He was too exposed standing out in the open and he had been away from Kala for far too long. He needed to get back to the Kingdom of the Black Sands before anyone noticed he was missing.

KALA

Bones breaking. Screams. *Her* screams. The pain came with every blow, sharp and cracking, blunt and unyielding. There was no escape. She was a child and they were fully grown men. Bigger than her. Stronger than her. Angry with her. She had made a mistake, broken the rules. She was a traitor and there was no forgiveness for that. Not in the Thaka. In her memory, she had lost consciousness, from a blow to the head or the avalanche of pain she didn't know. But in her dreams, she never lost consciousness. Their fists and feet kept striking her. Breaking her bones. Crushing her skull. Grinding her into the dirt until she was nothing. Until she was dead.

Kala screamed as she bolted upright in bed, her hands sprawled out in front of her to ward off the next blow. It took a moment to realize that she was not in the Thaka. She was in her bed, in her palace, safe. She was not a helpless little girl anymore. She was a fully grown adult. A queen. Kala swallowed hard and took a moment to steady her breaths as her pulse hammered inside her throat. Her skin and nightdress were soaked with sweat. The silk sheet on her bed was violently contorted as if she had been wrestling with it. Kala ran trembling fingers down her tightly styled braids, finding comfort in their familiar knots.

The dream was not new. Sometimes she would go for months with only pleasant dreams and peaceful sleep, but when the nightmares came, they were always the same. Kala swung her legs over the side of the bed and slowly stood up. Her knees felt a little weak but they carried her. The curtains around her bedchamber were drawn back, extending the room to join with the balcony that wrapped around it. The warm night air filtered inside, along with the smell of jasmine and oranges. The silver moon sat high in the sky amidst a constellation of shimmering stars.

Kala wrapped her arms around her middle as she stared at it. Its majestic light drew her out onto the balcony until she was standing at the balustrade. Below her, her kingdom was sprawled out as far as the eye could see. Thousands of flat sandstone roofs cloistered tightly together, a maze of narrow alleyways between them, along with several open-air bazaars. Oil lamps burned in the windows of houses but the streets were deserted. Not many people would be awake at this early hour. Not even the servants. Somehow, it made Kala feel like the loneliest person in the world.

At least she had the stars for company. Hundreds of thousands of souls watching her from the afterlife. Or so Merovians believed.

Kala wasn't sure what she believed. It was a beautiful thought, that when she died she would become a star, her soul burning bright for all eternity. But she had seen death. It was far from beautiful. She had witnessed bodies wither and disintegrate and rot. A large part of her believed that when she died, she would simply be dead. That thought was less comforting.

When she was a child, she never thought too deeply about death, despite it following her like a shadow. She had fought every day to live but she was never afraid to die. The end of her life would mean an end to her suffering, so perhaps in that way she welcomed it. But even her miserable existence hadn't extinguished the basic human instinct to survive. Now, as an adult, she rarely thought about death. When she did, it unsettled her. She had so much she wanted to achieve in her life that death would no longer be a sweet escape. It would be a bitter end.

Kala shook her head at herself in reproach for spiraling into morbid thoughts. She retreated back inside her chamber and lingered there, unsure what to do. She thought about waking Zaynab. Her friend wouldn't mind, but she would definitely ask questions, and Kala didn't feel like explaining why she was awake at this early hour. She thought about waking Samir. He wouldn't ask questions either, especially if she was naked, but they hadn't been intimate in a while, and she didn't particularly want to resume whatever it was that they'd once shared.

Cemir slithered in her bed, his slit pupils flashing in the darkness. Kala sighed and wandered over to a small table by the wall where an engraved silver tea set sat. She poured herself a glass of mint tea. It had long since cooled and was now crisp and refreshing. She sipped it slowly, savoring the flavor on her tongue. All too soon, though, her small glass was empty. The thought of going back to bed was not inviting. She wouldn't be able to fall back asleep, and even if she did, she would surely resume the nightmare that woke her. Kala decided to go for a walk. She set the glass down on the table and retrieved an oil lamp. Holding it aloft, Kala stepped outside into the silent, empty hallway.

Several guards were stationed around the corner at the entrance to her wing, but years ago, she had insisted that they not stand outside her door. She did not want to feel like a prisoner in her own bedchamber. Besides, Isa's room was just down the hall. He would hear her if there was ever a commotion or if she had need of him.

Except he hadn't.

She had screamed and he hadn't come running into her room. Kala frowned. Now that she thought about it, his absence was a little unsettling. She padded down the hall only to linger awkwardly outside his door. Part of her felt foolish. She didn't want to disturb him if he was sleeping. Nothing was wrong. Not really. But then she knew he would not mind being woken by her. He would ask her questions but he wouldn't push her to answer them if she didn't want to. He would let her sit in silence, keeping her terrors to herself while he kept her company.

Still, Kala hesitated. Something tugged at her gut. An instinct. It did not feel right. She had both trusted and ignored her instincts before and so she knew she should trust them. Always. Right now,

CHAPTER THREE 53

her instinct told her to walk away and return to her chamber. She ignored it. Kala knocked on the door lightly before pushing it open.

Isa's bedchamber was completely shrouded in darkness, which meant that the curtains had been drawn shut against the night sky. Kala lifted the oil lamp higher and closed the door softly behind her. Her eyes drifted over the sparse furnishings until they settled on the bed. The sheets were undisturbed. Isa wasn't there. Kala furrowed her brows, troubled, but she tried to remain calm. There had to be a rational explanation for his absence.

Maybe he was secretly seeing someone. A friend. Or a lover. After the last of the Naiab warriors left the kingdom, Isa had made no efforts to befriend anyone. Except for the purpose of official business, Kala never saw him speak to anyone. He ignored the admiring looks women threw his way and rejected the blatant offers for company. Isa kept to himself, dedicating his time and attention exclusively to Kala. But perhaps she had failed to notice something. Maybe he had met someone and preferred to keep his liaisons private.

Or, more likely, he could have been called away to deal with something urgent. Perhaps he didn't want to wake her and planned to tell her about it later. Kala decided she would ask the guards. She turned to leave but her gaze caught on something in the far corner of the room. Her steps were tentative as she approached it. She held the oil lamp higher to illuminate a small golden bowl, which was perched on a carved pedestal. It was half filled with water, scented with rose petals, and surrounded by ceremonial objects. The ash of burned incense smeared the surface of the wood, but the arrangement of flowers appeared to be fresh. Kala's heart stopped when she saw what lay beside them.

A band of silver bells.

With hesitant fingers, Kala picked the band up to inspect it but she already knew who it belonged to. Tahlia. Once the most coveted courtesan in Merovia, Tahlia had worn bands of silver bells around her ankles, wrists, and hips. The tinkle of the bells had added a hypnotic sound to every movement she made when she danced. Watching Tahlia dance felt like being lost in a dream. She had danced as if her body were not made of bones. Like the rules of gravity did not apply to her. It had been her source of power and she wielded it effortlessly. Anyone who watched her was spellbound and she held them prisoner, to do with what she wished.

The silver bells were almost weightless in Kala's palm. They should have been tarnished from years of neglect but someone had polished them, preserving their shine. Isa. This was a shrine to Tahlia. Isa was making offerings to a goddess.

Kala stood for a moment in stunned silence but then spoke aloud into the darkness. "Did you know about this?"

A voice danced into her mind like wind caressing silk.

Yes.

It was not a thought or a memory. The voice did not belong to Kala. The first time Tahlia wandered inside her consciousness, Kala had stood rooted on the spot, unsure what to do. But she knew without a doubt that the voice belonged to Tahlia. It was not a conjuring of her own grief or imagination. Tears had welled in her eyes and her heart felt like it might crack open because up until that moment, no one knew if Tahlia had ascended to divinity or not. After Isa burned her body in a desperate attempt to force her ascension, there had been no sign as to whether the God of Fire and Ash had received her and brought her soul to the gods. Every day, Kala had hoped for a sign but it never came. Eventually, she accepted that Tahlia had not ascended to divinity.

But she'd been wrong.

Months after her death, Tahlia had spoken into Kala's mind. She made her promise not to tell anyone about her ascension. She wished to remain connected to Kala, to help her grow into a powerful queen, but she did not want to disturb the peace that Henri and Malik had found after the war ended. She wanted them to carry on with their lives and rarely think of her. Kala had tried to convince Tahlia to change her mind but she was adamant. It was better to be thought dead and mourned than to know that she had ascended to divinity against her will, now doomed to be a goddess for all eternity. In the end, Kala conceded to her wishes and agreed to keep her secret. Even when Ele asked about Tahlia in his letters, Kala lied and said she didn't know what had become of her.

Since that day, Tahlia had spoken to her whenever Kala had need of her guidance. It was strange to hear a voice inside her head that was not her own. It felt like an echo in a pocket of her mind, tucked away and easily forgotten, but always there when Kala reached for it. What was more disconcerting than having a voice inside her head was when Kala allowed Tahlia to inhabit her body. Though

Kala had become somewhat used to the sensation over the years, it was never a comfortable experience. The essence of a divine was so powerful it flooded every inch of her mortal body and saturated every cell until she could hardly contain it.

Tahlia did not ask to inhabit her often but Kala never refused when she did. There was only ever one reason why Tahlia wanted to enter her body. To dance. To remember what it felt like to have a human form. The joy of movement. The expression of song.

"How long has he been doing this?" Kala asked aloud, though she didn't need to. She could just as easily ask the question in her mind, but somehow saying the words out loud made her feel like she was actually having a conversation with someone.

Since the beginning.

Since Tahlia's death. Kala felt her heart twist in pain as she carefully laid the band of silver bells down on the table.

"Why didn't you tell me?"

What does it matter?

"It matters because he is still holding on to you."

What made it even worse was that Isa was holding on without truly knowing if she had ascended or not. He was praying to a goddess he hoped existed. It was faith in its purest form. It made sense now why he had rejected every woman who ever looked his way. He was still waiting for Tahlia.

Kala shook her head in dismay. "This is no way to live."

Why shouldn't I let him live like this when he would not let me die?

Tahlia had a point. Still, it was wrong.

"He's still in love with you."

He never loved me.

Kala sighed. She knew she was not going to win the argument. "Do you know where he is at least?"

I am not his keeper.

"No. You're just his idol."

Go back to bed, Kala.

Kala felt Tahlia's presence slip away from her consciousness. Returning to her bedchamber was the last thing Kala wanted to do, especially when she still didn't know if Isa was safe. Clutching the oil lamp in her hand, she left the room and strolled down the hallway. Around the corner, guards formed a defensive line to the entrance of her wing. Their attention snapped to her, clearly surprised at her sudden emergence. Some of them dared to gaze at her thin white cotton nightdress before they either averted their gaze in shame or forced themselves to focus on her face. At any other time, she would have chastised them for it but right now she had bigger concerns than their roving eyes.

"Do you know where Isa is tonight?"

"No, Kafei," one of the guards replied. "Is everything all right?"

No. She didn't know. Her discovery in his room meant that Isa was clearly not visiting a secret lover. Most likely, he was carrying out official business, not that he had shared his plans with the guards or her. He could be lying dead somewhere, and she would have no knowledge of it because he hadn't told her where he was going. Kala pinched her eyes closed and forced a deep breath. She was being irrational. Isa was Naiab. A sand wielder. She had seen him take on dozens of men all at once and he'd cut them down like wheat in a field. He was alive.

Without responding, Kala spun on her heel and returned to her bedchamber. Once inside, she retrieved a light headscarf, wrapping it around her hair and shoulders, before strolling out onto the balcony. She let herself sink down to the cool stone floor and leaned her head against one of the pillars of the balustrade. Kala didn't want to sleep but she also didn't want to be alone. If the stars were the only company on offer, she would sit with them until dawn.

Kala stared down into the dark streets of her kingdom and wondered if Isa moved among them. There had always been secrets between her and Isa. They were the foundation of their relationship. But perhaps that needed to change. She couldn't protect him if she didn't know his weaknesses. He might be her guardian but she was his queen. She had a duty to him as much as he had a duty to her. Still, Kala would never betray a word of Tahlia's existence, not even to Isa. Kala could only imagine what Isa would do if he knew.

ISA

By the time Isa returned to the palace, dawn was breaking. He remained in his sand form, innocuous particles sliding across the tiled floor of the palace, maneuvering past the guards who stood watch outside the queen's wing. Once in front of his chamber, he collected himself to whirl up in a sand funnel before pouring silently through the door's keyhole. On the other side, he materialized into human form, feeling his bones solidify and his skin snap tight over his frame. Isa braced a hand against the wall as nausea suddenly threatened to erupt from him. Sweat began to bead on his brow and the room spun.

There would be no time to rest and recover from using his sand magic. Kala would wake soon, if she wasn't already, and he would need to accompany her as she carried out her duties. He couldn't recall what she had planned for the day but her schedule was always demanding. As queen, she insisted on being involved in every aspect of governing her kingdom. She inspected things personally and made adjustments as she saw fit. It was what made her such an astute leader. She kept her finger on the pulse of everything and everyone in her kingdom. He pitied anyone who tried to deceive her.

Isa quickly washed and pulled on a clean kurta before leaving his chamber. He waited outside Kala's door for her to emerge but as time passed, he became concerned. She was normally an early riser, keen to start the day to get through as many tasks as possible. Isa knocked lightly on the door. Silence was the only reply. He entered the room cautiously. The last thing he wanted to do was interrupt if she had company or was in a state of undress. But the chamber was empty. So was her bed. Adrenaline flooded his veins and his senses sharpened. The sheets were crumpled and twisted but there were no signs of a struggle. Cemal slithered across the pillows, clearly unimpressed by Isa's intrusion.

A warm morning breeze blew into the room, fluttering the edges of the silk curtains, which were drawn back around the chamber, framing the view from the balcony. Isa's heart plummeted as he spotted Kala slumped against the balustrade. He rushed to land on his knees at her side, scanning every part of her body for injury, but he found none. In fact, she was snoring softly.

Isa swore a string of curses under his breath. He gently shook her shoulder and Kala woke instantly, her expression briefly disoriented until her eyes met his and a look of relief washed over her face.

"You almost scared me to an early grave," Isa growled. "What are you doing sleeping out here?"

"I had a nightmare," she replied groggily as she wiped at her eyes.

Isa's features tightened in concern but he didn't pry. If she wanted to talk about the horrors that stalked her dreams, she would tell him. Instead, he offered her two hands and she took them, pulling herself to her feet.

"How was your night?"

Something about her tone sounded off but Isa ignored it. "Less eventful than yours."

Kala stared at him for a moment as if expecting him to say more but when he didn't, she recovered quickly. "I'll change and be out in a minute."

Isa gave a curt nod and promptly left the room. Standing out in the hallway, he wondered what had been so distressing that it had expelled her from bed and marooned her out on the balcony for the night. Had it been a fear of the future or a memory from her past? Isa did everything in his power to shield her from the world's dangers, but he couldn't protect her from her own mind. Sometimes the most dangerous battles were fought, not with blades, but with thoughts.

CHAPTER FOUR

ELE

Ele sat alone at a table outside the meyhane and observed life bustle around him in the busy bazaar. The Old City was a holy place dedicated to worshiping the gods and goddesses of Merovia, but that didn't mean it was quiet or without vice. The bazaar was a heady mix of color, carnival, and shrewd negotiations. The strong smell of spices assaulted his nostrils, and the cacophony of sounds resembled a chaotic but strangely harmonious melody. Prayer chants echoed in the distance, mingled together with harsh bartering and sharp musical instruments. It was deafening but this was exactly why he had chosen the bazaar.

Located in the heart of the Old City, just a short walk from most of the temples, the bazaar was the perfect place to meet. If Sabine was followed or if anyone grew suspicious of them, they could easily disappear amongst the crowd, weaving between hundreds of shops selling everything from hand-stitched rugs to silk slippers. The walls of the bazaar were painted with a wash of bright blue, and the streets were narrow beneath ornate stone archways. Overhead, glass lanterns shone a kaleidoscope of colors across the stone. Ele had spent the past two days mapping out every inch of the bazaar. There wasn't a corner, or shop, or vendor he wasn't familiar with. The escape routes were plentiful.

Ele tapped a finger impatiently against the painted glass in his hand but he didn't drink from it. His attention was singularly focused on scanning his surroundings for any sight of Sabine. They had arrived in the Old City almost a week ago, after crossing the Idris Desert by camel. Every day that passed without news of where the next sacrifice would take place made Ele's stomach turn tighter. If they didn't get the information by tomorrow, he wouldn't make Kala's birthday festival.

Ele wasn't sure what he would do if that happened. Probably write a contrite letter to Kala with a thousand apologies. It would never be enough. He would never forgive himself for letting her down. He *needed* to find the location. Except it wasn't up to him. Sabine was the one with the street credibility and contacts. Upon arriving in the Old City, she immediately slipped away to meet with them, offering great reward for the right information. But this kind of information was not linked to a black market of illicit drugs or a syndicate of rare precious stones. Its association was a small group of devout priests. Money was not their currency.

So far, Sabine's luck had run drier than the Idris Desert, and though she would never admit it, Ele knew her list of contacts was growing thin. If she failed to get the information, not only would her pride be wounded, but she would owe him a favor. It was a small consolation. Ele would much rather she gloat in his face about the superiority of her underground connections than spend the next few weeks trying to infiltrate a holy sect in order to assassinate them.

The flash of an emerald green kaftan caught his eye as a woman moved casually through the crowd. Sabine. Ele tried to keep his posture relaxed, as if he were content to idly pass time watching the comings and goings of people. It took more effort than he would have liked. His muscles were taut with tension, his senses on high alert. Sabine strolled over to his table and slipped into the chair opposite him.

She leaned forward to peer inside his painted glass. "Milk? Who drinks milk in a meyhane? Once a foreigner, always a foreigner."

Ele opened his mouth to retort, but Sabine snatched the glass out of his hand and smirked as she tipped the contents down her throat. He would have tried to stop her but—he didn't. It was Sabine, after all. A shit-eating grin slowly stretched across his face the second the liquid hit her tongue and her expression changed. She doubled over, coughing violently, almost throwing the liquid back up.

"Scorpion's milk," he explained smugly and her eyes widened in horror.

The liquid was not actually scorpion's milk, that was what Merovians called it because it had a wicked sting. It was twice-distilled alcohol that had a somewhat milky texture but could level a full-grown man after one small glass. Hence, why he had not drunk it.

"You son of a donkey," she swore viciously as she wiped her mouth with the back of her hand.

"That insult means nothing to me. Foreigner, remember?"

Sabine sprang to her feet, her fists clenched, but then splayed her fingers against the table as she swayed a little. "I should leave you to chase your tail in this holy city."

His hand gripped her wrist to stop her from leaving. "Does that mean you have information for me?"

She glared at him.

"I'm sorry," Ele offered, even though it was entirely her fault for snatching the glass from him. "Please, sit down."

She sank back down into the seat a little too quickly. Ele suspected that if she didn't sit down, she might fall down.

"If I pass out—"

"I promise I'll carry you home," he said sweetly.

They had been staying in the palace, entering and leaving discreetly through a private door in the courtyard. When they first arrived, Sabine had mocked him about the pompousness of staying in the palace, surrounded by luxury and servants to tend to his every need. But over the past few days, Ele had noticed her indulging in being waited on, and he would bet anything that her saddle bag held a number of items it shouldn't.

Ever since the last summit where Henri claimed this kingdom as his own, the palace had remained largely unoccupied, except for a few guards and servants who kept it in good condition. Henri rarely traveled to the Old City, preferring to send trusted viziers instead. Ele understood why. The city held painful memories for him.

"It's tonight," Sabine said, clearly struggling to keep her voice steady.

"The sacrifice?" His pulse jumped. "Where?"

"Where the veil between the mortal realm and the divine is thin," she repeated the words as if they were second-hand.

Ele's eyes pinged as his mind worked to decipher it. The phrase triggered a memory from long ago. It was said that beneath the foundations of the Old City were secret passages where the line between the earthly realm and the divine was delicate. Some even claimed that they could hear the echo of celestial voices from beneath the depths of the earth.

"The passageways. But there could be hundreds of them beneath the city. Were you given a specific location?"

Sabine swayed in her seat. "I'm going to throw up."

"No, no, no. Come on." Ele helped Sabine out of her chair, tucking her firmly under his arm as he led the way through the bazaar.

Her feet stumbled like a newborn goat but he managed to keep her upright. Ele scanned their surroundings as they shuffled past vendors and stalls, taking the quickest escape route he could think of. Thankfully, no one paid much attention to them. If he could just get Sabine to the palace, she could pass out in comfort and he could focus on tonight. It felt like he'd been given a gift. If he could find the location and prevent the next sacrifice, he could leave the

Old City tomorrow. He would be late for Kala's birthday festival but at least he would make it.

"Still with me?"

"I'm going to make you pay for this," Sabine slurred.

"The location, Sabine. I need you to tell me or all of this would have been for nothing."

She scoffed. "You'll never guess."

"I don't want to guess. I want you to tell me."

"Beneath the palace. There's a secret staircase just outside the gates that goes deep underground."

Sabine mumbled the details as Ele guided her through the city streets. They almost made it to the private door of the palace courtyard, but then she slipped from his grasp and collapsed on the ground. Ele scooped her up into his arms and carried her the rest of the way.

Inside the palace, the guards and servants discreetly averted their gazes, pretending not to notice that Ele was carrying an unconscious woman in his arms. He carried her to the guest chamber she had chosen for herself and laid her gently across the bed. The sight of her made Ele pause for a moment. Unconscious, Sabine looked young and peaceful and innocent, far from the vicious, violent truth of her. He wondered what she could have been like if she had been born into a different life. If she'd had a chance to be kind and hopeful and naive. He couldn't picture it.

Ele removed her sandals and tossed them onto the tiled floor. When he moved to take her scythe blade from her belt, she suddenly roused and shifted away from him like she was under attack.

"Sabine! It's just me. It's Ele."

Foggy recognition crossed her face and the fear dissipated, replaced by a drunken, saucy smile. "Trouble keeping your hands to yourself, Captain?"

"I was trying to take your blades. I would rather you not stab yourself in your sleep."

"You care for me." Sabine drawled as her eyes drifted closed again. "I always sleep with them."

Of course she did. It would be foolish not to in the Thaka. Ele decided to leave the blades be. She did not look particularly comfortable but within seconds, Sabine was snoring softly. Perhaps it was better this way. Sabine would have insisted on coming with him tonight, if only to prove that her information was accurate, but it was safer for both of them if he went without her. He had brought a few of Henri's best soldiers with him across the Idris Desert, in case he had need of them, but it sounded like he wouldn't. There would only be a handful of priests carrying out the ritual. Ele would slaughter them easily.

Leaving Sabine, Ele waited in his bedchamber until night fell. Then he stalked outside. He moved like a wraith, traveling between the shadows of the palace until he was beyond the gates. The secret staircase was surprisingly easy to find when one knew what to look for. The entrance in the ground was masked by wooden panels, slightly warped with age, but the metal latch was not locked.

The staircase descended beneath the earth, disappearing into endless darkness. With every step he climbed down, Ele's instincts screamed at him to go back up. His skin became clammy, his breaths short and shallow. He hated darkness such as this. The kind of darkness that swallowed him whole. When his sandals finally hit solid ground, Ele pulled a small torch from his belt and struck a firestone against the wall to light it. The flickering flame was small. Not enough to draw attention from a distance but just enough to light the next few steps.

Ele recalled the directions Sabine had slurred and began walking cautiously down the passageway. The air was cool and heavy, carrying the faint dampness of the underground. He kept his footfalls light but even so, there was a faint echo. Ele strained his ears into the stillness, trying to decipher what else he was hearing. There was nothing and yet there was something. Traces of whispers. Undertones of existence. The deep sigh of eternity.

Ele rested his hand on the hilt of his shamshir. If the rumors were true and he was indeed hearing celestial voices, the blade would do nothing to save him, but the familiar bone pommel in his palm was still reassuring.

Henri had gifted Ele his first shamshir at the age of ten. He had ordered it to be custom-made so it was smaller and lighter than a normal shamshir. The blade was made of Pelascene steel, the finest there was, and it was engraved and decorated. A short golden tassel had hung from the end of the pommel. It was the most beautiful blade Ele had ever seen and his heart swelled with pride to receive it. Henri had once told him that a sword gains its reputation from the one who wields it, not the one who forges it. That day, Ele had vowed that his sword would be renowned across the land for vanquishing Henri's enemies and safeguarding the defenseless.

When he grew into a man, Henri had commissioned a new shamshir for him. The blade had the same fine Palascene steel but the pommel was not ornamented with a tassel. The shamshir had served him well throughout many fights, its sharp edge reaping the lives of countless enemies. Tonight, it would claim a few more.

A faint noise drew his attention up ahead and Ele quickened his pace. He could now make out the distant rhythm of prayer chants. His stride slowed as he approached an opening into a side chamber. Firelight flickered from inside, so Ele placed his torch carefully on the ground and smothered the flame beneath his sandal before risking a peek around the corner. He counted five priests wearing dark cloaks and a man dressed in what looked to be a white sacrificial gown.

Ele assessed the stone chamber from floor to wall to ceiling. His brows furrowed in confusion. Historically, the most important sacrifices in Merovia were burned in an offering to the God of Fire and Ash, who received them and brought them to the gods. The less important sacrifices were buried alive in an offering to the God of Earth and Salt who acted as an intermediary for the gods. However, there was no tophet in the stone chamber and nowhere for smoke to escape. Nor had anyone dug a life-size hole in the ground. Which meant that the priests were not planning to burn or bury the man alive.

The chanting ceased. Ele immediately tensed. One of the priests moved toward their chosen sacrifice but another priest held out his arm to halt him.

"Musa is not here," the priest said.

"We can't wait any longer," the other priest replied. He retrieved a kard from inside his cloak and handed it to the man in the sacrificial gown. "You are ready for the gods. You know what to do."

They expected the man to stab himself to death.

"Or." Ele stepped inside the chamber and the priests spun around, their faces mirroring each other's surprise. "You could choose to live."

In a flurry of motion, the priests reached inside their cloaks and brandished shamshirs. It was an unexpected turn of events. Priests did not normally carry weapons, only ceremonial daggers, and they certainly weren't trained in combat. Still, five against one was not good odds. Especially not in such close quarters. The man in the sacrificial gown took up a defensive stance, holding the kard out in a threatening manner.

Ele raised a single brow at him. "Really? You too?"

Six against one, then. Ele was beginning to regret coming alone, but his thoughts scattered as the room exploded in a furious storm of sand.

ISA

The creature Isa became in his sand form sometimes felt like the truest version of himself. It was born from blood, sorrow, and death. It lived to inflict suffering and torment. Its purpose was relentless retribution. He was vengeance unleashed.

All too soon, the killing was done. He was nowhere near satiated, he craved more, but he strained to leash the dark urges. Isa stitched himself back together inside a carcass of skin and bone until he could feel his heart beating inside his chest once more. The floor and walls of the underground chamber were now slippery with blood. It splattered across the sacrificial gown of the man that remained standing, holding a kard out in his trembling hand.

"Go," Isa growled at him, jerking his head to the exit.

The man turned the kard inward and plunged the blade deep into his gut.

Isa shook his head. "Idiot."

He didn't really care, though, except to acknowledge the complete waste of life. In his experience, the zealots could be just as dangerous as the priests. Isa would gladly kill them all.

"Isa."

Isa turned around to see a young man standing at the entrance to the chamber. He looked stunned. His eyes traveled from the butchered bodies on the ground back to Isa as if he couldn't believe what he'd witnessed. Although the end of the war saw the restrictions on the Naiab lifted, allowing them to move freely across Merovia, it was rare that people saw them. Rarer still to witness the wielding of sand magic.

But the young man had also said his name, which was unexpected. Isa stared back at him. He looked familiar somehow but Isa couldn't quite place him.

"It's Ele."

Ele. The young man's features settled into Isa's memory of a ten-year-old boy, then a sixteen-year-old adolescent. He recognized him now in the sky blue of his eyes, the tight brown curls on his head.

Isa drew his gaze over Ele in a critical manner. "What is the Captain of the Guard doing here?"

"The same thing you are, apparently. Trying to stop a human sacrifice."

Isa pointed to the dead zealot on the floor. "You failed."

Ele's shoulders slumped slightly. His expression looked pained, as if the man's death weighed on him.

Ele sheathed his shamshir and then furrowed his brows in confusion. "What are *you* doing here? How did you know about the sacrifice?"

"Your king isn't the only one with spies."

"But Henri's spies have been trying to learn this information for months with no luck," Ele persisted.

In truth, Isa's network of informants weren't able to penetrate the priesthood either. Patience be damned, Isa had decided to slip away from the Kingdom of the Black Sands and travel to the Old City to get the answers himself. He'd followed a priest and then snatched him from the very temple he served. Isa was sure the priest had never prayed to a divine with more urgency as he had while screaming as Isa flayed his skin. The priest had given up the information almost immediately, but since there was time to kill before the sacrifice was due to take place, Isa had used it wisely. Excruciatingly. Marking each second in blood.

"So, your king sent you," Isa deduced, stepping over the bodies at his feet.

"And me." A young woman entered the underground chamber.

Ele's features shifted into irritation at the sight of her. "Sabine."

Sabine's eyes roved Isa's naked body unashamedly, lingering on certain parts with avid appreciation. "That was quite a show, sandman."

Isa flicked his gaze to Ele. "Friend of yours?"

"No," they echoed.

Interesting.

"Sabine was helping me to uncover the details of the sacrifice," Ele explained.

"And now you owe me a favor," Sabine returned triumphantly.

From Ele's tight expression, Isa got the sense that it wasn't a good thing.

"We're done here." Ele glanced around at the bodies, their blood still dripping down the stone walls. "You can return home, Sabine. My men can escort you, or you can make your own way."

Sabine looked a little taken aback. "You're staying here?"

"No. I'm traveling to the Kingdom of the Black Sands for the queen's birthday festival."

"You're going to be late," Isa grumbled.

It took days to travel between the Old City and the Kingdom of the Black Sands. Even traveling by sand, Isa would barely make it back in time. Kala would be crestfallen if she thought Ele wasn't coming.

"I'm a fast rider," Ele countered. "Besides, I'm sure Kala will forgive me given the circumstances."

"Kala? On a first-name basis with the queen, Captain?" Sabine jibed.

Isa took a threatening step towards him. "Kala can't know about this."

Ele blinked in surprise before his eyes narrowed in suspicion. "She didn't send you?"

Isa gritted his teeth. He had never meant to expose himself like this. Had he known that Henri was aware of the situation and would send soldiers to deal with it, Isa would have stayed away. On second thought, he wouldn't have. Ensuring that the practice of human sacrifice never occurred again was his responsibility. He owed Tahlia that much.

Ele witnessing his vengeance, however, had put them both in a difficult position. If Kala learned that Isa had been leaving the kingdom in secret, that he had kept a resurgence in human sacrifice from her, she would be more than enraged. She would be hurt. Kala trusted him implicitly but that trust would crumble like dry clay if she found out the truth.

"She didn't need to. It's my responsibility."

"Kala would want to know," Ele insisted. "She would want to make sure nothing like this ever happens again."

"And it won't." Isa's words were final, ending the discussion. He waved his hand around at the bodies. "You can clean this up."

Without another word, he strode out into the passageway, leaving Ele and Sabine behind. It was a gamble, not explaining himself further or pleading his case, but he didn't owe the boy anything. Kala was his queen, his duty to protect. He sheltered her from what he could and he would never apologize for that. If Ele was arrogant enough to believe that he knew what Kala needed better than Isa did, then he would quickly learn otherwise. Isa wasn't sure what he would do if Ele exposed him, but he was acutely aware that any action he took against the Captain of the Guard could start a war.

CHAPTER FIVE

KALA

"He's giving me the evil eye." Majid shifted uncomfortably on the bed as he watched Cemal slowly slither across the floor. "I swear he doesn't like me."

"He doesn't like anyone except Kala," Zaynab tossed over her shoulder. She was sitting on the floor opposite Kala, concentrating intensely on painting a design on her upper thigh. A collection of small ceramic pots of paint were scattered between them.

"It's unnatural," Samir agreed as he lay on the floor, a pillow beneath his head, inhaling the sweet smoke of dried balgarum from a water pipe. "Having a python for a companion, sleeping in your bed. Aren't you afraid he'll constrict you to death in your sleep, Kafei?"

"Most women sleep with snakes in their beds. They just don't realize it," Kala deadpanned.

Zaynab quirked an eyebrow without taking her eyes off her design. "That went dark."

Kala couldn't bring herself to crack a smile or lighten the mood. Cemal slithered beside her, his scales lightly grazing her leg in comfort. The paintbrush glided across the inside of Kala's wrist, leaving a wet trail on her skin, but she barely noticed it. Her mind was elsewhere. Two nights ago, in the late hour, she had risen from her bed and crept down the hall to check if Isa had slipped away again. It had become her nightly ritual ever since discovering him missing over a week ago. Each time she saw him shrouded in shadows, sleeping in his bed, a weight lifted from her chest. Two nights ago, that weight had crashed down on top of her.

Isa was not in his bed.

"How do you get the lines so neat?" Zaynab exclaimed in frustration, her eyes darting between her own design and the one forming on Kala's wrist.

"Practice," Kala replied.

Divine intervention. Tahlia's voice sounded amused. *There. A lotus flower for beauty.*

Kala glanced down at her wrist to see a delicate lotus bloom painted there. She felt Tahlia's essence moving her limbs as she made the final stroke. The goddess wasn't inhabiting her fully, but rather just enough to guide her hand. Tahlia had tried to teach Kala how to paint the designs on herself but they never looked as elegant as when Tahlia did them. Each symbol meant something different. Some were for prosperity or healing, others for wisdom or protection. The lotus bloom represented purity, strength, and resilience, but it was also known for its inner beauty.

CHAPTER FIVE 79

Tahlia transferred the brush between Kala's hands and rolled Kala's other wrist to expose a new canvas.

"Do you want some of this?" Samir held the pipe out to Kala.

"She definitely needs it. Why are you so cranky, Kafei?" Majid leaned over the end of the bed. "It's the first day of your birthday festival and yet here we are not enjoying it. I put a lot of effort into planning the perfect celebration. The least you could do is attend."

"Maj!" Zaynab admonished and Cemal flicked his forked tongue out in warning. Majid quickly retreated back onto the bed.

I agree with your friend.

Kala sighed. Even in her own head she was never left alone. It hadn't always been this way. Loneliness was something she had become intimately familiar with after becoming Queen of the Black Sands. She had gained a kingdom, a people, and a purpose, but she had lost her chosen family. It had been difficult to find people in her new kingdom she could trust. Her difficult childhood had made her guarded and her position as queen only amplified that. Everyone desired the favor of the queen. Women wanted to manipulate her, men wanted to control her, and genuine friendship was rare. The cost of trusting the wrong people, of exposing her vulnerabilities to those who might exploit them, was enough for her to keep most acquaintances at a careful distance. For years, she had thought it was safest to remain the loneliest person in the world. But fate, it seemed, had other plans.

Several years ago, she learned of an illegal body shop operating in her city. The owners were forcing people into the skin trade, some as young as children. Kala usually sent Isa to dispense justice on her behalf but on this occasion, Kala joined him. Along with a dozen soldiers, they raided the body shop and those responsible for such heinous crimes were put before her to be executed by her blade. The people who had been forced to work in the body shop were treated with care. Kala made sure that they were given money if they needed it or safe passage to return to their homes. Zaynab had stood out amongst them because she was similar in age to Kala. It had been like looking into the face of the future that she could have had if she'd stayed in the Thaka.

Zaynab didn't have a home or family to return to, so Kala had offered her a position in the palace. Such an offer would have been enviable to most people but Zaynab had refused. She didn't want to be separated from two other survivors of the body shop; Samir and Majid. As children, they had been thrown together into the depths of depravity. They had clung to each other like vines to a pillar. They were not bound by blood but they were each other's family. So, Kala had given all three of them positions in the palace.

Over the years, she observed them from a distance, the way they cared for each other, their unyielding loyalty to one another. Slowly, she carved out a place for herself within their family and they welcomed her. They never asked for anything in return. She felt safe in their company, as if they understood the girl she used to be before she became queen. Kala could be her true self around them. Share her fears and insecurities. They would listen without judgment. Instead of selling the information to the highest bidder, they guarded her vulnerabilities as if they were precious. Kala supposed there was a part of them that felt indebted to her, but she knew that there was a larger part of them that simply hated the act of exploitation. They would never do it to her or anyone else.

Majid, with his flair for showmanship, had come to oversee all her official events, as well as the city's annual festivals. Samir was a talented craftsman who had become a stonemason, which was convenient because whatever Zaynab designed, he would bring to life.

There.

Kala glanced down at the design on her wrist with mild interest. "A tree?"

"Why do you sound surprised? You drew it," Zaynab remarked.

Although her friends knew her better than almost anyone, they did not know about her affiliation with a goddess. Tahlia's existence was not Kala's secret to share.

For growth and longevity.

Kala rolled her eyes.

What would you prefer? Something for love?

It had been Tahlia's idea to paint Kala's skin for her birthday, to bring her blessings, but beauty and longevity were the least of Kala's desires. She would settle for honesty and reliability. Compounding her feelings about Isa's disappearance was the fact that Ele hadn't arrived yet. Her birthday festival had already started. She had hoped that he would arrive yesterday or last night so that she could wake this morning excited to spend the day with him. Instead, she had woken to disappointment.

"No," Kala sulked under her breath.

Ele will be here.

"If you want to stay cooped up in the palace, that's fine, but can we at least open a barrel of wine?" Majid suggested. "I ordered enough to last the entire kingdom through a drought."

Samir inhaled a long drag of balgarum smoke. "It would be a shame to let the wine go to waste."

Get up.

Kala could feel Tahlia urging her legs to move. Reluctantly, Kala stood.

"Oh, I see movement." Majid immediately sat up on the bed, his back ramrod straight with anticipation.

Kala let Tahlia steer her out onto the balcony.

"Let's not get too excited. She might be planning to jump," Samir quipped.

"With you two around, I don't blame her," Zaynab deadpanned.

Look down there.

Kala cast her eyes down into the city below and watched as a parade marched through the streets of her kingdom. The clashing symbols, sharp strings of the saz, and deep pounding of skin drums resounded in the air. From this vantage point, it looked like a sea of color had exploded. Everyone was dressed in vibrant tones as they danced, tossed flowers, and threw painted sand in the air. The streets were crammed with vendors selling wares, and food, and drink. Children laughed as they raced through the crowd with their friends. Her people were happy, joyous to have another occasion to celebrate.

The only person not enjoying herself was Kala.

CHAPTER FIVE

Never let a boy ruin a moment of celebration. Especially when that moment is celebrating you.

Kala lifted her chin. Tahlia was right. What was she doing? This was her kingdom, her birthday festival, and she was not enjoying it. She didn't know where Isa had disappeared to or even if he'd returned home. She didn't know if Ele would arrive over the next three days or whether he would miss her birthday festival entirely. Those things were out of her control. What she could control was whether she enjoyed today.

"I'm going down there," Kala announced.

She felt Tahlia smile before a rush of love squeezed her heart, then the goddess was gone.

"What was that, Kafei?" Majid called out to her eagerly.

Kala returned inside the chamber. "We're going down there. It's my birthday festival and we're going to enjoy it."

Zaynab squealed with excitement and then blew furiously on her thigh to make the paint dry faster. Majid jumped off the bed but then cautiously moved around the edges of the room towards the door, making sure to give Cemal a wide berth.

"I'll call for Isa," Majid said.

"No. No Isa. No guards. Just us," Kala replied.

Samir choked on an inhale of smoke. "Is that wise?"

"If anything happens to you, Isa will kill us," Majid agreed. "I've dreamed of that man's hands on my body but not like that."

Zaynab looked up at her with a mix of curiosity and concern, a clear question behind her eyes, but Kala ignored it.

"I'll need a headscarf," Kala said.

Normally, she wouldn't bother trying to conceal her identity when wandering about her kingdom but her birthday festival had attracted vendors from kingdoms far and wide. She couldn't trust that she would be safe amongst them, especially if Isa was not guarding her.

Satisfied that the paint had dried, Zaynab stood and retrieved a headscarf for both of them. Kala smiled at her friend in silent thanks.

"Not a word about this," Kala warned Cemal, who hissed in reply.

"We're going to need more than a disguise." Samir walked over to a lattice-work cabinet and opened the doors to reveal a small armory.

They concealed weapons beneath their clothes; Samir with his hammer and the rest of them with daggers. It felt strange to wander about the palace without Isa as her shadow but it was also a little defiant and thrilling. If his absence was drawing attention, Kala didn't notice. The servants and guards carried on with their duties. No one questioned them or tried to stop them as they boldly strode out of the front gates of the palace.

Once outside in the city streets, the smell of roasted meats, spices, and baked pastries hit her nostrils. The crowds jostled them as they moved between market stalls. Zaynab interlocked her arm with Kala, holding her close, while Majid and Samir stood on either side of them to provide a buffer. Kala felt herself smile for the first time that day. The atmosphere was pulsing with energy. It infused her with delight. There was so much to see. Merchants called out to them as they passed by, trying to draw their attention to their wares and lighten their purses.

They stopped by a vendor to buy honeyed pastries and ate them leisurely as they wandered from stall to stall. Majid made sure to speak to every trader, checking that business was going well and the festival he'd organized was a resounding success. Zaynab watched him with an admiring smile and Kala elbowed her friend in the ribs playfully. She'd noticed the change in the way Zaynab looked at Majid lately. Majid enjoyed the company of both men and women, which usually made him the most charming man in any room. Zaynab had always treated him like a brother but something had started to shift recently. Kala wondered if Majid had noticed.

It could be difficult to evolve from friends to something more. Kala had explored her feelings for Samir briefly before happily returning to their platonic friendship. It had mostly been curiosity on her part, to know what it was like to be intimate with a man. Samir was the only man she had ever been sexually attracted to. He was also the only man she felt safe enough to be intimate with. It had lasted a few short months before her curiosity waned and they returned to the way things were before. Kala was grateful no one's feelings had gotten hurt, but it was always a risk. She wondered if that concern was holding Zaynab back from revealing her true feelings to Majid.

"Are you enjoying yourself?" Zaynab squeezed her arm affectionately.

"I am."

"You deserve this, you know. You make all this possible. Your kingdom is prosperous. Your people are healthy and protected. It is your right to enjoy what you have built."

Kala tried to keep the smile on her face as a wave of sadness descended over her. She was proud of everything she had built, but it had come at great personal cost. She would never have chosen this path for herself, but the gods had a way of balancing the scales.

A small girl with flowers woven through her hair skipped up to them. "Would you like a flower bracelet?"

"We would," Kala replied and followed the girl back to her mother's stall.

She handed over a few coins, and the little girl fastened a flower bracelet around each of their wrists. The flowers were small and delicate but their violet color was vibrant.

"Mine's prettier than yours," Majid quipped to Samir, who grunted in reply.

They wandered through the streets, stopping briefly to listen to musicians or inspect the quality of garments at the stalls. Tonight, she would host a private festival in the palace for those who had supported her the most during her reign. From craftsmen to teachers, merchants and advisors, Kala had curated the invitation list carefully. Zaynab had designed a beautiful dress for the occasion. It was floor-length but strapless and featured glass embroidery. Kala couldn't wait to wear it. She had wondered what Ele might think of her when he saw her in it. Perhaps he would find her beautiful, maybe he might even say so, but now she no longer cared what he thought. She would be beautiful with or without him.

A jewelry stall caught her eye and Kala led the way across the street to browse the pieces. She knew Zaynab had probably already chosen the accessories she would wear tonight, but perhaps she might find something else she liked. The jewelry at the stall was beautifully crafted. From silver pieces designed with filigree work and set with colorful stones, to hairpins with intricate patterns featuring coral and amber. The necklaces and bracelets were made of glass beads, and the gold pieces varied from simple to elaborate designs.

The stall was popular, attracting enough customers to make it feel cramped. Majid was talking to a nearby merchant and Samir was standing beside Zaynab, so there wasn't much to protect Kala from being jostled about. Still, Kala held her position at the front of the stall with stubborn determination.

"Are you looking for something specific?" The female vendor leaned over to her.

There was a glint of recognition in the woman's gaze. Kala self-consciously adjusted her headscarf.

"Earrings to go with a dress," Kala replied.

The woman considered her collection of fine pieces and then selected a few to place in front of Kala.

"Rubies from Verenthia. Or perhaps black pearls from the Thelassian Sea."

Kala ran her fingertips over the perfectly round black pearls. They shone in the sunlight, exhibiting an array of colors ranging from deep charcoal to overtones of green, blue, and purple. Their lustrous sheen set the pearls apart from the other precious stones, yet their dark complexity seemed to hold the depths of truth. They were beautiful and elegant.

"The pearls," said a man who stood beside her. "They are almost as beautiful as you."

Kala stilled, her eyes widening at the unexpected compliment from a stranger. Part of her was desperate to look over at him, curious to see the face that would match such a deep velvet voice, but she kept her eyes fixed on the pearls in front of her. She didn't know what else to do. She was a coward. She had been told she was beautiful many times before, and she was content whenever she looked in the mirror, but to have a stranger admire her was completely foreign. Kala covertly peeked across at Zaynab, who was staring boldly at the stranger. The mesmerized expression on her friend's face told Kala that the man was indeed handsome. That knowledge made Kala's blush deeper.

"There you are! Buying something pretty for me?" A young woman bounded over to the handsome stranger.

Kala felt him unexpectedly bump into her side, as if the woman had pushed him playfully.

"Sorry," the stranger mumbled down to her.

Kala shook her head to dismiss his concern, but Zaynab's mesmerized expression morphed into a fierce scowl. Now Kala's cheeks burned with mortification. A man had flirted with her while shopping for a gift for his partner. Kala looked up at the vendor, who shrugged her shoulders slightly as if to say it happens all the time.

"I'll take them." Kala handed over a gold coin, far more than what the pearls were worth. "Keep it."

Kala snatched the pearls and linked her arm with Zaynab's before walking off into the crowd. Samir followed closely behind them, and Majid quickly ended his conversation with a vendor before jogging to catch up.

"Is it too early in the day to sample a barrel of wine?" Majid asked hopefully.

"I don't think so," Kala replied. "I could use a drink."

ELE

"What are you doing here, Sabine?" Ele exasperated.

After alerting Henri's soldiers to the dead priests in the passageway, Ele had promptly saddled his horse and left Sabine in the Old City to fend for herself. He'd ridden hard to make it to the festival on time. In fact, he'd ridden so hard he'd had to purchase a new horse halfway to the Black Sands just so that he didn't have to stop for rest. Ele had no idea how Sabine had managed to follow and keep pace with him.

When he arrived at the Kingdom of the Black Sands, Ele found the festival in full swing and had been swept up in the middle of it. He'd decided to tie up his horse on the outskirts of the city before diving into the throes of the lively crowd. The idea to buy

Kala a birthday gift was spontaneous. More born from guilt than anything else. He felt like he couldn't turn up at the palace with only an apology in hand.

"You invited me to a festival. How could I turn that down?" Sabine's smile was wicked.

"I didn't invite you," Ele retorted.

"Semantics."

Ele threw a look over his shoulder to find that the young woman had disappeared. He frowned as his eyes searched the crowd but there was no sign of her. He'd been browsing the merchant's goods for a birthday present for Kala when he noticed her standing beside him. Somehow in a sea of people, amidst a festival drenched in vibrant color, she drew his notice without effort. Her face was somewhat hidden beneath a headscarf, but he could see her skin was a warm, rich olive tone. Her fingers were soft and graceful as they brushed over the black pearls, her movements subtle and poised. She was most likely a wealthy merchant's wife. Not that it mattered. She was gone and he would never see her again.

Ele turned his focus back to the array of jewelry in front of him. He had no idea what Kala would like. Silver or gold? Diamonds or amethyst? The girl he used to know never wore jewelry. She barely washed her face. The last time he'd seen her, she was sixteen years old and still didn't wear jewelry. The whole visit had been incredibly awkward. Ele wasn't used to being around girls unless they were training to be soldiers. Reading Kala's letters was comfortable because he pictured her as he remembered her, his oldest friend since childhood, but in person, he found that he couldn't relax. It was impossible to ignore the time that had passed between them. Kala was no longer a girl, she was on the precipice of womanhood, just as he was growing into a man. Ele didn't know how to talk to her face-to-face. He didn't know what to say or how to act around her. It had taken days before he was able to simply be in her company without overthinking every little thing he said or did.

This time would be different. He was older, more mature, and he had certainly entertained enough women to feel confident in himself. He could be charming when he wanted to be and he drew his fair share of admiration. Ele hoped they would be able to pick up their friendship just like he picked up one of her letters. But all of that was not helping him to choose the perfect birthday gift. The Kala he had known in childhood was bold and daring but perhaps the years had refined her. Something dainty?

"Are we staying in the palace?" Sabine asked innocently, as she glanced around the festival.

"*I* am staying in the palace. *You* are not my problem anymore."

"You owe me a favor," she reminded him.

"And you are not going to waste that on something as trivial as staying in the palace," Ele countered as he studied the options in front of him.

"Perhaps I have developed a taste for the royal life," Sabine mused.

Ele huffed. This was a waste of time. None of the pieces looked right and he couldn't concentrate with Sabine chattering in his ear. Ele stormed off in the direction of where he'd left his horse.

"So how do you know the Queen of the Black Sands?" Sabine pursued him.

Ele rounded on her. "Stop following me!"

"You have to admit it's quite strange. When could you two have possibly met?"

"If I tell you, will you leave me alone?"

"Maybe," she grinned.

Ele shook his head and kept walking. Sabine kept stride beside him.

"We met when we were kids. When I first came to Merovia. Now go away."

"So, you met her before she was queen. I heard she was nothing before she was named heir. She wasn't even Rouhan."

"She was never nothing," Ele pitched his tone in warning.

"Listen to you defending her honor! I think you like this girl."

"She's not a girl, she's a queen, and she's my friend. Nothing more."

"Good. I was starting to feel jealous."

Upon finding his horse, Ele untied the reins from the post a little too forcefully and began to lead the tired animal in the direction of the palace. The beast was exhausted and Ele could relate. He was beyond tired. His stomach should have been rumbling with hunger, but he was too weary to think about eating or drinking. He would need to sleep before the feast tonight or he would pass out in the middle of it.

"That's her palace?" Sabine exclaimed as they approached the gates of a majestic building.

It was a masterpiece of black stone and white marble. Its exterior was adorned in rich mosaics and delicate calligraphy. Along the third story of the palace was an identical row of arched windows and carved stone balconies. Towering minarets rose gracefully from the corners of the building, each featuring golden domes.

"I'm starting to feel jealous again. Looks like it pays to be the first Queen of Merovia."

She was not the first queen. Ele wanted to correct Sabine but he swallowed his words. He approached the guards and gave them his name, along with a letter of invitation from Kala sealed with her insignia. They waved him through the gates and a servant promptly collected his horse. Sabine loudly cleared her throat behind him. Ele glanced over his shoulder to find her blocked by the guards and looking at him expectantly.

"She's not with me."

The guards tightened their line of defense in front of her and Sabine's eyes blazed.

"You camel's ass. You think this will stop me?"

Ele couldn't help but flash her a smug grin as he continued walking toward the palace.

ISA

Something was very wrong. When Isa woke, the harsh midday sun was streaming through his room. The bedsheets beneath him were soaked with sweat, as was his skin. He felt like he'd drunk an entire meyhane's worth of alcohol. His body burned, infected and inflamed with poison. His mind felt as if it had been cleaved in two and cast adrift in a haze of sand and fog. Isa managed to rouse himself from his bed and get dressed but each movement was painful and sluggish. He couldn't believe he'd slept through the entire morning. It was unprecedented of him. Worse, it was negligent.

He poured himself a short glass of apple tea, hoping it would give him a shot of energy and clear his head. Instead, he noticed the sounds of lively musicians filtering through the air, along with a boisterous crowd. Isa crossed the room in quick strides to peer down from his balcony into the city below. His stomach sank. Kala's birthday festival. It had started. Which meant he hadn't just slept through the morning. An entire day and night had passed.

Isa's last memory was of returning to the Kingdom of the Black Sands after slaughtering the priests in the Old City. He'd pushed himself hard as he traveled through sand to make it back in time. When he finally arrived at his bedchamber, his body was shaking from fatigue. Isa had collapsed into bed, utterly depleted, his mind still spiraling with the prospect of Ele exposing him to Kala. The only comfort he drew was the knowledge that he'd made it back in time.

Except now he was late.

Isa fled the room. His gut was still churning, polluted with sickness, but he ignored it. His sole focus right now was Kala. Isa went straight to her bedchamber but she wasn't there, which was not surprising given that it was the middle of the day. When he enquired of the guards standing outside her quarters, they told him that she'd left some time ago but were unsure where she was headed.

Isa began to search the palace, starting with the most likely places she would be. The training ring. The library. Zaynab's room. The kitchen. At first his search was discreet, so as not to spark unwanted rumors, but after an hour, he began to stop every servant that passed him to ask if they had seen their queen. No one had. When he had searched every room and spoken to what felt like the entire palace staff, Isa was left with a terrifying conclusion. Kala was not in the palace.

There were not enough curse words in the world for what he was feeling right now. Isa had allowed himself to slip into a mild coma, and Kala had taken the opportunity to disappear. It wasn't like her at all. She never left the palace without him as her escort. Perhaps she had found him asleep and didn't want to disturb him, so she took another guard with her. Even as the thought entered his mind, he knew it wasn't true.

Ele. Perhaps Ele had arrived and they were wandering the streets together, enjoying each other's company. It made sense. Ele was certainly capable of leading Kala astray. As Captain of the Guard, he would be confident in his ability to protect her from any danger.

Idiot. The festival would have drawn plenty of foreigners to the kingdom. Charlatans. Thieves. Murderers. Revelries often created the perfect storm for people to commit heinous acts. Kala was skilled with a blade but it had been years since she'd fought an enemy.

Isa clenched his jaw. If anything happened to Kala, Ele's death would not be swift. Isa would relish in his pleas for mercy, his contrition would not be enough to save him. Isa didn't care about the repercussions for him or the Kingdom of the Black Sands. His sole duty was to Kala. If any man hurt her or failed her, he would not live to draw breath, no matter who that man was.

Laughter echoed down a nearby hallway, along with the sounds of stumbling, swearing, and a frantic *shhhhh*. Isa stilled and waited, listening as the sounds drew closer. Kala stumbled around the corner in the drunken company of Zaynab, Samir, and Majid. He should have known. They stopped abruptly at the sight of him. Majid looked like he was about to throw up or piss his pants. Isa stood deathly still, his chest heaving with restraint as his stare bore into Kala. She was wearing a simple kaftan with a headscarf wrapped around her hair and shoulders. Her eyes were a little glassy and wide with surprise, but her features quickly hardened to anger, which was fucking perplexing given that he was beyond furious with her.

"Where have you been?" Isa demanded.

"Enjoying my festival." Kala lifted her chin slightly, trying to stare him down, but he towered over her and they both knew it.

Isa looked past her pointedly. "Without a guard?"

"With my friends."

Isa narrowed his eyes on her like the tip of a blade but his words were aimed at her companions. "Leave."

Her friends hesitated but Kala nodded her permission. Zaynab unlinked her arm from Kala and stumbled a little before Samir and Majid caught her between them. They carefully led her away but not before Zaynab cast him a warning glare. Even drunk, the girl was fierce and loyal to her queen. Isa admired her for that.

Once they were out of earshot, Isa unleashed himself. "You went out into the streets unprotected?!"

"I'm armed." Kala lifted a fold of her kaftan to reveal a hidden dagger.

"You can't even walk right now, let alone defend yourself."

"I'm walking just fine." Kala tried to march past him but he sidestepped to block her escape.

"What's gotten into you? You know better than this!"

"I know nothing!" Kala shouted back, her demeanor suddenly sobering. "I don't know where you go at night, or why, or what you do when you leave."

Isa stiffened. He took a moment to calculate exactly what to say to ascertain how much she knew without giving anything away, but Kala intercepted him.

"I came to your chamber a few weeks ago. You were gone. And then again, the other night, you weren't there. Have you only just returned?"

"No. I was sleeping. I overslept," Isa admitted. "You should have woken me to escort you."

"I didn't know you were back! You could have been lying dead somewhere, and I wouldn't have known because you tell me nothing!"

Isa exhaled a heavy breath, the tension in his muscles easing a little at the hurt and fear in her voice. He never wanted to cause her pain or make her worry.

"I'm fine."

"Well I'm not. I'm your queen!"

"It won't happen again."

"Where were you?" Kala demanded.

Isa considered his options. He didn't want to lie to her but he couldn't tell her the truth. If she knew all the things he shielded her from, if she learned what he had to do to keep the dark urges at bay, she would be horrified. And she would never trust him again. Most likely, she would banish him from the kingdom and that would leave her unprotected.

Kala's expression softened to curiosity. "Were you ..." Her voice was hesitant. "You are allowed to have a life outside of your duty to me, you know. If you were sneaking away to see your lover—"

Isa hissed, his anger suddenly flaring like a furnace stoked with dry wind.

Kala pinched her lips tight as she held her ground. "Well, maybe you should find one."

"I have no need for a lover."

"Only a goddess?"

Isa went unnaturally still.

"I saw the shrine."

They held each other's gazes, locked in a battle of wills. Isa saw the briefest flicker of guilt pass across Kala's face for invading his privacy, but she quickly masked it behind righteous indignation. He had built the shrine the day he returned with her to the Kingdom of the Black Sands. It was the only thing he could think to do to keep Tahlia close to him. He had hoped that if she ascended to divinity, she would hear his prayers. If she had, she'd never answered him. Still, he prayed. Every night. That was the power of faith. It was blind. Compelling. Irrational. Hopeful. He did not want to live in a world where there was no possibility of her existing. A life without her was a wasteland he did not want to wander alone.

"I didn't know …" Kala trailed off as Isa averted his gaze, trying to maintain control over his emotions.

The pain was too much. A decade had passed and yet it still felt as raw as the day it happened.

"She wouldn't want it." Kala clenched her hands into fists at her sides. "She would want you to move on, to live a full life."

"Enough." A tempest storm crossed his features.

Kala huffed in frustration. "We never talk about her."

He knew that a part of her wanted to uncover old wounds and let them breathe, while the other part of her didn't want to hurt him.

"I. Can't." Isa bit each word out, straining from the effort.

Though he couldn't look at her, he somehow sensed the tears threatening to spill from her eyes.

"Fine. Keep your secrets and your shrine. We'll just go back to the way things were, pretending that none of it ever happened."

Kala walked around him but he caught her wrist as she passed. His fingers brushed against the delicate petals of a flower bracelet. It was so simple yet beautiful, like something a child would make. Seeing it around her wrist somehow dulled the sharpness of his pain. But then his eyes caught on something else. He turned her wrist over and Kala quickly snatched her hand back as if he'd burned her. But not before he saw the design of a lotus flower painted on her skin.

"What is that?" Isa asked, even as a knowing ignited deep inside his soul.

The lines were perfect, the design intricate. It looked exactly like the designs Tahlia used to paint on her skin.

"I painted it this morning. For beauty." Kala's cheeks blushed self-consciously.

Of course. Tahlia used to paint Kala's skin when she was a child. Perhaps she had even taught her how to paint the designs.

"You do not need to pray for such blessings. You *are* beautiful."

It was Kala's turn to avert her gaze but she made no move to leave. Isa waited patiently as she debated whether to say more.

"I don't think Ele is coming," Kala admitted in a small voice.

"He is, I promise you. He's just been delayed."

"How do you know?"

"Because he knows I'll kill him if he disappoints you."

Kala's lips twitched to a brief smirk but then her features turned solemn. "Are you all right?"

The question held a thousand other questions but he knew she was trying not to push him.

"You are all that matters to me in this world. As long as you are safe, I am fine."

Kala didn't look entirely convinced but she nodded anyway. He got the sense that the conversation had ended for now, but it wouldn't be the last he would hear about it.

CHAPTER SIX

ELE

Ele smoothed a hand down his kurta as he stepped into the palace courtyard. It felt strange to wear such a fine garment, but Malik had commissioned it for him after he confessed he had not put much thought into what he would wear to Kala's birthday festival. The kurta was sapphire blue, made of the finest material, and light enough so that his skin could breathe through the lingering heat of the day. It featured a traditional pattern sewn in gold thread. The collar was high but Ele had left the top silver button undone. He was already feeling out of place in such fine attire, he didn't want to feel choked as well. Malik had tried to convince him to wear a silver earring, but Ele refused, just as he had refused the suggestion of various necklaces, bracelets, and rings. In the end, Malik gave up, mumbling something about him being dull. Ele did not feel dull. He felt like a peacock.

Thankfully, he was amidst a flock of peacocks. The expansive courtyard was already crowded with people, all wearing their finest garments to mark the event. They mingled amongst each other, painted golden glasses in hand, no doubt drinking the most expensive wine in the kingdom. Many of them had wide-eyed looks of awe on their faces, as if this was their first time being within the palace grounds and they could not believe their good fortune.

Before the great war, the Rouhan family had been the ruling family of Merovia and there were distinct social classes between courtiers and commoners. After the war, things changed. The social classes were disbanded, and people's ambitions were no longer limited by their blood or birth. This crowd likely included simple but industrious people who had worked hard to impress their queen and who now found themselves rewarded by receiving an invitation to attend her private birthday celebration.

It was certainly a spectacular event. Servants were stationed around the courtyard offering silver platters of dried fruits, mixed vegetables, pastries, grilled meats, and flatbread. The smell of spices was mixed with the scent of perfume. Oil from the lanterns that burned overhead infused the air. It was an unusual combination but it only added to the atmosphere. A small group of musicians played in the corner, plucking the strings of an oud and lightly patting the skin of a drum.

Ele moved through the crowd, trying to blend in, but it was impossible. As a child, he would often move through crowds like this to overhear court gossip and test the social temperature in a room so that he could report back to his king. The ability to walk freely and openly in a mass of people while remaining unnoticed was a skill necessary for a spy. But he was no longer a child or a spy and his presence drew curious glances.

Even so, through his brief observations, the mood of the crowd seemed merry. He hadn't overheard any grumblings, only polite conversation and salacious rumors, none of which involved Kala. Ele made his way to the magnificent water fountain in the center of the courtyard and decided to linger there for a moment. The base of the fountain was designed in a hexagonal shape and framed with thousands of tiny blue tiles. Water cascaded from a central spout down three levels of shallow basins into the pool below. The trickling sound of the water was rhythmic and soothing.

From this vantage point, Ele could take in the entire courtyard. It featured lush, fragrant plants such as jasmine and palms, but there were also rows of thick, hearty shrubs. Tall stone columns framed the courtyard, and the tiles beneath his feet were laid in an intricate geometric design. The sun dipped low in the sky, setting it ablaze with hues of crimson, burning orange, and golden yellow.

Ele scanned the crowd but he saw no sign of Kala. He assumed his arrival at the palace had reached her ears but he'd been too tired to see her before tonight. Instead, he had collapsed into bed and slept for a few blessed hours. Now that he felt semi-human again, he was anxious to see her. He wondered what she would look like now that five more years had passed. Thankfully, Ele wouldn't need to recognize her in a crowd of strangers. He would know her by the towering Naiab that shadowed her every move.

The long, hard ride to the Kingdom of the Black Sands had given Ele ample time to think about what had transpired between him and Isa. The knowledge that Isa was intentionally keeping things from Kala was unsettling, no matter the reasons for it. Kala was queen. She had a right to be informed, especially if her guardian was involved in the matter. It made Ele wonder what else Isa was keeping from her.

As a child, Ele hadn't had the opportunity to spend much time with Isa before fate had set Ele and Kala on different paths. But even so, Ele sensed that something had changed in the Naiab warrior. He was harder, crueler. In Ele's memories, Isa was a skilled warrior, cunning and clever, but also loyal and kind. The man who slaughtered the priests in the passageway was savage and relished in his savagery. Ele had seen it in men's eyes before, in the ones that enjoyed the suffering of others. Ele knew Tahlia's death had impacted Isa, but surely that alone would not have been enough to turn him vicious.

Isa's demeanor wasn't the only thing that had changed over time. His tattoos had not escaped Ele's notice. They were black as midnight. Ele recalled Naiab tattoos were turquoise, a gift from the Water Goddess. He wondered if the change in color was unique to Isa or whether the other Naiab warriors had also undergone a similar transformation. Ele searched the crowd but he couldn't see any other Naiab warriors. The last time Ele visited the Kingdom of the Black Sands there had been several Naiab stationed at various posts around the palace, loyal to Isa's command. Perhaps they had been ordered elsewhere for the night.

The crowd suddenly hushed and parted, creating a path as someone entered the courtyard. Ele immediately straightened and lifted his chin, trying to get a better look. He was taller than most people but he barely caught a glimpse of Isa over the heads of the crowd. The Naiab warrior looked severe as he escorted the queen. Ele froze. The woman walking beside Isa was stunningly beautiful.

The bronze skin of her heart-shaped face glowed in the warm, fading light of dusk. Her eyes were narrow but penetrating as they regally swept over the crowd. Beneath them were a set of full lips, slightly parted, as if she were breathing through the tremblings of nervous excitement. Two golden rings pierced her nose. Kala's dark hair was parted down the middle and captured in a myriad of long braids, which cascaded down to her hourglass waist. She was wearing a strapless dress the color of midnight, adorned with glass droplets that shimmered like stars.

Ele didn't realize his mouth was gaping open until Kala's eyes somehow found him amongst the crowd. At the same moment, Isa's attention also fixed on him and the warrior scowled. Ele promptly closed his mouth and shifted on his feet, trying to look poised but failing miserably. It was unusual for him to feel flustered but then he hadn't expected her to look like *that*. Kala politely acknowledged her guests as they approached to press her hand to their forehead in a sign of respect. She was gracious with them, though it was clear she was slowly forging a path in his direction.

Even after a decade in this country, it still felt strange to Ele that Merovians did not bow when their rulers entered a room. There were no trumpets blasting or herald's announcements. The musicians didn't even stop playing. Merovians' respect towards their leaders was more subtle. In Merovia, the word Kafei was a term of respect, used when referring to anyone who was considered worthy of more respect than the person saying it. Their parents. Their elders. They would use the title of king or queen on occasion, but most would refer to their leaders as Kafei.

When Ele first arrived in Merovia with Henri, he had wasted no time immersing himself in the culture and learning everything he could about his new world. It had been daunting but thrilling. There had been so much to take in. But as a foreigner, Ele had been on the receiving end of Merovian contempt. He had to earn the people's respect over years of service, much like Henri. Ele was glad to see that Kala had also secured the admiration of her people.

In her letters, she had often written about her ideas for improving her kingdom. The school she wanted to build, the changes to trade and law that would advance living conditions. She had accomplished so much in such a short time and her people were prosperous as a result. Kala's wisdom was beyond her years, her leadership a blessing to the realm, but at this moment, it was her beauty that held him in awe as she walked towards him.

With every step closer, Ele's heart kicked inside his chest. He felt like a wild horse bucking against confinement. When she finally stood before him, he was speechless. All he could do was stare, which is why he noticed that across her nose and cheeks was a smattering of freckles. He remembered those freckles. They had always been his favorite constellation.

"Ele." A shy smile bloomed on her beautiful face.

"My queen." Ele instinctively took her hand and pressed the back of it to his forehead before releasing it.

My queen? His cheeks burned in mortification. He almost couldn't meet her eye, but when he did, Ele saw something flicker across her features. She was pleased. It made him relax a little.

"You remember Isa?" Kala turned to the Naiab warrior at her side.

Isa's flat expression tightened. "You're late."

"Yes, I'm sorry. I arrived earlier today but needed to rest from the journey."

"You're here. That's all that matters," Kala replied smoothly.

Ele lowered his head in gracious acceptance.

"How was your journey?" Kala asked.

"Long and eventful." Ele's eyes briefly darted to Isa then returned to Kala. "But at least I didn't get raided by desert pirates."

Kala's brows knitted in concern. "That's the second time I've heard of desert pirates."

"We hear the rumors but we have yet to encounter them ourselves. Happy birthday, by the way. I'm sorry I didn't bring you a gift."

"Yes, you did. You promised to give me your gift tonight."

Isa took a threatening step towards him, his expression murderous, but Ele had no idea what she was implying.

"Ten years have passed, but I haven't forgotten that you promised to share a secret with me on my twenty-first birthday. It had better be worth the wait," Kala teased.

Ele laughed despite his nerves. He remembered that day so clearly. They were sitting on a precarious ledge in the Citadel, contemplating whether they would live to see another year, when Ele had promised to tell her a secret on her twenty-first birthday. The secret was his real name. When Henri had recruited him into his employ and asked for his name, Ele had given him a variation of the truth. It was the start of a new chapter in his life, a new identity. He was no longer a street thief but the king's spy, and so he needed a new name.

Not even Henri knew what his real name was. The coveted secret had captured Kala's attention and given her something to look forward to, something to live for. The promise had also given Ele a sense of reassurance. That no matter what happened or how life separated them, they would find their way back to each other on her twenty-first birthday.

"You'll have to wait and find out," Ele replied and Kala's eyes sparkled in anticipation. "Henri and Malik also send their love. They wish they could be here."

It was a lie, one they both recognized, but Kala didn't call him out on it. Certainly not with Isa standing there. The warrior's attention had drifted elsewhere, scanning the crowd for possible threats, but Ele knew he was listening to every word.

"How are they?" Kala asked.

"They are well. They think of you often."

"I miss them."

Ele hoped Kala would return one day to visit them or that Henri would set aside his grudge against Isa to visit Kala in the Kingdom of the Black Sands. It would be healing for Henri and Malik to see Kala happy and well. A long time ago, they had each chosen one another as family and even though Tahlia was no longer with them,

Ele wished that his family would come together again. A wave of emotion built in his chest but he clamped down on it.

"This is amazing." Ele indicated to their surroundings, keen to distract himself. "And the street festival today was impressive."

"You were at the festival?" Kala's eyes widened in surprise.

"Briefly."

"So was I. I bought myself a birthday gift." Kala lightly touched the black pearls in her ears.

Ele's face fell. "The woman at the jewelry stall. That was you!"

Kala's face mirrored his own startled recognition.

"They do look almost as beautiful as you." The words left his lips before he could rein them back in. Ele stared at her, horrified by his mouth's betrayal.

Kala's cheeks blushed at the compliment but she held his gaze as if daring him to go on.

Isa cleared his throat pointedly. "You should probably talk to some of your other guests, Kafei."

His words broke their stare and Kala looked up at Isa as if his suggestion displeased her.

"Of course. Go," Ele urged with a nonchalant wave. "I'll be here when you return."

"Are you sure? I don't want to leave you on your own."

"I've handled worse situations than a crowd of strangers. I'll be fine."

"I'll return soon," Kala promised.

Ele's eyes trailed after her as Kala walked away to mingle with her guests. Isa remained by her side and Ele noticed the people physically shrink in his presence. It was understandable. The man was a mountain. When he was a boy, Ele had been foolish enough to think he could take him. Now as a man, he wasn't quite sure he could. Isa's size alone would make anyone question their skills in a fight, but the fact that he was god-touched made any contest futile. No ordinary man could hope to win against a sand wielder. Their magic made the Naiab lethal warriors. Unbeatable. It was mesmerizing to see them in action but it would be terrifying to be their enemy.

Ele decided to occupy himself by patrolling the outskirts of the courtyard. On the way, he swiped a glass of wine and a piece of herb-coated goat's cheese from a silver platter. The cheese tasted tangy and earthy and made his stomach grumble in demand. Ele couldn't recall the last time he'd eaten properly. Several days ago in the Old City, most likely. Unable to resist, he sampled what he could from various platters. The wine was intense. It was lightly spiced and smooth on his tongue. He would need to be careful not to drink too much because he could already feel it affecting him.

As he strolled around the courtyard, the other guests eyed him with obvious interest but no one dared to approach. Occasionally, Ele looked over at Kala to see which guest she had moved on to. Right now, she was talking to a young woman of similar age. Kala's smile was warm and genuine and their conversation seemed animated. Maybe they were friends.

It made Ele wonder if she had many friends amongst the people gathered tonight. Or perhaps even lovers. Ele frowned at the thought. Kala rarely wrote about anyone in her letters, friend or otherwise. She only wrote to him about her projects, ideas, and hopes for the future. Then again, she probably wouldn't feel comfortable talking to him about such intimate matters. Ele studied the men in attendance with renewed interest. It was highly unlikely that she didn't have at least one of them keeping her bed warm at night.

"This wine is divine, wouldn't you agree, Captain?"

Ele whipped around at Sabine's voice. She was standing behind him, having snuck up on him like a bandit. He had been too preoccupied to notice, either that or his senses were dulled by the wine, but now he was acutely aware of every inch of her. Sabine wore a beautiful barely-there red dress with her dark hair swept over one shoulder. Gold bangles dangled at her wrists and a proud, secretive smile played across her lips as she lifted a glass of wine to them in triumph.

"What are you doing here?" Ele's eyes dashed around the courtyard as if it would reveal the answer. "How did you get in?"

"There's entertainment later. Though they are going to be short one dancer." Sabine glanced down at the dress, which hugged her curves like a second skin. "It looks better on me anyway."

"Tell me you didn't kill someone for that dress."

"All right, I won't."

Ele's face darkened and he grabbed her forearm roughly. "You can't be here."

"I love it when you're mean to me."

"Sabine," Ele growled in warning.

"What? I'm not going to hurt anyone. Else. I'm here to have a good time, that's all."

"You weren't invited."

Sabine drew closer and Ele realized that his hand was still on her arm. To anyone else it would look like they were embracing. Her eyes danced mischievously, as if she knew it too, before they dipped to his lips in silent invitation.

"I could be your special guest."

"Leave. Now," Ele bit out each word.

Sabine cocked her head. "Or what?"

"I'll make you leave."

She gasped and lifted a hand to her mouth in feigned shock. "That would cause a scene. But I'd like to see you try."

It was a blatant challenge. Ele had to admit she had him cornered. He couldn't force her to leave without drawing attention and he knew Sabine wouldn't go quietly. Ele assessed her as if he were sizing up an opponent, but it was hard to remain focused when the dress enhanced all her soft, supple assets. He was used to seeing her in a kaftan and pants, armed with her scythe blades. A pretty face but utterly ruthless. In contrast, this dress made her look delicate and feminine. Like an enticing flower.

A carnivorous one.

"By the looks of things, you're unarmed." He hated how his voice sounded sultry. "I thought you never took your blades off."

"From the looks of things, Captain, you like me disarmed." Her gaze dipped between them to his swollen crotch before meeting his eyes again, a feline smile spreading across her face. "I took them off for you. I'll take everything off for you."

Despite his aggravation and better judgment, Ele felt his cock thicken. It was the wine. Or the heat. Or the fact that it had been a while since he'd come to more than his hand. The same hand that was now gripping her warm skin. It made him wonder what the curve of her breasts would feel like in his palm. In his mouth. On his tongue.

"Ele."

Sabine's eyes darted over his shoulder, and Ele quickly dropped her arm as he turned to see Kala standing behind him. The expression on Kala's face was difficult to read, while Isa's expression was all too clear. It darkened with recognition and the promise of violence.

Sabine ignored Kala completely, directing her attention to Isa. "I was hoping to see you again, sandman."

Fuck.

"What is she doing here?" Isa demanded through gritted teeth.

"I don't know," Ele confessed.

His words turned to silence, though, as he observed Kala's face. She looked distant, paralyzed by a memory, rigid with fear and pain. When she finally spoke, the word was a hollow torment.

"Sabine."

CHAPTER SEVEN

KALA

It was the scar that gave her away. The faint pink slice of raised skin beneath her jawline. Easy to hide but noticeable when she lifted her chin, and Sabine had lifted her face to within an inch of Ele's lips. The scar was the remains of a blade held to a child's throat. It had torn through her skin when Kala tried to save her from the clutches of slavers. Thankfully, the cut had not been fatal and by some miracle, the wound hadn't gotten infected. But it had left a scar. Evidence of a child's stupidity and the cruelty of men.

Kala had noticed her from across the courtyard but she hadn't recognized her. She only saw a woman in a seductive dress, her beautiful face, and the fact that she had her hands on Ele. With his back to Kala, she couldn't see if Ele knew this woman or if they had just met. Kala wasn't sure if he was returning her flirtations or dismissing them. Either way, it was enough for Kala to promptly end the conversation she was having with a guest and cross the breadth of the courtyard to interrupt them.

Kala didn't know what she was going to say. Ele could flirt with whoever he wanted. She had no claim on him. But he had come all this way to see her, and she couldn't deny that she would feel angry and hurt if he decided to spend their limited time together with someone else. The moment she drew closer, though, her gaze had fixed on the scar beneath the woman's jawline. Kala's steps had faltered as she examined the rest of the woman's features like a puzzle she was trying to piece together. So many years had passed, a lifetime really. It wasn't possible, and yet the more she looked, the more she couldn't deny it.

"Sabine."

Kala heard the word but she wasn't sure she'd spoken it. She must have, though, because Sabine's flirtatious manner evaporated in an instant. Sabine studied Kala in stunned recognition and disbelief.

"No." Sabine shook her head as if she wanted to look away. "It can't be. You're dead."

Dead. She felt like it. As if she were a spirit floating above her body, a body which was standing there in dumb shock. Except Kala felt her limbs begin to tremble and tears threaten to spill. The sensation pulled her out of her suspended motion. She needed to leave. Now. A shot of adrenaline flushed through her system, or perhaps it was survivors' instinct, because she turned and fled.

Kala didn't care that her retreat would cause a scandal or that her birthday celebration was ruined. All she knew was that she had to escape. To breathe. Because she couldn't. There was suddenly no air in her lungs. They'd caught her. It all came flooding back to her in a barrage of images, smells, and sensations. Their anger. Their violent hands on her. The sharp pain as they smashed her bones while she crawled in the sand, desperate to get away. To live. Their acrid sweat invaded her nostrils. Hot tears streamed down her face. She tried to remind herself that she'd escaped, she wasn't there, but it felt like she was.

Kala bolted through the palace to no destination but she couldn't stop. She would run across the expanse of the Idris Desert if she had to.

Kala? Tahlia's panicked voice slammed into her mind.

"I can't. I can't." Kala's breaths came short and sharp.

She needed to escape. To be anywhere but here. They were going to kill her. She couldn't stand the pain any longer. It would destroy her to go back there. She wasn't strong enough to endure it. That's when Kala felt the rush of a force so powerful it flooded her body and saturated her mind, holding her soul captive in a prison of silk.

ISA

The moment Kala fled the courtyard, Isa felt torn. His instinct was to go after her, to make sure she was all right, but he had to deal with the intruder first. Isa didn't know why Sabine was here or what her intentions were but she certainly wasn't invited. It was a mystery how Kala knew her, but from the way Kala reacted, their dealings with each other had not been pleasant. Then there was the fact that Sabine had let slip that she knew him. Isa couldn't afford for her to say more, especially not in front of Kala.

"What is going on? How do you know Kala?" Ele demanded but Sabine was still staring blankly in the direction of Kala's escape.

"Come with me." Isa gripped her upper arm. He had expected Sabine to resist but she went limp in his grasp.

"Wait!" Ele stepped between them. "Where are you taking her?"

"That is none of your concern."

"And yet I am concerned." Ele's tone told Isa he feared for the girl's life.

Smart boy.

"She's trespassed onto palace grounds. The punishment is death."

"She's not your subject," Ele countered.

"She doesn't have to be. The law is the law."

"Sabine is one of Henri's spies. If you kill her, it will ignite a diplomatic incident."

Isa narrowed his eyes at Ele in disgust. Isa didn't give a shit about Henri or diplomatic relations, but he knew Kala would.

"Fine. She will be taken to the cells to await the queen's judgment."

Ele nodded, satisfied. "I'll come with you."

Clearly, Ele didn't trust that Sabine would actually make it to the cells alive. Isa growled in irritation. He cast a look over at Zaynab, Majid, and Samir who had gathered in response to the commotion. They stared at him in wide-eyed curiosity but Zaynab silently nodded her head in understanding. They would keep the guests entertained in the queen's absence, and somehow try to dampen the rumors that were sure to spread.

Isa and Ele escorted Sabine from the festival as discreetly as possible. The crowd watched them go, whispering fevered speculations amongst each other. Isa hoped the wine and entertainment would be enough to distract them. If they were fortunate, sore heads might forget the scandal entirely by morning.

They were silent as they moved through the palace and then down several flights of stone stairs until they reached a dark room. The air was dry and stale, like dust that hadn't been disturbed for years.

"Light the torches," Isa ordered and Ele complied, finding firestones located beneath the sconces.

Inside the room were two iron-barred cells, both empty and unguarded. Isa couldn't recall the last time they'd been used. It was rare to hold prisoners in Merovia. Justice was served swiftly and there was no point keeping a guilty man alive. Isa carried out sentences on the queen's behalf, both in secrecy and with her approval. The executions took place in private, but sometimes what remained of the bodies would be put on display in the market square as a warning to others. Trespassing on palace grounds was certainly an offense severe enough to warrant being made an example of.

Isa would have to station a pair of guards to watch the cell. He hoped Ele wouldn't be foolish enough to try to free Sabine, but he also didn't trust him. Isa wasn't sure what the relationship was between the two of them. Even as a boy, Ele had been fiercely loyal to those he cared about. If he cared for this girl, he might try to save her.

Isa lifted a set of iron keys off a hook on the wall and escorted Sabine into a cell. She didn't protest as he shoved her inside and locked the door. She simply stood there, as if she was still processing the night's events.

"I'll stay with her for a little while," Ele said.

Isa's expression tightened. "Guards will be posted outside."

Sabine rolled her eyes. "I'm not going anywhere, sandman."

"You have a habit of turning up in unlikely places," Isa returned.

Casting a wary glare at Sabine, Isa pocketed the keys and made to leave the room. He needed to find Kala. But as he began to ascend the stairs, he heard the exchange of their hushed voices. He stopped to linger just outside of view.

"You don't have to stay with me, Captain."

"I'm not here for you. I'm only going to ask you one more time, Sabine. How do you know Kala?"

Sabine's voice was dripping with sarcasm as she replied, "Don't you see the family resemblance? She's my sister."

ELE

Sabine stared back at him boldly as he critically assessed her features. There were slight similarities now that he was searching for them, but they were easily overlooked. Sabine was a year or two younger than Ele, which made her Kala's younger sister.

Kala had never told him much about her family except that they were the ones responsible for almost beating her to death as a child. The sight of her that night still haunted his nightmares. He had found her discarded, broken body in their usual meeting place, an alleyway across from the dilapidated building where she lived. Her skinny frame lay crumpled on the sandy earth, limbs at odd angles, an arm outstretched as if trying to ward off a blow. She was caked in blood. Her long, stringy hair was plastered to her face with it. He hadn't known what to do, how to save her, so he scooped her up into his arms and carried her back to the palace.

"I thought she died," Sabine muttered.

"She almost did."

The palace healer had done her best, but it was Tahlia that saved Kala's life by praying to the gods. The Goddess of Endings and Beginnings ignored Tahlia's pleas, but the Water Goddess answered them. The goddess had flushed the infection from Kala's blood, giving her a fighting chance at survival.

Sabine wandered over to the corner of the cell and slid down the bars to sit on the cool sandstone floor. She stretched her legs out in front of her while a strange, contemplative look crossed her face.

"You were the one she was meeting with, the king's man. That's how you met."

It was a deduction, not a question, so Ele didn't reply.

"You're the reason she almost died." Sabine shot him an accusing look. "She broke the rules for you."

Ele furiously gripped the iron bars in his hands, turning his knuckles bloodless. "I think you'll find it was for the gold coins. To feed herself. To feed her family. To buy fresh water. And yet her family repaid her by trying to kill her!"

"That's the penalty for breaking the rules in the Thaka," Sabine replied coldly.

Ele couldn't dispute that, despite his feelings of revulsion. He had lived in a place like the Thaka once. It too had its own rules. The first rule was the same as the last rule: keep your mouth shut. If anyone was found to be selling information to the authorities, there would be no defense that could save them, no mercy shown at all.

"You break the rules with me all the time," Ele pointed out. "Why do they let you live?"

"No one *lets* me live. If anyone tries to kill me, I kill them first."

Ele released the bars and forced himself to lean against them casually, crossing his arms over his chest. He had no doubt Sabine was telling the truth. She was ruthless and cunning. She would probably slice the throat of her own mother if it gave her an advantage. It was why she had risen so high within the ranks of her family's cartel despite her young age.

"Besides, times have changed. The old ways never helped us, so now we make exceptions on rare occasions when it benefits us to do so. We don't do it for a few coins. It's a business arrangement."

"For Kala, it was survival."

"We survived well enough without her."

Ele's anger flared and he pushed off the bars to prowl the length of the room. He couldn't stomach how blasé she was being about her sister. As if Kala had willingly betrayed them. When they first met, Kala had hated Henri, and was wary of Ele, but in the end hunger won out against her fear and hatred. She risked her life for a handful of coins that could feed her family for months, and her family had discarded her like trash.

"My sister, the queen." Sabine drew out the words as if she still couldn't quite believe it. "How did that happen?"

"It's a long story."

"You have a captive audience," she deadpanned.

"If Kala spares your life, you can ask her yourself. Not that she owes you an explanation. She owes you nothing."

"If she spares my life, that's not how my family will see it. We now have a powerful ally in the Kingdom of the Black Sands. A kingdom known for its lucrative trade in rare commodities. Do you know how much balgarum is worth in the underground market?"

Ele didn't but he could guess. The thought of Kala's family traveling to the Kingdom of the Black Sands and demanding an audience with her filled him with burning anger. The audacity that they would ever consider asking her for anything was beyond belief. But Ele knew the type of people they were. They had no morality. No shame. They would ask nicely with honeyed words and if she rejected them, they would threaten her. Kala was a queen now, with an army at her back. There was little they could do to her physically. Emotionally, though, they had the power to open old wounds.

"Don't worry, Captain, she won't let me live."

Ele frowned at her. "What makes you so sure?"

"Because we share blood. And if the roles were reversed, I wouldn't let her live." Sabine turned the gold bangle around her wrist nonchalantly, as if she had already accepted her fate. "We all have to die someday. Compared to life, death seems rather peaceful."

ISA

After ordering two soldiers to guard Sabine, Isa went looking for Kala. He had thought she would retreat to her bedchamber but she wasn't there. She wasn't in any of her favorite places, so he had no choice but to search the palace methodically, room after room. With every minute that passed, his gut turned to acid. His only consolation was that Kala was inside the palace, which meant she was safe. Still, he couldn't bear the thought of her alone and distressed. He would tear out his own heart if it brought her comfort or lessened her pain.

Isa supposed this was what it felt like to have a daughter, or at least as close as he would ever come to having one. The primal instinct to shield her from any hurt, to safeguard her peace and happiness at the cost of his own. In his quiet moments just before the dawn, Isa sometimes allowed himself to think what life might have been like if Tahlia had lived. Whether they would have raised Kala together as the chosen heir to the Black Sands. Tahlia would have been a remarkable queen. Strong yet compassionate. Graceful but unyielding. She would have guided Kala to emulate her rule. Instead, Kala had been forced to navigate her reign alone, guided only by her instincts.

Isa had tried his best to advise her but he knew there were times he had fallen woefully short. Once, he'd been gentle and kind, a leader amongst the Naiab. He had fought to usher in a new age for Merovia and his people. One of prosperity, and quality, and freedom. But he hadn't been that man for a very long time. Something had broken inside him the day Tahlia died. Something he refused to bury. It had festered and mutated over the years, rotting him from the inside out. If he ever saw his home again, the Naiab would not recognize him. He no longer felt like one of them. A warrior with honor. He had set fire to his honor long ago.

Isa knew there would come a day when Kala would no longer need him, yet the thought of her relying on anyone else perturbed him. If a boy was careless with her heart, if the people she chose to trust betrayed her, Isa wouldn't be able to control himself. Her tears would be the only evidence he'd need to condemn them all to the worst of fates.

If it wasn't for Ele, Sabine would already be dead. Isa didn't need to know who she was or what she'd done, Kala's reaction to the girl had been enough to convict her. The revelation that Sabine was Kala's sister only hardened her sentence. Kala had never spoken to Isa about her family or her life before she became Henri's spy, but Tahlia had formed a close bond with the girl, which told him two things. First, that those who should have cared for and protected her had failed to do so. And second, that Kala was worth defending. So, while Isa couldn't be everything Kala needed, he could at least be that. Her protector.

Isa briefly glanced inside the great hall, expecting to find it empty like every other room, but instead, what he saw turned him still as stone. Kala was dancing. Her feet glided effortlessly across the floor. Like a gentle breeze cascading over the desert dunes, her movements were fluid and elegant. Her silhouette was framed by soft torchlight, casting her shadow across the tiles. It mirrored the precise arc of her arms, the subtle twirl of her fingers, as if her shadow was dancing with her.

Although there was no music, Isa swore he could hear the beat in her movements, a melody in the harmony of her steps. She weaved a story of hope and pain, of love and loss. A story as old as the ages. Isa didn't realize he had subconsciously stepped further inside the great hall. It was as if he was being drawn to her. He couldn't look away, didn't want to. He was enraptured by her spell. The very air around her was electrified. She moved too swiftly for him to see her face but somehow he knew that it would be a canvas of emotion and passion. She was lost in the expression of dance, in the layers of her art. The world around her had faded to nothingness and the only thing that existed was her.

Except it was not Kala.

"Tahlia," Isa called out and the name echoed through the great hall.

In that moment, Kala collapsed to the ground as if someone had ripped every bone out of her body.

CHAPTER EIGHT

ISA

She was not Kala.

Isa had stood in this very hall and watched Kala take dance lessons for years. She had hated it. For someone who was lithe and nimble with weapons, she was surprisingly uncoordinated when it came to dancing. Isa suspected it was because she didn't enjoy the soft, quiet elegance of it. Nor the fact that it made her the center of attention for men's eyes. She had given up in utter frustration several times, only to return a week later, cognizant of the fact that it was a skill expected from royalty. If she ever traveled to other kingdoms or entertained royalty at her court, she may be required to dance. So she persisted, but once she was able to perform basic dances to her tutor's satisfaction, Kala declared her lessons finished.

Kala had never danced for the love of it, and her body had never responded to the command of a beat as if it were responsible for pumping blood to her heart. Isa had only ever witnessed one person move like that. To seduce a king. To entrap a god.

"Tahlia." Her name on his lips was the answer to all his prayers.

Each step was measured as he drew closer, quiet and careful as if he were approaching a ghost. Kala was still crumpled on the floor but he could see the soft rise and fall of her chest. Slowly, she began to command her limbs and climb to her feet. He couldn't see her face because she had her back to him. Isa stopped a short distance away and waited for her to turn around. He would have waited forever if he had to. When she finally turned, her eyes stole his breath away. They were otherworldly. Within their orbs flowed the mysteries of life, the silken threads of an eternity. They shifted constantly like smoke in the wind, reflecting the unfolding of destinies, the inevitability of death.

Isa tried to remember to breathe. He had dreamed of this moment a thousand times over. He'd yearned for it more than air. The chance to see her again, to know for certain that she still existed somewhere. To hear her voice would shatter his heart. To feel her touch would destroy him.

"Goddess."

She didn't blink. Didn't move. It was as if she was suspended in time, seeing everything and nothing all at once. But Isa knew that she saw him. He took another step toward her. Her eyes suddenly transformed back to human irises.

"No!" Isa rushed at her and Kala collapsed in his arms.

He held her up by the shoulders and stared down at her as she lifted her gaze to him. A confused expression crossed her features but then her pupils dilated at the realization of what had happened.

Isa's face darkened like a breaking storm. "You knew."

"I—" Kala's mouth gaped open but no words came out.

There were no words that could justify or explain such betrayal. Kala knew that Tahlia had ascended to divinity and yet she had said nothing. It was treachery. Blatant. Ruthless. Unforgivable. Isa's body coiled tight in rage, demanding violent release. His skin burned with the urge to split open and disperse into a million granules, to obliterate everyone and everything in his path. Isa could see panic rising in Kala's eyes as guilt tore at her edges, but it didn't dampen his anger, it only fueled it.

He gripped her shoulders tighter and she flinched. "How long have you known?"

"From the beginning."

Ten years. Kala had known about Tahlia for ten years. Every day he had prayed at her altar in fervent hope, and every night he had fallen asleep to her memory. Yet Kala had said nothing.

"She made me promise not to tell you."

Isa's brows knotted as he searched her eyes desperately. "Why?"

Kala returned a perplexed expression. "You know why."

He did. But he didn't. He hadn't respected Tahlia's wishes. She never wanted to be a goddess and he had burned her body anyway, offering her up to the God of Fire and Ash. He had done the unthinkable because he loved her. Because it was better to become a divine than to cease to exist for all eternity. Because he couldn't bear to live in a world without her.

"Isa! Let her go."

Isa looked over his shoulder to see Ele striding towards them, his hand gripping the hilt of the shamshir strapped to his waist. Isa scowled at him. That was twice now the boy had inserted himself into affairs that didn't concern him. He was stalking towards them as if he perceived Isa to be a threat to Kala. It was insulting. He was the one who had brought Sabine to the palace. Isa snarled at him viciously.

Ele marginally lifted his shamshir out of the scabbard, just enough to expose the glistening steel in warning. "Let. Her. Go."

A whimper drew Isa's attention back to Kala. Her eyes were wide and glassy with tears, her body tense with—fear? He looked down to see that his fingers were digging painfully into her shoulders. Isa immediately released her and stepped back, only to pace in a tight circle. Ele quickly closed the distance to stand at Kala's side, never taking his eyes off Isa or his hand off his shamshir. Worse than that, though, was the fact that Kala looked relieved to see Ele. That knowledge broke through Isa's blinding rage, forcing him to recognize that he'd lost control for a second. Shame simmered inside him but it was nothing compared to the inferno of betrayal.

"Did you tell *him*?" Isa jerked his head at Ele.

"No," Kala replied softly.

Ele's gaze pinged between them. "Tell me what?"

"Or her lovers?" Isa persisted.

If Henri had known this entire time, Isa would kill him. A three-kingdom army could not hold Isa back.

"She didn't want anyone to know."

Isa hissed through clenched teeth and shook his head in disbelief. Why would Tahlia not want him to know? How could she hear his prayers night after night for a decade and not answer him? How could she leave him to live his life in a perpetual state of desperate hope, never knowing for sure, when she had the power to end his torment?

"You betrayed me." Isa's voice was laced with threat.

Ele took up a defensive position in front of Kala but she stepped forward in bold challenge as her expression hardened. "You betrayed her first."

A gut-wrenching roar tore from Isa's throat, reverberating off the walls and sending shock waves through the desert sands. He was vaguely aware of Ele tugging at Kala's hand, urging her out of the great hall and away from danger.

Away from him.

Isa didn't watch them leave. He couldn't. His mind was chaos, his body an eruption of rage. He had never wanted to give in to the black sand so badly. To become the monster that festered beneath his flesh and hunt the streets until his teeth were bloody. His goddess had forsaken him. There was no point to restraint anymore. There was no point to anything anymore. Isa surrendered, letting himself dissolve into a maelstrom of obsidian sand. He welcomed its poisonous pain. It consumed everything he was until Isa could no longer remember what it was like to be human.

KALA

Kala lazily traced her fingers along the surface of the water. Her presence did not disturb the koi who swam within the fountain's waters. They were used to her company. The fountain was one of her favorite places to go when she needed time to herself. To think. To reflect. The tranquil sound of the water cascading over three shallow basins calmed her thoughts. The servants and guards knew not to wander through the courtyard when she visited, allowing her some measure of peace and solitude.

Kala lifted her gaze to take in her surroundings. Only last night, the courtyard had been richly decorated and filled with people celebrating her twenty-first birthday. She had been looking forward to the event for years. Majid had planned every detail meticulously. With the promise of Ele in attendance, the night had the potential to be truly magical. But she barely had a chance to enjoy it before the evening turned to disaster.

After leaving Isa in the great hall, Kala had retired to her chamber without even attempting to return to her guests or explain things to Ele. Instead, she spent the night crying and screaming into her pillows until she eventually fell asleep, exhausted. In the morning, she had woken to a raw throat, puffy eyes and an emotional hangover that made her feel nauseous. For a moment, she seriously contemplated not leaving her chamber all day but she knew she couldn't do that. So, she dressed and braced herself for the day.

According to the guards, Isa had not returned to his bedchamber last night. That knowledge filled Kala with unease. She had left him in such a state last night, he could be anywhere by now, but she hoped he would return home soon. Kala didn't know if they could work through her supposed betrayal, but she also couldn't imagine her life without Isa by her side. He was her family. The one person she could trust above all others. It had killed her to keep Tahlia's secret from him all these years, but it wasn't her secret to share. Kala didn't even notice she was crying until a tear hit the water, sending ripples throughout the basin. She quickly wiped at her cheek with the heel of her palm.

As if Isa's disappearance wasn't enough, the guards had also informed her that Sabine was being held in a cell beneath the palace, awaiting judgment. Kala had no idea what to do about that. She didn't want to see Sabine, yet she knew she couldn't avoid it. Sabine had committed a serious crime, one witnessed by a large crowd. Now her life was in Kala's hands, just like Kala's life had been in hers all those years ago. The irony. It was like the gods were taunting her.

She would have asked Tahlia for advice except the goddess was refusing to speak to her. Kala couldn't blame her for retreating into silence. No one was ever supposed to know that she had ascended to divinity. Tahlia had wanted everyone to move on with their lives, to hold her in their memories the way she wished to be remembered. As human. Above all else, Tahlia desired for Isa to remain unaware of her immortal existence. Now Isa knew, and Ele would surely tell Henri and Malik. Everything was a mess.

In the streets outside, the festival continued, untouched by the turmoil brewing inside the palace. The sounds of music and joy filtered through the air, along with the rhythm of approaching footsteps. Kala turned, expecting to find Zaynab, but instead saw Ele striding towards her. Fireflies stirred in Kala's stomach. In the heat of the day, Ele looked even more striking than he had last night. As a boy, he'd had the most unruly mop of tight brown curls and Kala had been convinced that, as a man, he would have grown out of them. But he hadn't. They fell carelessly over ceramic blue eyes.

Being a foreigner, Ele's skin was naturally lighter than Merovian's, but the sun had darkened it. Last night he wore a sophisticated kurta that made him look like a prince. Today, his kurta was casual and sleeveless, revealing the impressive contours of his muscular arms. It was clear that he trained hard every day. Kala had been tutored by the best sword masters in her kingdom but even they hadn't achieved such an impressive physique.

Kala tried not to stare but she couldn't help it. She immediately chided herself for not putting more effort into her own appearance. She'd been so preoccupied with last night's events she hadn't even thought about it. Her eyes were probably bloodshot and swollen. She'd chosen the least interesting kaftan in her wardrobe; a mild yellow that probably made her look washed out. At least her tight braids would neaten her appearance.

When Ele stood before her, he held out his hand, palm turned upward to the sky. He held something square wrapped in a white cotton cloth. Kala couldn't resist the knowing smile that spread across her lips as she took the soft parcel and unwrapped the cake. When they were children, Ele would swipe cake from the palace kitchen for her. Her favorite tasted like lemon and spices, roses and sugar, and had almonds and pistachios on top.

"It's a peace offering," Ele admitted as he gingerly sat down beside her on the edge of the fountain. "I'm sorry about last night. I didn't know Sabine would follow me, let alone infiltrate your palace. I certainly didn't know that she's your sister."

The smile vanished from Kala's lips. Sabine was *not* her sister. Kala had renounced her entire blood family the moment they tried to kill her. She had hoped she would never see them or the Thaka ever again. Kala put the cake aside, her appetite lost.

"How do you know her?"

"She gives me information sometimes," Ele answered carefully, "when I have exhausted all my other sources."

Kala narrowed her eyes slightly in question. Her sister selling information outside of the Thaka—to the Captain of the Guard, no less—was unfathomable.

"You said she followed you here?"

Ele's features turned sheepish. "The reason I was late to your birthday was because Henri tasked me with a mission in the Old City. Sabine accompanied me there because I needed her contacts. Afterwards, I mentioned I was traveling to the Black Sands for your festival. But I didn't invite her."

Kala nodded in understanding. "She was always impulsive and too curious for her own good."

"What will happen to her?"

Something in Ele's voice made Kala lift her gaze to study him. "Why? Does she mean something to you?"

"No," Ele replied but the second's hesitation made Kala's stomach sink.

The gods really were mocking her. Out of everyone in the three kingdoms, Ele was sleeping with her sister. The thought made her want to throw up.

"But she is Henri's subject," Ele pointed out.

"She invaded my palace," Kala snapped.

Kala was positive Henri had no idea who Sabine was or that she was helping Ele. If Sabine was giving Ele information, it was in exchange for something equally valuable. Coin, perhaps. Or an alliance. Ele wouldn't want Henri to know about that. Kala was confident she could kill Sabine without fear of repercussions.

They sat in tense silence for a moment.

"Kala, what happened last night between you and Isa?"

Kala averted her gaze to the koi swimming peacefully beneath the water. "Isa learned a secret that I've been hiding for a long time."

"About Tahlia?"

Kala nodded solemnly. "She ascended."

Ele's chest deflated as if he had been holding his breath. "She's a goddess. Of what?"

"I don't know."

It was common for those who ascended to divinity to have their power manifest as something significant from their mortal life.

Kala thought Tahlia might have become the Goddess of Dance or Desire but Kala had never asked her. It felt too personal.

"We've never talked about what it's like to be a divine. She watches over me. Gives me guidance when I need it. I let her inhabit me sometimes so she can remember what it feels like to dance."

Pain creased Ele's face, raw and unmistakable. Kala felt it too. They had both been there the day Tahlia died. It changed the course of their lives.

"I'm sorry I didn't tell you. She made me promise not to tell anyone."

"It's all right. I understand."

"Isa won't." Kala felt the tears threaten to spring forth again. "He'll never forgive me for keeping it from him."

"Isa has no right to judge when it comes to keeping secrets. He has plenty of his own."

Kala's attention snapped to him. "What do you mean by that?"

Uncertainty pulled at his features, as if he wasn't sure whether he should say more.

"Ele," Kala urged.

"He keeps things from you." Ele's eyes searched her face. "Surely you know that."

She did. But she had been too afraid to call him out on it. Afraid of losing him. Of hurting him. She justified her inaction by reminding herself that Isa would never keep something from her that was important. If she trusted him with her life, she could trust his secrets too.

"He's ..." Kala tried to find the words to explain.

"Dangerous."

"What? No. I mean yes, he's Naiab, but he's not a danger to me."

"Are you sure?"

Kala stared at Ele, dumfounded. "He would never hurt me."

Ele's gaze drifted down to her exposed shoulders, where Isa's hands had dug into her flesh only hours ago, hard enough to leave blooming bruises. Kala suddenly wished she was swearing a shawl around her shoulders.

"I need to tell you something." The change in Ele's tone made Kala's heartbeat slow. "The reason I was in the Old City was because Henri learned that the priests had resumed the practice of human sacrifice."

Kala's jaw dropped. It was not possible. After Henri conquered the kingdom, he put an end to the barbaric practice. The priests were disgruntled, but they were too fearful to oppose him so they adjusted their worship. If they had tried to resurrect the practice, Kala would have heard about it. Her spies would have told her. Or rather, they would have told Isa.

"Sabine found out where the ritual was being held and I went to stop them but Isa got there first."

"Isa?" Kala's brows shot up in surprise.

"He knew about it. He'd already tortured and killed one of the priests to learn the location of the ritual. He slaughtered them all."

Kala didn't blink as she absorbed Ele's words. That's where Isa had disappeared to that night. He'd traveled to the Old City to enact justice on the priests. Without her approval. Without her knowledge.

"He wasn't exactly thrilled to find me there. I think I interrupted his rampage. He asked me not to tell you about the priests. He said you didn't need to know."

White-hot anger flared deep inside her. How dare he think she didn't need to know! Those priests were responsible for the deaths of countless innocent, albeit devout, people over the decades. They had almost killed Tahlia as a child. If Kala had known they were trying to return to the old ways, she would have sent Isa to kill them herself. So why had he kept it from her?

"It made me wonder what else he's not telling you."

They exchanged a heavy look. Kala thought about the other nights Isa had been missing from his bed. What had he been doing? Enacting justice on others for crimes he hadn't told her about? The moment Isa returned she would demand answers from him. If he thought, as her guardian, he had the right to do whatever he wanted without her consent, he was wrong.

"Like the black sand."

"What?" Kala frowned, confused. "What about the black sand?"

"Haven't you noticed his tattoos? They used to be turquoise. Now they're black."

"The sand of my kingdom is black. All the Naiab's tattoos turned black when they served me."

"And where are the other Naiab now?"

She exhaled a regretful sigh. "They left."

It was yet another reason why she had never questioned Isa too forcefully. He had given up so much to be her guardian. Over time, his men had abandoned him to return to the Citadel. He had no friends left in the kingdom and no guarantee that he would ever see his home again.

"Why?"

Kala shrugged. "It's hard to be away from home. From family."

A moment of silent understanding passed between them.

"When Isa transformed into sand in the Old City, it was black. The sand did not change back to normal when he left your kingdom." Ele hesitated before adding, "He slaughtered those priests as if he enjoyed it."

"I would have enjoyed it too," she countered.

Ele shook his head emphatically. "He's changed, Kala."

"We've all changed. Even you."

Ele's expression turned perplexed. "What about me?"

"You're so ... tall."

Kala mentally kicked herself but Ele's chuckle broke the tension.

"Thank you for being honest with me. I will ask Isa about it when he returns."

"Where has he gone?"

"I don't know."

They sat in pensive silence for a moment, each lost in thought as they tried to make sense of everything that had happened.

"This was not how I imagined us spending our time together," Kala admitted.

"Me neither. But we can change that starting now." Ele shot to his feet. "What would you like to do, my queen?"

A thrill coursed through her at the term of endearment. Kala retrieved her discarded cake and sampled a corner, letting its deliciousness dissolve on her tongue. She thought she could be quite happy to simply eat cake all day and forget her responsibilities.

"Let's go for a walk." Kala stood up and continued eating as she led the way through the courtyard.

Ele fell into step beside her, clasping his hands casually behind his back.

"So how does it feel now that you've achieved your life's ambition to be Captain of the Guard?"

Ele considered her question for a moment. "It's an honor but a heavy responsibility. And not everyone is accepting of it."

"Sounds familiar."

Ele shot her a quizzical look. "Your people love you."

"They accept me now. It hasn't always been that way. I came to the throne as a child, and now I am an adult, but I am still a woman. There will always be those who long for the old days of Rouhan kings and annual summits fighting to the death."

Ele snatched a corner of her cake and she let out a yelp of disapproval.

He popped it into his mouth without apology. "I could see you fighting to the death to keep your crown. You would be terrifying."

Kala scoffed. "I would have to kill Henri and then you would be obliged to kill me to avenge him. Not that you would succeed, of course."

"I definitely would."

"Really?" Her smile was wicked as an idea formed in her head. "Let's find out."

CHAPTER NINE

ELE

"This is a bad idea." Ele ran his hands nervously through his hair.

Kala glanced around at the soldiers in the training yard as if she had only just noticed them. "Why?"

"Because you are their queen. It's not a good look to lose in front of your soldiers."

"I don't intend to lose."

"Kala."

"Captain."

Ele huffed as Kala surveyed the weapons displayed on a table outside the armory. Ele didn't bother. He always carried his shamshir but he was loathe to use it under these circumstances. The soldiers were training close by, supervised by their Captain, but the presence of their queen and an outsider had drawn their attention. Their movements were distracted as they went through their drills, watching Kala curiously from a distance.

"Can't we spar in private?" Ele suggested, not for the first time.

"Where would the fun be in that? We're recreating an arena. It's all about atmosphere."

"If I concede defeat now, can we do something else?"

Kala shot him an unimpressed look as she finally chose a blade. "If I think you're going easy on me, I may actually kill you."

"You use a bifurcated blade?" Ele couldn't keep the admiration from his voice.

The double-bladed sword looked like a shamshir except the tip of the blade was forked. The sword could be split in two to allow for dual wielding. Ele had trained in all manner of weaponry but he rarely saw anyone use a bifurcated blade. While it gave the wielder an advantage of two blades, when combined the sword was somewhat difficult to use.

"I can." She smiled sweetly, splitting the blades. "First to draw blood?"

"No!" He would indulge her insistence of a public performance, against all common sense and his better judgment, but he refused to actually hurt her. "First to claim a death strike."

"Fine." Kala moved to an open space in the training field and took up a defensive stance.

This was madness. Neither of them were wearing any protective clothing. Kala wasn't even wearing sensible clothing. Her shoulders were exposed to the harshness of the sun and she was wearing silk slippers for god's sake. As Ele reluctantly strode out to meet her, the soldiers stopped fighting, sensing what was about to happen. Ele shook his head as he muttered a string of curse words under his breath. The only thing he was grateful for was that Isa had disappeared. If the Naiab warrior was here, he'd kill him.

Ele had barely taken up a fighter's stance when Kala rushed at him. Their blades clashed as he deflected her blows in quick succession. He elbowed her hard in the chest, pushing her back so that he could gain a second to compose himself. He hadn't expected her to be so bold but he should have. This was Kala. The Kala he met as a child in the Thaka. Smart. Scrappy. Unafraid.

She was grinning at him with wild confidence as she assessed his posture, no doubt looking for weaknesses and trying to anticipate how he would move. She didn't wait long. Her attack was audacious and precise, her footwork impeccable. She moved with a lethal elegance he had rarely seen in his own men and he had trained hundreds of soldiers. Kala had clearly been trained by the best sword masters in her kingdom. But then again, so had Ele.

Kala spun around, aiming her blades in unison for his neck, but Ele blocked her arc, halting all three swords a hairsbreadth from his skin. A proud smile edged his mouth. Kala cocked her head to the side as if to concede that she was impressed, too. She lowered her blades and retreated a few steps to reevaluate the situation. That's when Ele noticed the crowd beginning to form around them. The Captain of the soldiers was standing in the front, his arms crossed over his chest in annoyance, but even he couldn't resist the spectacle. The soldiers were whispering amongst each other, and some were openly exchanging coin.

A shiver of warning crept down Ele's spine. This didn't feel right. He couldn't hear what the men were murmuring to each other but he knew soldiers well enough to guess. The female soldiers were watching with cautious concern laced with underlying respect, whereas the men's faces were a collection of arrogant sneers and smirks.

Ele didn't have time to think on it further before Kala attacked. She almost caught him off guard, executing a series of moves designed to trick him, but he recognized her feints and anticipated her countermoves. Shouts rang out from the crowd, jeering them on. He needed to end this now but in a way that preserved Kala's dignity as queen. He would let her win. She would be furious with him but there was no other choice. He shoved her backwards so that he could ready himself. He would make it look believable and the fight would be over in a matter of seconds.

Kala hesitated. Her eyes narrowed on him in question and then sudden recognition. Her nostrils flared as a scowl marked her face. She knew what he was about to do. He tried to convey a silent apology but he also stood firm, refusing to change his mind. He never should have let her talk him into this. They weren't kids anymore. He couldn't follow her around like he used to, conceding to her reckless whims simply because she asked him to. Kala was queen and he was Captain of the Guard. Their positions demanded more maturity than this.

Kala spun both blades in her hands and lunged at him. *Fuck.* Adrenaline and instinct took over as Ele deflected each blow in rapid succession. The crowd stood in stunned silence at the vicious attack. Her blades sang through the air as she wielded them with unforgiving expertise. Ele had no time to consider anything but surviving her strikes. Their playful contest had suddenly turned into a fight for dominance. He ducked beneath one of her arcs, shooting her a warning glare, but then he was forced to dodge again as the second blade came dangerously close to his head. It sliced through a wayward curl, the hair falling to the black sand at his feet.

Ele's eyes widened in a mixture of shock and anger as blood thundered loudly in his ears. If Kala wanted to know who would win between them, he would make it very fucking clear before he conceded defeat. Ele cut forward, his maneuvers swift and sophisticated as he forced Kala to lose ground. Her composure wavered for the slightest of seconds but it was enough. He swung her around to cage her from behind, holding his blade down to make it clear that he was not claiming a death strike.

Ele's exhale burned down the length of her neck. He could feel her chest rise and fall as she panted heavily within his corded arms. He could see the sheen of sweat on her honeyed skin, but this close he could also smell her. An exotic fusion of floral scents and spicy undertones. It paralyzed his senses for a second. It made him wonder what it would be like to taste her skin. Would it be sweet? Or spicy? Would she taste like all the other girls he'd had before? Something told him she wouldn't.

"What are you doing?" She growled at him.

What *was* he doing?

"Claim the strike," she urged.

"Hit me," he whispered into the arc of her ear.

He needed it. Deserved it really. He shouldn't be thinking about Kala in that way. He loosened his grip just enough so she could elbow him in the ribs. He hoped she didn't try to strike him in the groin because at the moment it was mildly swollen.

"No," she replied stubbornly.

"Do it!"

Sand exploded around them, sending Ele flying across the training ground. He landed hard, the flesh on his arms shredding on impact, but he barely had time to register the stinging pain before his cheek exploded. Screams reverberated in his ears. They sounded muffled as his head reeled in confusion. The blows kept coming, splitting his sides, detonating his face, sending his vision blurry and his thoughts stumbling for purchase. He was vaguely aware of the blood that was gushing from his nose and coating his chin. It felt like he was under siege, being attacked from all sides.

"Isa! Enough!"

Ele blinked through the watery haze to see Kala trying to wrestle the Naiab warrior away from him. It gave Ele the precious seconds he needed to scramble to his feet and grip his shamshir. Isa was naked and unarmed but that didn't make him any less deadly. The warrior held Kala back with one arm, as if he were shielding her from an enemy, but he pushed too forcefully, and the movement caught her off balance, sending her sprawling to the ground.

Ele dived to break her fall but Isa was on him in an instant. Ele sliced his blade in a downward strike as Isa dissolved into sand, only to reappear behind him. Ele swung around but barely had time to deflect the blow of a double-tipped spear Isa had conjured from sand. The warrior was relentless as he morphed rapidly from human flesh to black sand, slicing open Ele's skin repeatedly and forcing him to absorb the power behind each strike. It was like nothing Ele had ever felt before.

Because Isa was Naiab. He was god-touched.

The intensity of each hit was almost crippling. The crowd stood in muted fear, mesmerized. They had likely never seen a sand wielder fight before. Ele remembered the first time he witnessed it as a boy. Watching Isa cut down dozens of challengers during the summit had been both hypnotic and terrifying. He had sliced through skin and organ and bone with abandon. He had moved like a hurricane, reaping lives and leaving a carnage of bodies in his wake. Ele never thought he would fight a Naiab warrior. The very act was suicide. Every swing of Ele's shamshir met thin air and yet every swipe from Isa's spear tore flesh. Sand magic made the Naiab invincible. No ordinary man would ever be able to defeat one.

But Ele was no ordinary man.

He stopped thinking and let his instincts take over. Most times on the battlefield or during missions, Ele relied on his training when combating the enemy. But sometimes, in the rarest of moments, he leaned into something else. A consciousness. A pulse. Like an invisible thread in the air. He could sense the very essence of life as it shifted around him. Its fragility, its end. In battle, if he reached out, he could pull the thread, snap it. His sword would find its mark and the fight would be done. It was an immense and terrible power. Most times he tried to resist its allure but not this time. Isa was intent on killing him and Ele's training would not be enough to save him.

"Isa! Stop!" Kala screamed.

The spear slashed across Ele's chest, leaving a trail of crimson fire. Ele reached out to that invisible string and tugged on it. Isa faltered a step, his face contorting in sudden pain and confusion, but then his spear shot out in a deadly arc as he turned on the crowd behind him. Steel kissed flesh as he sliced through throats, splattering blood across the black sand. Cries of terror rang out from the crowd but Isa didn't stop. His movements were effortless as he executed soldiers one by one.

"Isa!" Kala yelled in horror.

The Captain and several soldiers tried to fight back, to defend themselves, but it was pointless. They were cut down with ease as the rest of the soldiers scattered, fleeing for their lives. Ele ran to Kala's side and clutched her hand tightly, urging her to run, but she refused.

"Stop him!" She pleaded.

Ele tried to think of his options but there was nothing anyone could do. Not against a rabid sand wielder. There was only one way to end this. Ele reached out with his mind to pinch the invisible string but before he could snap it, Isa collapsed.

The spear in his hand dissolved to sand at his side. The training field fell deathly quiet.

Kala choked out a broken whimper, a sound of sorrow and desperate relief. She staggered forward to Isa and landed heavily in the sand, assessing his body for signs of injury. He wouldn't have any. Ele approached cautiously, his shamshir raised and ready. Kala pressed two fingers beneath Isa's jaw and exhaled a shaky sigh when she found a pulse.

"Guards!" Kala called out frantically but only silence answered her.

Moments ago, they had been surrounded by an army, but now all that was left was a massacre.

KALA

"When I dreamed of Isa on top of me, it was a little different to this. Fuck, he weighs a ton!" Majid complained as he, Ele, and Samir carried Isa's body between them.

They moved slowly down each step and collectively groaned in relief when they finally made it to the underground cells. Behind them, Sabine stirred at the commotion, pulling herself to her feet. Kala tried not to look at her, but a quick glance told her Sabine was still wearing the barely-there red dress and golden bangles she had stolen. Her feet were bare and her hair was a mess but she looked alert.

"Put him in there." Kala indicated to the cell next to Sabine's.

Zaynab moved to stand beside Kala, squeezing her arm in silent support, as they watched the boys stagger toward the second cell. Majid stumbled on the lip of the cell door and dropped Isa's head, smashing it into the ground and causing everyone else to collapse under the weight.

"Majid!" Samir swore.

"Sorry! But it's not like the guy could get any more fucked in the head. He's already gone insane."

Kala opened her mouth to defend Isa but what could she say? He'd murdered her soldiers right in front of her in a very public, unprovoked attack.

"Trouble in paradise?" Sabine asked as she casually strolled over to peer inside the neighboring cell. "I've been wondering what he looked like naked."

Kala ignored her. Majid and Samir limped out of the cell, clearly exhausted, while Ele lingered to stare down at Isa's unconscious body. She wondered if he was looking for answers. If he was in shock like she was. Probably not. Hadn't he warned her only hours ago that Isa was dangerous? She hadn't believed it. Didn't want to believe it. The man who had protected her with his life, who had brought her comfort on her loneliest days, who had helped her grow into a queen—he'd gone mad.

"Isa has the only key to the cells," Ele said before he strode out. He closed the iron door behind him anyway.

Ele looked like a violent mess. His kurta was ripped in several places, his skin sliced open across his arms, chest, and torso. He had wiped most of the blood from his face but some was still caked to his throat and his hands were stained with it. It was a miracle he was still alive.

"You do know it's pointless holding a sandman in a cell anyway, right?" Sabine drawled.

They all slowly turned to look at her. She raised her eyebrows at them as if they were stupid.

"What exactly happened out there?" Zaynab directed the question to Kala.

"I don't know. Ele and I were sparring and then Isa suddenly appeared, and he must have thought Ele posed a threat to me because he tried to kill him but then he slaughtered all those soldiers."

"Gods." Majid's face paled as he looked back at Isa. "I guess the rumors are true."

"Rumors? What rumors?" Kala demanded.

"That he's psychotic," Majid replied. "You must have noticed how everyone's terrified of him."

Kala blinked, taken aback. "He's Naiab. He's intimidating."

"There are stories about what he does to your enemies. How he rips them apart tendon by tendon and revels in their pain," Samir said.

Kala furrowed her brow. "I've never heard of them."

"Of course not. No one would dare say anything to you," Zaynab said softly.

Kala stared back at her incredulously. She couldn't believe her ears. Isa had kept secrets from her. Her own friends didn't dare to tell her the truth. The only one in the room who had been completely honest with her was Ele.

"How did you stop him?" Samir asked.

"I didn't." Kala looked at Ele.

Ele shook his head. "It wasn't me."

No one could have stopped him. Isa was god-touched. No mortal would have stood a chance against him.

"What are you going to do with him, Kafei?" Zaynab asked hesitantly.

Their collective stares felt like a weight pressing down on her chest. Her heart spluttered under the pressure and her breaths turned shallow with panic. The question wasn't really a question. She had no choice. He was a murderer.

"You could banish him. Send him into exile," Majid suggested.

"He committed a massacre," Samir retorted.

Samir was right. The only punishment for such a crime was death. But how could she sanction that? Who would carry out the sentence? Isa was the one who delivered justice on her behalf. He was the one she trusted above all others. How could she sentence him to die? To say the words out loud would be impossible. To watch him die would be like stabbing herself in the heart. She would never forgive herself for doing it. The idea of ruling her kingdom without him, even for one day, was inconceivable. It made her hands tremble and her stomach turn to acid.

"Kill me."

Kala inhaled a sharp breath at Isa's strangled voice. They all looked over into the cell as Isa sat up, wincing in pain before he rubbed the back of his head. Majid quickly stepped behind Samir.

"Isa." Kala tried to approach the bars but Ele stepped in front of her. His shamshir was already drawn in her defense and his expression was severe. "He's not going to harm me," Kala snarled at him.

It was unfair to take her emotions out on Ele when he was only trying to keep her safe but Kala had no composure left. She was furious and frightened. She didn't know what to do. There was only one person she turned to when she felt this way, but he was currently sitting in a cell, having put her in this position to begin with.

"Kafei, his eyes," Zayna's voice was sharp in warning.

Kala glanced over Ele's shoulder to see Isa looking up at her from where he sat on the ground. His pupils were blown out and dark rings surrounded them, as black as ink. Majid swore repeatedly. Sabine took a few steps back from the bars.

"The black sand. It's infecting him," Ele observed.

"Isa." Kala pushed past Ele and shoved the cell door open to kneel on the ground in front of him.

She stared at his grave face, studying his eyes, trying to read the truth in them. "Tell me."

Isa's expression softened a little. "I'm sorry."

"No, not that. Tell me everything else. Everything you've been hiding from me. What's happening to you?"

The length of a blade was suddenly at Isa's neck, forcing him to tilt his chin away to avoid the sharp edge. Isa bit down on his teeth in clear irritation but he didn't fight it. Kala scowled up at Ele as he positioned himself strategically behind Isa, like an executioner.

"If I see so much as a speck of sand you're dead," Ele cautioned him.

"Ele!"

"He's right," Isa admitted through clenched teeth. "The black sand has been poisoning me for years."

Kala's gaze traveled down to the tattoos covering his naked body. Once, they had been a turquoise color that shimmered in the light of the sun. Now they were dark rivers that writhed beneath the surface of his skin.

"I've done everything I can to fight it, to resist its influence, but every day I feel myself changing, becoming more aligned with the darkness."

"The darkness?" Kala's voice trembled, as if she were afraid to ask.

"I have dark urges. The sand heightens everything, all my emotions. It turns anger into rage. Lust into mad desire. Power into complete dominance."

"That explains so much," Majid muttered from behind Samir.

Kala shook her head, perplexed. It explained nothing. It didn't explain where he disappeared to at night, or how he had managed to hide the urges from her all these years. It didn't explain why he suddenly snapped and murdered her soldiers without cause or remorse.

"Why didn't you tell me?" Kala demanded.

"There was nothing you could have done."

"Is that why the other Naiab warriors left the kingdom?" Ele probed.

Isa's expression told Kala the answer before he spoke. "They stayed as long as they could."

Kala's lips parted in disbelief. She hadn't thought too much about the warriors leaving, except for the impact it would have on Isa. There was nothing suspicious about the Naiab wanting to return home and be with their people. But now she felt like a fool. She should have paid more attention, asked more questions, not looked away when the truth felt too personal.

"Last night I lost all reason to ..." Isa's words drifted off, as if he couldn't bring himself to say it out loud.

He stared into nothingness, unable to meet her eye. He was ashamed. Of losing the battle he'd been fighting all these years. Of letting her down and committing an unspeakable act. Kala slid her hand in his and held it tight. It was all she could do for him, and yet it felt too little too late.

"The soldiers insulted you, their words were treasonous, but I shouldn't have killed them. I can't control it anymore. There are moments where I almost black out from the rage." Isa slowly returned his gaze to hers, a raw look in his eyes. "You have to kill me."

"No." The word burst forth like a reflex. "No, this isn't your fault. It's the black sand, it's not you."

"The sand *is* me. It's inside of me. There is no getting rid of it. It used to flush from my system when I left the kingdom but now it doesn't. It's become a permanent part of me."

"If the sand is evil, why doesn't it affect anyone else?" Zaynab interjected.

Kala glanced back at her friend. It was an excellent question for which she had no answer.

"It only affects the Naiab," Ele deduced. "Because you can wield sand. That's how it infects you."

Isa nodded, as if he had come to the same conclusion long ago. "The Water Goddess said it was cursed."

Kala raised her brows in surprise. "The Water Goddess knows about this?"

"There is very little she doesn't know about. She warned me not to return."

"You knew about the effects of the black sand and you returned anyway?" Kala exclaimed, horrified. "Isa! You should have never come back with me!"

"I gave my vow. To you and to Tahlia."

Kala scoffed and was about to argue when Zaynab interrupted again. "If the Water Goddess knows about the curse, maybe she knows how to lift it."

A spark of hope ignited in Kala's chest. "Zaynab's right. Maybe the Water Goddess will know how to heal you and the land. We have to ask her."

Kala closed her eyes and tried to concentrate, which was near impossible given the frenzy of thoughts and emotions currently churning inside her. She wasn't sure how to do this, where to begin or what to say, but she had to try. All she could think to do was talk to the Water Goddess in her head as if she were there in person.

"Is she praying?" Sabine's tone was skeptical. "She can't think the goddess will actually answer her."

"The Water Goddess has helped Kala before. She saved her life once," Ele explained.

"My sister is Queen of the Black Sands *and* favored by the gods?" Her question was met with silence. "So, she's praying for what? A miracle? The Water Goddess to snap her fingers and heal him?"

"She's probably asking the goddess to come and speak with us. The gods can inhabit any human vessel as long as they're willing," Ele replied.

"I'm not willing, just for the record," Majid said. Others murmured their agreement.

The room fell to stillness. Kala formed the words in her head, explaining the situation and asking the Water Goddess for help. If she was like Tahlia, the goddess could speak into her mind or perhaps ask to inhabit her. Kala would let her. She would do anything if it meant saving Isa's life.

She waited but the quiet stretched on. After a few minutes, Kala switched tactics and reached out to Tahlia. Perhaps Tahlia could talk to the Water Goddess and convince her to help them. Normally, Kala would speak aloud to Tahlia but there were too many people listening, including Isa, so she said the words in her head. Silence followed. Kala tried to be patient but each minute that passed made her more restless. Her polite requests turned to desperate pleas turned to angry retorts before she finally opened her eyes.

Nothing.

She could feel everyone staring at her, waiting for her to say something.

Kala's voice was small when she admitted, "They won't answer."

CHAPTER TEN

ELE

Ele wiped the condensation from the mirror and stared back at his reflection. He'd removed his ripped, blood-stained kurta, discarding it on the bathroom floor, and wrapped a soft towel around his hips. His body looked as though it had fought a war and lost. Badly. Blood caked his skin and dark bruises were starting to bloom. The slashes across his arms and ribs were mostly shallow but the one across his chest was deeper. Not deep enough to require stitches but enough to know that it would leave a scar. Ele sighed. His body was already a patchwork of scars, he supposed it didn't really matter that there was one more.

Retrieving some medicinal supplies from his saddle bags, he laid them out on a small octagonal table in the bathroom. Myrrh would serve as an antiseptic and anti-inflammatory, while honey would treat his wounds. He turned to the bath behind him and poured in a vial of rose water to further reduce the swelling.

The bath was a square design and set deep into the floor, enough for him to plunge his body entirely beneath the surface of the water, but not wide enough for him to swim. The bath was lined with thousands of tiny moss green tiles and surrounded by a raised lip featuring an intricate mosaic pattern. Above the bath, a round skylight had been cut into the sandstone ceiling, casting a beam of sunlight into the water. Ele's room back home was located in the king's quarter and yet he didn't have a bathroom like this. He wondered who had designed it.

Steam curled off the surface of the water, promising a glorious heat that would soothe his battered body. He strode over to the bath and unfurled the towel.

"We need to go to the Citadel," Kala announced as she stormed inside.

"Fuck!" Ele quickly re-wrapped the towel around his waist and almost tripped backwards into the bath. "Kala! What are you doing here?"

She cast a cursory glance at his half-naked body before averting her gaze as if it wasn't worth a second look. Ele bristled at the blunt dismissal.

Kala perched her hands on her hips. "Making a plan."

"Can't it wait?" Ele gestured to the bath behind him.

Kala simply sat down on the tiled lip of the bath, crossed one leg over the other, and propped her chin in her hands thoughtfully.

"Guess not." Ele begrudgingly sat down beside her.

Barely an hour had passed since they decided to leave Isa in the cell and regroup tomorrow to discuss their limited options. Kala had protested the need to keep Isa locked up but even Isa insisted he needed to be contained. Not that the bars would hold him if he shifted into sand. Sabine had a point there. Otherwise, Sabine had been uncharacteristically quiet as they left, which made Ele somewhat wary. Still, there wasn't much Sabine could do from behind bars. Especially not with Isa keeping an eye on her. Two eyes. Ringed with darkness.

"I don't understand why the Water Goddess won't answer me. You remember how she doted on Isa. She would help him if she knew."

"She does know. She warned him not to return to the Kingdom of the Black Sands and he didn't listen to her."

"He made a vow," Kala retorted.

"He chose you over her," Ele pointed out. "Weren't you the one who used to say the gods don't forgive and they don't forget?"

Kala grimaced. Ele still didn't know a lot about Merovian gods, despite living in the country for over a decade. There were too many to remember, and there were endless rituals and festivals to honor them all. He knew that the Gods of Merovia once walked the earth as humans before they were chosen to be divine, but being immortal made them lose all memory of what it was like to be human. How fragile and delicate life was. To be here one day and gone the next. To be forgotten. He knew the gods could be fickle. They basked in the admiration of mortals but took grave offense to the slightest insult.

Most of the time, the gods were only satisfied with human suffering. They delighted in playing their games, manipulating humans like pawns on a chessboard. Causing carnage and then walking away, like a child smashing their favorite toy. Eternity was eternally boring. They needed some form of entertainment to pass their existence. They didn't care who they killed or what they destroyed as long as they were briefly amused.

The Water Goddess had always seemed kinder than most gods. When the ancestors of the Naiab were cast out into the Idris Desert to die, the people clung to the threads of life for days and fought with everything they had to survive. Their fighting spirit led them to a narrow canyon within a desert mountain range. Unbeknownst to them, it was the sanctuary of the Water Goddess. Impressed by their obstinacy, the goddess sheltered the people. They had co-existed there ever since, carving a home for themselves in the canyon walls. They named their home the Citadel.

The Water Goddess had been benevolent towards the Naiab. She had also saved Henri and Kala's lives. But her kindness was not selfless. Looking back, it was clear to Ele that everything she did furthered her own agenda. If saving Isa did not fit into her plans, she wouldn't do it.

"Tahlia is not speaking to me either," Kala sighed.

"She will. She probably just needs time."

Ele was certain Tahlia would never abandon Kala but would be shocked if Tahlia was willing to help Isa. Surely, as a goddess she would have known about the black sand and what it would do to him. She hadn't tried to stop the poison from polluting him. At best it was indifference. At worst it was revenge. Perhaps there was no way to cure Isa or lift the curse from the land. The Kingdom of the Black Sands had been established generations ago, which meant the curse was very old.

"We don't have time," Kala exasperated.

Ele gripped the side of the bath as he contemplated his next words carefully. "I know you don't want to hear this, but curse or no curse, Isa still murdered your soldiers. The people will demand justice."

Kala glared at him. "I am not going to condemn him for something outside of his control."

"It wasn't outside of his control. He let go of control because he learned about Tahlia. That's a choice."

"It's more complicated than that."

"Love always is."

Kala furrowed her eyebrows curiously as she glanced at him sidelong. "What do you know about love?"

Ele ducked his head self-consciously. "Nothing."

"Are you in love with someone?"

"No," he scoffed.

"Have you ever been?"

"Can we not talk about this?"

"Why?" Her wide eyes stared back at him openly. "We're friends. Friends talk about these things."

Ele averted his gaze. He wasn't sure why he felt so embarrassed. Friends did talk to each other about such things, but for some reason, he didn't want to recount to Kala the girls he'd pursued and won over. It didn't feel right to talk about his first kiss or the best sex he'd ever had. It would make him sound like a cad if he admitted he'd never had true feelings for any of them.

"Fine." Kala got up and dragged the small octagonal table over to them before sitting down again.

She grabbed a linen cloth and dipped it into the bathwater before lining the cloth with myrrh.

"What are you doing?" Ele asked as he observed her.

Kala pressed the cloth unceremoniously to a wound across his ribs and Ele jolted in pain. "Fucking hell!"

"Sit still."

"So you can torture me? No thank you." He snatched the cloth from her and began gently dabbing at his own wounds.

Kala sat in silence watching him but her mind was clearly elsewhere.

"You should have taken the death strike when you had the chance," she grumbled. "Maybe then none of this would have happened."

"Isa would have lost control regardless, and you would have lost face in front of your soldiers."

"My reputation can handle losing one fight." Kala dipped two fingers into the ceramic jar of honey and leaned closer to smear it across a wound.

Ele jumped back an inch. "What are you doing?"

"What? Am I not allowed to touch you?"

Ele swallowed hard. She was so close it was unnerving, which made no sense at all. As children, they would fall asleep side by side in the same bed, often holding hands. In a harsh world, they had

CHAPTER TEN

found comfort in each other and drew strength from one another. They were always close, rarely leaving each other's side. Now years apart had put a distance between them that was not so easily closed. Ele wasn't sure how to act around her because he was acutely aware of everything about her. From her proximity as she leaned in closer, to her fingers hovering just above his split skin, to the subtle scent of her lingering in the space between them.

He was overthinking it. He needed to stop thinking.

"Of course you are. Just be gentle."

"You don't like it rough. Got it."

He stared back at her, stunned.

Kala burst out laughing. "Relax."

She smeared the honey across his wound and he repressed a hiss against the pain.

"What about you?" Ele asked through gritted teeth.

"I don't like it rough either."

"No, I meant have you ever been in love?"

He wasn't sure if he wanted to know the answer but he couldn't help asking the question.

"No."

A strange relief flooded his chest but he frowned anyway. "I find that hard to believe. You're Queen of the Black Sands, you're beautiful, you're … you. You must have endless suitors."

"I said I've never been in love. Not that I'm a virgin."

Ele forgot to breathe. His cheeks warmed and the flush continued down his neck, much to his embarrassment. Kala didn't seem to notice, though, as she kept applying honey to his wounds. Ele let the conversation die and tried to focus on tending to his injuries. He didn't want to know the details of Kala's romantic liaisons. He didn't want to think about who had taken her virginity or made her come in her first earth-shattering orgasm. The thought made his muscles flex and his fingers curl.

Suddenly, Kala shifted from sitting on the lip of the bath to kneeling down between his legs. Ele went rigid as she reached across to rub honey on a wound just above his hip bone. Her fingers were light, her face pinched in concentration. Ele's balls tightened. Her nearness set fire to his very blood. If she moved her hand a little lower, or her mouth—

This was wrong. He needed Kala to leave the room right fucking now.

"Wow." She lifted her head abruptly.

"What?" If she'd noticed his dick twitching beneath the towel, he'd die right here.

"I've never seen it before."

Ele followed Kala's gaze to the center of his chest. She was staring at his oldest and most prominent scar, where a king had once stabbed him through the heart. Kala studied the scar as if it were a holy relic. She hadn't been there that day to witness his death but Ele had told her what happened. How Henri had prayed to the Goddess of Endings and Beginnings and made a deal; Ele's ending in exchange for someone else's ending or beginning. Henri did not get to choose who would pay the price, the goddess would make the choice, but it would be because of Henri. His bargain on that auspicious day.

Kala had been horrified when Ele told her about it. He wasn't sure what shook her more, the fact that he died or that Henri had made a deal with a goddess to bring him back to life. As a child, Kala had mistrusted the gods more than anyone. Now she seemed almost comfortable with them.

"Ele." Kala's voice sounded tenuous. "How did you survive Isa's attack in the training yard? He's Naiab. God-touched."

They held each other's gaze and Ele's pulse gave a nervous kick. After the Goddess of Endings and Beginnings brought him back to life, he remembered Malik telling him that he was god-touched now. Malik had asked him if he felt any different, concerned it would change him in some way.

"You're god-touched too," Kala said as if she'd only just realized it. "Is that how you stopped him?"

"I didn't stop him," Ele insisted.

"I stopped him."

They both shot to their feet as Zaynab walked into the room, but one look at her eyes and they knew it was not Zaynab. Inside their otherworldly depths lay the secrets of the universe, the delicate strands of eternity.

"Tahlia," Kala breathed in relief.

Ele blinked furiously as if he could change the image in front of him by sheer will. It was all wrong. Zaynab looked nothing like Tahlia. It wasn't Tahlia's body or her voice and yet Tahlia inhabited her. Tahlia smiled slowly and approached Ele to put her arms gently around him. He stiffened in the embrace, his limbs unwilling to open to a stranger.

"My brave warrior," she murmured against his shoulder.

Ele's reservations obliterated at the words and his arms crushed her, holding on as if he were afraid she might vanish. Tears burned in his eyes but he fought to keep them from falling. It was not Tahlia's body or her voice but those words were Tahlia's. They were the last words she'd said to him before she died. Grief flooded his system. It felt like a tidal wave, sweeping all his defenses to ruin until he was completely exposed. Tahlia pulled back a little and Ele forced himself to let her go. She stared into his face, memorizing every detail, then she cupped his cheek in her soft hand.

"I have watched you every day grow into the man you were born to be. I am so very proud of you. You are, and always will be, my hero."

Ele couldn't stop the tears from falling onto his cheeks but Tahlia gently wiped them away.

Ele's voice broke. "I can't believe I get to talk to you again."

The moment was too surreal. It was both joyous and heartbreaking. Every second a miraculous torture. He only wished Henri and Malik could be here too.

"Zaynab let you inhabit her?" Kala interrupted, her tone skeptical.

"I told her I could help you." Tahlia stepped back from Ele and turned to Kala. "She is a true friend. You chose well."

"Are you going to help us cure Isa?" Ele asked.

"No. I'm going to save you time by telling you that he can't be saved. The Water Goddess knows the truth about the curse of the Black Sands but she can't lift it. Being a divine does not make us all-powerful. There are limits to our domain. We are bound by the rules of our creation."

"If she knows the truth about the curse, then she knows who created it," Kala surmised.

"It had to be the God of Earth and Salt, right?" Ele's eyes darted between them. "If the gods are bound by the rules of their creation, only he would have the power to affect the earth. But why would he poison his own dominion?"

"For fun?" Kala guessed. "To watch us suffer?"

She was right but still Ele wasn't convinced. If the God of Earth and Salt wanted to watch humans suffer, why constrain the curse to the Naiab? A people who rarely traveled outside the Idris Desert?

"The curse was not cast by a god," Tahlia corrected them. "It was cast by a witch."

Ele looked to Kala. "A witch?"

"I didn't know witches existed. But then again, I only just learned about desert pirates."

"The witch who cast the curse died long ago. Without a witch, the curse can't be lifted. So you see, Isa can't be saved." Tahlia folded her hands in front of her as if the matter was concluded. "You are Queen of the Black Sands, Kala. You cannot let personal feelings get in the way of your duty to your people. Isa made a choice to return to the Black Sands, fully knowing—"

"He returned because he made you a promise," Kala shot back. "Must he now pay for it with his life?"

Tahlia pressed her lips into a thin line. "We all die."

A fragile tension hung in the air as they stared each other down, a formidable queen and an indomitable goddess.

"Not like this." Kala set her jaw in determination.

Tahlia lowered her gaze in disappointment. "You asked for my help and I have given it. What you choose to do now will have consequences."

Tahlia offered Ele a small smile before pulling him into a warm, parting embrace. He fought the urge to cling to her or plead with her to stay.

"Protect her," Tahlia whispered in his ear.

"Always," he murmured back.

Tahlia pulled away and turned her attention back to Kala, her expression heavy with implication, before her eyes suddenly changed to mortal irises.

Zaynab stumbled and Kala grabbed her friend's arm to steady her.

"Zaynab, just breathe. It can feel strange when she leaves you."

Zaynab glanced down at her body as if she didn't recognize it. "I feel empty. And small."

"You are brave. You didn't have to do that for me."

"She said she could help."

"There's nothing we can do to save him." Ele sat back down on the lip of the bathtub and braced his hands on either side of him.

Zaynab's eyes lingered on his half-naked form. At least she had the decency to appreciate it.

"I refuse to believe that," Kala said stubbornly. "We're going to the Citadel. I need to know the truth behind this curse."

"There's no point. You heard Tahlia, the Water Goddess can't lift it," Ele countered.

"I did hear Tahlia. She said without a witch the curse can't be lifted. We need to find a witch."

"How exactly do you intend to do that?" Zaynab asked.

Kala gave Ele a look that made him swear under his breath. He didn't know what her plan was but he already knew he wasn't going to like it.

ISA

Isa sat with his back against the stone wall, staring into nothingness. One of the guards had given him a kurta earlier at the queen's request so at least he wasn't naked. An evening meal had also been delivered but it sat untouched just inside the cell door. A cell door he could easily get through if he wanted to. But he didn't try. This was where he belonged. Caged. Like the animal he'd become. Despite apologizing to Kala earlier, he didn't regret killing the soldiers for one second. Their vile words had signed their death warrants the moment they uttered them. They were fortunate their deaths were quick. His actions, however, were indiscreet and now he had put Kala in an impossible situation.

There was no other outcome. He would have to die.

As queen, Kala had no choice. If she didn't have the stomach to order his execution, he would do it himself. His only concern was who would protect her once he was gone. Most of the people were loyal to her, but there were some who would see his death as an opening. An opportunity to infiltrate and destabilize power. Kala would need someone at her side, defending her.

The obvious choice grated on his nerves. He knew he should ask the guards to fetch Ele so that they could talk. If Isa asked him to be Kala's guardian, would he agree? His sense of duty to King Henri was unwavering, his loyalty absolute, but he cared for Kala. He would never betray her. He would be able to advise her well enough, having grown up around court politics. Surely Henri would release him from his duty as Captain of the Guard for as long as it took to keep Kala safe.

Still, the idea perturbed Isa. Ele was a young man, after all. He was prone to being distracted by a pretty face. If he set his charms on Kala, that would be even more dangerous. To Isa's knowledge, Kala had never fallen in love or been besotted by any man. She was far too sensible for that. But if she already shared a deep connection with the man, such as her closest childhood friend, perhaps that would be different. Especially if she was grieving Isa's death. Grief did strange things to people.

"Contemplating your end, sandman?"

Isa didn't respond. He was acutely aware that Sabine had been staring at him for hours, probably plucking up the courage to say something.

"Aren't you bitter that the queen you've dedicated your life to is going to end you? Seems a little ungrateful to me."

He wasn't bitter at all. A part of him was relieved. He had been fighting the black sand for so long he was exhausted. Death would put an end to it all. At least he'd learned the truth about Tahlia's ascension before his death. If he had any regrets, it would have been dying without knowing. Now he could go to his grave in peace.

"We could make a deal, you and I. If you free me, my family will pay you a rich sum. They are the most powerful cartel in the Thaka. You could travel anywhere you want. Start over again. Find a wife. Make sand babies."

Isa remained expressionless.

"She's not worth dying for."

"Shut your mouth," he growled in warning.

He wouldn't mind giving in to the dark urges one last time to end Sabine. He would be doing his duty to his queen in carrying out her sentence. Sabine seemed to realize his train of thought and promptly closed her mouth.

The tenor of footsteps pounded down the staircase prompting Isa to lift his gaze. Kala and Ele stepped onto the landing, followed by Zaynab, Majid, and Samir. Isa frowned and got to his feet. They had agreed to reconvene tomorrow to decide his fate, which meant something had happened to change that plan.

Kala bypassed him to march directly up to Sabine's cell. Sabine spared her an unimpressed sidelong glance.

"What do you know about witches?" Kala demanded.

Isa's gaze shot to Ele, who shook his head subtly. Something had definitely happened.

Sabine kept her features neutral as she considered the question. "Why? Are you looking to break a curse?"

"Do you know where to find one?"

"Maybe." Sabine cocked her head in thought. "For the right price."

"Your life."

"Not enough. You have so much, sister, you really should share some of it with your family."

"Do not call me that. Ever." Kala's voice was pure venom.

Sabine flashed a poisonous smile in response.

"What do you want?"

"Fifty percent of all profits from your kingdom's trade."

Zaynab drew a sharp breath as Majid scoffed and Ele scowled murderously.

"Kala," Isa's tone urged caution.

"Ten percent," Kala returned.

"I don't think you're in a position to negotiate."

"Neither are you if you want to keep your head."

Sabine turned the gold bangle around her wrist indifferently. "I am not afraid of death. I've lived longer than anyone thought I would and I've had a good run. No one will mourn the loss of me. But if your sandman dies, will you ever be able to forgive yourself?"

Kala squared her shoulders. "If you're so ready to die, I won't stop you. I don't really need you anyway. You were only my first plan." Kala turned her back on her and walked over to Isa's cell.

"Tomorrow we leave for the Citadel. The Water Goddess will help us."

Isa tried to keep the skepticism from his voice. "You've spoken to her?"

"We spoke with Tahlia," Ele replied carefully.

Isa felt his insides clench at her name. The fact that Tahlia had spoken to Kala and Ele but had not deigned to speak to him made him want to roar until the stone walls of the dungeon collapsed to dust. He had never stopped worshiping her, not for one day, yet she ignored his devotion. He would give anything to hear her voice again, even if it cost him his ears.

"You can't leave your kingdom ungoverned," Isa insisted.

"It won't be." Kala turned to face her friends, who were standing by the far wall. "I'll appoint Zaynab as regent in my absence."

Zaynab's jaw fell open. "What?!"

Majid and Samir looked stunned into silence.

"Ele, Isa, and myself will leave the kingdom in secret tomorrow, but after a day or two you can formally announce my absence. I will leave everything you need to rule in my place. Hopefully I won't be away for too long."

"Kafei, I can't," Zaynab spluttered, her face turning pale with dread.

"Please do this for me. I trust you. And you will have Majid and Samir to help you."

Majid quickly slipped his hand into Zaynab's and Samir offered her a curt, reassuring nod.

"As long as I don't have to take care of Cemal," Majid muttered under his breath.

Ele pinched the bridge of his nose in aggravation. "You are taking a grave risk."

"I agree." Isa stalked up to the bars closest to Kala. "This won't resolve anything. Even if the Water Goddess cures me, your people will still demand my death for what I've done."

Kala shook her head. "It'll be fine."

"You could lose your kingdom," Ele countered.

Kala shot him a lethal look but he weathered it without apology. Perhaps Isa's earlier fears were unfounded. They were both stubbornly standing their ground against each other.

"I will not sacrifice Isa to a death that is unworthy of him. Nor will I allow my kingdom to remain poisoned by a curse. As Queen of the Black Sands, I have a duty to protect this land and its people. I will break the curse and then I will return. If there is any price to be paid, I will pay it."

Isa knew better than to argue with her when she was like this. Once Kala made her mind up about something, no one could deter her. His thoughts reeled from the prospect of returning home to the Citadel. He had long ago accepted that he would never see it again in his lifetime. He thought of the people he used to know, his family and friends, the men he used to command. Everything would have changed, moved on without him.

"We leave before dawn," Kala announced and made to ascend the stairs.

"What about me?" Sabine shot to her feet.

Kala threw a puzzled look over her shoulder as if she'd forgotten Sabine was there. "You said it yourself. You will die tomorrow and no one will mourn you."

Sabine gritted her teeth. "Fine. Ten percent."

"I really have no need of you."

"My life then."

"Deal." Kala lifted her chin in triumph as she stared her sister down.

Isa didn't know what Tahlia had told them but he knew one thing for certain; Kala needed a witch. Sabine's sour face told him she knew it too and that she didn't like being bested.

"How do we know you're telling the truth about the witch?" Ele directed the question at Sabine.

"Have I ever given you bad information, Captain?"

Ele's reply was silent but he looked far from reassured. It seemed Ele had come to the same conclusion as Isa. Sabine would betray Kala the first chance she got.

CHAPTER ELEVEN

KALA

In the early hours of the morning, before the sun had a chance to wake, Kala led the way through her city. They moved like bandits, traveling in the shadows, their feet silent against the sand. Their faces were obscured by the headscarves that were wrapped tightly around their heads and necks, leaving only their eyes exposed. The floor-length, long-sleeved tunics they wore were necessary to protect against the harsh conditions of the Idris Desert, but they also served as convenient disguises. If anyone spotted them, they would not be recognized.

Despite the eerie quiet, Kala sensed Ele at her back. Sabine would be behind him with Isa bringing up the rear, no doubt making sure that they weren't seen or followed. Normally, sneaking out of the city would be easy, but her birthday festival meant that the revelries continued long into the night, crowding the streets with people. Even when the crowds finally dispersed, all the inns were full. People had to sleep where they could find room. Usually on roofs, down alleyways, or on street corners.

It was difficult to move swiftly whilst trying to avoid sleeping bodies obscured in darkness. There was also an increased chance that thieves would target them, looking for drunken victims. They would be the unluckiest thieves in the world if they tried to rob them. At her request, Isa had agreed not to use his sand magic again until he was cured, but even without it he was lethal.

Once they were safely outside the city, Kala breathed a little easier. She spotted Zaynab waiting up ahead, standing between two camels saddled and laden with supplies. Handwoven dyed saddlebags sat on either side of the animals and tassels hung below their bellies. They would sway with the camel's gait and deflect flies. Sometimes wealthy merchants decorated their camels with brightly colored embroidery or beads, but these beasts were unembellished.

"Samir and Majid are at the border, just in case you have trouble getting through," Zaynab informed her.

"We won't. Not with this official letter." Kala held up a parchment she had written last night and stamped with her insignia.

In order to enter any kingdom in Merovia, people needed permission from the reigning king or queen. Even rulers could not visit each other without prior consent. Guards patrolled the borders of each kingdom and anyone found entering without the necessary papers were detained for treason. The letter she had written last night claimed they were merchants who had entered the kingdom to trade during the queen's birthday festival.

"I've packed everything you need, Kafei. Please send word when you can."

Kala nodded and squeezed Zaynab's hand lightly in thanks. Her friend's face was harried with concern, though she was trying to mask it behind formalities. It was no small task to be regent, especially when they didn't know when Kala would return. She had faith in Zaynab, though, and trusted her implicitly.

"You two ride together," Isa ordered Ele and Sabine. "I ride with the queen."

"Why don't we have one each?" Ele frowned at the camels.

"It's less conspicuous this way," Kala replied.

Camels were expensive. Only the wealthy merchants could afford them. It would raise suspicions if a small traveling party could afford a camel each. Sabine followed Ele to one of the animals and he grabbed the bridle with confidence, urging the animal to fold down onto its legs. He offered Sabine his hand to help her mount the beast and she took it with ease.

Kala frowned in disgust. They were too comfortable around each other, it was irritating. Even if they hadn't slept together, which she highly doubted, there was a familiarity between them. It made sense since they had already traveled together across the Idris Desert to the Old City. They had spent plenty of time in each other's company. Perhaps that was when their relationship had evolved beyond mere business. Or maybe it had happened earlier. They might have been casual lovers for years.

"Be careful with that, Kafei."

Kala didn't break her stare, she knew that Zaynab was following her gaze. Ele ensured Sabine was comfortable behind the second hump before he took his place in the saddle behind the first hump and urged the beast to stand.

"I know how to handle her," Kala replied curtly.

Sabine had already tried to hustle her and lost. Her pride would be gravely wounded. A wounded animal was the most dangerous of all because it was vulnerable and desperate to survive. Kala didn't trust Sabine for one second, but she was the only hope they had of finding a witch. Kala needed her alive.

For now.

Once she delivered her end of the bargain, Kala would kill Sabine herself. She couldn't risk her family finding out about her. She knew the kind of trouble they would bring to her door.

"It's not her I'm worried about," Zaynab murmured under her breath.

Kala broke her stare to cast a questioning look at her friend.

"We need to go," Isa called out to her as he patted the bridge of the camel's nose.

"I will send word when I can." Kala pulled Zaynab into a quick hug, but her friend locked her inside the embrace and whispered fervently in her ear.

"I saw something when the goddess inhabited me."

Kala froze. "What?"

"Something I wasn't meant to see. I swear I didn't know what I was doing. I just pushed back a little and then I saw it. At first, I thought it was a memory but now I don't think so. I think it's yet to happen."

"You invaded her consciousness?!"

"I didn't mean to!"

Kala couldn't believe it. She had no idea that was even possible. Whenever Tahlia inhabited her, Kala took the opportunity to let her soul rest. It felt like sitting quietly in a corner of her mind, taking a break while someone else took the reins of her body. But Zaynab hadn't sat quietly at all. She'd used the opportunity to infiltrate Tahlia's consciousness, whether she meant to or not.

Kala doubted anyone else had ever had the courage to push back while a divine inhabited them. If the gods knew this was possible, they would never inhabit mortals again. And if they ever found out that a mortal had breached their mind, death would be the least of their punishment.

Kala's first instinct was to beg her friend to be silent, to never speak of it again, but instead the question burst from her lips. "What did you see?"

"An island, I think. I'm not sure. The image wasn't clear. It was like a dream. Something important is about to happen. Something even your goddess is afraid of."

They pulled away from each other slowly and exchanged a foreboding look. Tahlia hadn't mentioned that anything was troubling her, but then again, a lot had happened recently, and Tahlia was good at keeping secrets. The idea that a goddess could be afraid of something was inconceivable.

"Kafei," Isa urged.

"I'm coming," Kala called back before squeezing Zaynab's hands one last time. "Be safe."

"You too."

Kala strode over to Ele's camel and held the parchment up to him. "When we get to the border, you need to do the talking. They mustn't see Isa's eyes or recognize my face."

Ele took the letter and Kala walked over to where Isa was waiting for her. She mounted the camel to sit behind the second hump while Isa secured himself behind the first hump. They set off for the border with Ele leading the way.

Kala wondered if she should reach out to Tahlia in her mind and ask her about what Zaynab saw, but she didn't want to put her friend at risk. Tahlia would not kill Zaynab, but if any of the gods found out about what Zaynab had done, they would certainly end her. Besides, Kala had a feeling that if she asked Tahlia directly about it, the goddess wouldn't tell her the truth.

Tahlia would not want to worry Kala. Whatever was going on, she would try to deal with it herself. Or perhaps she wasn't allowed to talk about it. It might be a matter of divinity, a secret of the spirit world. It didn't matter. If Tahlia really was in danger, Kala needed to find a way to help her. But what could possibly threaten a goddess?

"Isa." Kala leaned forward and lowered her voice. "Do you still carry the vial you gave Tahlia?"

Isa retrieved a brass vial that hung around his neck, hidden beneath his kurta. It was strung on a silver chain and shaped like a teardrop with a beautiful floral design etched into it. Before she died, Tahlia had imprisoned the God of Beauty and Fertility in it. Isa had guarded the vial ever since, ensuring that the god never escaped. Kala leaned back in relief.

"Why do you ask?" Isa probed.

"No reason."

"Don't lie to me."

Kala pinched her lips. "I was wondering how the Water Goddess would feel about having it near her, knowing it contains her ex-lover." It sounded smooth as she said it but it wasn't a particularly convincing lie.

"The god can't harm anyone as long as he stays trapped in the vial," Isa replied.

Which meant the God of Beauty and Fertility was not the one putting Tahlia in danger. Kala tried to think of a way to uncover more information. Perhaps the Water Goddess might know something. There was nothing Kala could do about it right now. She needed to focus on the task at hand: crossing the border.

Kala stared past Isa's shoulders at Sabine's back. If Sabine wanted to sabotage them, the border would be the perfect place to do it. If she gave them away, the knowledge that the Queen of the Black Sands was leaving her kingdom would spread faster than a desert storm. It wouldn't stop them from leaving but it would make things harder for Zaynab. Kala had hoped to give her friend at least a day or two to settle into things and allow the people who had traveled for her birthday festival to leave the city. A quiet city was easier to rule.

Sabine had nothing to lose by revealing them. In fact, it would be a smart move. She knew Kala couldn't kill her just yet and it would be an easy way to get revenge for being humiliated last night. There was nothing Kala could do to stop her. She just had to wait and hope that Sabine would keep quiet. Just like she had to trust that Sabine actually knew where they could find a witch. She could be lying.

Now that she'd achieved her freedom, Sabine might be looking for an opportunity to slip away from them. She had to know that Kala would not follow her back to the Thaka to enact revenge on her. Ele wouldn't kill her either, that much was clear. If she managed to elude them and escape back to the Thaka, she would be safe.

It didn't take long before the border was in sight. A decade ago, a towering wall had marked the border, sitting several feet high and disappearing in both directions. Guards had patrolled the top of the wall continuously but no one ever dared travel into the Idris Desert. After the war, though, the walls had been torn down.

As they approached the soldiers at the border, Kala shifted nervously in the saddle. Sabine covertly cast a look over her shoulder directly at Kala and a coy smile stretched across her face. Kala stiffened. A soldier motioned for them to stop and their caravan came to a halt. Ele leaned down to pass the letter to the soldier who unfurled the parchment to read its contents.

He eyed them curiously. "Where are your goods?"

"All sold, my friend," Ele replied cheerfully. "There's no point staying with no goods to sell so we thought we would leave early. Beat the other caravans."

"My husband is keen to return home." Sabine leaned forward to affectionately wrap her arms around Ele's neck. "There's not a lot of privacy in the inns, if you know what I mean."

Dead. Kala was going to murder her.

Ele cleared his throat self-consciously but raised a hand to Sabine's interlocked arms and patted them awkwardly. The soldier glanced over at the second camel. Isa kept his head down to avoid eye contact but Kala made no such attempt. She was too busy staring daggers into Sabine's back.

"Oh, that's just my sister and our servant," Sabine said. "We had to bring them along for the help, though honestly, they just got in the way. Not very bright, either of them."

"Be kind, wife," Ele said tersely.

"You know it's true, husband."

"Help yourselves!" A loud voice called out. Everyone looked over to where Majid was leaning casually against a very tall barrel, a short distance away. "Doesn't seem fair that you all have to guard our border while the rest of the city celebrates the queen's birthday festival, so she sent you a barrel of her best wine."

Samir stood beside him with a tray of ceramic cups. The soldiers muttered amongst themselves before they slowly began to leave their posts and gather around the barrel. Majid greeted every single one of them like a long-lost friend as Samir handed out cups of wine.

"That was the best wine I've ever tasted." Ele indicated to the barrel. "Your queen is very generous."

Kala scowled beneath her headscarf. At least the soldier had the good sense to look embarrassed as he handed the letter back to Ele. When she returned to her kingdom, she would have to do something about the fact that her border soldiers were easily brought down by a charming smile and a barrel of wine.

"We might have indulged in it a bit too much," Sabine giggled as she nuzzled Ele's neck.

Kala had to look away as she swallowed the bile that rose in her throat.

"You're free to go," the soldier announced.

Ele led their caravan forward. Ahead of them was a vast, endless sea of golden sand. Rolling dunes stretched on for miles in every direction beneath a cloudless blue sky. Kala couldn't resist looking back at her kingdom. Amidst a crowd of merry soldiers, Samir and Majid were soberly watching her. Majid raised a cup of wine in covert salute. Kala wanted to wave at them, to give some kind of signal that she was thankful for their interference, but she didn't dare draw attention to herself. Instead, they stared at each other until neither of them was visible anymore.

"That was unnecessary," Ele rebuked over his shoulder.

"It worked, didn't it?" Sabine had already leaned back in her saddle and was observing the scenery with distaste. "I can't believe I'm back in this forsaken desert."

Neither could Kala. She hadn't entered the Idris Desert in ten years. Isa maneuvered their camel to take the lead since he was the only one familiar with the route to the Citadel. Kala and Ele had visited the place once as children but they had been escorted by the Naiab. Kala had no idea how to find it herself.

The Idris Desert was a dangerous, desolate, unforgiving place. Most Merovians didn't dare enter it. Everywhere she looked was the same: miles of sand, sand, and more sand. The landscape never changed. The dunes rolled into one another seamlessly as if there was no beginning or end. There were no landmarks to signal the passage of time or distance. There was no foliage or wildlife to distract the eye. Even the sky was cloudless. A vast expanse of turquoise blue with a scorching sun at its beating heart.

The temperature soared to new extremes. Her skin was already damp with sweat, but she was grateful for the material that protected her from the sun's scorching rays. Her eyes burned every time a hot, dry wind blew and she squinted against the glare of the sun reflecting off the golden sand. It was blinding and relentless but she would endure it. She would endure anything if it meant saving Isa.

"How long will it take before we arrive at the Citadel?" Sabine directed the question to Isa.

"Three days."

Three days with nothing to see or do except contemplate how to convince the Water Goddess to help them. It had been years since their paths had crossed and yet Kala had always felt some kind of connection with the goddess. She'd saved her life once and kept her company when death came for her a second time. Kala hoped that meant something, that she could draw on her kindness once again. If the Water Goddess refused to help them, Isa would remain cursed forever.

ELE

Ele divided the couscous into small ceramic bowls as Kala sat beside him tearing the flatbread into four pieces. He'd added some dried goat and vegetables to the couscous but there wasn't a lot of seasoning to the dish. Still, it would fill their stomachs. From dawn, they had traveled across the Idris Desert, only stopping to make camp when the sun began descending in the sky.

"I didn't know you could cook," Kala smirked as she observed him.

"You learn a lot of basic skills as a soldier. I can even do my own laundry."

Kala laughed. "Impressive. As queen, I had the best tutors for everything: politics, business, penmanship. But I never learned how to cook."

"I can teach you."

She wrinkled her nose in disgust. "Why would I learn when I have you to cook for me?"

"He's a man of many talents." The innuendo was clear as Sabine sauntered over to them. "Which one is mine?"

Ele handed her a bowl and Sabine took a seat around the campfire. Kala ignored her, not even attempting to give her a piece of bread. Ele released a long-suffering sigh. This journey was going to be painful. He glanced over at Isa, who was busy setting up the tents, one for each of them. They were only large enough to fit a bedroll but they would keep the dry winds and vermin out. Ele passed a bowl of couscous to Kala and she handed him a piece of flat bread in return. He passed the bread along to Sabine, who flashed him a saccharine smile. Kala pretended not to notice but Ele could feel her ire. She also didn't pass him another piece of bread.

Cutting his losses, Ele took his bowl and gingerly sat by the fire, putting a small distance between him and Sabine. He knew the move would upset Kala further, it looked like he was taking Sabine's side, but he wasn't. Kala despised Sabine and Isa was one command away from slitting her throat. If Ele could convince Sabine that he had a shred of feeling for her, even if it was pity, it might give him an advantage. They couldn't trust her, that much was certain. It was only a matter of time before she bared her teeth. But he was more likely to see the bite coming if he kept her close.

Having finished setting up the tents, Isa strode over to the fire and Kala handed him the last bowl of couscous with a piece of flat bread. He sat down and they all ate together in silence. The only sounds were the crackling of the fire and the scurrying of nocturnal animals beneath the sand. Now that the sun had melted from the sky and the temperature had dropped, the animals were coming out of their hiding places in search of food and water.

"Well, this is depressing," Sabine drawled. "Did you have your servant pack any wine? We could get drunk and tell stories around the fire."

"She's not my servant," Kala shot back.

"Your regent then, your high and mightiness."

Ele wished there was wine.

"What about balgarum? We could get high."

Kala leveled her with a flat look.

"You do realize that by breaking the curse of the Black Sands, you will cripple your kingdom's economy? No more balgarum. No more rare onyx wares to trade. How will you provide for your people?"

Ele had to admit Sabine had a point. Though Kala showed no signs of being concerned, Ele knew that she would be acutely aware of the consequences for her kingdom. He could only hope she had a solution in mind.

"Fine. Sober stories it is. I know how you and the Captain met, but I have yet to hear how you and the sandman met. How did you become her guardian?" Sabine directed the question to Isa.

"That's none of your business," Kala objected.

"Oh, is it a tragic story? It has to be. The position of guardian is beneath you. A complete waste of your particular skills."

"Shall I cut out her tongue, Kafei?" Isa's expression was deadly serious. "She doesn't have to speak, she can write down the location of the witch. She only needs one hand to do that."

Kala flicked her gaze to Sabine as if she were deciding which hand they should cut off.

Sabine rolled her eyes. "That's right, you have dark urges. Anger spirals to rage. Lust morphs to mad desire. Power becomes an undeniable craving. Tell us, how long have you desired to rule the Kingdom of the Black Sands?"

Ele almost choked on his couscous. At first, the question sounded absurd, but Isa's expression tightened as shame pulled at the edges. Kala stiffened.

"I'm loyal to my queen."

"That wasn't my question. If you crave violence and power, you would covet the throne. Being her guardian would give you ample opportunity to take it from her. You can't say you haven't thought about it."

"That's enough," Kala warned.

"Have you two ever had a thing?" Sabine's eyes pinged between Kala and Isa. "If you're so mad with lust, you wouldn't have been able to resist her. A young queen and her warrior guardian. It's cliche, but—"

"How dare you!" Kala shot to her feet and Isa mirrored her movements. Ele extended his arm out to shield Sabine, preventing Kala from charging at her. "He's like a father to me!"

Sabine held her hands up in mock supplication. "I'm just looking out for you, sister."

"Don't call me that!"

"Your trusted guardian turned out to be a psychotic murderer who has kept secrets from you for years. Do you even know what other horrors he's committed in your name? You should be more careful about the people you trust."

"I suppose I should trust you? I did that once and look what happened."

"Poor you. You became queen."

"I almost died!"

"Stop this, both of you," Ele ordered.

"I'm done." Sabine passed her empty bowl to Ele with a satisfied smile. "I'll be in my tent. No need to carry me to my bed this time, Captain. I can undress myself just fine."

Fuck.

Sabine strode over toward the tents, leaving Ele speechless. Kala's nostrils flared as she whipped her wrathful gaze in Ele's direction. She didn't say anything, which was even worse. It was as if she was waiting for him to deny it.

He couldn't.

Surely she knew Sabine was trying to rile her. To pick and pick until she found a scabbed wound she could rip open and make bleed. He thought Kala would have had more composure than to rise to Sabine's taunts. But then again, the Kala he knew had always been hot-headed. Not one to back down from confrontation or guard her words.

To Ele's surprise, Kala turned her fierce glare on Isa. "Tell me."

"What?" Isa's sombre tone hinted he knew exactly what she was asking.

"Tell me what else you have done because of your dark urges. I already know about the priests you slaughtered in the Old City."

Ele winced, the sting intensifying as Isa's scrutiny fell on him like a thousand daggers. This night couldn't get any worse.

Isa inhaled a deep breath, as if he were bracing himself for the fallout of his confession. "I dispensed justice. If a thief was caught, if a man assaulted a woman, if traitors were uncovered, I would deal with them. I never targeted the innocent."

"But you didn't give them a fair trial either," Kala countered. "Or a swift death. You dealt with them by yourself, in secret, to feed the darkness inside of you. I can only imagine how slowly they died."

Isa clenched his jaw. "You'd rather I showed them mercy?"

"Not if they were judged fairly and found guilty by law, but you never wanted me to find out about them. Especially the priests."

"I didn't want to burden you. I swore an oath to protect you, which includes protecting your peace of mind."

"Keeping me ignorant does not protect me. It weakens me and gives my enemies a weapon to use against me. I thought I knew everything that happened in my kingdom but I knew nothing about the person closest to me."

A muscle feathered in Isa's jaw as he lowered his gaze to the fire. It looked as though he was weighing her words in the flames.

After a few moments Isa conceded, "I should have been honest with you."

"I'm at fault as well. I should have paid more attention, asked more questions. I never should have trusted you so much." Kala's voice was heavy with regret.

Isa steadied himself as though he'd just absorbed a blow. Kala said nothing more as she trudged away in the direction of her tent. Ele resisted the urge to go after her. A decade ago, he wouldn't have questioned his place at her side, that she would want him there to comfort her, but now he wasn't so sure. He suddenly felt like an outsider in her life, as if he shouldn't have even witnessed such a private moment. So he kept eating, the routine act giving him an excuse to avert his gaze and pretend that he hadn't heard a word.

After he finished, Ele cleaned the dishes and checked on the camels. They grumbled at his presence. Although he was no stranger to camels and admired their resilience under harsh conditions, he still preferred horses. There was something about the steady thud of a horse when compared to the swaying gait of a camel. Horses were also better natured. Still, he scratched one of the camels behind the ears as he stared out into the dark horizon.

At night, the desert held a quiet kind of peace. The land, which in daylight was a raging fiery furnace, now calmed to exhale cooler winds. Stars multiplied across the black sky and the moon cast a pale, soft light on everything. Shadows stretched across the dunes that sat in a vast expanse of stillness. The sight filled Ele with a sense of serenity.

His mind wandered, wading in a sea of his own thoughts. When he left home for Kala's birthday festival, he could never have predicted that he would end up traveling to the Citadel in the hopes of finding a witch and breaking a curse. His only thought had been Kala. What it would be like to see her again. He'd been determined not to let her down. But now she was heartbroken and, although it wasn't his fault, he had contributed in some small way to the rupture in her relationship with Isa.

He needed to see her. He wouldn't be able to sleep without knowing that she was all right. If she told him to go away then so be it, at least he tried. Ele wandered over to Kala's tent but halted. Isa was sitting on a bedroll outside the entrance. Both of his legs were arched as he balanced his arms on his knees, tending to one of his daggers with a sharpening stone. Isa didn't acknowledge Ele but the rhythmic movement of stone against steel spoke the warning loud and clear. As long as Isa lived, Ele had no chance of getting close to Kala.

CHAPTER TWELVE

ISA

Two days passed in a slow, steady rhythm of camel hooves, blistering hot winds, and suffocating silence. With every mile they traveled, Isa felt an uneasy peace descend on him. He was going home. The Idris Desert was as familiar to him as his own heartbeat. He could navigate it by the pulse of the sands alone. He was born of this land and he had been away from it for far too long.

But even as he savored its familiar surroundings, Isa couldn't ignore the feeling that something had changed. Him. He belonged here once. The Idris Desert had been a part of him, its golden sand swirling beneath his skin. Now the black sand festered beneath his flesh. It made him wonder whether he still belonged.

On the third day, as the afternoon sun hung high in the cloudless sky, the landscape began to change. Dramatic rock formations emerged, leading the way to a rugged terrain of mountains. As they trekked further into the mountain range, they found themselves beneath the cool shadow of a narrow canyon. Towering steep walls of sedimentary rock rose on either side, surrounding them. The rock was layered with waves of vibrant red, burning orange, and salty pink. Each layer testament to a time that had come before.

Isa's thoughts drifted back to the last time he had trailed through this canyon. He and his warriors had captured a caravan wandering in the desert; King Henri, his lover Malik, his courtesan Tahlia, and two small children. That was the first time Isa's path had crossed with Tahlia's. Isa knew she would come. He'd been waiting for her. The Water Goddess had told him about the beautiful woman he had seen in his visions. She'd told him who hunted her. How to save her. Now those two small children were grown and Tahlia was dead.

"Why is the sand changing color?" Sabine's head jerked from side to side, her eyes scanning the ground as a crease of worry furrowed her brow.

The sand was gradually fading from a coarse rusty red to a fine powdery white. He could feel them now as they pushed deeper into the mountain range. The Naiab. The guardians of this sacred place. They did not stand in position like sentries or patrol its boundaries like soldiers. They were woven into the very fabric of the land. In the sand beneath the camels' hooves. In the sediment of the high stone walls. No enemy could ever hope to pass through the canyon undetected.

"It means we're close," Ele replied. "The Citadel should only be a few miles up ahead."

"Thank the gods," Sabine grumbled.

Kala remained silent as she sat behind Isa but he knew the journey would be wearing on her, too. The walls of the gorge tightened around them, narrowing until they were forced to walk in single file. As they drew closer, Isa tried to fortify himself for whatever awaited them. Kala was confident that the Water Goddess would help them but Isa wasn't so sure. He respected the goddess, in truth he owed her everything, but he also knew her. She was patient and cunning, and she held grudges long past eternity.

Isa's attention snapped to a lone figure standing in the distance, melting in the air like a mirage. The figure waited just outside the entrance to the Citadel, in front of an opening that had been carved into the sheer face of the canyon. Isa instinctively knew who she was. She had probably been expecting them for days now. Isa wondered if Tahlia had spoken to her or if she had learned about their plans through another source.

"Who is that?" Sabine shouted from behind them.

"The Shahri of the Naiab," Isa replied.

"Their queen," Ele explained.

Queen wasn't exactly accurate but Isa didn't correct him. A Shahri was more than a leader wielding significant power and influence over the people. They were mother to the people. Caretaker of the land. They also shared a unique connection to the Water Goddess, acting as her vessel to inhabit when needed. Shahris were appointed by the Water Goddess and bound to serve their people until their final breath, at which point the goddess would choose another.

When they arrived in front of the Citadel, Isa halted their caravan, and the camels folded onto their knees as if they were bowing to the Shahri. Isa had hoped to see a woman with long, wild hair, white with age, and hands as dark as leather. Instead, a young woman stood before them, wearing a brown salwar kameez with no shoes or other adornments, her hands folded serenely in front of her. Isa felt his heart swell in sadness as he dismounted. Ten years had passed. He had returned too late.

Kala walked ahead with Ele following close behind her, but Isa remained by the camels. Sabine lingered near him, watching the Shahri cautiously, as if she could sense that something was not quite right. The girl had few redeeming qualities but Isa had to admit her instincts were sharp. When the Shahri's eyes locked onto her, Sabine froze. Because they were not human irises, they were otherworldly. Windows into a tempestuous sky, swirling with the dance of storm clouds and the promise of rain. Within their depths were the raw, untamed forces of nature, the electrifying energy of lightning, and the clap of thunder.

"Is she—?" Sabine choked with fear.

"The Water Goddess," Isa confirmed.

The goddess's gaze appraised Sabine before ignoring Isa completely to land on Ele and Kala.

"After all these years, you have returned. It's almost as if fate led you here." A secretive smile tugged at the goddess's lips.

Kala loosened her headscarf to reveal her face and Ele followed suit.

"Where is Lunara?" Kala asked.

"Her life came to its natural end. This is Dema." The goddess waved a hand over the body she was inhabiting. "She is the Shahri now."

"You knew we were coming," Kala observed. "Did Tahlia tell you?"

All amusement faded from her features. "The goddess and I are not exactly on speaking terms. We have some ideological differences of opinion."

Isa furrowed a curious brow.

"Do you know why we're here?" Ele asked.

"You seek to break the curse of the Black Sands."

"Will you help us?" Kala's voice held a fragile note of hope.

The goddess pinched her fingers together slightly, the only sign that she was uneasy. "You have had a long journey. We will talk more once you are rested."

It wasn't the answer Kala wanted but Isa knew she wouldn't press the matter. They would rest and then Kala would plead their case.

"Thank you," Ele replied, ever the peacekeeper.

He'd likely learned the skill from Malik. That man had always been a smooth politician. Isa moved to approach but the goddess turned on him in an instant.

Her eyes flashed lightning in violent warning. "You're not welcome here."

Kala and Ele looked back at him, stunned. Sabine stepped away as if to distance herself from him. Isa's expression remained neutral because he was not surprised. In fact, he would have been surprised if the goddess welcomed him home. He had turned his back on her a decade ago when he chose to serve Kala over her. He had also turned his back on his people. It was a betrayal in her eyes, one that was unforgivable, and she was nothing if not spiteful.

Naiab warriors suddenly materialized out of the sand, one flanking either side of the Water Goddess, while another rose behind him to stand between the camels. Isa watched out of his peripheral vision as the warrior took the reins of the beasts and promptly led them away to be taken care of. Isa returned his attention to the goddess and that's when he recognized one of the men standing next to her.

"Arsyn."

Arsyn had been one of the men under his command until Isa left to follow Kala to the Kingdom of the Black Sands. They had been friends once, but now Arsyn was looking at him as if he were the enemy.

"What do you mean he's not welcome?" Kala challenged.

"The curse has taken hold of him. He's a danger to himself and others," the goddess replied cooly.

"He can control it."

The goddess assessed him, her eyes lingering on his black rimmed pupils, his ink-colored tattoos, and then piercing through skin and bone to see his tainted soul. Her nose twitched as if she could smell the foul poison inside him.

"No. He can't."

"But the Citadel is his home," Kala argued.

"He is no longer Naiab."

The words hit him like a slap across the face. They scooped out his insides, laying his guts bare for the eagles to pick at.

The goddess eyed him with disdain as she said, "Nor were the others who tried to return."

Isa went preternaturally still. "You turned them away?"

"The black sand had taken hold of them."

He shook his head in defiant disbelief. "That's not true."

The black sand would have drained from their bodies the moment they left the kingdom. It was not too late for them. They had waited as long as they could and then got out just in time. Isa's muscles tensed with barely restrained anger, every fiber in his body teetering on the precipice of murderous rage.

"Where are they now?" he demanded.

"Dead. They returned to the desert and the desert judged them."

The dark creature inside him roared and lunged, its eruption caged only by Isa's skin and bones. It thrashed about, demanding blood, the slaughter of everyone standing before him, starting with the goddess. He would rip out her heart with his teeth. Isa knew she would flee her human vessel in an instant—mortals could not kill gods—but he would enjoy tearing apart her vessel all the same. Slowly, over days, until she was nothing but pieces of meat at his feet. The goddess would be forced to listen to the mortal's screams as she watched on from the spirit realm. Sweet music to his ears. And he wouldn't stop there. He would turn this canyon into a river of blood. There would be no end to his vengeance until everyone in the Citadel was dead.

He took a menacing step forward, but bursts of sand erupted around him until he was surrounded by Naiab warriors armed with double-edged spears, all leveled at him. It didn't matter. He would slaughter them all. A powerful force crashed into his mind, flooding his nervous system until white-hot pain exploded behind his dark-rimmed eyes. Isa doubled forward as he clutched his head in his hands and gnashed his teeth in agony. His body wrestled against it, demanding satisfaction, but the world around him tilted and he swore he was going to pass out. Instead, his back straightened and his limbs moved as if they were being propelled forward by invisible strings, blindly stumbling away down the path of the narrow canyon.

"Isa!"

Kala's voice sounded far away as it penetrated his consciousness but somehow it brought him back to himself.

Dead. His men were dead.

His mind slowly cleared like the sands dissipating from a red storm. They had died because of him. They had chosen to stay with him, to serve him, and that decision had cost them their lives. They never reunited with their families. They never saw their home again.

Kala was suddenly in front of him, yelling in his face. It took him a moment to recognize her, to filter her words. "Where are you going?"

Where was he going? He lifted his gaze to the horizon and instinctively knew.

"The desert."

He kept walking.

"What?! You can't. Without supplies, you won't survive. Stop." Kala pushed her hands firmly into his chest.

Isa stopped at her command. "I knew the moment I chose you, the Water Goddess would never let me return. But I didn't realize my men would pay the price as well."

They stared at each other, a shared grief passing between them, helpless to change any of it. Isa knew Kala would feel the weight of their deaths on her conscience, just like he did, but she was not to blame.

He was.

"Whether I live or die, you still need to cure your kingdom. Rest in the Citadel. Speak to the Water Goddess. She knows something."

Kala looked past him to where the camels had stood moments ago but they'd been taken away, along with the saddle bags and provisions. There was nothing she could offer him.

"Don't worry about me," he urged. "You need to watch your back. Sabine is likely to turn on you at any moment."

"I'll keep her safe," Ele promised as he approached them from behind.

Kala looked pained and torn, but there was no other option and she knew it. "I'll get the information as quickly as possible and then we'll leave. How will we find you?"

Isa knew that wasn't going to happen. The goddess would drag this out for days. She was forcing him to go through the trial again, but this time it wasn't to prove himself worthy of being a Naiab warrior. It was for revenge. She wanted him dead.

"Have the Naiab send a vibration through the sand. I will feel it and come to you."

If he was still alive.

Kala nodded weakly but she didn't look any less worried. Isa turned his attention to Ele, his expression hardening. The idea of leaving Kala unprotected for even a minute was making his blood simmer and his skin itch, but the prospect of leaving her in Ele's care set his nerves on edge for completely different reasons.

"I need to have a word with the Captain. Alone."

Kala glanced between them and opened her mouth like she might protest but then she closed it again. She hesitated a moment, as if she was unsure how to leave him. Isa wanted to pull her into his chest and hold her in a tight embrace, but given what had passed between them over the last few days, he remained still and left that decision up to her. Kala reluctantly walked away and Isa's shoulders wilted in disappointment. He waited until she was out of earshot before he spoke, his fierce gaze pinning Ele to the canyon wall.

"You will not take advantage of my absence, do you understand? If I find out that you so much as touched her without her permission—"

"I understand the concept of consent. Do you?"

Isa punched him in the face. Irritatingly, Ele didn't even lose his balance. He simply swiveled his head back to stare at him, vicious murder in his eyes.

KALA

Kala flinched as she watched Isa punch Ele in the face. The force behind it would have laid any other man out in the sand unconscious but Ele stood his ground. They were too far away for her to overhear what had sparked the violent response but she could guess. It had to do with her. She held her breath for Ele's retaliation but it never came. After staring Isa down, he simply walked away, his strides long and controlled, as if he were forcing himself to breathe through every step.

Their gazes met from across the distance and Ele's expression remained unrepentant. Normally, Kala would have defended Isa's actions but she remained silent. She'd been blind to Isa for years, never questioning him, failing to see what he was keeping from her. Now she felt like a fool. Like she couldn't trust her own judgment.

"You've been changed." The Water Goddess's sharp eyes latched onto Ele with new understanding.

She said nothing more before disappearing through the crude opening carved into the wall. The Naiab warriors waited expectantly for them to follow. Ele complied, leading the way. Sabine trailed behind him, looking unnerved at the prospect of entering the dark passageway into the unknown. It was understandable. Kala still remembered how terrified she had felt as a child to step inside the mysterious void. But then Ele had taken her hand, and her fear had dissolved instantly as they crossed the threshold together.

Now she was standing alone, a light breeze stirring the white sand at her feet. Kala cast her gaze back to Isa, watching as he gradually faded from sight, vanishing into the maw of the canyon. She promised herself it wouldn't be the last time she saw him.

She was a terrible liar.

He had no food. No water. No shelter. He would be dead by sundown tomorrow. Which meant there was no time for rest. She needed to speak to the Water Goddess and convince her to help. Kala stepped inside the sandstone wall. The temperature plummeted as darkness swallowed her whole.

Despite not being able to see anything, she kept walking, reassured by the knowledge that it would eventually lead her out into a vast chamber. The air in the tunnel was thick and heavy with moisture. It suffocated her breath, amplifying the feeling that the walls were closing in on her. Still, she moved her feet forward until a faint glimmer of light beckoned ahead. When she emerged, she stepped out into a spacious cavern. Light filtered through a natural opening in the ceiling and the air was mercifully dry. Kala inhaled a deep breath.

"This is the Citadel?" Sabine gaped in awe.

"Amazing, isn't it?" Ele replied.

They were standing side by side a short distance ahead of her, captivated by the sight in front of them. Etched into the cave walls that stretched high toward the sky stood a vertical city. Despite her memories of the Citadel, Kala's jaw slackened with awe to see it again.

The city defied gravity itself. Each layer of mineral formation in the wall created a distinct level. Narrow walkways curled around each level, yet there were no railings to stop anyone from plummeting down the sheer face of the cliffs. Each landing featured a maze of corridors hewn from the very rock that encased them. They wound through the city, while natural bridges and carved stairs clung precariously to the sandstone walls. Kala recalled that every corridor and walkway eventually led back to the center of the cave. To the heart of the Citadel.

At ground level, enclosed within the towering walls of the vertical city, was a field. It was tall with wheat and surrounded by fruit trees and fertile vegetable gardens, all of it growing in fine white sand. With the scarcity of water, the crops defied nature. Yet they were thriving.

The city was alive with activity. People were tending to the field, checking the wheat heads and clearing debris. Others bustled along each level, going about their daily lives, except that there was a distinct air of excitement.

"I'm afraid you've caught us at a busy time." Dema stood quietly to the side, observing her people.

Kala's heart plummeted at the sight of her eyes, which had returned to a light hazel color. "I need to speak to the Water Goddess."

"She will speak to you after the harvest," Dema replied.

Her features, even her voice, seemed younger now that the goddess was no longer inhabiting her.

"Harvest?"

Dema inclined her head to the wheat field. Of course, the people were checking the wheat to see if it was ready to harvest and store.

"How long does the harvest take?"

"A few days."

Kala's face fell to stone. "Isa doesn't have a few days. I need to speak to the goddess. Now."

"I'm sorry," Dema said but she didn't seem sorry at all. "Arsyn, will you please show our guests to their rooms?"

Kala was surprised to find that both Naiab warriors had followed her through the entrance. Arsyn didn't say a word as he walked off toward the first level of the city. Ele and Sabine followed while Kala speared a resentful look at Dema before she reluctantly fell into step behind them. She would need to find a way to get the goddess's attention. If the goddess's plan was for Isa to die in the Idris Desert, paying the ultimate price for his supposed betrayal, then she would be bitterly disappointed. Kala refused to let her enact her divine judgment.

For now, though, she needed to calm the anger raging through her body. It would do her no good. She could almost hear Isa's voice in her head, urging her to remain focused and alert. As they were escorted through the city, the Naiab observed them with interest, their demeanor warm and welcoming. Kala knew it was rare for the Citadel to receive visitors. Despite the walls that separated each kingdom from the Idris Desert being torn down after the war, very few people dared to travel into the Idris, let alone travel to the Citadel. There was still a lot of mystery and fear about the Naiab. And if large desert warriors with sand magic weren't enough to cause concern, there was the prospect of coming face to face with a goddess.

Kala forced herself to make eye contact and smile back at the people. She was yet to formulate a strategy to get the goddess's attention, but she might need help so it was in her best interest to be friendly. As they moved upwards through the city, the passageways became more cramped, forcing them to squeeze to the side in single file whenever someone needed to pass them. The ceiling was also unnervingly low. Ele almost had to duck his head.

After ascending several stories, Arsyn turned down a path that Kala recognized. It led to a corridor of guest rooms. The rooms had no doors, only crude openings that had been carved into the sandstone wall. Woven tapestries hung down from a frame bolted into the rock, providing some semblance of privacy, but in reality conversations would be easily overheard.

"You can have these three." Arsyn indicated to two rooms next to each other and one directly opposite. "Your saddlebags will be brought to you. I'll have someone bring food and water as well."

"Thank you," Ele replied.

Sabine looked a little unsure as she lifted the tapestry and disappeared inside one of the rooms.

"Wait." Kala grabbed Arsyn's arm as he made to leave. "You're Isa's friend, right?"

Arsyn stared down at her hand as if it were the jaws of a snake. "Not anymore."

"Because he fell victim to a curse?" Kala challenged.

"Because he left us. He abandoned his people."

Kala jerked her hand back. "He's the only reason you're alive today. This entire city would have perished without water if it wasn't for Isa."

"You returned our water. Not Isa."

It wasn't that simple, but Kala knew it didn't matter what she said, the narrative had long ago been etched into stone.

"Then you owe me. Find Isa. Give him food and water to keep him alive for a few days."

Arsyn shoved past her. "I can't do that. It's between him and the desert now."

Kala cursed a string of expletives at Arsyn's back but he kept walking.

Son of a donkey.

Kala shoved the tapestry aside and stepped into her room. Small did not begin to describe it. It was only large enough for a round table and two chairs. A flat surface had been carved into the end of it, resembling a bed, with a blanket and pillow tossed on top. The walls were rough, adorned with natural patterns and jutted rocks, and the ceiling felt like it might collapse at any moment. A dense, earthy smell filled her nostrils.

"Kala?" Ele called out before slipping inside behind her.

Now the space felt even smaller.

"What?" She didn't mean to snap at him. Or maybe she did.

"I know you're worried about Isa but he'll be fine. He's Naiab."

Not anymore. The goddess had said those words to wound him but it was also the truth. He was no longer part of the desert. He was melded with the black sand. But she didn't have the energy to argue with Ele. There was nothing more she could do for Isa right now.

"I'm tired." The exhaustion of three days traveling across the Idris Desert was suddenly hitting her in full force.

Despite the clear dismissal, Ele lingered. Kala raised her gaze to him in silent question.

"Maybe without Isa here to protect you, I should ... stay."

This time the snap in her voice was intentional. "I'm perfectly capable of protecting myself."

"I know you are but—"

Kala pinched her eyes closed and inhaled a long-suffering breath. "Just leave."

She felt his wounded stare boring into her before he batted the tapestry aside and left.

ELE

Ele halted at the sight of Sabine standing by her doorway, leaning against the stone wall, her arms crossed casually over her chest.

"Rejected," she crooned. Ele scowled which only made Sabine's grin grow wider. "What? Afraid I'll kill her in her sleep?"

Yes. He was. He knew without a doubt that her twin scythe blades were hidden beneath the folds of her tunic.

"Are you going to insist you wouldn't stoop so low?" He retorted.

"Not at all. I kill my enemies the first chance I get."

"She's not your enemy."

Sabine's features crumpled in mock confusion. "She refused to be my ally which makes her my enemy."

Ele had no patience for this argument. "I'm going to get some rest."

"Sure." Sabine shrugged. "If you think you'll be able to sleep knowing she's directly across the hall from me."

Ele narrowed his eyes at her.

She returned a venomous smile before sauntering up to him, her gaze roving over the contours of his body. "Or you could keep me company. I'm less likely to cut her into tiny pieces if you're distracting me."

She had a point. He wouldn't be able to sleep unless he knew Kala was safe. But even as he followed Sabine to her room, he knew he was going to regret this.

CHAPTER THIRTEEN

ISA

Isa removed his headscarf and tunic and lay them out over the jagged rocks. He had wandered through the desert mountains looking for a place to find refuge and eventually spotted a natural bridge. Beneath it was a small cave-like structure with an opening at either side. It was an ideal shelter, exposed enough to provide ample light but shaded enough to escape the intense heat of the sun. Within the shadow of the bridge, Isa crouched down, cupping his hands together to dig in the sand. It didn't take long before he had dug a hole large enough to resemble a shallow grave.

If he was going to survive, he needed to control his body temperature. He never had to worry about that as a Naiab warrior. The sand magic changed the composition of their skin, turning it a golden color. The sun did not burn them like it did others. They felt the warmth from its rays but it did not scorch them. They could move through the desert freely, morphing from sand to man, and they would never feel its rage. But the black sand offered no such protection. The heat from the sun seared into his flesh like a brand. Sleeping during the day would protect him and help control his body temperature by avoiding unnecessary exertion. It would also conserve his sweat.

Isa lay down in the shallow grave and closed his eyes, trying to ignore the drought in his throat. Sleeping in the ground would be cooler than on the sand's surface. Tonight, when the heat had dissipated from the day and the animals were emerging from their homes, he would hunt for food and water. While he could endure a few days without food, the lack of water posed an immediate threat. He would not last another day without water. If he were a stranger to this land, he might entertain the hope of finding a lake or an oasis, but the Idris Desert held no mystery for him. Though he hadn't returned for nearly a decade, he could sense the terrain, and not much had shifted in all that time. There was no large water source anywhere. The only free flowing water was within the Citadel itself, courtesy of the Water Goddess.

Isa considered shifting and staying in his sand form until Kala found a way to call him back to her. It would negate the need for food and water, but he wasn't sure how long he could last in his sand form. He had never remained changed for longer than a day. If he let himself go for several days, would he be able to shift back? Or would he lose his humanity? In the end, it didn't matter. He had promised Kala he wouldn't shift again until he was cured of the curse. He needed to keep his word, even if it cost him his life.

Isa tried not to dwell on the thought of death. If the desert wanted to claim him, it would. Kala was safe. That was all that mattered. With or without him, she would find a way to cure her kingdom. He couldn't be by her side forever. Regardless of the curse, at some point something would have separated them. She was strong and smart and her friends were loyal. They would keep her safe if he couldn't.

Sleep took him swiftly and the day melted from his consciousness. His mind drifted aimlessly like granules of sand on a hot, dry wind. Memories of his trial flooded back to him. He had been so young then, on the cusp of manhood. For years, he'd dreamed of the day when he would walk out into the desert and return triumphant, proving himself worthy of being a Naiab warrior. He knew the desert would test him but he was confident he could endure it. He had no idea what awaited him.

The first two days alone in the desert were tolerable but then dehydration and heat-sickness set in. Delirium seized his mind. The hallucinations were vicious, his own senses paralyzing him. The desert played its tricks, forcing him to confront his deepest fears. He was not worthy. He would die here. A dishonorable death. Eventually time lost all meaning, and death felt like a welcome relief. But then he saw her.

Thick dark curls billowed around a heart-shaped face, contrasting against the soft hue of her warm, honeyed skin. Emerald eyes held him captive within their gaze. Beautiful was an inadequate word to describe her. She was everything. Exquisite light fractured into a kaleidoscope of colors. The chorus of a thousand voices singing in harmony. A magnificent force of nature, raw, untamed, and eternal. She had looked at him as if she knew the secrets of the universe. She saw him right down to the marrow in his bones. His weaknesses. His strengths. His carnal desires.

When her rosebud lips parted, as if to breathe him in, his heart had exploded. In that moment, Isa knew he was hers. Only hers. All the days he was yet to live, every night, every minute belonged to her. She commanded the very beat in his heart. There would never be another who could compare. He would wait an eternity for her.

Jasmine, fig blossoms, and rose petals filled his senses. The scent of her. Raw desire ignited Isa's body. The force of it ruptured through him, sending his heart galloping. It felt so real. Like she was standing before him. Like he could reach out and touch her. Was this a memory or a dream? Every night since Tahlia died, he had tried to see her in his dreams. He longed for her to haunt his nights but she never did. The only way he could see her was to remember her in the harsh light of day. To pray at her shrine and worship her memory. But now the desert had conjured her like a vision. Dream or memory, it did not matter. Isa never wanted to wake from this. Let death come for him, he would surrender himself willingly, because this was paradise.

Tahlia's calm, ethereal presence shattered in an instant, replaced by a blazing intensity as her features sharpened with boundless fury.

Your death will not be so easy.

ISA

Isa startled awake, his senses alert. It may have been the drop in temperature that woke him, or the faint sounds of scurrying creatures moving along the sand's surface, but all he knew was Tahlia's voice echoing in his ears. A familiar sound. A forgotten song. But now he recognized every note.

"Goddess." Isa breathed into the darkness.

The darkness didn't reply.

Isa couldn't bring himself to move. He desperately wanted to close his eyes and return to wherever he had been. Wherever she was. It hadn't been a dream. Perhaps it had started as one but then Tahlia appeared to him. She was there, inside his mind. Isa didn't care about her wrathful words or promise of vengeance. He didn't care that the desert lay in waiting, ready to claim him. That the Water Goddess had condemned him to death. Until he saw Tahlia again, he dared not die.

Isa sat up from the shallow grave and took in his surroundings. Night had fallen, bringing with it blessed relief from the heat. His body felt cool and rested, but his tongue was stuck to the roof of his dry mouth and his lips were beginning to crack. Isa got to his feet and pulled his tunic over his body, grateful that muscle cramps and vertigo hadn't set in yet. He would need to make the most of the next few hours before his body started shutting down.

Isa set out into the Idris Desert. The full moon cast a soft, silver glow across the sand, but within the gorges between the mountains, the darkness was so dense not even the moon's light could penetrate it. Though he could navigate by the stars and sense the landscape through the sand that crawled beneath his skin, Isa tried not to travel far from his shelter. He was all too aware that it had been several hours since he last drank water. His mind was becoming sluggish. Soon his head would start throbbing with splitting pain. Confusion would come next. If he lost his bearings, it could be deadly.

Through the hours of the night, Isa wandered, gathering sticks as he found them so he could light a fire. Mercifully, his firestones and dagger were on him when he'd dismounted his camel earlier. Otherwise, he would have had to fashion crude tools out of rock and hope they would suffice.

The land was sparse with vegetation. Only a few plants clung stubbornly to life in between the rocks. He admired them for their resilience but they were useless to him. He couldn't eat them. They provided no medicinal benefit. But he let out a groan of relief when he saw a small cluster of hearty shrubs ahead. Saltbush. Isa gathered as many of the pale green leaves as he could, stripping the shrubs bare and chewing on the leaves as he worked. Though he couldn't taste it, the leaves held traces of water. It wouldn't sustain him for long but it would buy him a little time.

When the sun threatened to peek over the dawning sky, Isa began to make his way back to the cave. He carried a small pile of sticks in one hand and a collection of leaves within the folds of his tunic. The night had been unexpectedly successful. Perhaps Tahlia had been right and he would not die so easily. The memory of her voice set his pulse hammering. He didn't know if she would come to him again, if she regretted breaking her silence, but he would do everything in his power to see her once more.

Vibrations in the sand caught his attention and he halted to listen to them. He wondered if his mind was playing tricks on him, but the truth became clear when he marked a horned viper slithering across the sand. Isa laid the pile of sticks down and removed his tunic, careful not to crush the saltbush leaves. The viper moved quickly but Isa was able to track it easily. His dagger sailed through the air, nailing his prey to the desert floor.

By the time the sun spilled into the sky, Isa had returned to his shelter and lit a small fire. He would have preferred a rat or lizard. They were much easier to prepare and there was no risk of venom. He also didn't care much for the taste of snake. It was firm and chewy. Still, it would pacify his empty stomach. Isa slit the viper from behind its head down to its tail, careful to avoid the internal organs. He peeled the skin off in one sleek piece, removed its organs, and cut off its head. Slicing it into small pieces, he speared one on a stick before holding it over the flames.

The meal was filling but not particularly enjoyable. Knowing that he couldn't preserve the meat in the heat, it would quickly spoil and go to waste, Isa forced himself to eat every piece. Then he chewed on the rest of the salt bush leaves. Afterwards, he smothered the flames of the fire and settled down into his shallow grave.

Closing his eyes, he tried to calm his restless heart. It was thumping in anticipation. He had been counting down the minutes to this moment since he opened his eyes. He needed to hear her voice again. To have her scent fill his soul. Isa waited impatiently for sleep to take him. He would have waited until the end of time.

When Tahlia appeared, she did so like a mirage, slowly dissolving and shimmering into focus. A silk kaftan draped over her figure and loose dark locks tumbled down her back. She was hypnotically beautiful and he was forever spellbound. He thought he had preserved the memory of her in his mind but it was a poor substitute. It was like seeing the sun break free from behind a veil of clouds, its radiance no longer dimmed as it flooded the sky with brilliance.

Tahlia looked almost caught off guard to see him, but her initial surprise quickly shifted into a lethal glare.

How are you summoning me here?

A current of raw power surged toward Isa, consuming him like a raging brushfire racing through dry grass. Any other mortal would have wilted beneath its divine force but all he could do was behold her magnificence. Tahlia. His goddess.

Isa tried to remember to breathe, to speak, to form thought. "I'm not. Are you not coming to me?"

Tahlia huffed a cruel laugh. *Why would I come to you? I prefer to forget your existence.*

The enchantment splintered as his heart impaled itself on her words. He couldn't recall her ever sounding so cruel and indifferent. Isa wasn't sure how to respond. He had convinced himself that she was finally prepared to face him but she was somehow here against her will. His gaze swept over the inside of the cave in his dream and beyond to the desert surrounding them.

"It must be this place. It's where I first saw you in a vision all those years ago."

That seemed to hold her attention for a moment as she considered it.

There are places where the veil between the mortal realm and the divine are thin.

Like beneath the palace in the Old City. Isa remembered hearing the echo of celestial voices as he navigated the underground passageways in search of the priests. They had whispered to him from beneath the depths of the earth, but none of them were the voice he wanted to hear.

Isa took a step toward Tahlia, but she speared him with a dangerous look that halted him instantly. A muscle clenched in his jaw as his hands flexed. If she truly never wished to see him again, this would be his only chance to speak his peace. He refused to waste it.

"I called out your name every night. I prayed to you and worshiped you every day. Why didn't you ever answer me?"

I do not owe you peace! The air around her trembled in awe. *You did not honor my choice. You betrayed me. In death, you stole my power. I do not owe you anything!*

Her emerald eyes flared as she assessed him from toe to head, her hatred palpable.

You are no better than that god that hangs around your neck. You can worship me every day for the rest of your miserable, mortal life. Redemption will never come.

Isa felt like he'd been obliterated into tiny particles set loose upon the wind. The devastation of it made him want to crash to his knees, beg her for mercy and forgiveness, but he couldn't stop the desperate truth from rushing out of his traitorous mouth.

"I couldn't just let you die, I had to try. I would have done anything. I love you. I loved you long before I knew you. And then I found you, and I did everything in my power to save your life but it wasn't enough. How could I just let you go?"

Don't you dare speak to me of love! Love is not selfish. It is putting someone else's needs and wishes above your own. It is an unyielding devotion despite no guarantee of receiving anything in return. Love is trust in action.

Tahlia forced herself to inhale a deep breath. Her body shuddered with restraint against the torrent of words she clearly wanted to unleash on him. He could see it was taking all the strength she had to keep herself composed.

I am a casualty of your love.

Isa wasn't sure he was still alive. His body was motionless. Speechless. Breathless. He felt utterly diminished, like he was the smallest grain of sand beneath her feet, not even worthy of her notice. Everything she said was true and yet he couldn't accept it. He had failed her in life and he had failed her in death, but he couldn't bring himself to regret his decision.

She was still here.

If he could go back in time, would he choose differently? Could he love her enough to let her die?

Tell me again how much you love me. I dare you.

A treacherous tension crackled between them as their gazes locked, a pause in the battle before the battle cry.

"I'm sorry," he offered instead. "It was my weakness that did this to you. I needed you. I still need you. I can survive with nothing but not without you."

He sounded pathetic, even to his own ears, but it was true and the truth was all he could offer her. He couldn't go back and change the past. They were here now.

Your words are worthless to me. Your life means even less.

Isa lowered his gaze. He couldn't bear to see her look at him like that anymore. It tore open old wounds. He felt like he was bleeding out.

"Then take it. Take your vengeance. I am yours to do with what you will. I have only ever been yours."

And give in to my nature as a goddess? Be spiteful and hateful and sanctimonious? They cannot force me to submit to my divinity and neither can you.

Isa's eyes snapped to hers as his senses sharpened. "Who is trying to force you?"

The thought of anyone forcing her to do anything against her will had his blood rushing in his ears.

The irony was not lost on him.

Tahlia lifted her chin, observing his reaction with cold disdain. In her eyes was a piercing accusation; he was a hypocrite.

You will suffer but not because of me. You have condemned yourself.

Isa forced himself to hold her gaze and bear her judgment. She was right. All the choices he'd made since the day she died had led him here. He knew the black sand would infect him and still he'd chosen to return with Kala.

"I kept my vow to you." At least he had not failed her in that.

At what cost? Tahlia's voice softened ever so slightly as she observed the dark rings around his eyes.

"I would have kept it at any cost. I would have sacrificed everything to honor my promise to you. To keep Kala safe."

Now Tahlia's gaze held only pity as she stared back at him. "You will."

CHAPTER FOURTEEN

ELE

Ele's eyes shot open at a sudden sound but his muscles unclenched when he realized it was only Sabine turning on her side in the bed. He stared up at the crude ceiling waiting for his heartbeat to return to its regular rhythm. Even across the room, he could feel her eyes on him.

"You didn't have to sleep on the floor, you know."

She'd said the same thing three times yesterday, and even made suggestions for what they could do if they shared the tiny bed, but Ele had ignored her. He'd retrieved the pillow and blanket from his own room and fashioned a bed as best he could on Sabine's stone floor. It was uncomfortable to say the least. His spine ached no matter what position he was in, but there was no way he was giving in to Sabine's offer to share the bed. He knew she was trying to manipulate him, just as he was trying to manipulate her. She would use him as a weapon against Kala, to drive a rift between them. There was already so much distance between him and Kala, he couldn't bear for it to widen further.

"I'm fine."

He wasn't really. He'd hardly gotten any sleep. The slightest of sounds had jolted him awake, from their saddlebags being delivered, to food and a bucket of water being left outside their door. Ele had brought them all in and set them down on the table as Sabine slept. Not once did she stir or try to leave the room. Ele wasn't sure whether that was because he was guarding the exit or whether she was simply too exhausted to try. Probably the latter.

Sabine leisurely rose from the bed and walked over to the table to inspect the platter of food. There was an assortment of flat bread, dried fruit, pickled vegetables, and bulgur. Ele had helped himself when it arrived last night, but was mindful to leave enough for Sabine. She handed him a piece of flat bread as she chewed on a dried fig. Ele took it gratefully and sat up, leaning his stiff back against the wall and resting his elbows on his knees.

"So what now?" Sabine asked as she chewed.

Ele shrugged. "The Water Goddess has refused to speak to Kala until after the harvest."

"Do you think sandman will survive that long?"

"I don't know."

Despite what he'd said to Kala yesterday, Ele was not confident Isa could endure the Idris Desert for several days without food or water. It would be a near-impossible trial for any man, but Isa was also infected by the black sand. Ele had watched him closely over the past few days and noticed the way it weighed him down. Heightened his emotions and fed off them. It was possible that the black sand would make the harsh conditions even worse.

"Shame," Sabine said, as if it didn't bother her at all. "In the meantime, you can give me a tour of the Citadel." She stood up but then sniffed her kurta, her nose wrinkling in disgust. "After I bathe."

"I think that's what the water is for." Ele inclined his head to the bucket.

It had been delivered with a threadbare cloth and a thin towel.

"You might be used to your fancy baths, Captain, but this would have been a luxury to me as a child. We would go weeks without washing. This bucket of water would have been fought over to the death."

"I remember." That desperation was what had pushed Kala to sell information to Henri.

Sabine lifted her tunic over her head in one swift motion and Ele almost choked on his flatbread before he quickly averted his eyes.

"Don't look away on my account," she purred.

"I'll leave." Ele kept his gaze nailed to the ground as he got to his feet.

"Am I making you blush, Captain?"

Ele feigned boredom even as he cleared his throat self-consciously. "You have nothing I haven't seen before."

"You haven't seen *me*."

"I'll be just outside."

"You really are no fun."

Ele batted away the tapestry to step outside into the hallway. He released a breath he didn't know he'd been holding and stared across at Kala's room. A platter of food, a bucket of water, and her saddlebags had been left outside the door. Ele tentatively walked over and tried to listen. It sounded quiet inside. He carefully pulled back the tapestry to peek inside. Kala was sleeping soundly, despite her body being twisted in an awkward position to fit the tight space.

Ele retrieved the food, water, and saddlebags and put them on the table. Lingering in the doorway, he cast a look back at Kala but she didn't stir. She'd collapsed on the bed fully dressed, not even bothering to take her sandals off. Ele thought about slipping them off her feet but he didn't want to risk waking her. He returned to the hallway and waited for Sabine to emerge. When she did, her skin was clean and she was wearing a fresh kaftan the color of the sun. Sabine flashed him a playful smile and he scolded himself for paying attention to her appearance. It would only encourage her.

"How long did you stay here last time?" Sabine asked as they began navigating their way through the maze of corridors.

"Only a day or two."

But in that time Tahlia had entrusted him and Kala with the responsibility of scouting the Citadel and learning as much as they could about the Naiab. They weren't sure what the Naiab wanted from them at the time or whether they could be trusted. Kala had been convinced the Water Goddess had ulterior motives for sparing their lives.

"Do you even know where we're going?" Sabine asked as they turned down a passageway that looked like every other passageway.

"Such little faith," he chided.

The Citadel was a nightmare to map out, but all roads eventually led to the heart of the cave. After walking a while longer, they stepped out onto a narrow landing that overlooked the field down below. From this vantage point, it looked like a circular carpet of wheat, ringed by tree tops.

"How many levels does this place have?" Sabine leaned out as far as she dared and stared up at the different landings, all the way to the top of the canyon.

"Too many," Ele muttered.

"Great. How exactly do we get down?"

Their attention locked onto the stone stairs at the same time. The stairs were so narrow only one person could fit at a time and there was no rope to cling to should they stumble on a step.

"No," Sabine said resolutely. "That's not the way we came up. There's got to be another way."

"Afraid of heights?" Ele smirked at her and Sabine's scowl deepened. "Your sister isn't afraid of heights."

"She's not afraid of anything. That was always her problem."

Ele pondered the remark as he peered over the edge at the ground below. "Come on. We'll find another way down."

They headed back into the corridors and Ele tried to keep his bearings. He knew he shouldn't pry, but Sabine's comment stirred up a list of questions he wanted to ask about Kala. Now that they were alone, it seemed like the perfect opportunity.

"What did Kala mean the other day when she said she trusted you once and look what happened?"

"Isn't it obvious? She blames me for what our father and uncles did to her."

"Why would she blame you?"

Sabine pressed her lips together as if she didn't want to say. Ele waited patiently. He wouldn't press her if she chose to keep it to herself but he couldn't deny he was curious.

"Because I was the one who told them about her. What she was doing with your king. I saw the coins she was trying to hide and she told me the truth but swore me to secrecy."

"A secret you didn't keep."

"I was worried about her. We'd only just got her back from the slavers. What would you have thought if your sister was meeting a powerful man in a dark alleyway for coin?"

Ele tried to keep his features neutral but she had a point. Kala had been taken from the streets of the Thaka by slavers as a child. If it wasn't for Henri discovering the slaves chained in the hull of the ship, it would have set sail and Kala would have never seen her home again. Henri had released the slaves and ended human trafficking by taking full control of the Merovian coast.

"Henri never would have harmed her."

"King Heroux was a depraved warlord. How was I to know King Henri would be any different?"

That name still sent a chill down Ele's spine. As a boy, he had been unfortunate enough to spend a few hours in King Heroux's dungeons, used as leverage in the torture of Henri. Ele had barely escaped with all his limbs.

"You should explain that to Kala."

"Why? It doesn't change anything."

"It might. She thinks you betrayed her."

"I did betray her. But she betrayed us first, so I guess we're even."

A muscle feathered in Ele's jaw at the accusation but there was no point arguing. They fell into a silent stalemate until they finally wandered out onto the ground floor. It was bustling with people, everyone carrying out various duties to assist the harvest. Even the children were helping. Everyone looked so joyful, as if it were a celebration and not hard labor. Ele supposed it was a miracle to harvest anything in these conditions.

"You're awake."

Ele glanced over to find Dema approaching them, a warm smile on her face.

"Yes. Thank you for the food and lodgings," he said.

"Where is your queen?"

"She's not his queen," Sabine replied tersely.

Ele ignored her. "She's still sleeping."

"You two will have to do then. We could always use extra hands at harvest time."

Sabine's eyes widened in objection. "I am not a farmer."

"No. You're a smuggler, which means you get to come with me. You and I have much to talk about."

KALA

When Kala woke, she felt groggy, as if she had slept too long. Her muscles were stiff and sore, her head was hazy. She gradually sat up and took in her surroundings. Someone had placed a platter of food, a bucket of water, and her saddlebags on the table. It was disturbing enough that a stranger had entered her room, but the fact that she didn't wake was downright alarming. Isa would be horrified and gravely disappointed in her if he knew. Kala vowed to never tell him.

She forced her sluggish body over to the table and began to eat. The exhaustion was likely due to the rationed food and water over the past three days, as much as it was to the harsh desert heat. If this was how she was feeling after several hours of sleep, she couldn't imagine how Isa was faring out in the elements.

"Tahlia, how is he?" Kala asked out loud, hoping the goddess would take pity on her and answer.

She didn't. The silence was condemning.

Kala ground the dried fruit between her teeth. She understood Tahlia's anger toward Isa but she also wished the goddess could have a little more empathy. Isa had wronged her, there was no disputing that, but he had done it for the right reasons. Surely intent should hold a little weight, enough to sway some understanding in his favor.

"Help him," Kala pleaded. "Do it for me. Please. Don't let him die."

Kala didn't know if Tahlia was listening or if she even cared. It made her feel so powerless. She needed to speak to the Water Goddess right fucking now. Kala quickly washed the desert from her skin and changed into clean clothes before stepping out into the passageway. She gingerly peered into Ele's room but wasn't surprised to find it empty. She didn't have to check Sabine's room. Wherever Ele was, Sabine would follow.

Kala recognized the sting of jealousy but she didn't have time for it. They could wander off wherever they liked together. She had responsibilities to take care of. Isa's life depended on her. Kala marched down the corridor, weaving in and out of passageways until she finally came to a landing. Below her, she could see the field of wheat surrounded by fruit trees.

It looked like the entire population of the Citadel was down there. Men worked in the field in neat rows, bending down to scythe the stalks close to the ground. Others stood in a production line, passing the wheat stalks down to the ends of the field where more people stood, gathering the wheat into tight bundles. Kala's gaze followed as the sheaves of wheat were passed to another group of people who were beating the stalks against a flat stone surface.

It was clear that everyone in the Citadel knew their role and worked together to ensure the success of the harvest. As Shahri, Dema had to be amongst them. Kala spotted a narrow stone stairway and didn't hesitate to descend it. She concentrated as she took each step. Sand and dust crumbled beneath her feet, flying off the edge down to the ground below. It didn't slow her. She found a rhythm and refused the temptation to look out at the view. It would be easy to lose her balance if she did.

When she jumped off the final step to the ground floor, her calves burned. She had no idea how many stairs she'd just descended but it was enough to make her breath labored. Kala walked around the expanse of the cave, scanning the people's faces as she moved amongst them, but she couldn't find Dema anywhere. Her attention diverted to a group of young women standing nearby, giggling amongst themselves as they worked. They were filling woven baskets with fruit and then pouring the produce into larger barrels.

As Kala approached them, she noticed they were harvesting grapes from the ground. The dark vines snaked along the sandy earth in a spiral shape, looking coarse and tangled. The women unsnarled them with ease as they talked, plucking the fruit and filling their baskets. Kala had never seen grapevines like this. She hadn't spotted the vineyard from above because the tall wheat had concealed it from view, but now she could see the vines sprawled for quite a distance. She must have been staring because one of the women looked up at her and smiled.

"Keeping the roots close to the ground helps them conserve moisture. The lower they are, the more shielded they are from the heat and sunlight."

The woman indicated to the natural opening in the roof of the cave where light poured in. The sun's rays beat down on the field mercilessly but the men scything the wheat didn't seem to mind.

"I'm Aiyla," the woman offered.

"Kala."

"Queen of the Black Sands." Amusement danced on Aiyla's lips. "We know."

The girls behind her snickered as if they were all in on a joke she wasn't privy to.

"Is there something funny?" Kala asked.

"Forgive them. They're just admiring your Captain."

"My what?"

"We so rarely have visitors at the Citadel. Any new face is sure to draw attention. Especially one like his."

"It's not his face I'm looking at," one of the girls jeered and the other girls burst into a fresh wave of giggles.

Kala followed their gaze to see Ele standing in the field, bent down with scythe in hand, hacking at the wheat. Shirtless. His well-defined arms were bulging. Every movement he made sent his back muscles rippling, his abdominal muscles constricting. Sweat sheened his sun-kissed skin, his dark curls were soaked with it. Kala had seen Ele shirtless before when she helped him tend to his wounds after his fight with Isa, but somehow this was more erotic. It conjured images in her mind of what he would look like if she was the one causing him to sweat. To move atop of her. Or behind her.

Kala shook her head, banishing the thoughts from her mind. Perhaps she had been curious whether something could spark between them when they reunited during her birthday festival, but so much had happened since then. They'd barely had time to talk or reconnect as old friends, let alone explore anything else that may or may not be there.

Then there was Sabine.

Kala strode past the women towards Ele, determined to show them that she was immune to his sweaty, sculptured body. But then Ele straightened at the sight of her and a warm smile graced his beautiful face. By all the gods. Kala was vaguely aware she was having an out of body experience. She felt her body propelling forward of its own accord while her mind tripped over itself, drunk on desire. Air pumped in and out of her lungs, but when had her heart stopped beating?

"You're awake. Finally," Ele teased as she stopped to stand in front of him like an awkward statue. "I was getting worried."

"Worried?"

"It's past midday."

"It is?"

"You must have needed the rest."

She had. She'd been exhausted. In fact, she still felt a little light-headed. And warm. Kala's hands flew to her cheeks, praying to all the gods that they weren't flushed.

"Are you all right?" Ele reached out to graze her forehead with the back of his hand before he brushed his rough knuckles over her cheek.

Kala knew he was only checking her temperature but somehow the movements felt strangely intimate. Her body froze beneath his touch even as her skin warmed at the sight of him.

"It's the heat," Ele said.

Kala nodded mutely.

She glanced around, eager to look anywhere but at his glorious frame or handsome face. "Where is Sabine?"

"With Dema."

"What? Why?" Kala didn't even try to keep the suspicion from her voice.

"The Shahri said she wanted to discuss trade."

Sabine had been here for less than a day and already she was asserting her influence with the Shahri.

"I need to speak to the Water Goddess."

"There's a feast tonight to celebrate the start of the harvest. Dema will be there. Perhaps that's your chance."

Kala returned her gaze to Ele and she immediately regretted it. He was running a hand through his damp hair, pushing the curls back from his face, but some stubborn strands escaped to fall over his azure eyes. Sand and dirt was smeared across his face. He was mesmerizing. A tingling warmth began to pool between her thighs.

"Water?"

Kala startled as one of the young women approached with a bucket of water, a wooden ladle, and a hopeful smile. Clearly, Kala's presence had emboldened her to try her luck. Ele gratefully accepted the ladle, filled it with water, and drank eagerly. Water dribbled down the sides of his mouth, onto his stubbled chin and down his tanned neck. Kala was ashamed to admit that she couldn't tear her eyes away as his Adam's apple bobbed at every swallow.

Ele filled the ladle again and held it out to Kala, almost putting it to her lips before she instinctively leaned away from it.

"I can do it." She took the ladle from him with mild irritation. She didn't need to be spoon-fed.

Ele shook his head at her as she swallowed the water in one lengthy gulp.

"What?" Kala demanded, wiping her mouth with the back of her hand.

"Nothing." He bent forward and resumed scything the wheat, the conversation apparently over.

Kala returned the ladle to the young woman who looked rather disappointed. She reluctantly retreated back to her friends and Kala, unsure what to do next, followed her. She knew she could look for Dema but the odds of finding her before the feast tonight were not in Kala's favor.

"You look strong," Aiyla observed. "Can you help move and empty the barrels?"

Kala glanced over at the barrels stacked together on a low-lying cart. "Empty them where?"

Aiyla indicated for Kala to lift one of the long wooden handles attached to the cart while she took the other. Together, they pulled. The cart was so heavy Kala felt her feet sinking into the sand and her knuckles turning white. The wheels moved slowly. She felt like an ox. Surely there was a better way to transport barrels of grapes than this. Once they had a little momentum, though, the cart moved easier. They hauled it down a wide passageway into a smaller chamber of the cave. Inside was a spherical wooden trough standing at waist height.

"What is that?" Kala panted.

"A winepress," Aiyla grunted as she dropped the cart's handle in the sand.

Kala followed suit and flexed her hands, trying to bring feeling back into them. She was relieved that their task was done until Aiyla indicated to the barrels on the cart. Kala sighed. Together, they lifted each barrel down from the cart and poured its contents into the trough. By the time they had emptied four barrels, the muscles in Kala's arms and back were screaming.

"Do you fill this entire trough?" Kala perched her hands on her hips as she surveyed the winepress.

"If it's a good harvest," Aiyla replied.

It was easy to haul the cart back to the vineyard now that the barrels were empty, but then Aiyla tossed her a basket.

"Want to help collect the grapes?"

She had nothing better to do, so Kala found a place amongst the women and began to battle with the vines to retrieve the grapes. She listened as the women gossiped and laughed amongst each other. Occasionally, she glanced over at Ele but he never looked her way. He seemed completely focused on scything the wheat, as if he were happy to be performing manual labor. Ele had always wanted to be a warrior but maybe he could have also been happy as a farmer.

Kala wondered what kind of life she might have been happy with if she hadn't inherited Tahlia's kingdom. Most likely she would have trained as a soldier like Ele. She was confident that she was never meant to live an ordinary life. Even if she never met Henri or escaped the Thaka, her life wouldn't have been simple. Perhaps she would have turned out like Sabine, clawing her way to some kind of position of importance in the Thaka.

"Aiyla, is the Shahri looking to open trade between the Naiab and the rest of Merovia?" Kala kept her voice light, as if she wasn't particularly interested in the answer.

"Trade? I doubt it. The Water Goddess doesn't like strangers. Especially not in her sanctuary."

It was the same conclusion Kala had drawn. Either the Shahri had ulterior motives for speaking to Sabine or Dema was simply using her to avoid Kala.

"Your people fought in a war to tear down the walls so they could come and go across Merovia as they pleased, yet the Naiab rarely leave the Citadel," Kala observed.

"Freedom lies in the power to choose," Aiyla returned.

She was right. In many ways the Naiab had more freedom than Kala did.

The women worked at a steady pace, harvesting the grapes and then transporting the barrels to the trough. By midafternoon the vines had been stripped bare and the winepress was filled to the halfway mark. Kala stood at the edge of the wheatfield, tipping a ladle of water down her throat, when she heard the strum of an oud. Cheers instantly went up amongst the women as if an announcement had been made. Some of them ran ahead, disappearing inside the small chamber. Even the men in the wheatfields stopped what they were doing to watch the sudden stampede of excitement, knowing grins on their faces.

Kala looked over her shoulder at Ele, who stared back at her in shared confusion.

"Are you married, Kala?"

Kala returned her attention to Aiyla who was holding a calloused hand out to her.

"No. Why?"

Aiyla grasped her hand and yanked her into a sprint. They dashed inside the chamber to find three older women playing the oud in a lively tune and singing a song Kala had never heard before. Some of the young women kicked off their sandals and jumped into the trough, shrieking with excitement, while others gathered around the wooden edges, clapping loudly in encouragement.

Kala had to shout to be heard above the noise. "What's going on?"

"It's tradition. The unmarried women crush the grapes to bring fertility to the next harvest." Aiyla tossed her sandals to the ground and gestured for Kala to do the same.

Kala barely had time to think about it before a group of women shoved her forward, stripped the sandals from her feet, and hauled her over the lip of the trough. She landed unceremoniously, the wet slap of grapes collectively squishing beneath her. Kala sat for a moment, stunned. The women danced around her, weaving in and out of each other's linked arms as they crushed the grapes to the spirited music.

Kala's hands tried to find purchase but she couldn't even feel the floor of the trough. All she felt was the skins of grapes breaking open, releasing their sticky pulp and juices everywhere. She turned over onto her stomach and tried to get her feet beneath her. When she finally managed to stand, she struggled to stay upright. The floor was so slippery it was hard to keep her balance. The sensation of fruit slipping between her toes was repulsive.

Kala eyed the edge of the trough with trepidation. It was only a few steps ahead of her, but she wasn't confident she would be able to make it without falling over in a soggy heap. She was already submerged halfway up to her calves. A familiar laugh made her look up. Ele was standing with his elbows casually resting over the wooden lip of the trough, snickering at her. Kala could only imagine what she looked like, it would certainly be comical, but she wasn't in the mood. She bent down to grab a mushy handful of grapes and threw it at him.

Ele's mouth fell open as the grapes hit his naked chest with a sodden smack. As juice and pulp slid down his torso, Kala lifted a smug single brow, satisfied that she'd made her point. But then Ele fixed his eyes on her in a dangerous promise. He yanked off his sandals and leapt over the barrier into the trough. The women squealed in delight, but Kala yelped in alarm as he tackled her around the waist, sending her sprawling back beneath the squelching grapes.

She was going to kill him.

Except she had to get air back into her lungs first. His solid body was on top of her, crushing her deeper into the soggy mess.

Instinctively, she pushed both hands against his chest, trying to heave him off and put some distance between them, but then she became all too aware that her palms were touching his slippery, naked chest. Kala balled her hands into fists, as if touching him less would make the situation any better.

"Get off me!"

Ele pulled back a little, a wild grin on his face. It only served to infuriate her more. Kala fisted a bunch of pulp and slapped it against his cheek. The bastard laughed. Apparently, they had started something because around them the women exploded into chaos, hurling grapes at each other and knocking each other to the floor of the winepress. Pulp flew in every direction. Kala was so distracted that she didn't notice Ele taking a handful of grapes before he shoved them down inside her kaftan. She shrieked and squirmed as the sudden cold wetness hit her breasts.

"You camel's ass!"

Kala brought her knee up into his groin. Ele half groaned, half laughed as he rolled off her. Clearly, she hadn't hit him hard enough. The women clumsily fell over him and he quickly recovered to join their childish antics as they all tossed grapes at each other. Was this what passed for flirting in the Citadel? By the looks on the young women's faces they were enjoying his attention. Ele reached for one of the women's ankles and pulled her down into the mush before turning to defend his back against an onslaught of pulp.

Kala couldn't help feeling a prickle of jealousy. It was irrational, she knew that. It wasn't like she wanted him to hurl grapes at her but she also didn't want him to enjoy himself quite so much hurling grapes at anyone else. She hated that her feelings for Ele had become so complicated. That she'd been reduced to this kind of pettiness.

Kala stumbled to a standing position, trying to dodge the attacks but it was pointless. Grapes rained down on her. Juice dripped from her face and torn skins were embedded in her braids. She was soaked. Through the deluge, Ele must have noticed her standing in the middle of the trough being pelted mercilessly from all sides because he awkwardly waddled through the slush on hands and knees to get to her.

He made a valiant attempt to try to stand but he kept slipping, falling back into the slop. Kala begrudgingly offered him both her hands. Instead, he grasped her forearms, pulling himself up. The bastard was still laughing. His laughter was almost infectious. Kala stubbornly tried to resist the smirk that tugged at her lips. She was mad at him, no matter how funny it was.

Ele shook his head like a wet dog and Kala winced as juice and grapes went flying everywhere. She glared at him, infuriated, but he simply grinned at her as he ran his hands from her shoulders down her arms, flicking the fruit and juice from her skin.

Kala narrowed her eyes at the kind gesture. "Don't try to make amends now."

"This is your fault," he chuckled. "Don't start a war you can't win, my queen."

Kala shoved him hard in the chest but then lost her footing and they both fell in a heap. Ele landed on his back, his arms reflexively catching her, preventing her from tumbling face-first into the mushy pit.

"If this is your countermove, I might just concede defeat."

Kala lifted her head a little to blink at him in surprise. What did he mean by that? Their faces hovered inches apart as she searched his eyes for an answer. He held her gaze, brazen, waiting, but then his eyes lowered to her mouth. This couldn't be happening. Not now. Not like this. Kala scrambled backwards, her hands trying to find purchase on the floor so that she could push herself up, but instead she felt something else.

"Oh gods! Sorry!" She immediately retracted her offending hand as if it had caught fire.

She'd touched it. She'd touched *his* ... and it was *hard*.

"It's all right." Ele shifted away from her awkwardly.

Kala sat there in the wet mush, absolutely mortified, wishing the trough of grapes would swallow her whole.

CHAPTER FIFTEEN

ELE

On the way back to their rooms, Ele and Kala swiped a fresh bucket of water each. It was tiring lugging them up several stories through winding, narrow passageways but eventually they made it. Kala immediately retreated inside her room, leaving Ele to stand awkwardly in the hallway. They'd hardly said a word to each other since they climbed out of the winepress, but Ele had hoped it was because they were conserving their breath and energy for carrying the buckets. Now he suspected that wasn't the case.

Ele walked into his room and promptly stripped off his soaked pants. They were ruined, stained beyond repair, so he discarded them in the corner. Now two buckets of water sat on the table as he hadn't had a chance to use the one left at his door yesterday. Ele plunged the washcloth into the water and began scrubbing the juice and pulp from his skin. As he did so, his thoughts drifted back to the chaos of the winepress.

Kala had to know she was asking for trouble when she slogged grapes at him. The memory made his lips twitch to a wicked smirk. He had only meant to enact friendly retaliation by tackling her to the bottom of the trough but he couldn't deny that the moment he was on top of her, his need for revenge melted into a different need altogether. In the struggle, Kala's kaftan had ridden halfway up her thighs. She hadn't noticed him discreetly covering her body until he was able to pull it back down.

The material had been soaked and it clung dangerously to her curves. No man could have ignored curves like that. His cock had swollen involuntarily, which made it all the more painful when she'd kneed him in the groin. In a way, he'd been grateful for the pain because all his efforts to make it calm the fuck down had failed. But then she'd tumbled on top of him, her lips so close to his that he could almost taste their sweetness. Savage desire had flooded his shaft, which made it even more humiliating when her hand accidentally found his cock. He could still feel the slick warmth of her palm sliding against his pants. It had been for less than a second but somehow her palm was now imprinted on his skin. He wanted to feel it again.

If she was any other girl, Ele wouldn't hesitate to pursue her but this was Kala. He could never use her like that. Besides, they had only ever been friends and right now even their friendship felt precarious. It was normal to be attracted to her, he reasoned. She was beautiful. Of course, his body would react to her lying on top of him. But he refused to let himself fantasize about her.

He wouldn't think about what her lips would taste like. How it would feel to run his hands along her wet, olive thighs. He especially wouldn't think about the way he would have licked the juice from them, slowly moving his tongue upwards towards her center. By the time he reached it, she would have been slick with wanting him. He would have nudged her legs open and pulled aside her drenched underwear so he could feast on her.

"Fuck," Ele panted as he fisted his swollen cock and pumped hard.

It wasn't his palm on his shaft, it was Kala's, working him mercilessly. With her other hand, she lifted her kaftan further up her wet thighs until she exposed herself to him. Her sex was perfect. Pink and glistening. She was ready for him—

Ele spilled himself into his hand as the orgasm shuddered through his body and down his legs. He crumpled to the floor, unable to move. Every nerve ending in his body felt electrified. Satiated. And yet he instantly craved more. It had been a long time since he'd experienced an orgasm that strong, especially from his own hand.

It was wrong. It was glorious.

Perhaps this was the only way he was going to be able to control himself around Kala. He would permit himself to fantasize about her but that was it. He would remain her friend. *Only* her friend. That's what she needed the most right now. There was too much going on with Isa, the curse of the Black Sands, and her sister. No wonder Kala had been annoyed at the situation in the winepress. She didn't want to waste precious time on silly antics. They didn't know if Isa was still alive or if he had already perished. Her thoughts would be consumed by it.

Ele wondered if she'd devised a plan yet for coaxing an audience with the Water Goddess. If not, he needed to help her think of something. Ele finished washing himself and pulled on a fresh kurta. He wandered across the hallway to stand outside Kala's door and called out to her.

"Come in."

Ele lifted the rug and stepped inside. Kala was standing at the table in a fresh kaftan, her skin clean, leaning slightly over a bucket of water with her fingers tangled in her sopping braids.

Ele frowned. "What are you doing?"

"Trying to wash the grapes out of my hair." She gritted her teeth in frustration.

Ele walked over and peered into the bucket. The water was a cloudy mess.

"Hang on."

He collected the bucket of fresh water from his room and upon returning, he noticed a large empty bowl that had presumably once held food. He poured the water inside it.

"Sit down." Ele spun a chair around and positioned it directly in front of the bowl of fresh water. "Lay your head back."

"I won't be able to see," Kala protested.

"But I will."

Kala's hands stilled in her braids as she stared at him in surprise.

"Sit," he insisted.

Gingerly, Kala took a seat. "We need to undo them."

Ele inspected one of the braids. They looked complicated. "How?"

"Start at the ends and work your way up. Use your fingers to separate the strands."

He took one side of her hair as Kala worked the other.

"Do you do these yourself?"

"No. Zaynab does them for me."

"You seem pretty close to your friends," he observed.

Kala smiled softly. "They've become like a family to me."

Ele flinched. He knew he should be grateful that Kala had found people that she could trust but for some reason the comment hurt. Once upon a time he had been her family. They had chosen each other. He never wanted that to change, but now she had chosen someone else.

"How did you meet them?"

"It's a long story and not a particularly happy one, but it has a happy ending. They were already each other's family and then I kind of inserted myself."

"Sounds familiar," he jibed.

Kala whacked him. He feigned injury to which she rolled her eyes. It made Ele grin. This moment right here, this familiar rhythm and ease, made it feel like ten years had not passed between them. Time lost its meaning. Distance lost its significance.

"I thought perhaps you might have been sleeping with one of them." Ele was careful to keep his tone nonchalant.

"Why not all of them?"

Ele baulked but Kala's teasing smile made him relax.

"Samir and I used to," Kala admitted and Ele's stomach plummeted, "but it was casual and it didn't last long."

Ele thought of Samir, his gray eyes and messy brown hair, his calm and reserved demeanor. Was that Kala's type? How long, exactly, had it lasted between them? Did she pursue him? Surely not. Samir was reasonably good-looking, he supposed, but Kala could have had anyone in the kingdom so there was no reason for her to have become infatuated with him. Perhaps that's why she ended it. Samir certainly wouldn't have ended it. If Samir had broken her heart, Ele would have something to say about it the next time he saw him. After his fists had spoken, he might even use words.

"Ouch!"

"Sorry." Ele released the braid he'd been strangling.

All the braids were now undone so he flattened his palm against her forehead, gently tipping her head back as he gathered her hair into the bowl. There was a lot of it. His hands pushed it down beneath the water, swirling it around, before grabbing a bar of soap. He stole a glance at Kala. Her body was tense, as if she couldn't relax while submitting to this. Ele smiled a little as he lathered the soap between his hands and began working it through the strands, pulling out broken grape skins as they floated to the surface.

"Being intimate with each other didn't ruin your friendship?" Ele probed.

"No. I think because we both knew it was just sex. There are some bonds that can't be broken by anything."

A muscle feathered in Ele's jaw at the knowledge that she had that kind of bond with Samir.

"But you know that," Kala added swiftly. "You and Sabine seem to be fine."

Ele almost dropped the soap. "Me and Sabine? We're not even friends, let alone anything more."

"But you two have—"

"Never," he said adamantly. "We kissed once. Nothing more."

It was hard to read the silence that followed. Whatever she was thinking, her expression was carefully guarded. He wasn't even sure she believed him.

"She insinuated that you were lovers."

Ele sighed as he began to knead the soap into her scalp.

"I carried her to bed when she was drunk one time. And I didn't remove her clothes. She was just trying to rile you. I wouldn't have thought you would rise to the occasion so easily."

"You're my oldest friend, Ele. Of course I don't want you tangled up with someone like her."

He flicked his gaze to her face only to find that her eyes had closed and her body was no longer rigid. She had relaxed beneath his hands. Ele smiled, satisfied, and kept massaging. Her lips parted slightly in pleasure.

Ele couldn't resist leaning down to whisper in her ear, "Or you're jealous."

Kala's eyes shot open and they stared at each other, mere inches separating them. "Why would I be jealous?"

Ele straightened again. "I am incredibly good-looking."

Kala made a choking sound.

"Strong. Charming," he continued.

"Conceited."

"Thoughtful."

"Irritating."

"Sexy."

"Average."

Ele froze. Was she talking about …?

Kala cleared her throat. "I meant average looking."

"I think it's all clean." Ele helped her to sit up before handing her a towel to dry her hair.

"Thank you."

"No problem."

Kala ducked her head, twisting her hair to wring the water from it. It was long, thick, and unruly. He could see why she preferred to contain it in braids.

"I'm sorry I can't braid it for you. My talents end there."

Kala cracked an awkward smile. "That's fine."

She patted her hair dry with the towel and then flicked it back over her shoulders. The movement was somehow sensual. It made Ele swallow hard.

"The feast will be starting soon. We should probably join them," Ele suggested, keen to distract himself. "Do you have a plan for luring out the Water Goddess?"

"Of course I do."

"Care to share?"

"No." She patted the center of his chest as she strolled past him towards the door. "Just watch and learn."

KALA

The ground level of the Citadel had been transformed into a dining hall. Long low-lying tables had been laid out in several rows with cushions lined up on either side of them for people to sit. A multitude of small dishes were set on each table in ceramic bowls, the smell of grains and meats wafting in the air. It made Kala's mouth water. She hadn't eaten for several hours and now her stomach was protesting her neglect.

The space was crowded with people. Some had cleaned up from the day's labor, putting on fresh clothes, but others clearly hadn't washed or changed for the occasion. They were still covered in sweat and dirt. Even so, everyone mingled freely, talking and laughing. As Ele and Kala joined them, they were handed two shallow cups of clear liquid that were definitely not water.

"If this is wine from the grapes we crushed, I don't want it," Kala muttered as she inspected the suspicious liquid.

Ele drained his cup in one gulp before doing the same to hers. He winced against the taste as she gaped at him in shock. But then her attention caught on two figures entering the chamber. Dema and Sabine were an odd pair. One was a poised, calm leader, the other was a criminal. They separated as soon as they joined the crowd. The moment Dema walked ahead, Sabine's features shifted from polite to aggravated. Clearly, the negotiations had not gone well. Dema showed no signs of disappointment, though. She beamed at her people as they welcomed her, and she gradually made her way toward the front of the cave.

Kala scanned the gathering. At least a dozen warriors were in attendance, their turquoise tattoos making them easily identifiable. They didn't look armed but then again, they wouldn't need to be. The floor was sand. They could conjure weapons in an instant. If her plan didn't work, there was no way she and Ele would escape with their lives.

There was only one entrance to the Citadel and Kala knew it was guarded. Even if they made it through the tunnel and out into the narrow canyon, they wouldn't make it far. The Naiab were dispersed in the very earth. They would apprehend them in the blink of an eye. Kala glanced over her shoulder, covertly assessing the passageways. There were two exits from the chamber but to her knowledge neither of them led anywhere except back to the heart of the cave.

In her peripheral vision, Kala noticed Ele staring at her. When their eyes met, there was a sharp warning there.

"Don't even think about it."

She tried to feign innocence but his expression told her he didn't believe it for one second. She had no choice, though. This was the only way. Kala started to move.

"Fuck," Ele cursed under his breath as he followed closely, guarding her back.

They moved like predators through the crowd, slowly approaching their prey, her focus never wavering from her target. A hushed, reverent silence fell over the gathering as Dema stood at the front of the cave to address her people.

"Tonight, we gather to celebrate the first day of the harvest."

A high-pitched cry echoed in unison from the crowd, a sound of celebration that was unfamiliar to Kala but was apparently commonplace among the Naiab.

"We are truly blessed to have the favor of the Water Goddess who ensures our people prosper every year and grow stronger with each generation. May we always honor her and live by the principles of our forebearers, respecting the land that birthed us and the sanctity of our home, the Citadel."

Another unified yowl pierced the air, and in that moment, Kala leapt from the crowd, seizing Dema in a tight grip and pressing a hidden dagger to the underside of her jaw. Shrieks of terror echoed in the chamber while Ele took up a defensive stance in front of her, his weapon drawn and ready.

"Don't move!" Kala ordered the Naiab warriors who were already twitching with magic.

The air grew heavy with tension as everyone froze. Dema stood motionless as a statue, her eyes fixed forward, as if having sharp steel pressed against her jugular was not enough to raise her pulse. As Kala surveyed the crowd for threat, she realized Sabine was nowhere to be seen. Typical. Like a cockroach, she'd scuttled off, leaving Ele and Kala to fend for themselves.

Kala lowered her voice into Dema's ear, "I need to talk to the Water Goddess. Summon her. Now."

"No one can summon a goddess," Dema replied calmly.

"Fine. Then tell her I'm going to kill you in the next five seconds if she doesn't show herself."

"You wouldn't dare."

"She dares to try to kill my guardian, now I dare to kill her vessel. Fair's fair." Kala pressed the blade deeper until it broke Dema's skin.

The warriors jolted with restraint at the sight, causing Ele to reinforce his position. If they lunged at him, he would be dead in an instant. He was a strong fighter but no match for a dozen sand wielders.

"Three, two," Kala whispered.

"Don't kill them."

Dema's eyes had shifted, a tempest storm swirling within their depths. But that's not what caught Kala by surprise. The goddess was directing the plea to Ele. He didn't respond. He simply maintained his defensive stance, awaiting Kala's orders.

"We need to talk about the curse of the Black Sands," Kala insisted, keeping the blade to her throat.

"I should have let you die," the goddess hissed.

"We all have regrets."

The goddess took a moment to consider her options. "Not here."

"Lead the way then."

The goddess lifted her chin and projected her voice to the crowd. "Please continue the celebration. There is nothing to fear. I will deal with these outsiders and return your Shahri to you."

The implied threat sent a shiver down Kala's spine but she kept the blade level even as they shuffled toward the passageway. Ele stayed close, vigilantly guarding their backs to make sure the sand wielders did not try to be heroic.

It was a slow journey to wherever the goddess was taking them. For once, Kala was grateful that the passageways were so narrow, it made it easy to defend their position. Eventually, they turned down a short private path and followed it around until it opened up into a wide chamber. Kala recognized it straight away. This was where she had first met the Water Goddess as a child.

The walls were a natural wave of stone, their colors resembling a rainbow of layered sediments. A shallow river meandered across the floor of the cavern, and water dribbled down stalactites that hung from the ceiling. The space was strategically secluded from the rest of the Citadel, set back from the main passageways. The only sound to be heard was the trickling of water over rocks in the riverbed, which meant this place afforded them some measure of privacy.

"Now," the Water Goddess drew out the word as she slowly turned around and leveled Kala with a volatile stare, "give me one good reason why I shouldn't drown you in your own blood."

Ele immediately moved to Kala's side, though what protection he thought he could offer her against a goddess, Kala didn't know. Still, his presence was comforting as she stood her ground.

"It would be interfering with another god's realm. And I don't think the Goddess of Endings and Beginnings would take kindly to it."

The goddess's expression tightened. "I don't have to kill you to make you suffer."

"We didn't mean any disrespect," Ele intervened, holding his hands out in supplication. "We simply want to break the curse and save Isa."

The goddess's sharp gaze never left Kala's face as she asked him, "What if he can't be saved?"

Ele pressed his lips together in strained silence. It was clear he thought that Isa couldn't be saved either.

"We need to try," Kala answered for him. "Isa said you know the truth about the curse of the Black Sands."

The goddess turned her back on them and paced to the edge of the shallow river, as if considering whether to speak or not. Finally, she said, "I cannot break it."

"We know," Kala replied. "The curse was cast by a witch. Only a witch can break it."

"If you already have a goddess to give you answers, why come to me?"

"Tahlia doesn't know the truth of the curse."

The Water Goddess cocked her head slightly, the movement subtle but telling.

"Or if she does, she didn't share it with us. She didn't want us to come here at all."

The goddess looked over at the natural wave of stone in the wall. "Fate is chance threaded with choice. But there is always a creator of design."

Kala and Ele exchanged a blank look, unsure what she was trying to say.

"I will tell you the story of the black sand and then you will leave the Citadel."

"Agreed," Kala replied.

"Do you know how I came to be a goddess?"

Kala remembered the story. Tahlia had explained it to her and Ele after meeting the goddess all those years ago.

"When you were mortal, you fell in love with a man who sold your love story to the gods for a chance at divinity," Ele recalled. "After your sacrifice and ascension, you learned he was not the man you thought him to be. He had many lovers and many children. He desired to be divine so that he could collect beautiful women who would worship him and sacrifice themselves at his altar. He became the God of Beauty and Fertility."

"That's why he pursued Tahlia," Kala added. "Because of her beauty. He not only chose her to be sacrificed but also to ascend, so that she could be with him forever."

The Water Goddess turned around to face them. "The gods knew, of course. They thought it would be amusing for me to be doomed to exist for all eternity with his treachery and my own foolishness. I mourned and I raged for lifetimes, but then one day I found unexpected solace. I found my sanctuary."

The goddess lifted her hands to the wondrous cave around them. Kala had always thought it strange that a desert cave was the sanctuary of the Water Goddess. She would have thought a mighty lake or ocean would be more fitting. However, watching the water drip down the stalactites, feeding the shallow river which snaked across the floor, Kala finally understood why the goddess had been drawn to this place. Its beauty lay in its scarcity. Its strength in its adversity. The resolve to endure and live, even when faced with the most unforgiving or unforgivable conditions.

"Later, I sheltered a destitute people," the goddess continued, "granting sand magic to those who proved themselves worthy. But the God of Beauty and Fertility was not pleased to find that I had given such power to the Naiab. He did not see them as my people. All he saw was an army of god-touched."

The goddess flicked her gaze to Ele, who shifted uneasily beneath it.

"Why would he care?" Kala frowned.

"Perhaps he was worried I would send my army to destroy his precious kingdom."

"His kingdom?" Ele interjected. "He used to rule the Kingdom of the Black Sands?"

"When he was mortal, yes."

Ele's brows crowded in tight. "So, he sought out a witch to curse the land to ensure the Naiab could never conquer it?"

"Men can be petty like that. A woman gains a morsel of power and they see it as a personal threat."

Kala knew that truth all too well. While her people loved and accepted her now, there had been many men over the years who had tried to take her throne from her. As a child, she'd been vulnerable. As a woman, she was not suitable. Tahlia had been the first Queen of Merovia but her reign had been tragically cut short after a matter of days. Kala had fought hard to protect her people and ensure the prosperity of her kingdom, but that dream and purpose had threatened others' personal agendas.

"That's why the black sand only affects the Naiab," Ele concluded.

The goddess gave a curt nod. "The curse was cast long ago, the magic has weakened over time. Now the sand acts as a slow poison, where once it would have killed instantly. Isa has survived longer than I expected. He has defied the curse, but it will still kill him."

"Not if we can find a witch," Kala countered. "Sabine says she knows where to find one."

The goddess's expression turned cynical. "Witches no longer exist. Their line vanished after the one who invoked the curse died."

"Sabine could be lying," Ele acknowledged, "but if a witch does exist, she would know about it."

"The girl is cunning. You should not trust her so easily."

"We have no choice," Kala admitted.

Ele didn't look comforted by the thought either. "We'll go now."

They turned to leave but the goddess called out to them. "You will need more than a witch to break the curse of the Black Sands. You will need something only I can give you."

Kala cast a curious look over her shoulder. "What's that?"

The goddess's cold expression told Kala that she had no intention of revealing it.

"Fine. Tell me your terms."

"Do not make a deal with a goddess," Ele urged under his breath.

"The boy is right. Such covenants lead to unexpected outcomes." The words were laced with subtext as the goddess paused for consideration. "You can stay one more night. I will have an answer for you before you leave in the morning."

CHAPTER SIXTEEN

ELE

"What in the hell kind of plan was that?!" Ele raged. "Threatening to kill the vessel of the goddess in a room full of Naiab warriors. Fucking suicidal!"

"It worked, didn't it?" Kala threw back at him.

"You could have been killed! And then Isa would have died, your kingdom would be lost, and this whole fucking mess would have been pointless. It would be all my fault for listening to you. Just blindly trusting you ... where in god's name are you going?"

He had mindlessly followed her through the winding passageways of the Citadel, too absorbed in his anger to give any consideration to where she was leading him, and now they were standing in front of a dead end.

"I can't believe it's still here," Kala marveled as they both stared up at the sheer cliff face.

Ele's stomach plummeted at the memory of climbing that cliff face as kids. "I can't believe we didn't die."

No sooner had the words left his mouth before Kala reached for a rock that jutted out of the wall. She hauled herself up with ease, her hands and feet moving in tandem along cavities that had been carved into the wall long ago. Ele glanced up at the final destination: a narrow ledge. Then he looked out over the stark drop. There was no end to it. His palms began to sweat.

Kala climbed with unnatural speed and pulled herself up onto the narrow ledge to dangle her legs over the side. She was beaming with a dangerous combination of pride and adrenaline.

"Don't tell me you're still afraid of heights," Kala called down to him.

"I'm not afraid of heights. I'm afraid of falling ... from a height."

Ele gritted his teeth, pinched his eyes closed, and sent a silent prayer to all the gods. Then he began to climb. It wasn't as harrowing as he remembered. His body was stronger now and the distance was not so significant. In minutes, he had reached the narrow ledge. Kala shuffled over to make room for him to sit beside her. Even so, their thighs were flush against each other.

Above them, a rupture in the cave's ceiling revealed a glimpse of the starry sky. It resembled a rich dark tapestry with thousands of sparkling gems stitched into it. They shimmered with a soft, serene grace as gentle moonlight filtered through.

"Why did you want to come here again?" Ele asked as he brushed the sand and grit from his hands.

Kala stared up at the sky, a pensive look on her face. "The last time we sat here we didn't know if any of us would survive. Henri was facing the summit. Tahlia was being hunted by the gods. Malik was—being Malik."

Now they didn't know if Isa would survive the curse. Kala was worried about losing her family all over again.

"Isa will be fine. We'll find a way to save him, I promise."

"I'm not a child anymore. I don't want you to make promises you can't keep." She nudged his shoulder playfully. "Besides, you still haven't fulfilled the last promise you made me."

Ele's eyes widened in sudden realization. He still hadn't told her his real name. Kala looked at him expectantly. He didn't know why, but he suddenly felt self-conscious, as if he was about to show her the most vulnerable part of him. It didn't make sense. He hadn't used his real name in years and it held no particular significance to him. It belonged to the boy he used to be. The boy before Henri.

Unable to meet her eye, Ele averted his gaze and cleared his throat. "Eleuterio."

"Eleuterio," Kala repeated, as if testing the sound on her tongue.

"It means liberator."

"It suits you."

Ele peeked at her out of the corner of his eye to find that her face was sincere.

"You're the only person who knows that about me."

And, for some reason, it felt right that she did. The secret belonged to just the two of them.

Kala flashed a smug smile. "That's better than any present you could have bought me."

"Happy birthday." Ele took her hand and turned it over, pressing a kiss to her wrist.

When he released it, Kala continued to stare at her wrist as if his lips had branded her. She seemed stunned, which made him go wholly still. He hadn't expected to do it, hadn't planned it, it just happened. By the look on her face he'd overstepped.

"I'm sorry," he said quickly.

"No, it's fine. You can kiss me. If you want to."

Did she mean—? Ele's gaze dipped to her lips involuntarily. They were perfect, her bottom lip full and rosy. He knew he was staring, but he couldn't tear his eyes away, couldn't get the thought out of his head. The invitation lingered in the air between them. Kala sat very still, almost like she was anticipating or hoping that he would make a move. Or maybe he was misreading things. Ele felt himself lean closer, like a magnetic force was drawing him in. There was hardly a breath between them now but still Kala didn't move. Her eyes never left his face. She was going to let him kiss her, he realized. Panic flooded his system but it was too late to overthink it now.

His lips touched hers. They were as soft as flower petals, exactly how he imagined they would be. The kiss was tentative and gentle. He didn't dare to press against her heatedly or explore her mouth with his tongue. His hands didn't reach for her body, though he instinctively wanted to. He wanted to cup her face between his palms, to brush his thumb in tender strokes along her cheekbone, to encircle her waist until she was flush against him.

Ele had never kissed someone like this before. It wasn't born from passion, an excited frenzy of desire and carnal lust. It was born from wonder. A precious gift. A breath shared between two souls. It felt familiar and rare all at the same time. He was about to pull away when Kala tilted her head up, pushing her lips firmer against his. She wanted more. But no, that couldn't be right. She was simply returning the kiss. She didn't want it to go any further.

Ele pulled away and Kala jerked back, awkwardly casting her eyes anywhere but on him. Her cheeks looked a little flushed. His cheeks were probably flushed too now that his heart had started beating again. He wasn't sure what to do or say, but as the seconds passed, it became painfully clear that he should do or say *something*. Thanking her for the kiss sounded too formal. Commenting on the kiss would be crass. Ignoring it altogether was an option. He could remark on the stars, how beautiful they were tonight. Not that they compared to Kala's beauty. Or the warm glow he'd felt whilst kissing her. God damn it, why couldn't he think of anything to say?

"The Water Goddess was afraid of you tonight," Kala said.

He supposed they were ignoring it then.

She still refused to look at him, which made him stare even more. He couldn't help it. He had kissed those lips a moment ago. A part of him couldn't believe it. Another part of him longed to relive it.

"She begged you not to kill her sand wielders. No mortal can kill a sand wielder, let alone a dozen of them. You have magic."

The words immediately sobered him. She said it so matter-of-factly that it left no room for doubt or argument. Not that Ele would have lied to her. He had just never acknowledged the truth out loud before. Henri and Malik suspected, of course, but they had never asked him outright. Henri was afraid of the answer. Ele was god-touched. Changed. And it was all because Henri had made a deal with the Goddess of Endings and Beginnings to save his life.

"I wouldn't call it magic," Ele replied carefully. "It's more like an ability."

"To do what?"

"End lives," he said simply. "When things are heightened, I feel it. Like a pulse or a current. Life. If I reach out, I can snap the thread."

Kala finally met his gaze, her wide eyes flickering with awe and fear. It made his insides twist. The last thing in the world he wanted was for her to look at him like that. As if he were dangerous. Someone to be feared.

When she spoke again her voice was a trembling whisper, "You stole a kernel of the goddess's power."

"No," Ele insisted, his brows pinched in confusion at the accusation.

Kala nodded covertly, like the Goddess of Endings and Beginnings might be watching them. It wasn't true. His ability had come from the goddess but he hadn't stolen it. At least not consciously.

"The Water Goddess knows," Kala breathed in alarm. "Does anyone else know?"

"No."

"You must never tell anyone."

Ele set his jaw in irritation. He knew that already. He wasn't stupid enough to go announcing it to the world.

"We should go," Kala said suddenly, pulling her legs up over the ledge.

Ele tried to concentrate on his footholds as he climbed back down the cliff face but his mind was a jumble of thoughts. He wasn't sure if Kala feared him or feared *for* him. If the Goddess of Endings and Beginnings ever found out about his ability, she would surely kill him. But the Water Goddess had no reason to betray him by revealing his secret. Ele got the impression that she wasn't exactly close with the other divines or loyal to their deific cause. Besides, she had protected Tahlia's secrets for years when Tahlia was mortal. Then again, she did so because it served her agenda. To deprive her ex-lover from having the one thing he wanted most in the world; Tahlia.

Now that the God of Beauty and Fertility was imprisoned in a vial around Isa's neck, Ele wasn't sure whether the Water Goddess had moved on and found peace, or whether she was still plotting against those who had wronged her in the past. Perhaps his secret could serve as a strategic move in her eternal game of revenge. Perhaps Kala was right to be afraid.

KALA

Kala barely noticed the walk back to their rooms. There was so much to process from the night's events. She should have known the origins of the curse would be tied up with the Water Goddess's schemes. The goddess had held a grudge against her mortal ex long past her death and into her eternal divinity. Kala feared his suspicions about her raising an army against his homeland were not unfounded.

Then there was Ele's secret. After he survived Isa's attack in the training yard, Kala had reasoned being god-touched made him faster and stronger than others. She couldn't have predicted that he would also have magic. The power to end lives. It was unthinkable. And dangerous. If the Goddess of Endings and Beginnings learned of it, her retribution would be swift and lethal.

"Goodnight." Ele's flat dismissive tone jolted Kala back to the present. She was standing mindlessly in front of her room and Ele was walking in the direction of his.

"Wait. Aren't you worried Sabine will try to murder me in my sleep?"

"I thought you were perfectly capable of protecting yourself," Ele mimicked her words.

"I am," she replied defensively.

He was mad at her, she realized, though she didn't know why.

Ele threw a droll look over his shoulder. "You didn't even wake when I brought your food and water in."

Kala flushed with embarrassment. "Because I knew you weren't going to stab me!"

Ele's expression told her he didn't believe her for one second but didn't argue. He simply lifted the tapestry to enter his room.

"Wait! Just ... stay with me. Please."

He looked back at her. "Why?"

Because she was worried about him. His ability made him the most dangerous person in Merovia but it also made him a target for a powerful goddess. Kala wasn't sure what the Water Goddess would do with the information. Logically, Kala knew there was little she could do to protect Ele against a divine, but the thought of leaving him alone terrified her. It was safer if they stayed together.

"Because I've asked you to?"

Ele weighed up her plea for a moment before releasing a resigned sigh. "Fine."

Relief flooded her chest.

"I'll just grab my bedding." Ele paused but made no move to go inside his room, instead his gaze drifted to Sabine's room and his face fell a little.

"What?"

"Nothing."

"Is your bedding in Sabine's room?"

Ele winced. "It's not what you think. I slept on the floor."

Kala's brows shot up and she scoffed in admonishment.

"You wouldn't let me guard you! It was the only way I could be sure she wouldn't try to kill you. I'll sneak in and get them."

"Don't bother, you might wake the beast. You can share my bed."

Ele stilled but Kala feigned indifference as she batted the tapestry aside to disappear inside her room. She could hear Ele follow behind her. It would be a tight fit. The bed was nothing more than a flat surface that had been carved into the end of the room, with a blanket and a pillow tossed on top. Kala made a show of looking busy, dragging a comb through her unruly hair and then finishing the last of the fruits on the table. Ele lingered near the entrance like he was unsure where to stand or what to do.

Kala held a dried fig out to him. "Want some?"

"No thanks."

Perhaps it was better to put him out of his misery and just go to sleep. Normally, she would get changed but she wasn't about to undress in front of him. Her kaftan would be comfortable enough to sleep in. Sudden movement caught her eye and she glanced over to see Ele pulling his kurta over his head. Kala almost choked on the fig. His sculpted chest was a work of art, marred only by his scars, the most prominent of which was across his heart. A dagger was wedged in between the waistband of his pants, which hung low around his hip bones.

Clearly, Ele had no qualms about getting undressed in front of her. Of course he didn't. They were friends. She'd been foolish enough to embrace the kiss when she should have accepted it for what it was: a birthday kiss between friends. Chaste and respectful. He hadn't even tried to touch her.

"I can turn around if you want to change," Ele offered.

Kala realized she'd been standing there staring. She nodded hastily and made her way over to the saddlebags to retrieve her nightdress. She peeked over her shoulder to find Ele facing the wall, his hands perched on his hips as he waited for her. A tremor pulsed through her as her eyes traced the contours of his powerful back.

What was wrong with her? Kala mentally kicked herself before pulling off her kaftan and sliding the nightdress on.

"You can look now."

Kala crawled onto the stone slab and tucked herself tight against the corner of the cave. Ele pulled the dagger from his pants and slid it beneath the pillow before stretching out beside her. Kala knew the space would be cramped but this was ridiculous. She almost sucked in a breath to make herself smaller. There was absolutely no space between their bodies. Their foreheads were almost colliding.

"Do you want to swap sides? You could hit your head if you turn in your sleep." Ele eyed the jagged wall behind her with concern.

"I'm fine." She would rather hit her head than be pushed out of the bed entirely.

Ele shifted, putting his arm above her head and then curling it around defensively. If she turned in her sleep, his hand would prevent her from knocking into the wall. Kala couldn't help the smile that bloomed on her lips but she kept her head down so he couldn't see it. If she tried to lift her chin, their noses would brush, and she didn't want him thinking she was trying to kiss him again.

Kala tried to relax but it was impossible. Lying this close to Ele felt like sitting too close to a fire. Hot and dangerous. Kala tried to ignore the waves of heat that emanated from him, just like she tried to ignore the sight of his naked pectoral muscles inches away from her face, or the dip at the base of his throat. She pinched her eyes closed, willing herself to think of anything else, but that just heightened the scent of him. He smelled faintly of earth, sweat, and oranges.

Perhaps the orange scent came from the soap he'd used to wash her hair earlier. She still couldn't believe he'd done that for her. The act had felt so intimate. His large hands had been so gentle as they massaged her scalp, sending waves of pleasure through her body. The deftness and strength of his fingers made her imagine what else they were capable of.

Kala's eyes shot open as something tugged at her awareness. Ele was lightly twirling strands of her hair between his fingers. She wondered if he even knew he was doing it or if it was subconscious. Kala tried not to overthink it. She had read too much into the kiss earlier, she refused to read too much into this. It felt nice, though. It would almost be soothing if she knew what it meant.

Kala huffed a breath of annoyance at herself. She was used to sharing her bed with a snake, not a hot half-naked man. It was affecting her more than it should. Every nerve ending and molecule in her body was acutely attuned to every part of him. Kala wondered if Ele was feeling any of this. Probably not. He likely shared his bed with many girls, but it had been a long time since Kala had allowed anyone to get close to her.

The lack of intimacy usually didn't bother her. She knew how to take care of herself. Abstinence did not make her crave sex. Yet here she was, her body lit like an oil lamp. Her center practically melting with arousal. Ele, on the other hand, showed no signs of agitation. He lay still, calm, but he hadn't fallen asleep yet. His breathing hadn't changed and his fingers were still coiling her hair.

Kala swallowed deeply. "Ele?"

"Hmmm?"

She had nothing to say. Why had she spoken?

"Thanks for the kiss today." She cringed as the words left her mouth before she could call them back. The last thing she wanted to do was remind him of that awkward moment.

"You're welcome."

"I'm sorry if it was weird." Damn it! She needed to stop talking. *Now.*

"It wasn't. Nothing could ever be weird between us."

Kala stared at the pulse beating in his neck. What did he mean by that? Perhaps he'd just said it to make her feel better. Or perhaps it was a veiled invitation. She'd said earlier that some bonds could withstand anything. Perhaps this was his way of suggesting that their bond could too. She could reach out and touch him, see how he responded. But if he rejected her, the humiliation would haunt her forever.

"You pulled away so fast, I thought maybe I'd done something wrong."

"No. I'm sorry, I didn't mean to make you feel like that."

If it were possible, she was even more confused now than she was a moment ago. Kala sighed. It didn't matter. Whatever this was, whatever it could be, it wasn't a good idea. She needed to sleep.

Tomorrow she would forget all about this and everything would go back to normal.

Except the damn throbbing between her legs wouldn't fucking stop.

"I promise next time I won't pull away," Ele murmured against her hair.

Next time.

The words sent her heart hammering to the pulse of her sex. He thought there would be a next time. Kala slowly lifted her head to meet his gaze and their noses brushed. Even in the dim light, Ele's eyes flared like warm embers, darting from her face to her mouth and back again. Like he was asking a question. Like he was daring her.

All Kala's doubt dissolved in an instant. He wanted her. The desire on his face was unmistakable and yet he didn't make a move. It was like he was waiting for her to decide. A thousand unspoken words passed between them. Kala knew all the reasons they shouldn't, but she also knew that if she didn't, she would regret it for the rest of her life.

Kala tilted her head up and closed her eyes as she pressed her lips against his. Ele opened his mouth to her immediately, welcoming the kiss, their tongues meeting in tentative exploration. A shiver coursed through her and her senses electrified. Ele's arm enclosed protectively around her, pulling her flush against him until there was no space left between them at all. She almost yelped as her pelvic bone was impaled by his erection. She knew he'd wanted her, but she hadn't realized he was *that* aroused by her.

Ele lifted his hand to cup just below her jaw, holding her gentle but firm as he commanded the kiss. Everything about it was intoxicating, from the way he held her to the strokes of his tongue. Ele knew how to kiss. Of course he did. She shouldn't be surprised. Perhaps she was more surprised by the way she was responding to his kiss. Like it was the last drop of water in the desert. Like she was feverish for him.

Kala had ever been kissed like this. She wanted to melt into him, abandon every thought she'd ever had and surrender herself completely. She was so lost in the moment Kala didn't realize she'd gone limp in his arms. The thought that he might be disappointed in her own abilities was intolerable. She pressed her hips firmer against the length of him and Ele moaned into her mouth. He sounded just as desperate for release as she was. That knowledge tore away any lingering reservations she had. Kala reached for him, slipping her hand inside his pants until his shaft was in her palm.

Ele jerked back slightly, startled by her boldness. "Wait."

"For what?" She breathed impatiently.

"What are we doing?"

Kala blinked, confused. "Don't tell me you're a virgin."

"No," he huffed a breathy laugh. "I mean us. What is this?"

"Sex."

"Just sex?"

Kala's features shifted in sudden understanding. He was worried that she might expect more from him afterwards that he was not willing to give.

"Don't worry, I won't fall in love with you. You have your duties and I have mine."

She could control her emotions. It was her damn body that she couldn't control. She needed him. Everywhere. Inside her. *Now*. Kala began to stroke his cock in heated demand. It felt thick and solid in her hand, the tip wet with pre-cum. Ele abandoned all protest as his mouth closed over hers in renewed hunger. His hand grasped her breast and his teeth scraped against her lower lip. A floodgate of desire burst open, leaving her unbelievably wet.

"Kala."

It was so strange to hear him say her name like that. A panting, breathy plea. She hoped he wasn't pleading for her to slow down because she couldn't. One of her hands yanked his pants down while the other guided his cock beneath her nightdress to her entrance.

"Holy gods," Ele groaned as she pulled him into her.

Kala wrapped her leg around him and he gripped her hips as they moved together, finding a rhythm, but it wasn't enough. She needed faster. Deeper. Kala pushed Ele onto his back and straddled him, sinking down between his legs until she filled herself to the hilt. An animalistic noise of pure pleasure escaped her throat. She ground against him, charging into a carnal chase, a delicious tension building inside her.

Kala arched her back as she rode him, rapt in the heady sensation of each thrust. When she looked down at Ele, she found him watching her intensely. His pupils were dilated, his swollen lips parted in awe. Then he lifted his hips and pressed a hand against her stomach, deepening the angle. She shattered.

The orgasm ruptured through her, leaving ripples of devastating pleasure in its wake. She had never felt anything like it. With Samir her climaxes had been good but not like this. Kala felt utterly destroyed. Ele shuddered and released himself into her with a groan. The warmth of his seed spread through her core. Her head was still spinning as she rolled off him. Ele immediately made room for her on the bed, cradling her body so that she didn't hit the wall. She wouldn't feel it if she did. She'd gone completely numb.

"Are you all right?" Ele brushed strands of sweaty hair back from her face.

"Much better," she breathed.

It was hard to form thoughts or words in her drunken haze of orgasmic pleasure. Silence passed between them, only disturbed by the sound of their panting breaths. Kala knew she should probably say something but as soon as the thought came into her head sleep dragged her under.

CHAPTER SEVENTEEN

ISA

When Isa stirred awake at dusk, his first thought was water. Tahlia's presence lingered in his consciousness like smoke on a garment but his arid mouth demanded his attention. Even before he pushed himself up into a slumped seated position, Isa already knew his body had deteriorated. His skin was painfully dry but sticky. His muscles were stiff and cramped. The pain in his head throbbed violently and his eyes were irritated. Isa had hoped he would have more time before the symptoms set in but there was no denying them. If he didn't hydrate his body in the next few hours, he would die.

It was impossible.

He had already stripped the saltbush bare. Even if by some miracle he was able to find another one, the little moisture in the leaves would not be enough to sustain him. Not anymore. Isa cast his gaze out from beneath the natural bridge to the night sky. It was a hush of orange, violet, and obsidian. The stars were only starting to emerge.

Perhaps this would be the last night of his life. If so, he was fortunate. To die in such a peaceful and beautiful place was more than he could have hoped for. There was a time he had been convinced he would die in battle, blood soaked and torn apart by the edge of a sharp blade. Slipping into an eternal sleep beneath a blanket of stars was a far more pleasant way to go.

Isa wondered if this was what it had been like for his Naiab brothers when they were refused refuge by the Water Goddess. Maybe their bones lay in a desert cave not far from here, their bodies reunited with their homeland but not their loved ones. If so, it was fitting that he would join them soon. He owed it to them to share their fate.

Isa forced himself to stand in his shallow grave, his tendons stretching and scraping against each other. The world swayed around him and he stumbled backward, trying to find balance. He managed to step out of the grave and braced a hand against the rocky wall for support as he pulled his tunic over his body. Just outside the cavern, a few sticks lay discarded in the sand but there was no point in lighting a fire. He had no game and the night wasn't that cold.

The remnants of the snakeskin from last night had already withered away to dust. Isa shuffled forward until he was standing out in the open beneath the canvas of night. He already knew he didn't have the strength to wander the desert in hopes of salvation. There was no hope. He had already accepted that.

Isa had never really given much thought to the afterlife. Whether he became a star or fed the earth did not matter to him. What mattered was the way he lived his life. He had always longed to be a Naiab warrior, to protect his people, and die an honorable death. But he was no longer Naiab and his honor had been burnt to ashes years ago. Tahlia was right. He'd betrayed her. He didn't deserve forgiveness and he was not worthy of her love.

At least he had gotten to see her one last time, to hear her voice, to have her gaze upon him, even if it was only with anger. He was grateful to whatever force had brought them together all those years ago and had chosen to reunite them one final time. Isa had once hoped to share a lifetime with Tahlia but the gods had deprived him of that. Still, he would have waited all the ages of the world for her, even if their life together was limited to a single day.

"I am sorry, goddess." Isa swayed on his feet as he called out to the night sky. "You are my one regret in this life. I need you to know that I would do anything to make it right. I would suffocate if it meant you could breathe again. I would give my mortality so that you could feel again. If it meant being condemned for all eternity, I would do it. Even then, you would not owe me anything. Some betrayals can never be forgiven. But I also need you to know that, even though my love is unworthy of you, it has and always will be yours. I will love you beyond my death into whatever existence comes after."

A gentle wind moved over the desert sands as silence stretched on forever. He did not expect a reply. The goddess had told him his words were meaningless to her, his life meant even less. Her sentiments had been cutting but clear. Whether in life or death, she was indifferent to him. He did not resent her for it. On a night like this, ten years ago, he had not been strong enough to let her die. But tonight, death would claim him, and only then would he truly lose her.

KALA

He's dying.

Kala's eyes shot open as the words pierced her mind, sending her heart bolting out of her chest. Ele woke instantly at her sudden movement, whipping the blade from beneath the pillow, but there was no enemy.

"Where is he?" Kala demanded, tossing the blanket to the floor and scrambling out of bed.

I can lead you there but you might not make it in time.

Kala pressed her lips together in determination. She would make it. Kala spared no thought for privacy as she stripped naked and changed into a tunic suitable for riding.

"What's happened?"

Kala glanced over at Ele to find him already getting dressed, strapping his shamshir to his belt and wedging his dagger inside his pants.

"Isa is dying. We need to leave. Now."

Thankfully, she hadn't had time to unpack her saddlebags so she simply threw them over her shoulder. She spared a minute to fill her waterskin. Isa would need it when she found him. Alive.

"I'll get Sabine and we'll meet you at the entrance," Ele offered.

Kala was glad for it because she wasn't going to wait. She sprinted out into the passageways, skidding around corners until she came out onto a narrow landing that overlooked the field down below. She darted down the stone staircase as fast as she dared. It was the quickest route to the entrance and she was determined to take it, even though one false step would send her careening over the lethal edge.

The Citadel was quiet, not a soul wandering about. Kala risked a glance up at the opening in the cave's ceiling. The sky told her it was roughly an hour before dawn. She jumped the last few steps to the ground and rushed to the entrance. The darkness of the tunnel engulfed her, forcing her to slow to a walk, but she put a hand out along the jagged wall to guide her. It wasn't long before she burst out into the Idris Desert.

Ahead of her, two camels sat in the sand, saddled and laden with supplies. The Water Goddess had obviously given orders that the beasts be made ready for their departure. Just then, two warriors materialized from the sand on either side of her. Kala recognized one as Arsyn but the other was unfamiliar. Both held spears made of sand, which they crossed directly in front of her.

"The Water Goddess has not given you permission to leave yet," Arsyn said.

"I do not need her permission. I am not a prisoner!"

"Go back inside," the other instructed.

"No! Isa is dying. I need to go to him."

Kala tried to push past them but Arsyn shoved her back with ease. Before she could think, she'd punched him in the face. Pain exploded in her hand but Arsyn didn't budge an inch. His fellow soldier did, though. The Naiab grabbed Kala's arm with such force she thought he might break it, but just as she was about to retaliate, a scythe blade whizzed through the air and sliced clean through the upper bicep of the arm that seized her. The warrior immediately released her, cursing as he grasped at his gaping wound while blood ran down his fingers in rivulets. Arsyn took up a defensive stance, but a second scythe was already at his throat while the first one had rebounded back to its owner.

Kala's mouth fell open as Sabine stood toe to toe with Arsyn, which was ridiculous considering Arsyn towered over her. The warrior glared down at Sabine with violent promise but she met his stare with spitfire of her own. She would do it, Kala realized. Sabine would slice the blade across his throat without blinking. By the hard glint in his eyes, Arsyn knew it too.

"Don't even think about shifting," Ele warned.

Kala wasn't sure when Ele had arrived but his shamshir was leveled at the other Naiab warrior who was still clutching his arm, now dangling limp at his side.

"Kill us and my brothers will slaughter you," Arsyn spat at Sabine.

Sabine's smile was practically feline. "But you'll still be dead."

"Kala?" Ele prompted over his shoulder.

"They won't let us leave without the goddess's permission," Kala explained.

"She said to break the curse we needed something only she could give," Ele reminded her. "Are you sure you want to leave without it?"

"Isa is dying! We can't afford to wait."

Ele lowered his chin in concentration, his features tightening as his eyes sharpened on something Kala couldn't see. Was he using his magic?

"Let us leave." His voice was pure predatory power.

The Naiab warriors flinched, as if the vessels of their hearts were being squeezed by an invisible force. Seizing the moment, Sabine clocked Arsyn with her fist, knocking him out cold.

"Son of a donkey!" Sabine swore, shaking her hand. "What are they made from? Stone?"

Kala swung a blow to the other warrior's face, sending him flying into the sand. Ele immediately relaxed an inch, heaving an internal sigh of relief. He hadn't wanted to kill them but he'd been prepared to do it. Thankfully, he'd weakened them enough for Kala and Sabine to render them unconscious.

"Come on." Kala ran to the camels and mounted behind the first hump before urging the beast to stand.

Ele and Sabine mounted the second camel and followed her lead, compelling the animals into a gallop. As they hurtled down the gorge, Kala held her breath, waiting for funnels of sand to launch up from the ground in front of them to prevent their escape, but nothing materialized. Either the Naiab were toying with them or they were letting them go.

Kala didn't have time to question it.

"Where is he?" Kala shouted.

Tahlia's calm voice entered her mind, directing her path. Kala forged ahead, praying it would be enough. The camels would only be able to travel at speed for a short burst before slowing to a steady pace. The animals were built for endurance not speed. Kala gritted her teeth and held tightly to the pommel as she braced her body against the jarring movement. Sitting high on the camel's back, she felt every sway and jolt, even as her saddle kept her firmly in place. It felt less like running and more like being wildly tossed about.

Kala wasn't sure how much time had passed before Tahlia ordered them to stop. By then, the sun had risen over the dunes, bringing the first taste of heat with it, and the camels had long since slowed to a more energy-efficient stride. Kala's eyes darted around the desert, desperately searching for any sign of Isa. A rock formation in the shape of a bridge caught her eye. Its shade would offer shelter from the sun. Kala forced the camel to kneel and Ele followed her lead. Once she dismounted, she ran for the bridge, already knowing in her heart what she would find.

Kala skidded to a halt at the sight of him, sending up a plume of dust in her wake. Isa lay sprawled on his side in the sand, his arm outstretched as if reaching for something. His skin looked dry and tight, like flaking fish scales. His lips were cracked. His eyes were sunken in.

"No, no, no," Kala muttered as she rushed to him, sinking to her knees and cradling his head in her lap.

She fumbled to uncork her waterskin and opened Isa's mouth before pouring a small amount of water down his throat. He didn't swallow. Didn't move. Kala was vaguely aware of Ele and Sabine standing nearby, giving her space but watching on with concern.

"Is he even alive?" Sabine asked.

Kala hadn't thought to check his pulse or breath. She didn't want to, because what if—

"Tahlia!" Kala cried out desperately.

"He has minutes," Ele said gently, his tone conveying what he couldn't say. He could see Isa's lifeforce fading.

"No!" Kala refused to believe it. She poured more water down his throat but it only spilled over the side of his mouth, dribbling down his chin.

It was impossible. Isa couldn't die. He was a formidable force in her life. Strong and fearless. Like a mountain, unmovable, withstanding whatever nature threw at him. He had stayed by her side even though it cost him everything.

Save him.

Kala's head snapped up in confusion at Tahlia's voice, but her gaze immediately locked onto Dema, who was casually striding towards them, leading a camel behind her. Ele, Sabine, and Kala exchanged wary looks. Dema must have followed them from the Citadel, though Kala wasn't sure why. The Shahri peered down at Isa's body as he lay limp in Kala's lap. Her expression was unreadable, but then her eyes shifted, suddenly holding the ebb and flow of tides.

"You save him," the Water Goddess replied sharply, the comment clearly directed at Tahlia. After a beat of silence, a bitter smirk carved across her face. "Oh, that's right. You refuse to embrace your divinity and lower yourself to be like the rest of us. If you won't save him, why should I?"

Because the time hasn't come.

"Careful. You sound almost prophetic."

Sabine leaned into Ele to hiss under her breath, "Who is she talking to?"

"Tahlia," Ele deduced.

"Please," Kala begged. She didn't know what they were arguing about, but if someone didn't do something, Isa would die in her arms. She couldn't bear it.

The goddess crouched down slowly, her eyes running over Isa's body from head to toe, presumably assessing the internal damage. "I can only do what is within my power."

"Then do it," Kala urged.

"Give him more water," the goddess instructed.

Kala complied, pouring water down his throat. The Water Goddess raised a hand and lifted her fingers as if she were playing chords on the wind. She was manipulating the water in Isa's body, Kala realized, directly infusing it into his bloodstream. Kala poured a little water onto his face and brushed it across his forehead and cheeks. Once the Water Goddess was done, she lowered her hand and met Kala's hopeful stare.

"That's all I can do. He needs rest if he has any chance of recovering."

Kala stared down at Isa. There was no noticeable change. The color of his skin hadn't improved, and he was still unconscious, but if anyone could claw their way back from death, it was Isa.

"How is he meant to rest? You won't permit him in the Citadel," Ele pointed out.

"No. He will need to go with you, wherever you are going. I have asked the Naiab to make a stretcher. It will be here soon. One of the camels can pull it."

It wasn't ideal but it would have to do.

"Thank you," Kala said.

"Don't thank me yet. He may not survive." It almost sounded like the goddess hoped he wouldn't. She turned her attention to Sabine who froze under her stormy gaze. "Where is your witch?"

Sabine hesitated a moment, as if she were unsure whether to give up the information. It was understandable considering it was the only thing keeping her alive.

"The Kingdom of the Salt Plains."

Kala raised her brows in surprise. The kingdom bordered hers.

"I'm coming with you," the Water Goddess announced.

CHAPTER EIGHTEEN

KALA

The journey to the Kingdom of the Salt Plains felt excruciatingly long. The hours crawled by slowly, and Kala couldn't resist looking over her shoulder every few minutes at the stretcher that dragged behind her camel, trailing two deep lines in the sand. She had wrapped Isa in light linen cloth soaked in water to keep his skin damp but she knew it was futile and wasteful. The sun's rays would have absorbed the water in minutes. Still, the cloth would protect his skin from burning. It was all she could do for him.

They traveled in silence which meant that there was nothing to distract Kala from her thoughts. They battered her mind like the hot wind battered her body. Mostly they were consumed by Isa, whether he would live or die. In the moments they drifted elsewhere, they circled around the Water Goddess. Kala wasn't sure what to make of her sudden decision to join them. She still didn't know whether the goddess was on their side.

The goddess had known about the curse of the Black Sands since its creation and yet she had done nothing to neutralize the threat it posed to her people. The Water Goddess was not usually one to stand idle or let things go. Especially when it involved her ex, the God of Beauty and Fertility. Maybe she genuinely believed the witches had died out and there was no way to break the curse. But it was also possible she didn't want the curse to be broken, and now they were leading her straight to the only witch in existence.

That's if Sabine wasn't lying to them.

Then there was Tahlia. If Isa lived, it would be because of her. Kala was still reeling from the fact that Tahlia had asked the Water Goddess to save him. It was unfathomable. Whether Isa lived or died was of no concern to Tahlia, which meant she had another motive to save him. The thought made Kala uneasy. She could confront Tahlia about it, demand answers, but she already knew the goddess would not give her any. Ever since her divine existence had been revealed, she had become even more distant and withdrawn.

When the sun began to set, they made camp. Ele set up the tents and Sabine took care of the camels while Kala carefully unwrapped the white cloth from Isa's face. He was still unconscious but at least he was breathing.

"Hold on," Kala whispered to him. "For me."

She poured a little water down his throat and soaked the cloth, patting it gently over his skin.

"His condition has stabilized," the Water Goddess said as she walked up behind her.

Kala's shoulders sagged in relief. "Will he wake soon?"

"If fate allows it."

Kala stood up, her eyes surveying Isa's body for any signs of improvement. She wasn't used to seeing him like this. Weak and vulnerable.

"I have something for you." The Water Goddess held a vial out to her.

Kala appraised it skeptically before she took it. "Is this what we need to break the curse?"

"It's what *you* need to break *your* curse. I told you once, it is a privilege to be a creator, and it is rare to find true love, but it is rarer still to rule. You're a queen. You cannot afford to be so reckless."

Kala frowned, confused.

"It's a contraceptive," the goddess said drily.

A flush bloomed across Kala's cheeks. She hadn't even thought about the potential consequences of last night, she'd been too caught up in her own lust. The goddess was right. She'd been reckless and impulsive.

"How did you know?"

"Tahlia. The goddess claims to stay out of mortal affairs but I'm beginning to question whether that's true."

She wondered what Tahlia thought about what had happened between her and Ele. Perhaps she had always hoped their friendship would develop into something deeper as they got older. Or maybe she thought it was a mistake they would come to regret. Either way, Kala was grateful for her interference. She wouldn't make the same mistake again.

"It must be hard to let go of the mortal world and the people you love," Kala said in defense of Tahlia.

"You are wrong. Most find it easy. Once death has taken their loved ones, nothing tethers them to this place."

"You're an exception then. Your people keep you tethered."

The goddess tilted her head slightly in disagreement. "I choose my bindings."

As the goddess turned to walk away, Kala wavered a moment, unsure whether she should say anything more, but she couldn't stop the words from bursting forth. "Do you know anything about an island?"

The goddess went wholly still. It was obvious she was trying to keep her face carefully neutral but a spark of fear flashed in her eyes before it was drowned in the sea.

"You do." Kala couldn't hide the spark of hope in her voice.

"Tahlia should know better than to share the secrets of the spirit world with mortals."

"She hasn't shared any secrets with me. All I know is that something important is about to happen. If Tahlia is in danger, you need to tell me."

"Why? What could you possibly do? You of all people should know that mortals who challenge the will of the gods are doomed."

"That's not true," Kala countered. "Tahlia evaded the gods for years and even trapped one."

"Tahlia is dead," the Water Goddess snapped. "After all that has happened, do you still not understand? There was always going to be a reckoning."

Dread curled inside Kala's gut like a serpent. "What does that mean?"

"Do not speak of it again. You'll only draw attention."

The goddess stalked away as if she hadn't just detonated the very ground Kala walked on. Zaynab was right. Something was about to happen, a reckoning, and Tahlia was caught up in it. Kala clutched the vial in her hand, her heart pounding. But if Tahlia and the Water Goddess were unwilling to talk about it, there was no other way to find out what was going on.

"Isa's tent is ready." Ele's voice startled her as he approached. "I'll take him inside. What's that?"

Kala quickly hid the vial inside her kaftan. "Nothing."

She glanced around, trying to find a task to occupy her. She opted for unpacking food supplies from the saddlebags in preparation for dinner. There were meat, and vegetables, and grains, which sounded wonderful except she had no idea how to cook. Ele was still setting up the tents, and the Water Goddess had disappeared somewhere, though Kala doubted very much the goddess would know how to cook. Kala glanced over at Sabine, who was standing nearby, tending to the camels. Sensing her attention, Sabine met her stare.

"Can you cook?" Kala held up a small bag of grains.

"You can rule a kingdom but can't boil water?"

Kala scowled. "Never mind."

Sabine begrudgingly strolled over and assessed the supplies she'd unpacked. "I can make a shorba out of this."

"Great."

"And by me, I mean you. I'll tell you what to do."

"Fine."

If Isa woke from his unconscious state, the soup would certainly help him hydrate. They sat by the fire and Sabine instructed her on how to prepare the vegetables and meat, taking great delight in pointing out her many errors. Kala endured it. If Sabine wanted to lord something over her, this was probably the only chance she would get. Still, it felt odd to perform such a normal task together. It was what family did every night around the dinner table. Except they were not family. Not anymore.

Kala poured the ingredients into a pot and settled it over the fire.

"Now watch it and make sure it doesn't burn," Sabine ordered.

Kala wasn't sure how to tell if the shorba was burning or not but she didn't say anything, she just kept stirring.

"Who taught you how to cook?" Kala wasn't sure what prompted the question. It sounded too personal and she immediately regretted asking it.

"No one. I taught myself. Just like everything else."

Kala cocked her head sardonically. "You taught yourself how to wield scythe blades?"

The twin blades were still tucked between Sabine's belt and kaftan, one at the front and one at the back. Dried Naiab blood stained one of the blades.

"I know many ways to kill my enemies. Scythe blades just happen to be my favorite."

"You're impressive with them," Kala admitted. "Your disappearance last night was also very impressive. Looks like sometimes you run away from your enemies."

Sabine's nostrils flared angrily, but Kala pretended not to notice as she continued to stir the pot.

"I know how to read a situation and calculate the odds of survival," Sabine shot back. "You threatened a goddess in her own sanctuary in front of a dozen sand wielders. Suicidal doesn't even begin to cover that."

"Then why did you fight with us this morning? We were defying a goddess's orders in her own sanctuary and facing a legion of Naiab warriors intent on stopping us from leaving."

"Because against all odds you survived," Sabine exasperated. "Somehow, you always survive. You seem blessed with more lives than I can count. I haven't figured it out yet but I will."

"What?"

"What's so special about you," she spat the words like they were poison.

Kala self-consciously tucked a strand of hair behind her ear. There was nothing special about her. Ele had been the one to save her as a child. Without him, she would have died broken in the streets. Even now, Ele was still saving her. The only reason the Water Goddess hadn't killed her was because Ele was god-touched and could obliterate her Naiab warriors with a single thought.

Sabine huffed out a tight breath. "I don't owe you anything, and this is not an apology but about what happened ... it wasn't what I wanted."

"Let's not," Kala interjected, her tone laced with warning.

"I didn't know that would happen," Sabine persisted.

"What did you think was going to happen?!"

"I was worried you were in trouble again."

"Again? I was only taken by the slavers because of you!"

"Exactly!" Sabine shook her head infuriated. "Never mind."

Kala's mouth gaped open. There were too many words she wanted to say, all of them like daggers to a target, but they caught in her throat, so she swallowed them down and tried to remember to breathe.

"You might not have known that would happen to me, but it did happen, and you still defend them. I am nothing but a traitor to you."

"You were older than me. You knew what you were doing."

"Trying to live! Trying to make sure my brothers and sisters lived. Tell me, who else is alive today? Out of all of us, how many survived?"

The pressure of silence was a physical thing. It sat on her chest, restricting her airways and crushing her arteries. Sabine looked solemn for once, as if she couldn't speak, like she was lost in the painful memories of young faces. Children who used to have names. Skinny bodies that had slept beside them in cramped spaces. Now corpses, withered away to dust. Only called to mind by the occasional thought. Sabine's silence told Kala everything she needed to know.

"If you want to hate me, hate me. But at least be honest about why you hate me." Kala tossed the spoon in the pot and stood up. "I'm not hungry. You make sure it doesn't burn. I doubt it will be salvageable if it does."

ELE

Ele dragged Isa's stretcher inside the tent and was about to leave when he heard Kala and Sabine talking. Sabine was instructing Kala on how to cook and it was going about as well as a hostile alliance negotiation. He lingered just inside the tent, listening carefully, hopeful they would find some common ground. Instead, it deteriorated into the equivalent of a military deadlock. Kala stormed off to her tent and Sabine was left to salvage the food.

Ele sat down on his haunches, giving Sabine a moment of privacy to process the heated exchange. Unlike Kala, he hadn't been surprised that Sabine fought with them against the Naiab. She hadn't acted out of a sense of loyalty. It was simply in her best interest to leave the Citadel, and her odds of survival improved significantly if she traveled in their company. If she tried to escape the Citadel and cross the Idris Desert by herself, she would never make it back to the Thaka alive.

What did surprise Ele was that Sabine had taken his advice and tried to talk to Kala about what had happened between them. He hadn't thought Sabine cared enough to bother but he'd been wrong. The bonds of family were strange. Trauma could shatter people apart but it could also bond them, and time had a way of reshaping perspective.

"Goddess."

Ele spun around at the garbled moan. Isa was stirring on the stretcher, his eyes slowly opening to narrow unfocused slits. Dark rings circled his pupils. He looked terrible, and yet markedly better than what he had looked like hours ago.

"I'm afraid not. It's just Ele."

Isa's gaze roamed the tent until it landed on him. "Kala. Where's Kala?"

"She's safe. She found you unconscious in the desert. The Water Goddess saved your life."

Isa's features creased in confusion and Ele nodded, agreeing with his cynicism.

"Why would she do that?" Isa croaked.

"Because Tahlia asked her to."

Isa barely breathed as he stared back at Ele in disbelief.

"We're in the Idris, making our way to the Kingdom of the Salt Plains where Sabine says the witch is," Ele explained. "The Water Goddess is traveling with us. She says she has something we need to break the curse."

Ele uncorked a waterskin and moved closer to tilt it to Isa's lips. Isa sat up a little, swallowing a few mouthfuls before pushing it away and lying back down. He looked very weak. It would likely take days before he regained his strength.

"I'll fetch you something to eat."

Ele stepped out of the tent to find Sabine still sitting by the fire. She'd taken the pot off the flames and served herself a bowl of soup. Ele glanced around the campsite but Dema was nowhere to be found.

"How is it?" Ele asked as he walked over and ladled some of the soup into a bowl.

"Edible."

Ele considered saying nothing more, it was probably best if he stayed out of it entirely, but he couldn't help himself. "You did the right thing."

"Once a spy always a spy, huh, Captain?" Sabine finished her soup and put the bowl down in the sand. "It doesn't change anything."

"It might. In time."

If Sabine kept her word and didn't betray them. Or sell Kala out to her family. Sabine looked up at him and unfurled a slow, saccharine smile. It didn't fill Ele with confidence.

He returned inside Isa's tent to find the warrior staring up at the woven fabric, his mind clearly reeling. Ele couldn't fathom it either; why Tahlia would lead them to Isa or plead with the Water Goddess to save his life. Ele already knew Isa would cling to it like a lifeline. He would interpret the goddess's actions as proof that she still cared for him.

Maybe she did.

Ele put the bowl down beside the stretcher. "It's shorba. Kala made it."

"I must be dead."

Ele snorted as Isa reached for it and sniffed the contents but his features immediately melted in avid gratitude. Of course, he would be starving. The man hadn't eaten in days. Ele watched as Isa ate. He got the impression that Isa was forcing himself to do so slowly. If he ate too much too fast, he would only bring it up again.

"You had us worried," Ele said.

Isa remained focused on his meal as he replied, "I was resigned to die."

Ele couldn't blame him. If their situations were reversed, he wasn't sure if he would have been able to survive in the Idris Desert without food and water. When faced with such bleak odds, one had to accept the most likely outcome.

"Well, I'm glad you didn't. It would have broken Kala's heart."

Isa didn't reply, he just kept eating.

With the conversation seemingly over, Ele turned to leave. "I'll tell Kala you're awake."

"Don't. I'll see her in the morning once I've had some rest."

Ele frowned but then he understood. Isa didn't want her to see him like this. He was her guardian, her protector. It would pain her to see him so weak, to hear that he'd been resigned to die.

Isa lifted his gaze to him, his eyes turning shrewd. "Did anything else happen that I should know about?"

Fuck.

Ele was skilled at lying and he was used to keeping his affairs private, but he had a feeling Isa would see straight through him when it came to Kala. He perched his hands on his hips while his forehead lined in thought.

"Kala threatened to kill the Shahri in front of a dozen Naiab warriors."

The spoon paused on its way to Isa's mouth before he resumed eating, as if he expected as much.

"Thank you for protecting her."

"There's no need to thank me. I'll always protect her."

"Good. Take up guard outside her tent tonight."

Ele bristled at the overt order coupled with the dismissive tone, but he bit his tongue and left. Sabine was still sitting by the fire as Ele helped himself to two more bowls of soup.

"It's not *that* edible," Sabine protested.

Ele lifted one of the bowls pointedly as he walked away. "Kala."

Sabine pressed her lips tightly at the explanation but returned her gaze to the fire. As Ele made his way over to Kala's tent, he could see her silhouette through the fabric illuminated by the oil lamp inside. It made his balls tighten. Even her shadow was stunning.

A part of him still couldn't quite believe what had happened between them last night, like it must have been a fever dream. But it wasn't. He remembered every little detail. He had relived it over and over again in his mind. He just wasn't sure what it meant. Or if it would happen again. Especially since he hadn't put in his best performance. He'd been so caught off guard by her boldness and overwhelmed by the fact that it was Kala gripping his shaft and riding him to the edge of pleasure that he'd simply let her take control. He regretted it now. She probably thought he wasn't capable of offering her more.

"Come in," Kala called out to him, despite the fact that he hadn't said anything.

It dawned on Ele that he'd been standing outside her tent like a dumbstruck idiot. He stepped inside to find Kala sitting on her bedroll, having changed into her nightdress. Her nipples peaked beneath the cotton fabric but Ele tried not to notice. He was acutely aware that he had only briefly explored her breasts last night before Kala pinned him to the bed. He craved to see them in the light, naked and exposed, ready for him to caress and suck as he wished.

Kala's gaze flicked up to him and then down to the bowls in his hands. "I'm not hungry."

It was obvious from her flat tone and sour demeanor that she was still working through the conversation she'd had with Sabine.

"Isa's awake."

"What?" Kala instantly reached for a shawl.

"He said that he wanted to rest and he'll see you in the morning."

Kala's shoulders sank in disappointment.

"Eat." He held the bowl out to her. "We both need to if we're going to make it to the Salt Plains."

Kala reluctantly accepted the bowl and Ele sat down beside her. She blew lightly across the spoonful of soup before bringing it to her lips and swallowing it down. The movement shouldn't have been erotic but it was.

"Do you think there really is a witch?" Kala asked pensively.

"I don't know."

"Sabine could be leading us into a trap. Think about it. She tried to recruit Isa for his sand wielding. She tried to negotiate trade with the Naiab. Both attempts failed but it wouldn't matter if her true intention is to deliver us to our enemies."

"You mean deliver us to your family."

"The Shahri of the Naiab, a sand wielder, Captain of the Guard, and Queen of the Black Sands. What a bounty."

Ele had to admit it made perfect sense. A formidable cartel notorious for underground dealings would be very interested in securing a partnership with the Queen of the Black Sands and the Shahri of the Naiab. And if they refused such a partnership, there was always the option of blackmail or murder. A sand wielder would be a powerful addition to their ranks. As for Ele, he'd likely be tortured and slaughtered for spite, his head delivered to Henri in a box or speared just outside the palace gates.

Kala licked her lips anxiously. "They can't hurt me in my own kingdom but alone like this?"

"You're not alone."

"You know what I mean."

He did. Without soldiers guarding her borders and an army at her back, she was vulnerable. He would protect her with his life, as would Isa, but Isa was currently in no condition to fight. If Sabine truly was leading them into a trap, they needed to proceed with caution.

"We'll be careful," Ele promised her.

Once they finished eating, Ele collected the bowls. "Sleep well. I'll be right outside if you need me."

Kala's brows furrowed even as her lips twitched to an amused smile. "Are you guarding my tent?"

Ele winked at her. "Isa's orders."

When he strolled outside, the fire had been doused to ashes, and Sabine had presumably retired to her tent for the night. Ele washed the bowls and repacked them before retrieving his bedroll from his tent. At least if he was guarding Kala's tent for the next few nights, he wouldn't have to bother to erect his own. Ele unfurled the bedroll and stretched out onto his back, interlacing his fingers behind his head. He didn't mind sleeping out in the open. He'd slept in places far worse than this, with more vermin to contend with.

As he lay there staring up at the night sky, Kala's words crawled inside his mind. They unsettled him. What was even more unsettling was the fact that he hadn't come to the same conclusion. As much as he hated to admit it, he'd become too comfortable around Sabine. He knew he couldn't trust her to care about anyone but herself, but he'd underestimated the threat she posed. His hands instinctively reached for the shamshir strapped to his side and then checked the dagger hidden beneath his kurta.

The Kingdom of the Salt Plains was ruled by Malik, who was rarely in residence and trusted its governance to a regent. But Ele knew Malik would mobilize his army in a heartbeat to defend Kala. The thought gave him some measure of comfort.

"Ele?" Kala called out to him, interrupting his thoughts.

He tilted his head back toward the tent. "Yes?"

"I need you."

Ele got up and slipped inside the tent. Kala was sitting on her bedroll, the linen nightshift hanging loosely on her frame. Her dark hair was unbound and wild around her shoulders making her look like a true desert queen.

"What is it?"

"I need some water."

Ele's gaze immediately caught on the waterskin next to her bedroll, within easy arm's reach. His forehead lined with curiosity as he bent down to pick it up. He could feel the weight of it, there was water inside. He passed it to her. Whispers of a smile danced on her lips as she took a sip before putting it back down in its original spot.

A corner of his mouth twitched as he asked, "Anything else?"

Kala slowly lowered herself to rest on her elbows but she kept her knees bent. Ele watched as the nightshift slipped down her legs to bunch at her thighs. Her olive skin glowed in the lamplight and the shadow between her thighs beckoned him like a siren's call.

"I need my lamp blown out."

Ele lifted the oil lamp to his face, never taking his eyes off Kala as he blew out the flame. The tent pitched into darkness.

"Anything else?" His voice pitched dangerously low.

"I need—"

"I know what you need." Ele lunged, caging her body between his, one arm braced on either side of her and his cock between her legs.

She gasped at the hard pressure pressing against her sex. He lifted his hips a little and her breathy whimper protested the absence of him.

"Trust me," he whispered.

Ele could hardly see her in the dark, but he could feel her warm breath on his skin and the taut sexual tension that hung in the air between them. His face hovered inches above hers, his lips precariously close. He traced his thumb over those gorgeous plump lips and they obeyed his silent plea to part for him but he wouldn't kiss her. Not tonight. There were so many things he wanted to do to her but they weren't what she needed.

Ele trailed the pad of his thumb down her chin, her throat, and then splayed his fingers wide as they moved down her chest. The cotton shift prevented him from feeling her bare skin but that only heightened his desire. He ran his hand over her right breast, giving it a small squeeze and pinching the nipple between his fingers. Kala arched her back in response, lifting her hips to meet his, generating a spark of delicious friction as she ground against him. But Ele lifted himself higher, just out of reach, and Kala groaned as she sank down in frustration.

His hand resumed its leisurely descent. It trailed down her stomach until it found the bunched-up shift at her hips. He yanked the material up, pulling it out from beneath her bottom so that it gathered around her breasts. Greedily, his palms ran down the length of her body and then gripped the inside of her thigh. Kala jolted at the possessive touch and Ele smirked in the dark. Then he lowered his lips to her abdomen.

She tasted faintly of salt and sand. His tongue skimmed along her stomach, his teeth grazing her skin torturously until he felt it pebble with anticipation. Kala's hands grasped either side of his head, her fingers buried deep in his curls, but she didn't try to push him down or guide him towards her center. Ele got the impression that it was taking all her willpower to restrain herself.

He left a trail of burning kisses from her navel to just above her pubic bone. He could already smell her, the delicious wetness of her core. Ele lingered above her, breathing it in like sweet perfume, savoring the enticing scent. Then his hands gripped the insides of her thighs and pushed them out so that she was spread before him. His cock pulsed painfully, demanding entry, but Ele ignored it. Instead, he flicked his tongue out and licked the tip of her sex.

Kala shivered and Ele felt all his nerves ignite at once. It was hedonistic, the knowledge that he commanded her body. It was soft and supple in his hands, desperate for his touch, responsive to his every whim. It was a power beyond anything he had ever aspired to and he couldn't remember why he hadn't dedicated his life to this singular pursuit.

He was ravenous for it.

Unable to resist, he captured her nub in his mouth, sucking it hard but slow. Kala's groan was loud enough for Ele to immediately raise his head in reproach.

"Quiet. You'll wake the camp."

"You try to—" Her words were swallowed by a moan as Ele licked her slit.

She tasted incredible. She was so slick and ready for him it made his cock tremble. His tongue worked her thoroughly, plunging into her center the way that his cock longed to do. She writhed beneath him, opening wider for him. He gripped her hips, steadying her. When he sucked her again, her groan was positively feral.

Ele darted above her body to slam a hand over her mouth. "Do you even know how to be quiet?"

A muffled retort came from beneath his hand but he only chuckled.

"If you can't behave, I'm going to have to fuck you like this."

Her garbled answer sounded like a blatant challenge.

Ele reached down and slipped his fingers between her entrance, stroking her. Kala inhaled deeply through her nose and her body clenched in response. He wished he could see her face. Her cheeks would be flushed, her eyelashes fluttering as she tried to maintain her composure against his ministrations. Kala was not shy about her wants or needs, he had learned that much last night. She was used to taking charge and demanding satisfaction. But submitting herself to someone else, trusting them to fulfill her desires, was not something she was accustomed to. The fact that she hadn't tried to take control of this told him that she trusted him. And that was an honor that he was eager to earn.

Ele thrust two fingers into her center and she squeaked beneath his hand. He felt her walls immediately contract around him, her thighs clenching eagerly. His fingers moved in and out of her, soaked with her heat. Fuck, he wished he could watch his hand. He never thought he would be jealous of it. He wanted to bury his mouth in her slit and his cock in her sex, but his hand was currently getting the best of her. Ele hooked his fingers inside her, plunging them deeper and Kala whined. He pressed his hand firmer over her mouth. The sense of domination was intoxicating. He was restraining her and unleashing her at the same time. He could make her come. He could make her scream. He could make her beg. He controlled her every sensation.

Ele increased the pace until Kala was panting beneath him. Her body pleaded for release while he never wanted this to end. He wanted to drag her pleasure out for hours, witnessing every erotic second of it, but tonight wasn't about what he wanted. Ele felt her walls pulsing around his fingers, building to climax, and he finally gave in by pumping her hard whilst flicking his thumb over her sex. Her body erupted beneath him, her head arching up against his hand in pure pleasure and abandonment. He kept working her through the throes of the orgasm, gradually bringing her down until her body was satiated beneath him.

Ele lifted his hand away from her mouth and grabbed the nightshift that was bunched around her breasts, pulling it down to cover her. Kala sat up a little and reached for him but he grasped her hand.

"Sleep now. I'll be just outside." He brought the inside of her wrist to his lips and kissed it lightly before he slipped outside into the night.

CHAPTER NINETEEN

ISA

He sensed her before he saw her. The signature of her essence called to every part of his being, carrying him across worlds until he found himself before her. Nothing existed around them and yet there she was, as real as she had ever been. The only thing that tainted her mesmerizing beauty was the barely controlled rage as she prowled towards him.

You need to stop this!

Isa went completely still. He had thought he would never see her again. He had accepted death as it reached for him, the price he would pay for the choices he'd made. Yet he lived. And now he was drinking in the sight of her one more time.

"Stop what, goddess?"

Summoning me.

"If I could summon you, I would have done so every waking moment for the past ten years."

Tahlia huffed irritably. *We are no longer in the canyon where the veil is thin. How is this still possible?*

He didn't know but he was eternally grateful for it.

"I was thinking about you," Isa said, then faltered for a moment. "Were you thinking about me?"

Don't flatter yourself.

He recognized the truth despite her harsh words. "You were."

The knowledge made his heart swell with hope but he tried to temper it. Hope was a fragile thing. Like a seedling sprouting through rocks in a desert ravine. Easy to burn to cinders by the sun before it had a chance to live.

"It could be that if I push from the mortal realm and you pull from the divine realm, we make the connection."

I'm not pulling anything. That's not how it works.

Isa narrowed his eyes in gentle challenge. "Then tell me, goddess, how does it work?"

Tahlia crossed her arms over her chest in stubborn defeat. Even angry she was the most beautiful woman he'd ever beheld. Isa didn't understand what was happening to them and he didn't care, as long as he could be with her.

"A part of you must want this."

Trust me, I don't.

"Then why did you save me?"

It wasn't your time to die.

Her words were so simple, so devoid of emotion, she could be recounting any fact of life. Except he didn't believe her. She had intervened by guiding Kala to find him, by imploring the Water

Goddess to save him. Gods interfered in mortal matters all the time, but they did not interfere in the realms of other gods. By right, the Goddess of Endings and Beginnings should have claimed him. Instead, Tahlia had risked herself to save him.

"You know my end." It wasn't a question. He already knew the answer.

I know many things. The privilege of divinity.

"You said I would sacrifice everything."

Tahlia released her arms so that they hung loosely by her sides. *Haven't you already?*

"No. But I would, gladly. For Kala. For you."

He searched her face as they held each other's stare. There was something else she was keeping from him. It shifted behind her features. During their last interaction, she'd let slip that she refused to submit to her divinity, to give in to her nature as a goddess. He still wasn't sure what she meant by that.

"Tell me what it's like being divine."

A spark of rage ignited her emerald eyes and she stormed away. He watched her put distance between them until her pace finally slowed and her steps dragged to a stop. Even then, she kept her back to him, as if she couldn't stand to look at him. He couldn't blame her. He was the reason why she was divine, and now he had the audacity to ask her what it was like. Isa wasn't sure she would answer him but when she spoke her words were hollow.

Lonely. I have everything in abundance. Time. Knowledge. Power. But it's all meaningless. Without love there is no purpose to ex-

istence. Everything becomes blunted over time. I am losing feeling. Memories are fading. I am forgetting what it was like to be human.

Isa let the truth settle between them, a raw wound unable to heal. "Is that why you inhabit Kala?"

Tahlia nodded pensively. *To remember.*

His steps were slow and careful as he closed the distance between them until he was standing at her back. He couldn't resist the draw of her. She was like gravity and he would never stop falling into her. Isa didn't speak. He was content just to be near her.

The slight turn of Tahlia's head over her shoulder told him that she was aware of his proximity, but she didn't move. A flicker of courage made him reach for her hand but his fingers passed through it like air. Tahlia stared down at where their hands should have met. Her expression showed no signs of surprise, only a resigned sadness.

"I can't feel you," Tahlia said, though neither of them withdrew their hands.

"Don't worry," he murmured against her ear. "I can hold you without touch. I still feel you even though you're gone. You are everywhere to me."

Isa could have sworn she shivered. At least it was proof that he was not dreaming. If he were dreaming, there would be no barriers between them. She would forgive him for his wrongs against her, and he would take her body and heart and soul and bury himself within her until the end of time. In this reality, though, Tahlia would never forgive him. He'd never had her heart. He could only hope for these precious moments with her. To see her but not keep her. To hear her but not touch her. To go to her and yet never truly stand at her side.

"Your power. It's not like the Water Goddess. It feels infinitely stronger."

Tahlia took a step away from him. *I am a lesser god, just like the others.*

All lesser gods had been human once. Upon their mortal deaths, the gods chose them to ascend to divinity and bestowed upon them a realm of power in the living world. The realm was often tied to what had held significance for them during their mortal life.

"What is it? Your power?"

Tahlia turned to face him, her features hardening with fierce resolve. *It doesn't matter because I refuse to wield it.*

KALA

When Kala woke, her first thought was of Ele. His hot mouth on her skin, his tongue expertly licking her center. She squirmed as her core tingled at the memory, a secret smile forming on her lips. The moment he'd left her tent, she'd drifted into a deep sleep, relaxed and satisfied.

Kala's second thought was of Isa. She quickly sobered from the afterglow of last night, got dressed and rushed outside. To her surprise, everyone was already awake. Ele was dismantling the tents while Sabine was preparing the camels. Dema stood a short distance away on the fringes of the camp, the hem of her kaftan fluttering in the early morning desert winds. Her face held a strange look, but it only took a second for Kala to figure out why. Isa sat in front of the doused campfire finishing his breakfast. He rose to stand when he saw her.

Kala flung herself at him, tossing her arms around his neck and squeezing her eyes tight in sharp relief. He stumbled back a bit, obviously still weak, but his arms encircled her, strong and familiar. She tried to breathe through the onslaught of emotions. She'd been so afraid. The thought of losing him was unbearable. And his death would have been her fault. She had already cost him so much, she couldn't bear for him to lose his life as well.

"I hear you saved me."

Kala forced herself to let go and pulled away. With the sleeve of her tunic, she quickly wiped away a tear that had escaped down her cheek.

"The Water Goddess saved you." Kala flicked her gaze over to Dema, who was watching them carefully. "I only found you, with Tahlia's help."

"The gods can be unpredictable," Isa mused.

"We should get going," Ele interrupted as he dragged the stretcher toward the camels.

"I don't need that anymore," Isa said.

Ele paused and shot him a dubious look. "Are you sure?"

"You almost died yesterday," Kala pointed out. "Your body is still recovering. You might not be strong enough to sit in the saddle all day."

"I'm fine," Isa replied tersely.

He did look significantly better than yesterday, but Kala also knew he would never admit when he was struggling.

"Then you can ride behind me and rest against me if you need to," Kala offered.

Isa grimaced as if it were an insult.

"Don't make me order you," Kala warned and Isa had no choice but to begrudgingly accept.

They finished packing up the camp and mounted their camels as the first rays of dawn stretched across the sky. The morning air was already tinged with the first stirrings of heat, foreshadowing the impending scorch the day would bring. Only Kala's eyes and hands were exposed to the elements, the rest of her was safely hidden beneath her long-sleeved tunic and headscarf. Still, even with her skin protected from the sun, the heat had a way of invading the senses and organs until everything felt like it was baking in a stone furnace. The desert was merciless and unyielding that way. It pushed the limits of endurance, both physically and mentally.

"If we make good time today, we should meet the trading route this afternoon and cross into the Kingdom of the Salt Plains late tomorrow," Ele advised.

"When we arrive, I'll send a pigeon to Zaynab. She must be worried that she hasn't heard from me," Kala added.

Dema guided her camel to walk alongside Kala's. "You could have sent a pigeon from the Citadel like Sabine."

Kala whipped her head from Dema to Sabine, who were riding on opposite sides of her. "You sent a pigeon? To who?"

"My contacts in the Salt Plains," Sabine feigned innocence. "You want me to find your witch, don't you?"

Kala's stomach lined with nervous acid. "If you betrayed us—"

"You'll what? You had your chance to kill me. Now you need a witch that only I can provide. You have to trust me."

Kala gripped the leather reins until her knuckles turned white as she stared Sabine down. But Sabine was right. She had no other choice. For now. Once they found the witch, however, there would be nothing stopping her from slitting Sabine's throat. Perhaps by then it would be too late and her family would have already planned their attack against her. Kala flicked her gaze to Ele, who met her wary stare but she couldn't read his face as it was hidden beneath his headscarf.

They continued trekking across the desert. The camel's snorts and plodding of hooves were the only sounds that disrupted the silence. The rhythm of the camel's gait was soothing, a gentle rocking from side to side. Combined with the suffocating heat, it lulled Kala into fatigue. She wondered how Isa was coping behind her. She was yet to feel the slump of his body against her back, so she presumed he was still awake and upright.

Now and then the wind picked up, carrying a fine mist of sand that irritated her eyes and coated her lashes. Kala adjusted her posture every now and then, trying to relieve her discomfort of being in the saddle, but it did little to ease her pain. The muscles in her legs and lower back were stiff and aching. She comforted herself by thinking of what it would be like to return home. A warm bath of rosehip and myrrh oil would restore her body and relax her muscles, not to mention wash the grit of sand from her skin. An attendant could massage her joints and she could rest in her bed for as long as she wished.

A sudden jolt from behind caused Kala to halt the camel and glance around. Her eyes widened in horror when she saw that Isa had fallen to the ground. But it wasn't exhaustion that caused him to fall. A double-tipped spear was embedded in his shoulder blade.

"Ambush!" Ele cried.

Fucking Sabine! Adrenaline flooded her body as Kala turned to see half a dozen funnels of sand rising from the dunes in front of them.

Naiab.

Except the sand was black.

The plumes materialized into the solid forms of men and Kala recognized them immediately. Her former guards. They were armed with spears and blades crafted from sand, their expressions were carved from hate. But that's not what stopped her heart; their eyes were completely dilated onyx orbs.

"Go!" Ele shouted.

He had already leapt from his saddle to the dunes and unsheathed his shamshir. Kala's head spun back to Isa only to watch him dissolve into obsidian sand, the spear in his shoulder dissipating with him. The Naiab launched themselves into attack, and Isa met them in a furious storm of sand, each morphing from solid flesh to bursts of sediment as they battled. Ele took advantage of the split seconds when the warriors became solid forms to slice through their skin and draw blood, but it was like fighting wraiths. They quickly maneuvered to surround him, appearing then disappearing as they forced him to switch to a defensive stance.

Kala turned to Dema to see the roar of wild seas churning in her eyes. The Water Goddess was watching the conflict with cool detachment.

"Command them to stop!" Kala pleaded.

"I have no command over them," the goddess replied. "They are no longer Naiab. The black sand has corrupted their souls completely. They only know the dark urges; violence, power, lust, and greed."

Just then, a hand clasped Kala's ankle and yanked her violently to the ground. She landed hard in the sand, the air escaping her chest in a fierce gush, but she instinctively raised a hand above her head to defend herself. The sun reflected off the edge of a blade, blinding her as it was raised above her. Then something crashed on top of her, winding her anew and crushing her bones. She could feel warm wetness seeping into her clothes.

Blood.

A Naiab warrior lay collapsed on top of her, decapitated by a scythe blade buried in the sand not far from where his head sat. Kala resisted the urge to vomit. The metallic smell of blood filled her nostrils and she didn't even want to think about what else was soaking into her. It took considerable strength to shove him off her but she did it, drawing precious air into her lungs as she watched Sabine defend their supplies from two assailants.

This was no revenge attack, Kala realized. They were looting.

"Fucking pirates!" Sabine swore as she wielded her scythe blade with deadly accuracy.

Kala jumped to her feet, retrieved the bloody scythe blade from the sand and threw it back to Sabine, who caught it mid-attack. Ignoring her hidden daggers, Kala retrieved the bifurcated blade strapped to her camel's saddle and split it in two. She flanked Sabine as the assailants swung their double-edged spears towards them.

The fight was dirty, frenzied, and pointless. Every time she parried, her blades met air and she was thrown slightly off balance. When the warriors materialized again, she barely recovered in time to block the next blow. It was like trying to fight mist. Each spray of sand sliced her skin with a thousand tiny cuts. It was only a matter of time before a strike became fatal.

Kala was vaguely aware that Dema remained perched on a camel, watching the chaos unfold in front of her. Thankfully, her camel only carried minimal supplies so it was not a primary target for looting. Though she didn't know for sure, Kala would bet anything that the goddess had abandoned her human vessel to whatever her fate may be. The Water Goddess could have drowned the warriors in their own blood but instead she chose not to interfere.

Kala had no time to try to puzzle out her inaction. In her peripheral vision, Kala studied the fray, trying to discern where Isa was. Each brief second that he morphed into solid flesh and bone, he called out to his Naiab brothers, urging them to stop, but his words were snatched up by the wind. Ele was holding his ground but his tunic was sliced in several places and his wounds were bleeding.

Isa suddenly solidified and his body collapsed to the ground.

"Isa!" Kala yelled desperately, even as she deflected another strike.

One of the warriors landed a deafening blow across Sabine's face, sending her sprawling. Kala pivoted to defend her but in doing so she left the saddlebags exposed. Two of the Naiab snatched the supplies and fell back, but the rest of the warriors showed no signs of retreating.

Their motive was looting, but it was clear they had no intention of leaving anyone alive.

Kala's gaze cut back to Isa, her heart hammering wildly in her chest. He couldn't be dead. She refused to believe it. But without Isa stemming the tide of the sand wielders, Ele would be slaughtered in seconds.

"Ele!" Kala screamed.

He was surrounded, forced down on one knee with both hands holding his shamshir over his head to block half a dozen spears from penetrating his skull. The second's distraction meant Kala didn't see the Naiab warrior until he was on her, landing splitting blows to her body, overpowering her with unimaginable strength, and knocking the blades from her hands. She scrambled to fight back and managed to punch him in the face but he barely flinched. It was like hitting a mudbrick wall.

Pain erupted through her hand, though that was quickly eclipsed by the agony of him seizing her throat in both of his meaty palms. She clawed at his tattooed wrists and kicked with her feet but his grip was like a vice. He was too strong. Her vision was blurring at the edges and her lungs were screaming for air. But then he let go and sank to the dune with a sudden thud. They all did.

Kala's hands flew to her bruised, tender throat, and she coughed as she stumbled forward, looking around in desperate hope. Ele was alive. He was still bent down on one knee but he had lowered his shamshir. He was surrounded by bodies. A dozen Naiab warriors lay dead in the sand.

Sabine staggered to her feet and her jaw loosened in disbelief at the sight. Kala rushed over to Ele, her knees hitting the ground in front of him while her eyes scanned his body for fatal wounds.

"I'm fine," he panted. His voice sounded strangely calm.

He refused to look at her, even as she cupped his face between his hands. He didn't want to see the carnage that surrounded him, she realized. Because he had been the cause of it. He had ended the warriors' lives as easily as a thought. He had done it to protect them but the fact remained, he had just annihilated a dozen people.

"Ele, you had no choice," Kala tried to soothe him. "Look at me."

Reluctantly he raised his head to meet her gaze and in that moment he looked like the boy she met in the alleyway all those years ago. Wide eyed, street smart, but with a heart as soft as her own.

"You had no choice."

"What did you do?" Sabine accused as she drew closer to the slaughter.

Kala gritted her teeth and tossed over her shoulder, "He saved your life."

"But how?"

Movement stirred out of the corner of her eye, and Kala felt a wave of relief when she realized it was Isa. He was slowly crawling along the sand, dragging himself closer to his fallen brothers. When he reached them, he rolled them over one by one and studied their faces. A look of agonizing recognition contorted his features each time. Kala couldn't tear her gaze away from his raw anguish. She felt it too. These men had protected her for years. Chosen to stay with her, to follow Isa instead of returning to their home and their families. She owed them better than this.

Their dark tattoos remained but the inky liquid no longer swirled beneath their skin. Kala drew in a sharp breath as she stared into the black pits of their eyes.

"It's only a matter of time before the same will happen to you." Her aged voice gave away that the Water Goddess had reinhabited her vessel now that the danger had passed.

Isa looked up at the goddess with a hateful sneer. "If you'd let them come home—"

"It was too late. The black sand had already taken hold of them."

"They lived out here in the desert, robbing traders to survive," Kala concluded, drawing the pieces of the puzzle together. "Isa, it was almost like they didn't recognize us."

"They were rabid," the goddess replied. "In that state, they will kill anyone."

Kala recalled Isa had been the same when he massacred her soldiers. He looked almost inhuman, unreachable, like he didn't have control over himself. He simply annihilated everyone in front of him. Isa seemed to be thinking the same thing because his body slumped forward in the sand, utterly despondent, as he wiped a hand over his anguished face.

"Am I missing something?" Sabine interrupted. "Does no one else care that they all dropped dead for no reason?"

Kala locked eyes with Ele, silently pleading with him not to say anything. But his expression told her it was pointless to hide the truth. There was no other explanation for it and Sabine would never let it go.

"I killed them," Ele admitted.

Kala blinked slowly in dread. Now Sabine had even more reasons to betray them.

"You are god-touched," Isa said plainly.

Isa had been there the day that King Heroux killed Ele. He had witnessed Henri strike a bargain with the Goddess of Endings and Beginnings to save Ele's life.

Ele pushed himself up to stand and sheathed his shamshir. "Yes. I can end lives if I wish."

Sabine's features shifted to shock. "The rumors are true, then. You are gifted from the God of War and Valor."

Ele winced. "Not quite."

"If the Goddess of Endings and Beginnings finds out about your power, she will kill you," the Water Goddess warned.

"I'm well aware."

But now the likelihood of that happening had increased exponentially. A secret only remained a secret if it was held by one person, maybe two at best. Now everyone knew. The information was priceless. It could be used to further anyone's personal agenda. The Water Goddess's. Sabine's. It only reinforced Kala's plans. The moment they found the witch, Sabine had to die.

Kala stood up, the weight of the butchery surrounding them falling heavy on her shoulders. "I'm so sorry, Isa."

Isa closed each of the warriors' eyes, silently saying goodbye to them. When he was done, he surveyed the scene.

"We will not leave their bodies to rot in the sun. We will bury them here in the Idris Desert, the land that birthed them."

Kala nodded solemnly. They had no shovels so would have to dig the graves by hand. It seemed fitting.

ISA

The night sky hung in quiet stillness as Isa stood on a high dune looking out over his brothers' graves. It had taken hours to dig them by hand, one by one. Granules of sand were wedged deep beneath his fingernails, and every limb in his body strained beneath the weight of their deaths. Imprinted behind his eyelids was the memory of their blank faces staring up into nothingness, their lungs no longer drawing breath, their hearts shockingly still.

He was blind to everything else.

The others had set up camp a short distance behind him but he remained here. With his brothers. Lost in thought. Buried in guilt. His men had been loyal, and yet they were cast out of their home, rejected by their goddess, and condemned to wander the desert like pirates. They were once Naiab warriors, but instead of dying with honor, they had died cursed. He couldn't imagine what the past few years must have been like for them. To have no home. To rob and kill every day to survive. Did they even recognize themselves, or each other, for who they once were?

He wished they'd returned to him after the Water Goddess rejected them but he understood why they hadn't. They couldn't bear one more day of the curse corrupting their soul, and yet the Black Sands had never loosened their grip on them. It didn't make any sense. When his men left the kingdom, their eyes had been clear. Not a speck of black sand tainted their irises. Yet somehow, despite leaving, the black sand had continued to pollute their bodies until it seized control of their minds.

So why did he still have mastery of his?

Compared to his men, he had lived several more years in the Kingdom of the Black Sands, exposed to the poison every day. He should have lost his mind ages ago. Vicious memories of all the people he'd killed flashed in his mind, reminding him that he was not so sane. Traitors. Priests. Kala's soldiers. Isa's jaw tightened as the bodies piled up in his head.

It was true, he had lost command of himself at times and found alternative ways to feed the dark urges, but he hadn't lost himself completely. Even now, he could feel the black sand turning his stomach, fueling his emotions, but he reigned them in. Surely the curse was strong enough to overwhelm his resistance. So why wasn't he lying dead in a grave beside his brothers?

A shift in the sands told him someone was approaching. Instinct told him who it was. It reminded him of a night ten years ago when the desert had borne witness to a different atrocity. Both tragedies resulted from his choices. He always seemed to destroy the ones he loved the most.

"What have you done?" Her voice was dangerously soft as she came to stand beside him.

Isa's stare remained unbroken on the vast stretch of desert before them.

"You are not innocent in this," he growled in return.

"I have nothing to atone for. I warned you not to return to the Black Sands. You didn't listen. I wanted the Naiab to return home. Instead, they chose to follow you. Their deaths are on your conscience, not mine."

He had no strength left to argue with her, and in a way, the goddess was right. No matter her sins, his were far greater. They were his men. He had led them to their deaths. The truth was cold and sharp as it carved itself across his heart.

"I thought the black sand would drain from their systems the moment they left the kingdom," Isa murmured.

The goddess sighed as though she found his naiveté tiring. "The curse has weakened over time. When it was first cast, the black sand would have been fatal to any Naiab who stepped foot in the kingdom. Now it poisons slowly. Once it takes root, though, it is only a matter of time. There is no escape from its madness."

"Then why aren't I rabid?"

"You should be. I suspect someone has been interfering."

Isa's gaze cut to her, his expression a contortion of confusion and precarious hope. "Tahlia?"

The goddess met his gaze in silent confirmation but Isa shook his head, adamant.

"She has no reason to try to save me."

"I never said she was trying to save you. You, better than most, understand the nature of the gods. We are not benevolent. We do things because it suits our agenda. Perhaps she has another end in mind for you."

Isa considered her words. Tahlia had said that she knew of his death. That he would sacrifice everything.

So be it.

He would surrender his life to her without question. She could do with it as she pleased. His every breath had always been hers to command.

"She told me that she refuses to embrace her divinity."

The goddess's brows raised slightly in surprise. "She has spoken to you?"

Isa ignored her question. He didn't understand what was happening between him and Tahlia, he could hardly be expected to explain it to someone else.

"She resisted divinity as a mortal, she continues her rebellion as a goddess. She's stubborn like that." The goddess's lips twitched to a fond smile before quickly fading to a tight, uneasy line.

There was something she was not saying.

"Will she face retribution for it?" Isa probed carefully. "For not embracing her divine power?"

The goddess lifted her chin as if steeling herself against what was to come. She stared out over the desert realm, her eyes softening like it might be the last time she would see it. "We will all face judgment for our choices one day. Even the gods answer to a higher power."

CHAPTER TWENTY

ELE

As they drew closer to the Kingdom of the Salt Plains the landscape around them changed. Golden rolling dunes flattened out into a vast expanse of white, hardened earth. The ground became cracked and uneven, forming an endless geometric pattern that stretched to the horizon. The cracks were coated in a crust of salt which shimmered like diamonds under the sun. When the hot wind swept over the earth, clouds of salt swirled in the air. It coated everything from Ele's lips to his eyelashes. He couldn't get rid of the taste on his tongue.

Relief washed over him when they finally spotted soldiers up ahead, marking the border crossing. He threw a glance over his shoulder at Kala, who turned in the saddle to speak to Isa behind her. Isa pulled his head scarf tighter and lowered his gaze at her command. The price of wielding his sand magic to defend them against the Naiab was evident in the dark rings that now almost eclipsed his irises. It was impossible to know what the soldiers would do if they saw his eyes but Ele would rather not find out.

As their caravan approached, a soldier held up a hand to halt them while the other soldiers remained in their positions, holding a line of defense that stretched on for miles.

"Papers," the soldier demanded in a flat tone that indicated he had already been on border patrol for several hours.

"I don't have papers. I am Captain of the Guard for King Henri," Ele explained, hopeful that his position would carry some authority.

As Captain of the Guard, Henri frequently sent him across Merovia to his various kingdoms to oversee issues of governance or carry out missions. But the Kingdom of the Salt Plains was ruled by Malik. It was the one kingdom Ele had never traveled to. The letter Ele possessed from Henri gave him permission to enter and leave his kingdoms, but it did not extend to Malik's.

"Papers," the soldier insisted.

"I told you I don't have any. If you let us through, I can send a pigeon to King Malik and he'll confirm I am who I say I am."

The soldier spat on the ground in annoyance and waved his hand in dismissal, effectively shooing them back to wherever they'd come from. Ele glanced over at Dema and Kala who stared back at him blankly, unsure what to do next. The soldiers would not care about the Shahri of the Naiab, she held no authority over them, and Kala's identity had to be protected at all costs. Not that the soldier would believe that Kala was the Queen of the Black Sands. After several days traveling across the Idris Desert, they all looked haggard rather than regal. But they couldn't turn back now. They didn't have enough supplies to last the journey to either neighboring kingdom.

Ele set his jaw in determination and turned back to the soldier. "A pigeon is all I need."

"Leave or I will arrest you for treason."

The soldiers unsheathed their blades in perfect unison, the threat clear with the exposure of polished steel.

"Money," Sabine interjected. "We will pay you if you let us pass. My sister is very wealthy."

Kala glared at her and Ele flinched. They had little money between them, certainly not enough to tempt this disgruntled soldier or buy the silence of his comrades.

The soldier narrowed his eyes at her. "Bribing a soldier is treason."

Sabine shrugged. "Only if you get caught."

"Captain!"

Ele lifted his gaze at the familiar voice and his body immediately relaxed at the sight of the woman strolling towards them. "Inaya."

Malik had appointed Inaya regent of the Kingdom of the Salt Plains shortly after the war so that he could stay with Henri. As king, Malik occasionally visited his kingdom, but it was out of political obligation rather than a desire to rule over his dominion. He never stayed very long. Inaya was his most trusted friend and advisor. She had previously served Henri as Captain of the Guard before the war altered the balance of power amongst kings and kingdoms.

Inaya joined the defensive line of soldiers but her smile was warm and welcoming. "What brings you to the Salt Plains?"

"We're looking for someone." Ele hoped Inaya wouldn't take offense to the vague response or insist on more detail. The less people who knew about them and their business, the better.

Inaya's gaze moved past Ele to assess his companions one by one. It was clear he was not traveling with Henri's soldiers, which was suspicious.

"On King Henri's orders?" she probed.

"No. On the orders of the Queen of the Black Sands."

A flicker of recognition crossed her features and Ele knew she was looking at Kala.

"Then welcome to the Salt Plains." Inaya swept her arm wide as she stepped aside, gesturing for them to cross the border.

The soldiers shifted with unease but returned their shamshirs to their sheaths.

"They have no papers," the soldier hissed at Inaya.

"I will personally vouch for them to King Malik and the Captain will send a pigeon to confirm the king's permission. You will have your papers by tomorrow." Inaya turned her attention back to Ele. "I will escort you to the city."

"Thank you." Ele led their caravan past the line of soldiers, and they waited a moment for Inaya to mount a camel so she could join them.

Once they had traveled out of earshot, Inaya flicked her gaze over her shoulder to Kala. "Forgive me for not greeting you properly, Kafei."

"It's all right. I'm surprised you recognize me."

"The last time I saw you, you were a child," Inaya agreed.

"Inaya, this is Dema, Shahri from the Citadel. And this is Sabine from the Thaka. And Isa from the Black Sands, formerly from the Citadel," Ele said and Inaya nodded in greeting at each of them. "This is Inaya, regent of the Salt Plains."

"What is the regent doing inspecting a border patrol?" Sabine asked skeptically.

Ele cast Sabine a reproachful look but he had been wondering the same thing. It was a rare coincidence, which meant it was not a coincidence at all.

"Your king is worried about you," Inaya directed to Ele. "You were meant to return home days ago. He sent word to each of his kingdoms but no one has seen you for some time. Malik sent word to me to keep an eye out for you. You need to send a pigeon to King Henri straight away. I get the feeling he's one frayed nerve away from sending out his entire army to search for you."

Ele's cheeks flushed with a hue of guilt and embarrassment. He should have sent Henri word before he left the Kingdom of the Black Sands but there was no time.

"The city is not far. Who is it you are looking for?"

"That's none of your business," Sabine snapped.

"Sabine!" Ele chided before turning back to Inaya. "Apologies. The matter is sensitive."

"I understand. You can stay in the palace while you're here. Rest tonight and then you can start your search tomorrow. Let me know if I can assist in any way."

"Another palace?" Sabine exclaimed. "At this rate, I'm going to see the inside of every palace in Merovia. Though the last palace I stayed at was a bit too tawdry for my liking."

"That's because you were being held in a cell," Kala returned drily.

"Excuses, excuses."

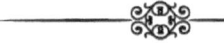

KALA

The moment they arrived at the palace grounds, Inaya sent the others ahead while she escorted Ele and Kala to the dovecote. Kala had always marveled at the mudbrick cylindrical structures. Hundreds of small openings dotted the exterior in what looked to be an artistic pattern, but it had a far more practical purpose of allowing the pigeons easy access to their home. Inside, the walls were lined with holes, each one a nesting place for a pigeon pair. Within its round walls, it was cool and comfortable, perfect for breeding and roosting.

After scribbling their messages, the caretaker of the dovecote assisted Ele and Kala to attach the parchments to the legs of two hearty-looking pigeons. Kala felt instantly lighter as she watched them take flight. Zaynab would be relieved to hear from her, as would Samir and Majid. She wondered how Zaynab was faring under the weight of the kingdom. Surely if anything disastrous had happened it would have reached Inaya's ears, but Inaya swore that she hadn't heard anything apart from the fact that the Queen of the Black Sands was mysteriously absent from her kingdom. Kala hoped Zaynab would send an immediate reply and put her mind at ease.

Ele was noticeably quiet as Inaya guided them back to the palace and showed them to the guest quarters.

"This is your room, Kafei, and this is yours, Captain." Inaya indicated to two rooms separated by a broad hallway. "The others have been given rooms nearby."

"Thank you for coming to our aid today." Ele forced a tired smile. "I'm not sure what we would have done if you hadn't."

Inaya smirked. "Knowing you, you wouldn't have left quietly. Really, I was coming to the aid of my soldiers. I fear they would be no match for a Naiab warrior and Captain of the Guard."

The sight of her slaughtered soldiers combined with the litter of dead Naiab warriors flashed in Kala's mind, making her wince. Inaya had no idea just how deadly Isa and Ele were.

"Can I request that a soldier be placed outside Kala's door?" Ele asked.

"Of course."

Kala stood there stunned as Ele nodded in thanks before disappearing inside his chamber. He hadn't even said a word to her, and apparently, he no longer cared to guard her. Inaya's eyes slid to her in quiet question before she bowed her head to acknowledge it was none of her business.

"If there is anything else you need, please let me know." Inaya walked backwards a few steps before bowing, turning and leaving.

Kala entered her chamber, but she barely noticed the rich furnishings, luxuriously soft bed, or stunning view from her wraparound balcony. Her mind replayed the interaction over and over again. Ele's casual tone. His dismissive manner. Even as Kala marinated in a bath that had been prepared with rose petals and chamomile, she couldn't stop analyzing it.

They hadn't really spoken to each other since he'd slaughtered the Naiab warriors. That night, Ele had laid his bedroll outside her tent, both of them instinctively knowing that Isa would be spending the night in silent vigil over his men rather than guarding her. She had thought about it then. Calling out to Ele, or even slipping outside her tent to check on him, but she hadn't. His quiet, distant demeanor as they dug each grave by hand made it clear to her that he wished to be left alone.

So she had.

But perhaps now he would be ready to talk about it. Kala knew it wasn't the first time Ele had taken a life. He would have killed countless men on the orders of his king or in defense of his own life, but this was different. The Naiab had been cursed. They weren't in control of their minds or bodies when they attacked, the need to survive and spill blood overriding all other senses. Their deaths had been like ending the misery of a creature too far gone, a dying beast too broken to save. Merciful but brutal all the same.

Kala wondered if guilt was weighing on him. She also wondered if it was the first time Ele had used his magic. Perhaps he had used it once before against a particularly formidable enemy, but he certainly wouldn't have used it against a dozen men. Kala pondered what it felt like to wield such a dangerous and terrible power. Maybe it felt euphoric, like an adrenaline rush. Or perhaps it drained him until he felt numb and empty. He certainly seemed strangely detached.

She needed to see him, she decided. With resolute determination, Kala stood up from the bath and dried herself before putting on a fresh kaftan. It was amazing to feel clean again, all traces of sand and salt washed from her body. She arranged her hair into a single braid down her back and stepped out into the hallway.

The two guards standing on either side of her door startled her. With annoyance, she recalled Ele asking Inaya to post them there. Any privacy she thought she had was now eliminated. They kept their eyes trained forward and showed no signs of acknowledging her as Kala gingerly crossed the hallway to Ele's chamber.

Standing outside his door, she hesitated. When they were kids, they had always turned to each other for comfort. They instinctively sensed when something was wrong and would always know how to make each other feel better. But they didn't know each other like that anymore. Kala wasn't sure what Ele was feeling, and she didn't know what he needed to feel better. She didn't even know if he would want her there. But as his friend, she had to try.

Kala knocked lightly and bounced on the heels of her feet as she waited impatiently. She glanced back at the guards but they were pretending to be blind and deaf. A minute passed. Surely, Ele wouldn't have gone to sleep already. The sun had only just gone down. Even if he had gone to sleep, he was a light sleeper. The sound of her knock should have woken him.

Kala knocked again, louder this time. Perhaps he didn't want to see her after all. Maybe this was a mistake. She felt her resolve slipping through her fingers. The door suddenly opened to reveal Ele standing there in a clean kurta, his curly hair damp from a bath. He looked surprised to see her. His gaze quickly darted to the soldiers stationed outside her door before returning to her in a puzzled expression.

"What's wrong?"

Suddenly, Kala was questioning everything she thought she'd observed. "Nothing. I just wanted to check if you were all right."

"I'm fine." He shifted his weight, bracing an arm against the doorframe. The stance made it clear he wasn't going to invite her inside. "Why wouldn't I be?"

"What happened with the Naiab was—"

"Necessary. Like you said, I had no choice."

"Yes, but ... those decisions are never easy."

"It was very easy," he replied matter-of-factly.

Kala's lips parted in confusion until her thoughts landed on the truth. He wasn't riddled with guilt. He seemed calm and detached because he was genuinely unaffected. It didn't matter to him that the Naiab were cursed and not in full control of themselves. They were the enemy and he had defeated them.

"I was seconds away from doing the same to Isa that day he slaughtered your soldiers. If Tahlia hadn't interfered when she did, Isa would be dead."

Kala sucked in a sharp breath at the thought.

Ele simply stared at her, his expression remorseless. "I will do everything in my power to help you break the curse. But you need to know that if we can't cure Isa, the moment he turns rabid like his men, I will kill him."

Her mouth fell open in abject horror. "It won't come to that," she stammered.

"His eyes are almost completely black," Ele pointed out.

"I know."

She had noticed them that morning. Kala suspected that using his sand magic against his brothers had made the poison in Isa's system spread further. They were running out of time. No one had dared to comment on his eyes, not even Sabine, but Isa probably knew regardless. He could likely sense it. The black sand's grip on him tightening, consuming him piece by piece.

Ele's gaze drifted to her neck, where bruises blossomed in shades of yellow and violet, like wilted petals. The Naiab warrior had almost strangled her to death. She had been powerless to stop him.

Ele set his jaw firmly. "I won't let him hurt you or anyone else."

"He would never hurt me," Kala insisted.

"You still think that after what we saw yesterday?"

Irritation crawled beneath her skin. "Is that why you're suddenly ignoring me? Because you think you're going to have to kill Isa like you did the others?"

"You care for him. He's become like your family. If I killed him, could you ever forgive me?"

No.

She couldn't.

He must have seen the truth in her face, heard it in her silence, because his fingers tightened on the doorframe. "That's what I thought. It's better this way."

"For who?" Kala accused.

"For both of us."

A door creaked open down the hall and Sabine stepped out, only to freeze at the sight of them. Kala narrowed her eyes at her in suspicion.

Ele cleared his throat. "Good night, Kafei."

He closed the door and Kala stared at it for a moment, confusion and rage simmering inside her. How dare he. It was like he had already given up on Isa despite everything they had been through to get here. Whether Isa lived or died was not his decision. Nor would she let Ele harm him.

"Trouble in paradise?" Sabine chimed.

Kala clenched her fingers into fists at her side but Sabine simply shrugged as she approached.

"Men. Once they've had you, they become bored of you. The Captain is no exception. In fact, he has a reputation for it. So many women have been lured into his bed and yet none of them have held his interest for longer than a night."

"He hasn't had me," Kala retorted.

"Please, sister. The tent fabric isn't *that* thick."

"Mind your own business."

"Oh I do, don't you worry."

They exchanged a heated stare, neither of them willing to blink.

"Where are you going? Trying to sneak outside the palace?" Kala challenged.

"I have a witch to find, remember? I need to speak to my contacts in the Salt Plains. It could take a day or two."

The words rolled off her tongue easily enough and her expression held no signs of deception, but Sabine was an expert liar. Kala had no way of knowing whether she was telling the truth or not. She could be meeting anyone. Plotting anything.

Sabine cocked her head as if she could read Kala's thoughts. "Don't even think about following me. If my contacts so much as sniff another person besides me, they won't speak to me, and your sandman will be dust."

Kala gritted her teeth and speared Sabine with a warning glare. A smug smile split Sabine's lips, and there was a slight swagger in her step as she strolled past Kala to disappear around the corner. There was nothing Kala could do except return to her chamber and wait. Whatever Sabine was up to, she would find out soon enough.

ISA

Isa prowled the length of the room for what felt like the hundredth time that day, his irritation growing with every step. In the early morning, Kala had informed him that it would take a day or two before Sabine located the witch. Until then, he would need to stay confined to his chamber because they couldn't risk anyone seeing his onyx eyes. If they did, rumors would spread like wildfire, not only whipping up fear about the Naiab warrior with dark eyes, but revealing Kala's identity in the process. It was well known that the Queen of the Black Sands was guarded by a Naiab warrior. It wouldn't take long for people to figure it out.

Imprisoned in this cursed chamber, a full day hadn't even passed, and already Isa felt like hurling himself from the balcony just to escape the walls that seemed to be pressing in on him. It wasn't normal. He knew the obsidian sand writhing beneath his skin was heightening his emotions. Ever since he'd shifted to defend them against the Naiab attack, the black sand had seized him more fiercely than ever before. It screamed at him to let go. To submit. It craved power like a drowning tide, violence like a lover's teeth, and pleasure like a fine wine. His body thrummed, invigorated but caged. It begged for release, but there was no one to fuck or fight, and repression was clawing him open from the inside out.

Isa roared as he clutched his head in both hands. His thoughts raged. He kicked a cushion across the room but its soft thud as it hit the wall brought no satisfaction. There were too many fucking cushions. Arranged in small clusters throughout the spacious room, they were clearly meant to encourage lounging or entertaining, neither of which he was inclined to do. Patterned rugs adorned the floor, and soft light filtered in through the latticed arched windows. It was a luxurious prison. He wanted to tear it apart until there was nothing left but feathers and rubble.

CHAPTER TWENTY

Steepling his fingers behind his head, Isa kept pacing. He had no idea when this torture would end. Hours. Days. Even if Sabine found the witch, there was no guarantee he would be cured. Isa was sure he would descend into madness before then. He tilted his head back to stare up at the painted ceiling. The geometric patterns in bright colors did nothing to calm his mood. They all seemed to trace back to the middle focal point, much like every thought racing through his head circled back to a singular truth that had been haunting him since the Naiab attack; he would rather die than turn rabid.

Isa cast his gaze out to the balcony. It was framed by delicate curtains flittering in the warm breeze. At this height, if he threw himself over the balustrade, the fall alone would kill him before he hit the stony ground. It would be a painless way to die. But then it did seem a touch dramatic. He could slice open his own throat. Puncture his own heart. It would be neater.

Just breathe. Tahlia's voice ricocheted in his head like the echo in a canyon.

"Goddess?"

Tahlia hadn't appeared to him for the past few nights, but then again, he hadn't been thinking of her. His every thought had been occupied by the loss of his men. When he closed his eyes, it was their faces he saw.

You need to fight it.

"That's what I'm fucking doing!" He roared and kicked another pillow across the room.

Throwing yourself to the stones is not fighting.

"It may be the only way to stop me from turning into ... them."

He could feel his control slipping through his fingers like sand. He refused to put Kala or anyone else at risk.

It's not.

"Then tell me what to do! Or do it yourself. I know it was you who rendered me unconscious after I slaughtered Kala's soldiers. It was you who forced me to walk away at the Citadel. You said you preferred to forget my existence, that my death meant nothing to you, but all this time you've been interfering. You've been slowing the poison."

I didn't do it for you.

Isa bellowed in rage and agony as he clenched his hands into white knuckled fists. He was so tired of everything. The games gods played. The sickness that plagued him. The depraved urges that corrupted his soul, never satiated. He'd been fighting the black sand for years. Controlling it. Enduring it. He was done. No man could be expected to withstand it for as long as he had. He would die cursed, like his brothers, but at least he would finally be free.

You made a vow to me. Tahlia's voice turned urgent. *You are not qualified to die yet.*

Isa beat his chest in rage. "This is me keeping my vow!"

Coward.

"Hypocrite! You're the one too scared to embrace your divine power."

A resounding knock caused Isa to still as he whipped his attention to the door.

Open it.

CHAPTER TWENTY

Sweat beaded on his brow, trickling into his eyes and sliding down his neck. He was burning up. The black sand was like a furnace, scorching him alive from the inside out. Isa shook his head, unsure if he was delirious or not. If Kala was at his door, he couldn't let her see him like this. He was not in control. He was too volatile.

Open. It. Now.

Isa planted his feet in defiance. If an entire army was at his door, they would need to break it down to get to him.

The lock clicked. Isa's heart stopped.

A young woman calmly stepped inside. She was dressed in the simple attire of the servants, her long brown hair falling loose to her waist. Her eyes were respectfully downcast as she strode towards him but they flicked up, sharp as daggers, just before her hand cracked across his face.

Shock, more than pain, struck him. He slowly turned his head back to the woman, only to see that her eyes were otherworldly, shining like stardust interwoven with fragments of eternity. Isa searched her face, not daring to believe it as his heart spluttered inside his chest.

"That's for sacrificing me to the gods." She punched him in the mouth, splitting his lip as well as her knuckles. "That's for your weakness and cowardice."

"Stop, goddess, you'll break your hand!"

She gripped his shoulders and slammed her knee up into his balls. Pain exploded, bringing him crashing to his knees before her.

"And that's because I hate you for it."

Isa tried to stifle his groan but it escaped through gritted teeth, a broken, pathetic rasp. For a moment, he was grateful. He could no longer feel the black sand because his senses were overwhelmed by the agony in his balls.

"You need to fight someone? Fight me." She sent a vicious kick to his ribs, knocking him onto his back.

Isa spat blood from his split lip, staining the plush rug beneath him. "If I fight you, I'll kill you."

Tahlia stood over him, looking down at him with disdain. "Mortals cannot kill gods."

"Your vessel then. You would sacrifice an innocent?"

"She was willing to be inhabited by a goddess. And she is no innocent. That's why I chose her. She has committed many crimes, and her pretty face has allowed her to escape justice. The curse is demanding satisfaction. So feed it."

Isa couldn't believe what he was hearing. He forced his body to move until he was kneeling before her once more. "You want me to kill her?"

Tahlia's laugh was bitter. "Don't act so sanctimonious. You have killed before to keep the dark urges at bay. If it eases your conscience, this vessel can't feel anything while I inhabit her, and she is willing to be sacrificed. So do it."

Isa considered it for a moment before standing up, bringing them face to face. Tahlia's expression was a bold provocation, daring him to act.

"I can't hurt you."

If Tahlia could feel everything through inhabiting a mortal vessel, he would never allow himself to cause her pain.

"Fine. Then don't hurt me. Fuck me."

Time stopped. Even the wind held its breath.

"What?"

"The curse demands power in its veins, blood on its skin, and pleasure in its mouth."

She couldn't be serious. But her face was deadly serious.

"No." The word came out as a choked reply.

"No?"

"You don't want me to fuck you. You hate me."

"I do hate you." Her eyes never left his face as she stepped up to him, bringing them toe to toe, face to face. "I have never hated anyone more in my entire existence."

She pressed the body of her vessel against him. Isa stiffened, his arousal immediately flaring and his cock broadening despite the lingering pain of Tahlia's assault. His reaction was involuntary but only natural considering he hadn't allowed himself to be with a woman for over a decade. It was part penance, part apathy. No woman could hope to compare to his goddess. He would have her or no one at all. The body pressing against him was soft and slender, whereas Tahlia's had been strong and curvaceous. Her face was pretty enough, but Tahlia's beauty had commanded the attention of kings.

Isa pressed his eyes closed as he tried to regain control of his traitorous body. "Tahlia," he breathed her name like a plea. "It's not you."

She rose on her toes, capturing his mouth with hers and savagely bit his lip where it had split. He jerked back slightly, but the sight of his blood on her tongue did something feral to him. His body turned hard, trembling with desperate need as his darkest cravings slipped their leash.

"I can taste you." Her husky voice turned his skin to gooseflesh. "I can feel you. And as your goddess, I command you to fuck me."

Isa wasn't sure what happened next because his hand gripped her throat as he forced her back until she tripped onto the bed. He pinned her there beneath him, his prey to devour. His other hand slid between her kaftan, pushing up her thigh until the material was bunched at her waist and her sex was laid gloriously bare. Isa yanked his pants down, freeing his cock and plunged it into her sweet center. Tahlia arched her back, tilting her head to the ceiling as she released a moan of pure ecstasy. He slammed into her over and over again, wild and savage. He couldn't stop. He was greedy for her. He wanted his length coated in her, the imprint of his teeth on her breast, and the mark of his hands on her skin.

He wanted to ruin her.

Tahlia shoved him in the chest hard, jolting him from his lust-drenched haze, and he immediately withdrew. She edged up the bed away from his reach. His cock dripped onto the sheets as he watched her in confusion. Kneeling in the center of the bed, she gripped the hem of her kaftan and pulled it up over her body in one swift movement, tossing it onto the floor. Isa took in the sight of her small breasts bouncing as she lowered herself back against the mountain of cushions.

Fucking cushions.

Isa held himself still as Tahlia lounged back provocatively and then ever so slowly opened her legs in invitation. Wicked woman. Her entrance was pink and wet with a mixture of her arousal and his pre-cum. He needed to brand it with his cock. To fill her up and dominate her until she was panting beneath him, begging him for more.

Isa lunged, caging her beneath his frame as he drove himself inside her. Tahlia wrapped her legs around him, drawing him deeper in silent challenge, and he growled as he hit her inner wall over and over again. She sucked a sharp intake of breath between her teeth.

"Goddess." He couldn't control himself. Couldn't stop.

"I can take it. I want to take it."

Fuck. She knew exactly what to say to make him unleash himself. If she wanted to be used, he would use her. He would hate himself for it later, if it was even possible to hate himself more than he already did.

Isa gripped her thighs as he slammed into her at an unforgiving pace. His tongue lashed at her neck as his teeth scraped against the hollow of her throat. In his mind, he was tasting Tahlia's skin. Warm like honey. He could see her so clearly in his memories. Her scent still haunted him; jasmine, fig blossoms, and rose petals. Intoxicating and maddening. He lost himself inside her. In the fantasy that he longed for with every fiber of his being.

Her fingers slipped through his hair and then gripped tightly. A reminder that whilst he was conquering her body, she was the one allowing him to do so. Isa's grin was vicious as they watched each other. There was pleasure in pain. Salvation in sin.

"Come for me, goddess."

Tahlia's sharp, breathy moans told him she was close. His thighs moved between her legs, driving her to combustion and this time when the flames ignited, they burned together.

CHAPTER TWENTY-ONE

KALA

Kala wandered the palace grounds aimlessly, eager to distract her thoughts but failing miserably. High sandstone walls surrounded her, enclosing courtyards of hearty shrubs and pomegranate trees. Fountains featured in shaded alcoves and reflection pools offered the opportunity to sit and admire the tranquility of the gardens. The sound of trickling water should have been soothing but it wasn't. Kala barely noticed it as her mind replayed the interaction with Ele last night over and over until she wanted to scream.

Her scream would certainly echo in the dome pavilion she'd just entered. Its roof was tiled, catching the sunlight and brandishing a marvelous mosaic of colors across the polished floor. The cheerful sight did nothing to brighten her mood. Kala was about to keep walking when she startled at the sight of Dema sitting on the stone steps on the other side of the pavilion.

The Shahri was staring out across the courtyard, no shoes on her feet, her chin resting casually on her folded hands. Kala considered turning around and slipping away silently but something made her speak.

"I don't suppose you've seen a garden like this before."

Dema glanced over her shoulder, clearly surprised to have company.

"I'm sorry, I didn't mean to disturb you," Kala offered.

"You haven't." Dema dropped her hands to her lap. "I was just thinking."

"I'm trying not to think," Kala admitted. "It's not going well."

Dema gestured to the step beside her. "Would you like to join me? We can think about not thinking together."

Kala grinned as she gingerly sat down beside her. Despite spending several days traveling across the Idris Desert together, Kala had to admit she didn't know much about the Shahri of the Naiab. She wasn't sure they would have anything in common to talk about. It was likely going to be an awkward, forced conversation.

"I'm surprised Isa is not with you," Dema remarked.

"He can't risk anyone seeing his eyes. I told him to stay inside his chamber until we learn the location of the witch."

Dema gave a curt nod of understanding. "And where is Ele?"

"I don't know. I haven't seen him." Kala tried to sound nonchalant but there was a bitter edge to her words.

He was avoiding her. She had tried knocking on his door that morning but if he was inside, he hadn't answered.

"Have you spoken to the Water Goddess?" Kala pried.

Dema shook her head pensively. "A lot has happened over the past few days. Perhaps we're all taking time to come to terms with things in our own way."

Kala made a non-committal sound. Ele wasn't coming to terms with anything. He'd already decided that Isa's life was forfeit. She knew that as Captain of the Guard, he was used to assessing situations quickly and taking action, but this was not some mission Henri had assigned him to carry out. It wasn't his responsibility or his decision.

"You must be missing home." Kala attempted to change the topic.

"I am." Dema sighed. "I have never left the Citadel before. Everything here is so strange. Even the air is different."

Kala couldn't begin to imagine what it was like for her, having lived every day of her life within the walls of a cavern, to now walk freely out in the open. It was her first time seeing a city. Ordinary dwellings would look foreign to her. She would have never seen so many people before.

"May I ask, how long have you been the Shahri?"

Dema only looked to be a few years older than her. It made Kala wonder why the Water Goddess had chosen someone so young.

"Not as long as you have been Queen of the Black Sands," Dema replied with a knowing smile.

Kala tilted her chin, conceding the point. Kala was used to being underestimated, not only because she was a woman but because she was young. As a child queen, some considered her to be easy prey, but she had learned fast. Perhaps Dema had experienced the same misgivings from her own people and had learned to adapt.

Dema stretched her legs out in front of her. "You and I were both given the opportunity to do something great with our lives, to be more than ourselves. We didn't ask for it, we wouldn't have chosen it, but it happened. It's a privilege and a burden."

"You didn't know the Water Goddess would choose you to be her new vessel?"

"No. One day I was ordinary, belonging to no one except my parents. The next day I was Shahri, belonging to everyone."

Kala inhaled a deep breath and allowed her shoulders to sag a little. "I understand."

When she first arrived in the Kingdom of the Black Sands it was jarring to think that everything she saw belonged to her. But what really overwhelmed her was the realization that every person was her responsibility to protect. Life wasn't just about her survival anymore. The lives of her people rested on her shoulders as well.

"There is something else you and I share. We are perhaps the only two people living who know what it's like to be inhabited by a goddess," Dema said.

It wasn't entirely true, Zaynab also knew what it felt like, but Kala didn't correct her. In fact, thinking about Zaynab made her thoughts snag on another possibility.

"Do you ever see things when the Water Goddess inhabits you?" Kala asked casually.

Perhaps Dema had also unwittingly stumbled into the Water Goddess's consciousness on occasion. Maybe she knew something about the reckoning.

"I can see and hear everything. I'm there, I'm just not in control. Is it not like that for you?"

"It is, but—" Kala chose her words carefully. "The goddesses see through our eyes. Do you ever see through the Water Goddess's eyes?"

Dema's expression turned thoughtfully blank. "No."

"Perhaps hear her thoughts or see her memories?"

"No."

"Me either," Kala said quickly. She needed to change the topic before Dema read too much into her questions. "By the way, I'm sorry for almost killing you that day. It wasn't personal."

"I understand why you did it. Isa is your family. You would do anything to save him. People have always used love to justify the worst of deeds."

Kala furrowed her brow, unsure if Dema was accepting her apology or rejecting it. She had a point though. Kala was willing to do reprehensible things to save Isa, just like Ele was willing to do unforgivable things to protect her. Who could say who was right and who was wrong? Perhaps they both were. Love was complicated. It could forge both martyrs and murderers. She only wondered which one she would become.

KALA

The bazaar was loud, crowded, and stifling. The heat of the day burned through her sandals as they slapped against the stone streets. Despite having Isa at her back and Ele protecting her from the front, Kala was still being jostled by people. Dema walked ahead of Ele but behind Sabine, who led them through a labyrinth of narrow alleys and endless stalls.

It had taken two days for Sabine to learn the location of the witch. Those two days seemed to stretch on forever as Kala wandered the palace grounds listlessly, anxious for news. Dema had provided her with company, but Kala almost wept when she received a message from Zaynab. It was brief and direct; they were well and her kingdom was fine in her absence. Kala had read the note at least a dozen times, wishing there were more words to devour. She craved to speak to her friend. She missed her so much it physically hurt.

When they finally left to meet the witch, Kala hadn't known what to expect but it certainly wasn't this maze of merchants and stalls. The vast array of smells was overwhelming. Sizzling meat and fine spices mixed with the pungent odor of donkeys and mules. Kala wished she was still wearing her headscarf so she could diminish the powerful scents assaulting her nose.

It felt like they had been walking for hours, going around in endless circles. An ominous dread seeped into Kala's bones at the unsettling thought that Sabine might not be leading them anywhere. Because there was no witch. Either that or she was luring them into a trap. The endless changes in direction could be to make sure they had no bearings for escape.

Kala glanced around warily but no one appeared to be following them. Vendors called out, inviting them to sample their wares. From dates to tea to jewelry and pottery, Kala politely declined each offer and kept walking. Still, she couldn't shake the feeling that something wasn't right. Suddenly Sabine stopped and pivoted to face them, causing everyone to halt abruptly. Kala strained to hear Sabine's words above the cacophony of the bazaar.

"We're here," Sabine announced.

"Which is where exactly?" Dema asked, her voice laced with skepticism.

"Are you saying one of these vendors is the witch?" Kala frowned, confused.

"Maybe. It could be anybody."

"Enough, Sabine," Ele said tersely. "Tell us where to find the witch."

Sabine's eyes sharpened on Ele. "I want to call in my favor."

"Favor." Kala glanced between them. "What favor?"

"We made a deal. I gave the Captain information he needed to complete his mission and now he owes me a favor."

"What is it?" Ele asked impatiently.

"The moment I tell you where the witch is, one of you, if not all of you, will try to kill me." Sabine looked at each of them pointedly. Nobody denied it. "You must promise to defend my life and ensure my safe return to the Thaka."

Kala's features tightened in barely restrained anger. "We already have a deal. I freed you and pardoned your treason in return for locating the witch."

Sabine shrugged. "I'm renegotiating."

"I'll kill you right now!" Kala lurched forward but Ele blocked her path.

He lowered his voice to a whisper only she could hear. "We have no choice."

Kala knew he was right but it didn't stop the blood from rushing in her ears. Sabine needed to die. She had likely already alerted her family to Kala's existence. For that alone, she needed to pay with her life.

"Fine." Ele turned back to Sabine. "I promise to protect you with my life and guarantee your safe return to the Thaka."

Sabine made a swooning sound as she pretended to faint against him. "You have a way with words, Captain."

"Where is the witch?" Isa demanded, his scowl the only thing visible from beneath his hooded cloak.

Sabine guided them down another narrow alleyway but this one was quieter and had fewer people passing through. She gestured to a market stall. The entrance was covered by a thin iridescent fabric, probably to offer the illusion of privacy to customers. Despite the curtain, Kala could see everything inside. The space was not particularly big, but it was cramped from floor to ceiling with dark wooden cabinets displaying glass bottles filled with liquids and small ceramic jars. From the roof hung tied bunches of dried herbs and flowers. A thick rug cornered off an area for private use.

There were no customers inside. In fact, the stall didn't even look occupied.

Before Kala could enter, the iridescent material was dramatically swept aside and a young man appeared. His face was strikingly beautiful; high cheekbones, amber eyes shadowed with kohl, eyelids painted with silver. Even his ears were pierced with copper rings. A single thin braid hung at the side of otherwise short and unkempt hair. It was adorned with shiny dark beads.

"Welcome, friends! Come in, come in. Thank you for visiting my humble dukkan."

He ushered them inside quickly. Suddenly, the space felt very cramped. Kala had to watch where she stepped to avoid bumping into one of the many wooden cabinets that surrounded them.

"Don't be shy, don't be shy. Anything that ails you, I can heal. Except death, okay? I can only buy you time. Give you enough time to have a good time before you die, okay?" He chuckled at his own joke, a high-pitched feminine giggle. "So many of you! Is it contagious?"

"You're a healer?" Kala asked, doubt creeping into her voice. He looked more like a street performer.

His smile brightened at the question, two perfect rows of shining white teeth. "Of course, my beauty! The best healer in all Merovia. That's why you came to see me, yes? I have a rare gift." He wiggled his painted fingernails in front of her and concentrated. "I know what people need just by looking at them. Here."

He scrambled over to a cabinet behind her and selected a small linen pouch.

Kala eyed the pouch curiously as he gave it to her. "What's this?"

"What you need. Some lucky man is getting your attention, my spicy flower." He winked as he elbowed her in the ribs mischievously.

Kala paled. Isa's scowl deepened from beneath his hooded cloak.

"And you!" The healer twirled around and dramatically clicked his fingers in front of Sabine's face. "I have exactly what you need, my treasure."

Sabine smiled in amusement as he clambered to retrieve a small stool before setting it against the cabinet and reaching for a glass vial on a high shelf. He exhaled proudly at the concoction as he brought it down and delivered it to Sabine.

"A love potion. A few drops in his drink and he won't be able to resist your juicy apricots." He shimmied his chest suggestively before chortling uncontrollably.

Sabine's features darkened violently but he had already moved on to Ele.

"And you, my dream, by the gods, there is nothing wrong with you." The man's hands hovered in front of Ele's face, framing it as if he were about to paint it. "In fact, you're a little too perfect. You and your beast of a friend make quite the—"

Isa jerked his hood back, revealing a fearsome glare and black rimmed eyes. The healer yelped as he fell backwards a step before his gaze switched to Dema as if she'd called out his name.

"A vessel," he mumbled as he stared at her in disbelief. "I haven't … I never …"

Dema's eyes immediately shifted from human to swirling pools of churning seas. The healer jolted as if he'd been struck by lightning and collapsed to shaking knees, his hands prostrated on the ground as his mouth panted for words that escaped him.

"Witch," the goddess hissed accusingly.

"Witch? N-no. Not me. I heal. I do tricks. I flirt. But no magic. Never magic."

"Word on the street is that you give divinations and they're eerily accurate," Sabine remarked coolly.

He half scoffed, half choked. "I tell people what they want to hear. You will meet the love of your life. Have great fortune. Beautiful babies. Mere stories. Nothing more."

The goddess clicked her tongue. "You have knowledge of the spirit world."

"No! I know nothing! I mean I know about the gods, everybody knows about the gods. They are powerful and vengeful, and I would never do anything to turn their eye toward me," he squeaked.

"I see you, witch."

He let out a strangled cry.

"She's not here to kill you," Kala insisted as she moved toward him, trying her best to look non-threatening.

"But I will if you fail to break the curse," the goddess warned.

The healer resembled a stone statue. Kala wasn't even sure he was breathing. She speared a disapproving look at the Water Goddess, who deftly ignored her. Kala sighed. She needed to change tack.

"I will pay you generously if you help us."

The healer peeked up at her from beneath long dark eyelashes.

"You could rent a bigger stall." Sabine waved her hand around the cramped space.

"You could buy the bazaar," Kala countered.

He considered her offer for a moment before stumbling to stand on shaky but determined legs. "You don't know what you're asking of me. Curses are powerful. The witch who cast the curse of the Black Sands paid for it with her life. The curse was so terrible, it sent every witches line into hiding so that no god would be able to exploit us again."

Kala's eyes lit up. "You know of the curse of the Black Sands?"

The healer glanced at Isa nervously, his expression almost apologetic. "The witch who cast it was my ancestor."

"Then you know how to break it," Ele prompted.

The healer crossed to the iridescent curtain at the entrance of his stall and peered down both directions of the alleyway. Satisfied, he turned back to them.

"Dark ingredients were used to cast the curse. Poisoned water. Polluted smoke. A corrupt flame. Sand stained with suffering. My ancestor wrote it all down before she died. To break the curse, you would need light ingredients."

"Such as?" Kala probed.

"Pristine water," the Water Goddess guessed and the healer nodded.

"White smoke," the healer continued. "A pure flame. And sand untouched by tragedy or suffering."

"Sounds easy enough," Sabine drawled sarcastically as she studied the endless rows of glass bottles and ceramic jars.

"When wood catches fire, it releases white smoke," Ele suggested.

"And a pure flame?" Sabine goaded.

The cramped room fell into uneasy silence.

It was Isa who finally broke it. "Sand untouched by tragedy or suffering is impossible to find. All sand has touched some form of tragedy and suffering."

"There is only one way to obtain it," the Water Goddess interjected. "From the God of Earth and Salt."

Suddenly, the space felt stifling and void of air.

"Will he help us?" Kala asked hesitantly.

"It is rare for the gods to help mortals. When they do, it is never given freely." The Water Goddess's gaze slid to Ele, and Kala knew she was thinking of the deal Henri made with the Goddess of Endings and Beginnings.

"The gods cannot be trusted," Sabine agreed, before glancing back at the Water Goddess. "No offense."

The healer clapped his hands in spontaneous delight. "I'm glad we all agree it's a bad idea."

"No one said that," Kala retorted.

"Look, even if you somehow managed to convince the God of Earth and Salt to take a break from ferrying lesser sacrifices to the gods, and you collected all the light ingredients you need, which is highly unlikely, you all seem to be forgetting one thing; breaking the curse would kill me."

The healer searched their faces for understanding or at least a trace of empathy. When he found none, his tone turned desperate. "I'm sorry that your friend is cursed—"

"My entire kingdom is cursed," Kala corrected.

He blinked. "You're the Queen of the Black Sands?"

A blade was at his throat before his next inhale, Isa's dark-rimmed eyes feral with violence. "If you want to live, you will keep that knowledge to yourself, witch."

"I want to live! That's what I've been trying to tell you!" He raised his trembling hands in supplication. "All my services are confidential."

Kala placed her hand on Isa's arm and gently urged him to put the dagger away. He complied reluctantly.

"What is your name?" Kala asked.

"Darius."

"Darius, I understand your fear but this curse has already cost people their lives. It must be broken."

"The magic is old and weakened. It may not take your life," the goddess speculated, though it sounded like she wasn't concerned either way.

"So comforting," Darius muttered.

"We'll return when we have all the light ingredients." Ele strolled over to stand by the entrance, pulling the curtain aside.

Dema and Sabine followed his lead and stepped out into the alleyway.

Isa pulled his hood back up and adjusted it so that only his mouth was visible. Even so, he leveled Darius with a lethal look. "Don't even think about running."

Darius released a high-pitched giggle that betrayed it was all he was thinking about. There was nothing Kala could say or do to reassure him, so she remained silent as she followed Isa out. Ele fell into step beside her as they collectively made their way back towards the bustling bazaar. Before the narrow alley joined the chaos of merchants and traders, they turned to face each other, their expressions a mirror of doubt and unease.

"He's going to run," Sabine said flatly.

Isa nodded. "I'll watch him. Make sure he doesn't try to flee or sell us out."

"Is that wise? Your eyes," Kala protested.

"I know how to stay hidden."

"Take the first shift. I'll relieve you at sunset," Ele offered.

Without another word, Isa turned back down the alleyway. Kala watched him go, anxiety pooling in her gut. The sooner they found the light ingredients, the sooner this could all be over.

"We need to find a pure flame," she muttered, more to herself than anyone else.

"Good luck with that. I've kept my end of the bargain, so I'll be leaving." Sabine linked her arm through Ele's. "Captain, would you kindly escort me back to the palace?"

Ele briefly glanced at Kala before he started walking away, making no effort to remove Sabine's arm from his. Dema followed behind them but Kala remained rooted in place. Ignoring her was one thing, insulting her was another, and using her sister to make her jealous was downright low.

Ele threw a glance over his shoulder and stopped mid-stride when he noticed she hadn't moved. "Kala?"

Kala turned on her heel and marched in the opposite direction, disappearing into the bustling crowd. She vaguely heard Ele calling after her, his shouts sharp with irritation before quickly fraying to desperation. Kala ignored him. She knew it was reckless, dangerous even to wander around on her own. She would most certainly get lost, but she would prefer that to returning to the palace. The only thing awaiting her there was more uncertainty, fewer answers, and a loneliness that was beginning to hurt her heart.

She missed home.

An angry tear escaped down her cheek but Kala quickly wiped it away. Crying would not help. She needed to find a pure flame and think of a way to convince the God of Earth and Salt to help them. She was loath to involve another god in the situation, but she had little choice. The God of Beauty and Fertility had known what he was doing when he enlisted the witch to cast the curse. Without the help of the gods, it was impossible to break it.

If the gods had stayed out of mortal matters, none of this would have happened. Her kingdom would not be cursed and Tahlia would still be alive. But then Ele would be dead. And the Naiab wouldn't exist. It was pointless to think about what could have been. Instead, she needed to focus on what was in her control; saving Isa.

Bodies knocked into her as she tried to push through the crowd, causing her to stumble and trip over her own feet. She was moving against the tide, she realized. She kept going anyway. It was pure stubbornness at this point. Kala put her weight into each shove, refusing to be deterred. It felt good to fight back. To move forward when she'd felt stagnant and trapped for days.

Except she had no idea if she was any closer to finding her way out of this maze or whether she had inadvertently done a loop and was back to where she started. She needed to find higher ground to get her bearings. Kala looked up above the market stalls, trying to see if there were surrounding buildings that she could climb. Suddenly, Kala felt something brush her kaftan. It was so subtle it could have been someone bumping into her except she knew it wasn't.

One of her daggers had been lifted.

Kala's eyes darted around until they caught a flash of a little boy moving through the crowd at a hurried pace. "Hey! Stop!"

Kala shoved people aside and weaved in between crowded stalls as she tried to give chase. The little thief was brazen thinking he could steal from her. But then again, the bazaar was a prime place for thievery and she should have been more on guard. With so many people crammed in tight, most wouldn't notice they'd been robbed. The boy glanced back at her, a calm focus on his young face, as if he was confident he could escape her.

Brat.

She knew he would have an escape route ready. She needed to catch him before he managed to get to it. Kala knocked into a stall, sending a pyramid of dried fruits and nuts flying, but she didn't stop. The merchant called curses down on her, causing the crowds to part a little to avoid being associated with the curse. It gave her the advantage she needed. She could see where the boy was heading now, a tight shadowed alleyway in between two buildings. Kala bolted, quickly closing the distance between her and the boy. When he shot into the darkness of the alleyway, she was almost close enough to reach out and grab him, but strong hands grabbed her first.

CHAPTER TWENTY-TWO

ELE

"Let her go, Captain." Sabine tugged at his arm, dragging him further away into the crowd. "She'll be fine. She has more lives than a scorpion."

Ele craned his neck, trying to spot Kala over the heads of hundreds of people, but everyone looked the same as they moved about like a herd of goats.

He clenched his teeth in irritation. "She's going to get lost."

"Hopefully," Sabine said cheerily.

"You underestimate her." Dema's tone was distracted as she took in the abundance of sights in the bazaar.

Ele arched a brow at Dema. The comment surprised him. Kala and Dema were not friends so she had no reason to defend her. Ele knew very little about the Shahri of the Naiab, but from what he'd observed over the past few days traveling together, she preferred to stay out of conflict and she usually kept her opinions to herself.

Ele slipped Sabine's arm from his own and begrudgingly followed as Sabine led them through the throng. He promised he would guard her with his life and he couldn't do that if he went after Kala. Besides, he had no chance of finding Kala now. She could be anywhere in the sea of people. That was the point. She didn't want to be found. At least, not by him. Ele scowled.

"Gods save me." Sabine tossed her head back dramatically. "You look like you're being tortured. What's wrong with you two? You're friends, you're more than friends, you're not friends."

"I will always be her friend," Ele shot back.

"There's no future for you two anyway. She's a queen. You're a captain. There's an entire desert that separates you. Regardless of whether the sandman lives or dies, she will return to her kingdom and you will return to yours. You've already fucked her. She should be out of your system. Move on."

Ele glowered at Sabine. He wasn't surprised that she knew. They hadn't exactly been subtle about it. He wished it were that simple to move on. If it was anyone else it would be, but it was Kala. He feared he would never get her out of his system. That fear made everything ten times worse.

"True connections don't fade with distance or time," Dema said, tracing her fingers along a row of hanging amulets as they passed a stall.

Sabine snorted. "You've been letting the goddess inhabit you for too long. You're beginning to sound like her."

CHAPTER TWENTY-TWO

"That's not what this is about," Ele grumbled.

"Then what's it about?" Sabine threw her hands up, exasperated.

A dispute suddenly broke out ahead of them, between who and over what Ele had no idea. He grabbed Sabine's elbow, and Dema moved to his side instinctively as he ushered them both down another row of stalls to avoid it.

"If the witch can't cure Isa, I will have to kill him," Ele explained.

"Shame," Sabine deadpanned as she sidetracked to a perfume stand.

Ele crossed his arms impatiently as he stood at her back and scanned the crowd for signs of threat. Dema joined Sabine as she sniffed at the tiny ornate bottles. He couldn't believe they had just found the witch, were faced with an impossible task to break the curse, and yet Sabine and Dema were taking the opportunity to shop. Finding one she liked, Sabine uncorked the bottle and tilted a few drops of the oil on her wrist.

"You're worried she won't forgive you?" Dema asked as she glanced over at Ele.

His features shifted uneasily but he tried to keep his expression neutral. Truth be told, he'd hardly slept the past few nights. All he could think about was Kala, the look on her face when he'd told her the truth, and what he might have to do to keep her safe. He held no ill will against Isa, though the warrior clearly didn't like him, but he refused to let the man be a danger to others. Especially Kala. An ordinary person could never stand a chance against a Naiab warrior. A rabid Naiab warrior meant mass slaughter.

"The act of forgiveness is deeply personal," Dema reflected. "She might surprise you."

Ele wished he could believe that.

"What are you doing?" Ele flinched as Sabine flicked some drops of a musky scent on him. He snatched the bottle from her hand and put it back roughly. "That's enough. Let's keep moving."

Dema followed his instruction but he had to herd Sabine forward with a firm hand on the small of her back. The contact only made Sabine grin.

"There are some things that can't be forgiven." Ele directed the words to Dema.

"Not in my experience," she countered.

Ele scoffed, then winced against the bright rays of sunshine that filtered down between strips of patterned cloth overhead. They cast a pattern of shadow and light across the stone path.

"Then you haven't been paying attention," he retorted. "The Water Goddess never forgave her mortal ex for his betrayal or Isa for choosing Kala over her. Tahlia will never forgive Isa for sacrificing her to the gods. Kala refuses to forgive Sabine for what happened when they were kids, and Sabine won't forgive Kala for her so-called betrayal."

"And if everyone had forgiven each other, would we still be in this mess?" Dema challenged. "When the Rouhan family took control of Merovia and my ancestors refused to submit to their reign, they were cast out into the Idris Desert to die. The Rouhan tried to commit genocide against my people. If it weren't for the Water Goddess, none of us would be alive. That trauma has taken generations to heal, but I have forgiven them. Refusing to forgive only ensures that one holds on to the pain and passes it to the next generation."

"That's not true." Sabine's expression suddenly turned deadly serious. "You can let go of the pain without forgiving someone. Sometimes withholding forgiveness is the only way people can reclaim their power."

Ele watched Sabine carefully. He had a feeling she was not talking about Kala's betrayal. A sudden flash of light seared his vision and he instinctively lifted a hand to shade his eyes. It wasn't coming from above. Light flared off a dozen small bronze curved mirrors hanging by leather bands in a market stall just ahead.

The merchant's face became animated at the sight of them. "Kafei! You look like a traveling man. Come, see my mirrors! The finest quality in all Merovia, No need for flint or firestones!"

Ele nodded politely and kept walking but Dema paused, her expression curious.

"Kafei!" The merchant turned his attention to her. "You look like you are devoted to the gods. The mirrors can be used for rituals and divinations!"

Dema wandered over to inspect the mirrors. Ele huffed impatiently as Sabine eagerly joined her. He had little choice but to wait for them. Dema held one of the mirrors up to the sunlight, a secretive smile spreading across her lips.

Ele's brows furrowed in curiosity. "What is it?"

"Parabolic mirrors. When positioned correctly, they focus the light of the sun to brighten dark places. We use them in the Citadel."

Ele recalled the large mirrors that sat in the corners of the cavernous spaces beneath the opening in the cave's rooftop. He hadn't realized their purpose.

"They can also be used to light fire," Dema added.

"A sacred fire for your sacrifices to the gods," the merchant suggested. "Untainted by flint. Lit by the Sun God himself!"

Ele's face brightened in sudden realization. "A pure flame."

KALA

In the space of a heartbeat, Kala ducked out of his grasp, slammed her assailant against the mudbrick wall and pinned him there with her forearm against his neck. A hidden dagger was now poised dangerously against his spleen, his fault for assuming that she would only have one weapon on her. The boy had obviously not chosen her at random. This was a trap and she had fallen into it so easily. Kala wanted to scream at her own complacency but she saved her rage for the enemy under her knife.

"Who sent you?" She demanded.

"Zaynab."

"Samir?"

His voice was the sweetest sound on earth and it immediately melted all the tension in her body. She let the dagger clatter to the ground and flung her arms around his neck, squeezing him tighter than she ever had before. He embraced her just as hard, cradling the back of her head in his hand. Kala felt the tears burn behind her closed eyelids but she refused to cry. She was too happy to cry.

"What are you doing here?" Her voice was a broken sob.

"We were worried about you."

"I told you I was fine. You got my message."

"I know but Zaynab insisted that I see you with my own eyes."

Kala smiled despite herself. Zaynab was being an overcautious regent and an overbearing friend and she loved her for it. Kala released Samir but they were still pressed against each other in the narrow alleyway.

"How did you get past the border?"

"Zaynab gave me official papers. Come." Samir took her hand and tugged her out of the alleyway and into the crowd.

Now that they were in the sunlight, Kala could see how exhausted he looked, as if he hadn't stopped to rest in days. His cloak was dusty from travel and his skin was a shade darker from riding beneath the desert sun. Samir looked her over from head to toe as well. Kala couldn't help but smile at him fussing over her.

"I'm fine," she insisted.

Worry lined his brow. "You've lost weight."

"You look terrible too."

"I never said you looked terrible. You always look beautiful."

Kala pointed a warning finger at his face. "You'd better have my dagger."

Samir smirked as he retrieved the hidden dagger, flipped it once in his hand and held the hilt out to her.

Kala snatched it back. "I can't believe you paid a kid to steal from me."

"I can't believe you fell for it."

"Neither can I. It's embarrassing. Let's never speak of it again." Kala frowned at a sudden thought. All morning she'd had a feeling that something wasn't right. "Have you been following me?"

"I was wondering if you would notice. I didn't know if it was safe to come see you directly. I wanted to get you alone first. I was going to find a way to get a message to you but then you suddenly left your companions. Not the wisest choice you've ever made."

Kala sighed. "I know."

Samir's brow furrowed in concern. "What's wrong?"

Kala opened her mouth to speak but she didn't know where to begin. From Isa almost dying in the Idris Desert, to the slaughter of the rabid Naiab warriors, to the canyon-sized rift between her and Ele. There was just so much to tell.

"Is it too early for a drink?"

ELE

Isa was going to kill him. The sun was pouring liquid gold in the sky, and Ele was yet to relieve the Naiab warrior from his post because Kala hadn't returned to the palace. Ele had searched the city for hours, combed every inch of the bazaar, and then explored streets at random. His heart felt like it was in a perpetual state of atrophy. Every minute that passed made him more certain that something terrible had happened.

If Kala had gotten lost, she would eventually have sought help and been pointed in the right direction. Once she found her way out of the bazaar, it was relatively simple to find the palace. Either she was refusing to return in order to punish him, or she was being held against her will.

Or she was dead.

The thought made his teeth clench and his hands flex into fists. If Sabine had alerted her family that Kala was in the Kingdom of the Salt Plains, would they be bold enough to try to cross the border without permission and snatch her from the streets in broad daylight?

Yes. They would.

Ele rubbed the back of his neck anxiously as he glanced around the open square. Perhaps another enemy had seized Kala. Sabine could have sold her out to anyone. There was no shortage of people who would profit from Kala's death. The Black Sands was a wealthy kingdom. The chance to rule over such a land could stain even the purest of hands with blood.

For what felt like the hundredth time, Ele called out to Tahlia, begging her to help him, but the goddess was infuriatingly silent. Perhaps she was punishing him, too. Surely, if Kala was in danger, she would tell him. Then again, perhaps she couldn't. The gods might be watching her. Tahlia had already intervened by saving Isa's life. Ele couldn't imagine that the Goddess of Endings and Beginnings had taken kindly to that.

Ele swore under his breath and tried to think. He was out of options. He should have known better. Should have seen through Sabine's act to keep him distracted. He would torture her if he had to. By sunrise tomorrow, he would know the truth. He could only hope that whoever had captured Kala hadn't killed her yet. Perhaps he would get lucky and the fools would try to negotiate a ransom. He would find wherever they were holding her and make them pay for daring to touch her.

But first, he had to tell Isa.

Ele moved quickly toward the bazaar's entrance. There were several entry points, but he was aiming for the one that would bring him closest to the healer's stall. He knew how the Naiab warrior would respond. Ele would be lucky to keep all his limbs, especially given the obsidian knife's edge that Isa was currently operating on. Ele could hardly use his power to protect himself when he deserved whatever the warrior would do to him. It didn't matter, though. Ele would pay any price as long as they saved Kala.

The bazaar was lively at night, though the air held a different atmosphere. One of revelry rather than shrewd business dealings. Glass lanterns flickered, casting an array of colors across the stone walls. Voices of vendors and customers echoed down the streets as children laughed and played, weaving in and out of the crowds. The smell of sizzling lamb and baked flat bread reminded Ele he hadn't eaten in hours. Sweet smoke curled from tucked away corners where old men sat to watch the commotion. Nearby, someone played a reed flute, the only tranquil sound in an otherwise chaotic place.

A raucous cheer erupted from a meyhane just ahead and a man's voice loudly announced the winner of a zajal. It sounded like it was an entertaining one. Ele had watched other people participate in the poetic dueling but he had never been tempted to try it himself. He was no poet and he certainly couldn't recite any from memory. He'd always hated reading and avoided it as much as possible. The words seemed to shift on the parchment, the characters becoming tangled in his mind. Even reading a simple letter demanded a lot of concentration. Kala's letters were the only words he'd ever been eager to read.

Boisterous laughter hit his ears as a group of patrons stumbled out of the meyhane and into the crowd. One of them recited a particularly bad line of poetry and they all began howling anew. Ele stepped aside, trying to avoid them, but then froze when he saw Kala standing amongst them. She was grinning widely, her cheeks flushed, as she enthusiastically relayed something to the others, which triggered a wave of hysterics. Ele blinked, stunned. She was not being held against her will, and she most certainly was not dead.

Ele's body trembled with barely controlled anger as one of the men slid his arm around her waist and tugged her close. That man was about to lose an arm. Except Kala looked up at the stranger adoringly and wrapped her arm around his middle as if she welcomed his embrace. Ele had to look away to try to regain control over himself. Maiming and murdering in the middle of the bazaar would only land him in prison and bring unwelcome attention to Kala. He needed to be calm. Strategic. There could be no witnesses to this bloodbath.

When he looked up again, the group had dispersed and Kala and the stranger were already walking away in the opposite direction, their steps a little unsteady, as if they were keeping each other upright. Ele trailed them at a distance, not close enough to overhear their conversation, but near enough to take in every smile and laugh they exchanged. It defied belief how comfortable Kala seemed to be in the stranger's presence.

Ele glowered in disgust. Kala had stormed away from him, recklessly putting herself in danger, only to go to the nearest meyhane and spend the rest of the day drinking and sparring in drunken poetry battles. While he had spent hours searching for her, frantically imagining the worst possible scenarios, she was flirting with a stranger who she now appeared to be going home with.

The man would never get to touch her. In fact, he wouldn't have a hand left to fist himself with. They leisurely wandered out of the bazaar and into the open square. It was dark and mostly deserted. The perfect opportunity. Ele moved fast, closing the distance between them and reached for the stranger's arm locked around

Kala's waist, but as he did so, she spun around and a blade pierced his flesh.

Ele stilled. His face crumpled in confusion, then pain. Kala's mouth fell open in utter shock while the stranger took up a defensive stance in front of her, a hammer gripped in his hand.

"Ele?" Kala spluttered as she swayed on her feet, her eyes pinging from the wound in his torso to the bloody dagger in her hand. "Why did you sneak up on me?"

Ele immediately applied pressure to the wound, watching in disbelief as blood trickled down his fingers. "Fuck, Kala, you stabbed me!"

"I thought you were trying to rob us! I only meant to threaten you. You were the one who rushed into the blade!"

"You're saying I stabbed myself?" He stared back at her, incredulous, but Kala only lifted her chin, indignant. "You're drunk! You can't even stand straight."

"I can too." She swayed.

Ele narrowed his eyes at her and then flicked them to her would-be defender. "A hammer? Really?"

The stranger lowered it slowly but his expression was severe, as if Ele was in the wrong. It only made Ele want to kill him more.

"Samir is a stonemason," Kala shot back defensively, "and is quite deadly with a hammer."

"Samir?" It was only then that Ele recognized the man. One of Kala's closest friends. And former lover.

"Yes. You two have met."

"What's he doing here?" Ele growled.

"He wanted to see me."

"Why?"

"He was worried about me."

"She's fine."

"Clearly," Samir deadpanned.

If he wasn't bleeding everywhere, he would have knocked that judgmental expression right off Samir's face. Kala seemed unaware of the violence pulsing in the air, though, because she tried to tuck her dagger back into the belt of her kurta. Her fingers were clumsy and she kept missing.

"Give me that." Ele snatched it off her and tucked it between his own belt.

"Hey! Why is everyone stealing my dagger?"

Kala shrieked as Ele swept her off her feet without warning. Pain exploded in his side, and fresh blood gushed from his wound but he gritted his teeth against it. Cradling Kala in his arms, he began marching in the direction of the palace.

"What are you doing? Put me down!"

To Ele's annoyance, Samir kept up with his relentless stride.

"You can't walk straight and you don't know where you're going," Ele insisted, his grip on her tightening.

"Over there!" Kala pointed to the large golden dome in the near distance, the pinnacle of the palace. It rose tall above the flat rooftops of the city. "It's hard to miss it."

"I wouldn't put it past you in your current state."

"Oh, of course. Like you've never had too much to drink."

"It was the scorpion's milk," Samir said. "We were fine until we lost the zajal. Losers had to drink scorpion's milk."

"Scorpion's milk?! How are you still conscious?"

"I have stamina! Something you wouldn't know about me." Kala pressed a finger into his chest before waving it at Samir. "He knows it about me."

A hint of a grin broke through Samir's serious expression. Ele's nostrils flared at the insinuation, and he adjusted his hold without warning, making Kala shriek again.

She entwined her arms around his neck, holding tight, but released a growl of irritation. "This is not keeping your distance from me."

"I thought you didn't want me to."

They glared at each other, their faces inches apart. The sudden urge to kiss her was bizarre and overwhelming. Ele's gaze dipped to her lips, so close to his own. He wondered if she would let him, if she would kiss him back or push him away. Samir cleared his throat, a not-so-subtle warning.

Ele forced himself to look ahead. "I'll escort you back to the palace but then I have to go relieve Isa."

Kala tensed in his arms. "But you're wounded."

"It's not deep. I'll be fine."

Ele walked the rest of the way in stubborn silence. When he felt Kala's head loll against his shoulder, he allowed himself to glance down at her. The little drunkard was asleep. A soft smile twitched on his lips. The usual stern lines on her face were smoothed away. She looked calm and peaceful.

As they passed through the palace gate, Samir turned to him and held his arms out. "Give her to me."

Ele hesitated a moment but then carefully unfurled Kala into Samir's arms. Ele's hands immediately went to the wound in his side. It had stopped bleeding but his clothes were soaked with blood. Ele grimaced. There was nothing he could do about it. As he turned to head back to the bazaar, Samir called after him.

"A word of advice. You don't get to decide what she can and can't handle. What she will and won't forgive. You only get to love her. And if you're lucky, she might love you back."

Ele stared over his shoulder at Samir, trying to assess his sincerity, but the man looked earnest. Clearly, Kala had told him what had happened between them. Part of Ele was surprised she would be so candid with an ex-lover, but she had said their bond was one that could withstand anything. If they were nothing more than close friends, it made sense that she would seek his counsel.

Kala sleepily tightened her grip around Samir's neck and nuzzled into his chest. It hurt to see her like that. Completely vulnerable and safe in another man's arms. It wasn't Ele's arms that were holding her and it should have been. Samir turned to walk in the direction of the palace while Ele stood there for a moment, considering his advice. Perhaps the stonemason was right. Ele's intentions were good but they had only ended up hurting Kala. Now that Dema had discovered a pure flame, perhaps Isa would be cured.

When Ele entered the bazaar, he quickly wove through the bustling market stalls. Thankfully, it was too crowded for anyone to notice his blood-stained kurta. Eventually, he slipped into the stillness of the healer's secluded alley. Moving silently and cautiously, Ele scanned his surroundings.

Isa stepped out of the shadows like a wraith, his expression fierce. "The sun set an hour ago."

"I know. I'm sorry."

Isa tilted his head curiously as he noticed the blood stain. "What happened?"

"Kala's safe, don't worry." Ele had hoped he could leave it at that but Isa continued to stare at him expectantly. There was no point trying to hide the truth from him. "Kala stabbed me."

Isa nodded as if he wasn't surprised and could relate to the urge. "You deserved it then."

Ele sighed. "I did."

A voice called out to them from inside the healer's stall. "Well, don't just stand there. Come inside and let me take a look at it. I am a healer after all."

Isa and Ele exchanged a look of surprise.

"If you thought I wouldn't notice two perfectly handsome men stalking me, you clearly don't know me. Now come in and take your clothes off."

CHAPTER TWENTY-THREE

ISA

Isa scanned his bedchamber the moment he entered it, his stomach sinking to find the room empty. Deep down, he knew Tahlia wouldn't be there but he'd still clung to a sliver of hope. The past two days had felt like a fever dream. He'd hardly eaten or slept or thought about anything else except burying himself between Tahlia's thighs and driving her to ecstasy over and over again. Nothing else existed in the world except her.

His appetite for her had been insatiable, the black sand demanding more and more, like a starving wild animal driven to madness. Isa had tried to restrain himself, concerned that Tahlia's vessel wouldn't be able to withstand it, but Tahlia had assured him she could. His efforts at restraint were obliterated the moment she seized his cock in her hand or placed her mouth on his skin. He was ravenous for her. It was not Tahlia's body but the intention

CHAPTER TWENTY-THREE

was hers. It was all that she could give him and he would take it. He would drown himself in her.

They'd hardly spoken the entire two days, at least not with words. Their bodies had spoken a language all of their own, telling a tale of longing and forbidden desire, of loneliness and aching need, intertwined with anger and bitter regret. There were moments that were calm and tender, but most were raw and savage. After everything that had happened between them, there were some things that could not be expressed in words. They needed to be felt. Deeper than the soul's core. In the meeting of skin. Along the line between pleasure and pain.

But then he'd woken this morning to find her gone.

Isa might have believed it was all a dream except the evidence was strewn around the room in the wreckage of broken furniture and the flurry of feathers from desiccated pillows. Though his emotions were still heightened, he was able to leash them. The darkness had receded a little from his eyes, and the beast that clawed at his insides appeared satiated. For now. Though how long it would last, he wasn't sure.

The witches' revelation had not given him hope. The light ingredients required to undo the curse seemed impossible to obtain. Even if they managed to find a pure flame, he couldn't imagine what it would take to convince the God of Earth and Salt to help them. The gods were not known for their benevolence. The only reason they interfered in mortal matters was to stifle the boredom of their everlasting existence with the one thing they found most entertaining: human suffering.

Isa wandered over to a mass of shredded linen and scattered feathers in the middle of the room. He'd tried to pray to Tahlia several times throughout the day but she'd refused to answer him. He was not surprised by her silence. She had offered herself to buy him time, to keep his dark urges at bay a little longer. She had not forgiven him. Ultimately, nothing had changed between them. They had used each other for their own purposes, and while he wanted to delude himself into believing it was more, he couldn't. Still, the absence of her hurt. It was a familiar emptiness, the sharp edge of agony worn down to a phantom pain over time.

Isa sank to the floor, stretching out on his back amongst the torn sheets and strewn feathers. He closed his eyes, surrendering himself to exhaustion. It felt fitting to sleep amongst the destruction of what they'd done to each other. Isa already knew Tahlia would not come to him tonight, not even in his dreams.

KALA

The feeling of hands nudging her body stirred Kala from unconsciousness. Someone was trying to maneuver her. They were tucking their hands between her waist and whatever she'd passed out on. It felt soft, so it was probably her bed. Kala knew she was too hungover to put up much of a fight, but it was instinctive to kick out at whoever was trying to manhandle her.

"Kala, it's Ele." His hushed voice ceased her feeble attempts and coaxed her heavy eyes to open.

Ele swam into her vision. He was standing by the side of the bed, leaning over her, his arms half tucked beneath her body. He looked a little weary but an amused smile tugged at his lips. Behind him, burning sunlight streamed through the lattice windows, almost blinding her. It was morning, then. Kala winced against the light and scowled at Ele's intrusion. She needed at least several more hours of sleep to recover.

"I come here bearing gifts only to find another man in your bed."

Kala's head lolled to the side, where she saw Samir sleeping next to her, both of them fully clothed, as if they'd simply collapsed onto the bed and passed out. She had very little memory of how they had gotten back to the palace last night but she recalled Ele had carried her at some point.

After she stabbed him.

Kala's eyes widened with panic and she opened her mouth to say something, but Ele scooped her up into his arms, the movement jolting her body to nauseous awareness. The room tilted and her stomach revolted but she managed to keep its contents from coming up through sheer will.

"What are you doing?" Kala protested.

"I don't think Samir is in any condition to look after you."

"I don't need looking after."

"Is that right, little drunkard? Shall we see if you can stand?"

Kala pressed her lips together, but she couldn't help going limp in his arms as Ele carried her out of the room, across the hallway, and into his own bed chamber. She decided the guards stationed at her door were useless. They didn't even question him, let alone stop him. It was true, they had been stationed there at his request, but still. They were doing a lax job of protecting her.

Her head pounded as Ele laid her down gently across his bed but her stomach seemed to settle at the sudden stability.

"Much better," Ele said as he took in the sight of her nestled in his sheets.

Kala's attention caught on his fresh kurta, concealing any sign of injury. "I stabbed you."

"I'm glad we agree on that. Last night you insisted I stabbed myself."

"Are you all right?" Kala clumsily tried to prop herself up on her elbows but Ele leaned across her, urging her to stay down.

"I'm fine. I've had worse injuries."

"I'm so sorry."

"Don't be. I will bear any scar you give me." Ele took her hand in his, lacing their fingers together.

Kala stilled at his words, at his unexpected touch. They'd held hands many times before but somehow this felt different. More intimate.

"Besides, I should be apologizing to you. I should have trusted you to make your own decision instead of trying to make it for you. I just never want to hurt you and I couldn't bear the thought of you hating me. But I ended up hurting you anyway. I'm sorry."

They held each other's gaze and somehow Kala recognized the deep fear he was trying to mask.

"You will never lose me, Ele." She tightened her grip on his hand. "I don't know what will happen if we can't cure Isa, but you and I will always be in each other's lives. Time and distance can't separate us, and neither will this."

Ele lowered his head and laughed softly, as if he felt foolish. "You know, when I was young, I worried you would outgrow me. You were always one step ahead of me. Smarter than me. Definitely braver. I was worried that our friendship would not be enough to keep you by my side. So when you chose to become Queen of the Black Sands, it felt like you'd finally chosen to leave me behind."

"I never chose to leave you," Kala insisted. "I only wanted to honor Tahlia's wishes."

"I know. I was afraid we would grow apart, but even after all this time, you're still one of the most important people in my life."

Kala's smile was slow and gentle as a feeling of warmth bloomed inside her chest. Words failed her. She hoped he knew she felt the same way about him. That she would always feel that way. Perhaps, she even felt something more.

"This apology comes with gifts." Ele turned to retrieve something from the nightstand and held a glass vial out to her with what looked like muddy brown water sloshing inside. "My first gift to you is a cure for your hangover, courtesy of our witch. He insisted that you don't smell it, just drink it."

Kala eyed the vial suspiciously.

"You were drinking far worse last night," Ele reminded her.

Kala scowled at him and took it. She knew it was only a matter of time before she either passed out or vomited all over Ele's bedsheets. She would rather avoid that fate if possible. If the witch's cure actually worked, she would be grateful for it. She emptied the glass vial down her throat. It tasted how it looked, complete with gritty bits. Kala slapped her tongue against the roof of her mouth in distaste.

"Good girl." A seductive smile curled at the corner of Ele's lips. It made her nauseous stomach flip for an entirely different reason.

Kala cleared her throat self-consciously. "Your second gift?"

"Dema found a pure flame."

Kala froze. "What? How?"

"Parabolic mirrors."

Kala recalled the mirrors that were used in the Citadel to channel the natural light that poured in through the cave's ceiling, but she had no idea they could ignite a flame. The flame would be pure, direct from the Sun God.

"So now we have all the light ingredients except sand untouched by tragedy or suffering," Kala said.

"Do you have a plan for convincing the God of Earth and Salt to help us?"

"Not exactly. But if I know anything about the gods, it's that they're not shy in making demands."

ISA

Crusted white salt crunched beneath their sandaled feet as they assembled outside the city. Not a single breath of dry air stirred. It was as if the earth knew what they had come to do and it didn't dare to exhale. The tense silence amongst the group betrayed their collective unease. Everyone had reservations about the plan, but now that they had come this far, there was little choice left except to follow through.

Ele and Kala laid down the pile of wood they'd gathered to create white smoke. Dema held a parabolic mirror in her hand, which she'd purchased earlier from a merchant in the bazaar. In between Isa and Samir, the witch shuffled nervously, feverishly tying a long white cord into a tight, intricate design.

Kala had ordered them to fetch Darius and escort him to the outskirts of the city, by force if necessary. The witch had blanched at the sight of them at his door, but he knew that if he tried to run or refused to help them, he would not live to see another day. So, he had accepted his fate and instructed Samir to bring a sizable incantation bowl with them. Despite his strength as a stonemason, Samir's arms trembled as he carried the bowl. He looked like he might buckle under the weight of it at any moment.

Isa wasn't sure why Sabine had insisted on coming with them. She'd fulfilled her end of the bargain by finding the witch and had no personal stake in whether the curse of the Black Sands was lifted or not. He could only speculate that she was bored and had nothing better to do with her time. Or perhaps she was afraid to be left alone. Maybe she thought Kala would send assassins to kill her.

"What are you wearing?" Sabine arched a curious brow at Darius.

The witch glanced down at his attire in confusion. He was wearing a peach colored kurta with small flowers embroidered on it. His eyes were shadowed with kohl and his eyelids were painted green. Rings pierced the arc of his ears, and a single braid remained the only thing that looked kempt amidst his tangled hair.

"Around your neck," Sabine clarified.

Darius lifted a handful of talismans that hung around his neck. "They're for protection and empowerment. I'm trying very hard not to die today. You all seem determined to kill me."

Isa looked closer at the talismans. He recognized some of them. They were *feliq*, symbols of the spirit world. Tahlia had painted one of them on her body every day for years to keep herself hidden from the gods. She had also used one to trap the god who hunted her. But the only reason Tahlia knew about *feliq* was because the Water Goddess had shared it with her. Which meant that, at some point, a god had shared the secrets of the spirit world with witches. Or perhaps such secrets had created witches. Maybe *feliq* was the source of their so-called magic.

Samir set the incantation bowl down on the cracked ground and then carefully stretched out his muscles, his face wincing in pain. Various symbols were inscribed on the bowl and a circle was crudely carved into the base. Isa didn't recognize the symbols but that didn't mean they weren't *feliq*. His knowledge of the symbols was limited to what the Water Goddess had been willing to share with him.

"And that?" Sabine indicated to the cord in Darius's hand.

"It's for you." He tossed the knotted cord to Isa who reflexively caught it. "It'll help unbind you from the curse. Hold on to it."

Isa studied the complex knot before casting a speculative glance at Kala, but she only stared at the knot as if it tied all her hopes together.

"We will need a vessel for the God of Earth and Salt to inhabit," Dema announced.

She was usually so calm and poised that it made the slight tremor in her voice hard to miss. Isa understood her trepidation. As Shahri, Dema was accustomed to the presence and nature of the Water Goddess, but she had likely never met any other divines. Most mortals never interacted with the gods beyond prayers and sacrificial offerings, content to derive meaning and answers from innocuous occurrences. But today they were about to invoke one of the most powerful gods to ask him to interfere in a mortal matter, and they had absolutely no leverage to barter with. The god could kill them all just for daring to interrupt his eternal existence.

"Not me," Sabine said resolutely.

"It can't be Isa or Dema," Kala pointed out.

"I'll do it," Ele offered.

"No!" Kala lowered her voice to a strained whisper. "The gods can't find out about you."

"I can do it." Samir stepped forward and braced his shoulders.

Isa wasn't sure if Samir was stretching his muscles from the strain of carrying the incantation bowl or if he was readying his body for the impact of receiving a divine power. Kala looked torn, like she wanted to talk Samir out of it, but she also recognized there was no other option.

"Is there anything I should know about letting a god inhabit me?" Samir asked.

"Just surrender yourself." Dema offered an encouraging smile. "It feels a little like being half-asleep. A part of you is conscious, but you're not in control of yourself, and you're not sure if any of it is real."

"Sounds like being drugged," Sabine quipped.

Kala shot her a disapproving look before turning her attention back to Samir. "I liken it to sitting down in a corner of my mind. Try to relax."

"Can you feel everything that's happening to you while the goddess inhabits you?" Isa probed.

He had never asked Kala what it was like for her when Tahlia inhabited her. Now he found himself curious. Tahlia had assured him that the vessel she'd inhabited over the past few days wouldn't feel anything, the pleasure or the pain, but perhaps she'd lied to him.

"Only if the divine wants you to. They are in complete control," Dema explained.

Samir nodded in stoic acceptance, his expression apprehensive but determined. They watched as Dema's eyes suddenly shimmered with the depths of ocean floors and the silver of moonlight on water. The Water Goddess looked around at each of them before speaking.

"I can only ask. He might not come. Gods are fickle creatures."

Kala inhaled a steadying breath. "We have to try."

The Water Goddess went unnaturally still, her gaze unseeing as if she were elsewhere but her vessel remained. Isa shifted closer to Kala and he noted that Ele moved to flank her other side. It was instinctive but futile. Isa was under no illusion that they could protect Kala from the wrath of a god should this plan go badly. No mortal could kill a god. Not even a god-touched mortal. Only the Water Goddess could protect them now. Except Isa wasn't sure which of the two divines was the most powerful.

Samir closed his eyes in willing submission but the clenched fists at his sides betrayed his inner conflict. They waited, keeping silent vigil on the Water Goddess. No one dared look away. When Samir's eyes finally tore open, they were no longer human. The orbs were forged from ancient stone, glittering with veins of crystal. Kala drew in a sharp breath.

The God of Earth and Salt turned his head stiffly, taking in every detail of his surroundings before tipping his chin to the sunburnt sky and then staring down at the salt-encrusted ground beneath his feet.

"How small your mortal existence is," the god marveled before lifting his gaze to the Water Goddess. "You enjoy diminishing yourself like this?"

"There are gains and sacrifices to every form of existence," the Water Goddess replied smoothly. "Even ours."

The god returned a non-committal sound as if he didn't agree but did not care enough to debate the point. Instead, his attention caught on the incantation bowl.

The lines around his mouth tightened. "Which one of you is casting a spell?"

The color instantly drained from Darius's face. If the witch's collection of talismans hadn't given him away, the stench of fear certainly would have. The god fixed his eyes on him, unblinking and pitiless.

"Hello, witch. I thought your kind were dead."

Darius swallowed audibly. "We're about to be."

The God of Earth and Salt tilted his head to crack his neck as if he found Samir's body too restrictive.

"We're not here to cast a spell. We're here to break one," Kala intervened. "The curse of the Black Sands. Do you know of it?"

"Silly girl, I am the God of Earth and Salt. I know everything that happens on the surface of this land, down to its molten core."

"Are you saying you allowed your realm to be cursed?" Kala asked dubiously.

The god looked bored as he traced his finger slowly around the rim of the incantation bowl, collecting a fine layer of dust on his fingertip. "The God of Beauty and Fertility once asked me to help him curse the sand of the kingdom he ruled when he was mortal. But I said no."

"Why?" The Water Goddess probed.

He flicked his gaze to her. "Why did he want to curse the land? Or why did I say no?"

"Both."

"He wanted to curse the land as a counter-move to you creating them." The god pointed a loose finger at Isa as if he were an abomination but an insignificant one. "And I said no because I've never much liked the prick."

"So, the God of Beauty and Fertility found a witch to help him instead," Ele deduced.

The god stared at Ele suddenly transfixed, as if he saw something in him but couldn't quite recognize it. Or worse, he recognized it but couldn't quite believe it. Panic flashed across Kala's face and she turned to Isa, silently pleading for him to do something, but there was nothing he could do. If the god discovered what Ele was, he was as good as dead.

"Why didn't you stop him?" The Water Goddess demanded.

The god broke his stare, resuming his bored demeanor. "Of course I could have, but he was so single-minded, and in the end, I didn't care enough to intervene."

Isa clenched his jaw. A land had been poisoned, his men infected, his own mind and body septic, all because a god did not care enough to protect the realm he'd been gifted. Apathy was the silent architect of destruction.

"How could you not care that your realm was poisoned?" Kala exclaimed.

The god scuffed his foot against the cracked earth, sending a spray of salt into the air. He watched the particles float then fall with mild interest.

"Mortals poison the earth every day. It is no greater sin when a god does it."

"Well we mortals care enough to want to set things right," Ele replied tightly. "To break the curse, we need sand untouched by tragedy or suffering. Only you can give us that."

"Why should I?"

"Because another god dared to interfere with your realm!" Kala retorted. "Doesn't it bother you? I thought that broke some kind of divine law or something."

The gods' eyes suddenly narrowed to slits of suspicion. "What do you know of our laws, mortal?"

Isa stepped forward to angle himself slightly in front of Kala. "We know the gods are territorial," he said carefully.

"And vengeful," Darius squeaked.

Either the God of Earth and Salt was truly indifferent or he had other reasons for letting the insult from the God of Beauty and Fertility slide. Perhaps a larger game was being played here.

"We have our rules, like every civilization, and there are consequences for breaking them." The words were casual but the god's tone hinted at some underlying meaning.

Isa suspected it was aimed at the Water Goddess.

"Rumor has it, though, that the God of Beauty and Fertility has already been punished. Captured and imprisoned around a mortal's neck. What a fitting fate."

The air snapped taut. Darius's mouth gaped open in disbelief.

"Maybe so but the curse remains," Kala replied. "Will you help us break it or not?"

The god paced a few steps as he feigned consideration. "I could but I would require something in return."

"Name it."

The god stopped, his stare clinging to the teardrop vial strung on a silver chain around Isa's neck. "I want your prisoner."

Isa blinked, the request catching him off guard for a split second, before he released a low growl. "No."

If the god wanted the vial, he would have to kill him first. Isa had sworn that as long as he lived, he would be warden to Tahlia's enemy and ensure that the god who hunted her never escaped. Isa had failed to protect Tahlia in her mortal life, but he would not fail to protect her in her divine existence.

"There is nothing else you have that I want."

"Why do you want it?" Kala pressed.

"As I said, I never liked the prick. It would give me joy to be his jailor."

Joy. An emotion the gods typically only experienced through *human* suffering. Granted, that was because the gods never suffered. Yet here was a god, trapped in a tiny mortal object, suffering. It made sense why the vial would be viewed as a prize. Except the god would not be able to take a mortal object to the divine realm. He would have to leave it somewhere in the mortal realm. Hidden. Or protected. But not by Isa. Which meant that he could not guarantee the vial would remain sealed. Once opened, the God of Beauty and Fertility would be unleashed.

Or perhaps the God of Earth and Salt had no intention of keeping the God of Beauty and Fertility imprisoned. The gods had been outraged when they learned that a mortal woman managed to imprison one of them. Maybe the God of Earth and Salt wanted to balance the scales by setting the God of Beauty and Fertility free.

Give it to him.

Isa tensed as Tahlia's voice pierced his senses. By the startled looks on Kala, Ele, and the Water Goddess's face, she had spoken into their minds as well.

"I will not," Isa ground out, the words rumbling low in his throat.

There is no other way.

"Then I will die, the land will remain poisoned, and as long as no Naiab sets foot in the kingdom, no one else will be infected. I will not endanger you for anything in this world or the divine one."

"Who is he talking to?" Darius hissed at Sabine, who simply shrugged.

It is not your decision to make. I imprisoned the God of Beauty and Fertility. He is my prisoner. Mine to do with what I will.

Isa clutched the vial in a tight fist as if he could prevent the god from taking it from him. He couldn't. But the God of Earth and Salt would have to pry it from his stiff, dead hand.

"Isa." Kala approached him, her expression full of conflicting emotions but also understanding, along with a silent apology.

Isa flinched to see it because he knew what she was about to do.

"You can't trust the gods," Isa beseeched her.

"I know. I don't trust them. I trust Tahlia." Kala held out an upturned palm expectantly.

Isa stared at it, stunned. This was madness. His life was not worth putting Tahlia in danger. He would rather die a thousand deaths than break his vow.

"Kala's right," the Water Goddess urged gently. "This is Tahlia's choice."

The words gutted his insides, exposing an entrail of failings. Years ago, he had not respected her choice. He had put his own selfish desires ahead of her wishes. If he refused to surrender the vial now, history would be repeating itself.

Kala waited patiently but Isa couldn't bring himself to do it. If he was no longer protecting Tahlia from her enemies, what was the purpose of him drawing breath? Kala must have recognized his incapacitation because she reached up and unclasped the vial from around his neck. Isa didn't stop her. The absence of its weight against his chest was haunting. It took all his willpower to stand there while Kala walked over to the God of Earth and Salt and dangled the necklace before him.

"Do we have a deal?"

"We do," the god smiled.

Kala dropped it into his hand and returned to stand between Isa and Ele.

The god settled the necklace around Samir's neck before he said, "Let's begin, witch."

Darius's gaze was riveted on the vial, his mouth still agape in nervous horror, but he managed to move his limbs towards the incantation bowl. He placed one of the wooden logs across the rim, and the Water Goddess passed him the parabolic mirror. He positioned the mirror to direct a ray of sunlight onto the log. Everyone seemed to hold their breath as they watched and waited, but within seconds, tendrils of smoke rose from the wood, white and wispy. Then a flame ignited.

Kala exhaled and shifted between her feet as if she were struggling to contain her fragile hope. The Water Goddess, however, was composed as she stood beside the incantation bowl and lifted her face to the cloudless blue sky. Water droplets formed from vapor in the air and dripped down into the bowl in singular drops of rain. It reminded Isa of the day that Tahlia had sat high in the saddle of her camel, claimed her new kingdom in front of her people, and then called on the Water Goddess to make it rain. Rain had poured from the sky like a heavy monsoon, and the crowds cheered for their beautiful queen, beloved by the gods.

Days later, the gods killed her.

The God of Earth and Salt stalked forward to stand opposite the Water Goddess. He stared down into the bowl with cool detachment before he held out his fist. Sand slipped through his fingers, refined and pure. It mixed with the water, a fine sludge forming.

"Your turn, witch," the god said impatiently.

Darius clutched his talismans and mumbled a silent prayer before he began citing a mantra. His voice was pitched so low Isa could barely make out the words. What words he could decipher didn't make any sense, but Isa didn't have time to contemplate it before blinding pain seized him.

Someone was ripping the veins out of his body. Pouring liquid fire down his throat. Cleansing his insides and melting his bones to ash. His mind fractured as his thoughts shattered into a million shards of onyx. There was no last thought. No final breath. Only the end.

CHAPTER TWENTY-FOUR

KALA

Kala threw herself over Isa's broad chest to listen to the rasp of breath escaping from his mouth. "He's breathing!"

Her heart was in her stomach and her stomach was clenched like a fist. She didn't know what to do. Isa had crashed to the earth like a mountain in a landslide. It was unnatural to see. He was the pillar of her world and yet he looked defeated, lying unconscious on the salt plains.

But he was not dead.

"He's alive." She repeated the words over and over again in an attempt to soothe herself.

Ele crouched down beside her, his nearness giving her a small measure of comfort. "Look at his tattoos."

Kala's focus shifted to Isa's arms, where his tattoos were no longer black. They were turquoise. They shimmered in the sunlight and moved beneath the surface of his skin like the ocean tide. The color of his skin was also changing, becoming lighter until it glowed with an almost golden hue. Kala recalled the golden coloring was due to the subaqueous sand beneath his skin. It was from the bottom of a deep pool in the Citadel, the womb of the Water Goddess's power, which she'd used to make the Naiab god-touched.

"And the knot." Sabine stood over Isa and pointed to the cord clutched in his hand.

Moments ago, it had been white but now it was black. Darius had said it would help unbind Isa from the curse. Had it really absorbed the black sand as it flushed from his system? Isa stirred, his head jerking back and forth as if he was experiencing sharp pains. Then he opened his eyes. Eyes that were no longer rimmed with ink.

Kala released a strangled sound of relief. "It worked. Isa you're cured!"

Shock collided with gratitude, and she couldn't hold back the tears that sprang to her eyes. She felt like she could burst out of her skin with joy and yet all she could do was cry.

Isa stared at her in dull confusion before his gaze moved past her to fix on the blazing sun in the sky. "I can't feel it," he breathed unsteadily. "It no longer burns me."

Kala wasn't sure what he was talking about, but she was elated because it meant that he felt *different*. The dark urges he'd battled for years without her knowing, the heightened emotions, the torturous agony; all of it would be gone. He would feel like himself again, if he even remembered what that felt like.

"You are Naiab once more," the Water Goddess said as she approached them, a pleased smile touching her lips.

Kala's joy tempered. She had been so focused on saving Isa's life that she hadn't realized the implications of what it would mean if he was cured. He could go home. To the Citadel. To his people. She wouldn't blame him if he chose to leave her. If that was his choice, she would let him go.

"Shift," Kala urged as she stood up, wiping at her damp cheeks with her sleeve.

Isa glanced up at her before he dissolved into sand. A pile of coarse, fine, golden sand sitting on a cracked salt-lined earth. The granules of golden sand began to move, rising up, swirling like a whirlwind until they changed shape and formed the profile of a man. Then Isa was standing before them, flesh and blood and bone, naked but alive, as if he'd been reborn.

Ele collected Isa's kurta from the ground and handed it to him. "You had us worried there for a second."

"You and I both know that if the curse hadn't broken, you would have killed me," Isa said as he pulled the kurta over his head.

Ele didn't deny it, nor did he look the least bit apologetic.

"And I wouldn't have stopped you," Isa added.

A look of understanding and respect passed between them.

Kala frowned disapprovingly. "No one is dying today."

"Not even the witch, it seems," Sabine remarked.

CHAPTER TWENTY-FOUR

They all turned to see Darius kneeling in the cracked earth next to the smoking incantation bowl, clutching his talismans. His face was gray, the kohl around his eyes smudged, and his body looked stiff as if he were waiting to be struck by lightning.

"Those things really do work," Sabine quipped.

The Water Goddess peered over at Darius as if he were being overly dramatic. "I told you that you might survive. The magic was weakened over time."

Darius's features turned indignant as he rose on shaking legs. "Each of these talismans once belonged to a witch. Only by channeling them did I have enough power. Otherwise, I would have ended up like my ancestor."

"We're glad you didn't and we're grateful for your help," Kala mediated. "When I return to my kingdom, I'll make sure you are rewarded."

"Does that mean I can go now?" Darius asked hopefully.

"Yes."

"But if you breathe a word of this to anyone, you *will* end up like your ancestor," Ele warned.

"Take your bowl with you," Isa added.

Much to everyone's surprise, Darius braced his knees wide and lifted the bowl into his skinny arms.

"No offense but I hope to never see any of you again," he grunted before slowly walking off in the direction of the city.

"Well, that was mildly entertaining." The God of Earth and Salt casually stepped forward. "Your kingdom is cured. The curse of the Black Sands is broken."

Kala almost couldn't believe it. She probably wouldn't believe it until she saw her kingdom with her own eyes. Even then, it would take some getting used to. The Kingdom of the Black Sands would no longer have black sand. Sabine had been right when she pointed out that Kala's kingdom relied on trade to survive. Without the black sand, she would need to find another way to sustain her kingdom. But not today. Today, she was simply grateful that the curse was broken and Isa was alive.

The God of Earth and Salt ran his fingers over the teardrop vial around his neck. "I will borrow this vessel a while longer before I return him."

Kala's attention snapped to him. "What? That wasn't the deal. Where are you taking him?"

"That's my business, mortal," the god replied dismissively before turning to the Water Goddess. "We will meet again very soon, goddess. These events will provide for interesting discussion at the trial."

The Water Goddess's expression soured, but she didn't say a word as the god followed the witch towards the city. Kala watched him go, helpless to stop him. The god had no reason to harm Samir, she reminded herself. He would be fine. Then again, when had the gods ever needed a reason to harm mortals?

"Trial?" Isa directed the question to the Water Goddess, his tone low and dangerous.

The Water Goddess composed herself, folding her hands in front of her. "Now that you are Naiab again, I must ask something of you. Return to the Citadel. Protect the Shahri. Support her and help her lead our people."

"Why?" Isa probed.

Her tone was grave as she said, "I might not be able to return."

Kala's lips parted in shock. "Return from where?"

"The higher gods have called for a trial."

"There are higher gods?" Sabine looked to each of them, confused.

"All lesser gods were human once," Isa explained. "At the moment of their mortal deaths, the gods chose them to ascend to divinity and granted them dominion over a realm in the mortal world. Unlike lesser gods, the higher gods have always been celestial beings."

The Water Goddess nodded subtly. She'd obviously shared these secrets with Isa long ago, just like she'd told him about Tahlia and how to trap a god.

"Higher gods existed before time or space or even thought," the goddess continued. "After creating the world and everything in it, the higher gods abandoned it to the lesser gods. They do not interfere in the mortal world like lesser gods do. They control vast realms, one of which is the divine realm."

"And they are more powerful than lesser gods," Sabine deduced.

"Yes. The divine court has only ever assembled on rare occasions throughout history. Its sole purpose is to bring lesser gods to justice."

"What kind of justice?" Ele's brows furrowed.

"Annihilation."

Kala froze. "You mean death."

"Gods can't die," Sabine scoffed.

"No mortal can kill a god. But lesser gods can be destroyed by higher gods," the goddess corrected. "It is rare but it has happened."

It was incomprehensible. A divine, an immortal, ceasing to exist. Their realm forsaken. Would they even become a star like mortals? Or would they simply become nothing?

Isa's face hardened. "Why is a trial being called now?"

"The higher gods have learned of Tahlia's crimes."

"Crimes?" Kala exclaimed in horror. "What crimes?"

"Rejecting her divination as a mortal. Hiding from the gods. Trapping a god and imprisoning him. Interfering with the realm of another divine."

"By saving my life," Isa muttered under his breath.

"The higher gods have been watching her. Collecting evidence."

Kala's eyes widened in fear. "We just gave the vial to the God of Earth and Salt! It will incriminate her!"

"And she just helped break the curse of the Black Sands," Sabine pointed out, before turning to the Water Goddess. "But so did you."

"Yes, I did. Which is why I might not return. I am not sure how many lesser gods will be on trial or how much the higher gods know, but my crimes are many."

Kala's thoughts raced as dread pooled like acid in her gut. The Water Goddess had given powers to the Naiab and shared secrets of the divine realm with Isa. She had also shared those secrets with

Tahlia, helped her escape from being sacrificed to the gods as a child, and assisted her in staying hidden from those who hunted her. The Water Goddess had once said that if there was one person the gods wanted to punish more than Tahlia, it was the informant who had helped her. If the higher gods knew the truth, the Water Goddess would be condemned.

"A reckoning." Kala recalled the goddess's words and then another realization hit her. "An island. Is the trial happening on an island?"

The Water Goddess sighed. "The Divine Isle. A sacred place here in the mortal world."

Ele raised a brow at Kala. "How did you know that?"

"I ... thought I saw it when Tahlia inhabited me. The image wasn't clear. But she was scared. It made me wonder what could possibly scare a divine."

"The island has various protections which make it undiscoverable, except by those who already know of its existence. Those protections are why Tahlia has only been able to see fragments of the future."

"Wait." Kala stilled. "Tahlia sees the future?"

"Do you still not understand her divine power? She is the Goddess of Fate."

Kala stared back at her, stunned to silence. The Goddess of Fate. It made perfect sense. A divine's realm of power was often linked to what held the most significance for them during their mortal life. Tahlia had spent her mortal life running from her fate, unable to change it and yet resisting it at every turn. The gods were being cruel. Giving her the ability to rewrite the fates of others when she had been powerless to change her own.

"I guess that explains why you're so hard to kill," Sabine deadpanned.

Kala narrowed her eyes at her but Sabine had a point. Kala knew Tahlia watched over her, guided her at times, but had Tahlia been actively changing her fate?

"No," Isa said sternly, as if he could read her thoughts. "Tahlia told me the gods were trying to force her to submit to her divinity but she refused to wield her power. She may know the future, but that doesn't mean she's altering it."

"Except when she saved your life," Ele remarked.

A tense silence stretched between them as they absorbed the uncomfortable truth. Tahlia loathed what she had become, she'd resisted her divinity even in her immortal existence, and yet when Isa's life had hung in the balance, she'd relented.

Kala looked up at Isa, heavy emotion lacing her voice. "She still loves you."

Isa's expression remained guarded as he asked, "Where is Tahlia now?"

"I don't know," the Water Goddess admitted. "She tries not to draw attention to herself. But she cannot hope to escape the trial. All lesser gods will be drawn to it by a force beyond our control."

"We have to save her," Kala insisted, though the words fell flat, even to her own ears.

CHAPTER TWENTY-FOUR

Everyone knew mortals could not defy the gods and expect to live. Confronting a court of higher gods and lesser gods was pure insanity. And yet Kala couldn't just stand by and do nothing.

"I'm coming with you to the Divine Isle," Isa said to the Water Goddess, his tone leaving no room for argument.

"You mean *we're* coming with you," Kala corrected him.

Isa shook his head. "No. You have to return to your kingdom."

"I'm not going anywhere except on a boat," Kala retorted.

"There is nothing to gain from either of you trying to save her," the goddess asserted. "At best, you will die with her. At worst, your presence will prove her guilt and seal her sentence."

"The fact that they've called for a trial means she is already condemned," Isa pointed out. "I will not let her die alone."

"She would not want you to waste your life. Or break your vow to Kala."

"I release you from your vow," Kala said promptly.

"Thank you," Isa replied, his gaze never leaving the Water Goddess. "I am free to make my own choice and I've made it. Will you take me with you or not?"

The goddess weighed his words for a moment before she nodded in reluctant acceptance.

"Great, I'm coming too. And before you open your mouth." Kala pointed a finger at Isa. "Don't."

Isa clenched his jaw as if the words might burst forth of their own volition, but then he looked to Ele in silent question.

"Wherever Kala goes, I go," Ele said.

Kala thought she saw a flash of approval ghost Isa's features but it quickly disappeared.

"You're all fucking suicidal, you know that? Besides, Captain, aren't you forgetting your promise to return me safely to the Thaka?" Sabine crossed her arms over her chest.

"That's exactly where we're going if we want to get on a boat," Ele replied. "Henri's kingdom controls the coastline. The only problem is that nothing and no one leaves or arrives on the shores of Merovia without his knowledge. And if Isa sets one foot in Henri's kingdom, he'll kill him."

"If Kala sets one foot inside Henri's kingdom and my family finds out who she is, they'll kill *her*," Sabine countered.

"Do you honestly think I believe you haven't told them already?" Kala shot back.

Sabine glared at her. "Believe what you want."

"We go in disguise," Isa suggested. "Ele will get us past the border and Sabine will smuggle us onto a ship. We'll be gone before anyone gets a chance to be discovered and killed."

Sabine didn't look convinced. Ele also seemed unsettled by the plan. Kala knew it would be hard for him to sneak around and keep secrets from Henri, but the last thing they needed was to dig up old grudges from the past.

"Will you do it?" Ele directed the question to Sabine.

Sabine nervously glanced between them before she scowled. "Fine. But you all owe me a huge favor."

ELE

Embers danced and snapped as everyone sat around the campfire eating dinner. The sun had already melted from the sky, taking with it the blistering heat of the day and leaving dry winds in its wake. The camels knelt in the cool sand nearby, chewing lazily on their feed. They had made good traveling time over the past few days and would reach the border of Henri's kingdom tomorrow night. Guilt scratched beneath the surface of Ele's thoughts but he tried to ignore it. Henri would understand his decision not to tell him about Isa crossing into his kingdom. Or Tahlia facing a divine trial that threatened her immortal existence. Or the fact that he was about to challenge the higher and lesser gods in their own court and would likely not survive to tell the tale.

Henri would understand. Eventually.

And if by some miracle Ele survived, he would ask for forgiveness. Surely after everything, Henri wouldn't deny him that.

Ele released an uneasy breath and glanced across the fire at Sabine, who was quietly eating her lentils. Ever since they'd left the Kingdom of the Salt Plains she'd been strangely subdued. He hadn't heard a snarky comment or attempt at flirtation in days. She was obviously apprehensive about returning to the Thaka but Ele wasn't sure how to interpret that. Was she feeling guilty about hiding Kala's identity from her family? Or guilty about already telling her family about Kala's identity and setting a trap for her?

Perhaps she wasn't feeling guilty at all, just anxious about her odds of survival.

Sabine was no fool. She would know that if she betrayed them, Ele would kill her. As for her family, not even the most formidable cartel in Merovia could hope to survive against a Naiab warrior and a god-touched. She would not risk it. Yet, if her family found out that she was keeping valuable information from them, she would either lose her place in the Thaka's hierarchy or she would lose her life.

Isa finished his bowl of lentils and cleaned the dish before silently heading in the direction of his tent. It wasn't unusual for the warrior to keep to himself, but even he seemed singularly focused on the task at hand. It didn't help that no one had heard from Tahlia in days. The Water Goddess had also gone dormant. They didn't know if it was by choice or if something had happened to them. Ele could only hope that when the time came to board a ship, the Water Goddess would appear to chart their course. He had a feeling that if she didn't, Isa would be desperate enough to set sail anyway.

"You're unusually quiet," Kala remarked as she observed Sabine from across the fire.

Dema exchanged a look with Ele that implied a tinder had just been struck.

"Did you pack wine this time?" Sabine replied. "Or the last remaining balgarum in the country?"

"No."

"Then I'll pass on sober story time."

Ele spooned some lentils into his mouth, hoping the conversation would die a natural death.

"You must be looking forward to returning home," Kala probed.

"I don't know, I've become rather fond of the palace life. I think I might miss it."

"You've been away for a long time. Will they even welcome you back?"

Sabine met her stare with a sarcastic look. "Are you worried about me, sister?"

"Just curious. And don't call me that."

"I'm touched." Sabine mockingly placed a hand over her heart before dropping it back into her lap. "I assure you I'll live. At least longer than you will."

Ele stiffened at the brazen threat.

Sabine's eyes darted between them before adding, "I'm not the one challenging the will of the gods in their own court."

Kala's features softened in reflection. "When you love someone, there's nothing you wouldn't do to protect them."

Ele stared at her for a moment. The glow of the fire illuminated the freckles on her olive toned cheeks and her eyes held a faraway look in them, as if she were lost in memories. He wondered what she was thinking about, or rather who she was thinking about, because when she uttered those words all he could think about was her. There was nothing in this life or the next that he was not prepared to do to keep her safe. He had always felt that way since the moment they'd met. For her, he would face any enemy, endure any hardship, outlast time, and outlive death. As his closest friend, he had always loved her but now his feelings felt changed. Deeper.

He wasn't sure what to do about that. If he should do anything at all. It was pointless to consider the future given that they most likely would not survive to see it. Still, Ele couldn't help wondering what life would look like if they returned to Merovia triumphant. Logic told him that he would remain in Henri's kingdom as Captain of the Guard, serving his king and living the life he had always aspired to.

Yet, the thought of watching Kala return to her kingdom was unbearable. It would feel like history was repeating itself, ripping his heart out of his chest, leaving him utterly destroyed. Who knew how long it would be before they saw each other again? In that time, would she find someone else to give her heart to? Perhaps she would return to Samir. Ele had to admit Samir was a good man, he might even be worthy of her, but the thought of anyone else claiming her heart or giving her pleasure made Ele feel murderous.

"I wouldn't know," Sabine replied.

Ele leaned closer to Kala. "Can I talk to you for a moment? In private?"

Kala's eyes searched his face, concerned, before they both discarded their bowls and stood up. Ele led the way to Kala's tent and held the flap open for her to walk through. He was very aware they'd lost all pretense of discretion. A glance over his shoulder told him that Dema at least had the decency to avert her gaze and pretend not to notice, but Sabine's eyes had followed them the entire way.

Ele stepped inside the tent and grasped Kala's arm, pulling her into his chest as his lips crashed against hers. She released a small sound of surprise, but then her mouth opened to him. Relief flooded his system, morphing into instant arousal. They hadn't had a moment alone together since he'd apologized for being a camel's ass, so he wasn't sure whether she would let him kiss her, but she welcomed his touch like nothing had ruptured between them at all.

It had been far too long. He'd almost forgotten the taste of her. Ele explored her mouth with his tongue, eagerly consuming the softness of her lips while his hands roamed the curves of her body. Her breasts were full and perfect, nipples peaked beneath her clothes. The need that had simmered just beneath the surface surged through him like a sudden desert storm. He wanted to claim every inch of her with his mouth, sucking and licking until she whimpered in his arms. He wanted to study the arc of her backside and the slope of her hips. He wanted to learn all the ways to make her come so that she trusted only him to make her body sing.

Kala cupped his face between her hands, slowing him down but deepening the kiss. She wanted this just as much as he did, wanted to savor it. He could feel it in the way she pressed herself against him. In the tender intensity of her touch. He was sure that if he put his hand between her thighs she wouldn't want him to slow down. His cock broadened at the thought of her breathy moans. He wanted to plunge himself inside her, to lap at her center until she screamed his name. They fit together so perfectly. Anyone else would feel wrong. They belonged together. They always had.

"What is this about?" Kala asked between breathless kisses.

"I've missed you."

"I've missed you too, but this is reckless. If Isa finds out—"

"I don't care." Ele dipped his head and set his mouth to her neck, trailing kisses down her throat. "What's he going to do? Kill me? I'm god-touched."

Kala pressed her palms against his chest, pushing him back until he was forced to look at her. "Be serious."

"I am. I don't care who knows about us. I just want to be with you."

"Is that because we're facing annihilation by the gods?" She smirked.

"No. It's because I can't imagine not being with you, not even for one day. Never again."

Kala stilled in his arms, her expression slowly falling. "What are you saying?"

What *was* he saying? The words seemed to be tumbling out of his heart, bypassing his head, and his mouth was doing nothing to stop them.

"When we started this, you said you wouldn't fall in love with me. That you have your duties and I have mine and this was just sex. Do you still feel that way?"

A line deepened between her brows as she tried to read his face. "I—Is that how you feel?"

She was scared, he realized. Normally Kala was fearless, far braver than he could ever be. This time, though, he would be the brave one.

"I've never been in love before so I have nothing to compare it to, but all I know is that when I see you, it's like nothing else in the world matters except you. When I'm with you, I feel like I'm where I'm meant to be. I don't want to write you letters anymore. I don't want to wonder about what you're doing. I want to know, every day, that you're happy. That you're safe. That you're mine."

Kala stared at him for a moment, stunned, before averting her gaze. She refused to look at him. His stomach plummeted in panic. He hadn't meant to say all those things and yet he meant every single word.

"Kala, please say something."

She opened her mouth but nothing came out. Then she cleared her throat, determinedly. "I wasn't expecting this."

"Neither was I, but I can't deny it."

"Sometimes feelings get the best of us and we lose sight of what's real."

Ele frowned. "What's that supposed to mean?"

She looked up at him, sadness and uncertainty clouding her eyes. "You would never leave Henri."

Not so long ago he would have agreed with her but now he wasn't so sure. Staying or leaving, there was no painless choice. But being with Kala meant more to him than any title or reputation or childhood dream. Henri wouldn't hold him back. He would understand Ele's choice because he knew love. The love Henri shared with Malik was truly rare. It was probably the reason why Ele had never fallen in love. He hadn't believed that he would ever be lucky enough to find a love like theirs.

"And even if you did," Kala added to his silence, "I would be scared you would resent me for it later."

"I could never resent you."

"You say that now." Her words fell away and quiet settled between them, the kind of quiet where hearts fracture in stillness.

"So where does that leave us?" Ele asked, his voice tight.

"I don't know," Kala admitted. "Let's survive defying the gods and then we can talk about the future."

Ele wasn't sure what to say. A part of him didn't want to let it go. He wanted to convince her that this was the right thing for both of them. But he couldn't force her to feel what he was feeling, nor could he promise her that everything would be all right. He shifted his weight awkwardly between his feet. Now that he'd just bared the most vulnerable parts of himself only to be let down gently, Ele didn't know what to do.

"Let's get some sleep," Kala suggested. "Stay with me?"

"Always."

Ele turned around to give Kala privacy as she changed into her nightshift. She lay down on the bedroll as he pulled his kurta over his head but kept his pants on. He slid his dagger beneath the pillow they shared as he lay down beside her. The bedroll was not designed for two people so half of Ele's body was on the desert floor. As they stared up at the canvas ceiling, their arms brushed. Kala's skin was so soft it made him itch to touch her. He kept his focus ahead and his hands locked beside him by sheer will, but he couldn't mistake the sound of Kala's breath becoming uneven. As much as he wanted to believe it was because she was thinking about him, secretly longing for him to take her, he knew she probably wasn't.

So much had happened in the past few days, everyone was feeling on edge. Before they left the Kingdom of the Salt Plains, Kala had sent a message to Zaynab to let her know the curse had been broken. They hadn't had time to wait around for a reply, so Kala didn't know whether Samir had made it back home safely or whether the God of Earth and Salt was still occupying him. Ele knew Kala had to be worried about him. She would also be thinking about how to sustain her kingdom now that she could no longer produce onyx wares and grow balgarum in the black soil.

Tomorrow night would also be playing on her mind. He couldn't imagine what it would be like for her to return to Henri's kingdom, to walk the familiar city streets again after a decade. She never would have returned by choice, he knew that. Not only was it too dangerous, it was too painful for her. She may have some good memories but most would be violent and traumatic.

Then there was Tahlia, the prospect of what might happen to her, to all of them. The last time they tried to save Tahlia it had ended in failure. Now it could end all their lives. From the moment they set sail, the mission could be doomed. Kala was willing to give up everything she had, her kingdom, her life, on the chance that she might be able to save Tahlia. But she was responsible for so many other lives. The decision would be weighing on her.

Ele shifted to lie on his side, facing her. Kala glanced over at him before following suit. They stared at each other in the dull light of the oil lamp, almost nose to nose, but they didn't say anything. They were simply content to share breath, and space, and silence. They had often fallen asleep like this as children, finding comfort in each other's presence. A peace they couldn't find anywhere else.

Ele remembered how he had slept by her side when Kala fought for her life after her family tried to kill her. He recalled how his last thought, after Kareem stabbed him in the chest, was of Kala's sweet smile. There were so many times in their lives when they should have died and yet they'd lived. Because they were survivors. They held on to each other, even in the darkness when all hope was lost.

Kala reached for him and placed their joined hands to rest on the pillow in the space between their faces. He knew what she wanted him to see, what she couldn't find the words to say. She was there with him. She always would be. Ele tilted his head forward to press a light kiss to her forehead. Satisfied, Kala closed her eyes, surrendering herself to sleep. They would live through this. He would accept no other outcome. And afterwards, he would never leave her side again. Because nothing in this life was guaranteed, except for the way he felt about her.

CHAPTER TWENTY-FIVE

KALA

They waited for nightfall before approaching the border to Henri's kingdom. Kala maintained careful watch from her camel as Ele handed an official letter to the border soldier. Despite immediately recognizing Ele and addressing him as Captain, the soldier dutifully checked the document. Then he lifted his oil lamp higher as if it could help illuminate the rest of the faces in the caravan. Anyone could see that they were not soldiers but he wouldn't be able to discern more because their headscarves were wrapped tightly around their faces, only revealing the whites of their eyes.

The soldier was clearly curious, but with Henri's seal on the parchment, and without any reason to detain them, he waved them through. Ele led the way and Kala and Dema guided their camels to follow in single file. The animals were weary after traveling all day, their steps heavier than usual and their pace slow. Fatigue was also beginning to settle over Kala. It felt like a weight dulling her senses and pulling at her limbs.

On the outskirts of the city, they stopped to dismount from the camels. Carrying as many supplies as they could, they continued on foot. It would be odd for wealthy merchants to ride their camels through the city at night, and the last thing they wanted to do was to draw attention to themselves. At this late hour, the streets would be quiet but the meyhane's would be bustling. It wasn't worth the risk.

"We should buy more supplies," Dema said as she adjusted the saddlebags she was carrying.

"There are no night markets in the city," Ele advised. "What we have will have to last us."

What he didn't say was how long it would have to last them for. Nobody knew where the Divine Isle was so nobody knew how long it would take to get there.

"I'll see what I can get delivered to the ship," Sabine muttered.

Kala looked over at her, surprised by the kind offer. If Sabine felt Kala's eyes on her, she didn't show it. Her focus never wavered from their surroundings as they made their way through the city. Some streets were pitched into darkness, whilst others had lanterns strung overhead between buildings. The streets were familiar to Kala and yet they looked different from her memories. Narrower. Aged.

She'd been a girl when she last ran along these roads. Bare feet, tattered clothes, wide eyes sunken into skin and bones. Pain was as constant as breathing. Danger waited at every corner, predators

CHAPTER TWENTY-FIVE 437

and prey both trying to survive. No one could be trusted, yet there were familial obligations and rules of the Thaka which had to be obeyed. Mistakes were paid for in blood.

Sabine halted suddenly, her wary eyes scanning the area. "Wait here. I'll be back soon."

Dema immediately put her load down, grateful for the reprieve, but everyone else instinctively moved to surround Sabine.

"What do you mean, wait here?" Kala challenged. "Where are you going?"

"To the Thaka. I think it's best you don't come, sister."

"Don't call me that."

"Why do you need to go to the Thaka?" Isa demanded.

Sabine arched a sardonic eyebrow. "To organize a ship, sandman."

Ele exchanged a look with Kala that mirrored her own thoughts. This was dangerous. Sabine could not be trusted.

"I'll come with you," Ele offered, dumping his bags on the ground.

"Because the Captain of the Guard tailing me wouldn't be suspicious at all," Sabine drawled.

"That was the deal, remember? I promised to protect you with my life and guarantee your safe return to the Thaka. I'm only trying to keep my word."

"I'm going by myself," Sabine replied curtly before turning to Kala and holding her hand out expectantly. "The money."

Kala stared at her defiantly.

"No money, no ship," Sabine taunted.

Before they left the Salt Plains, Sabine had warned her that she would need money to bribe her contacts and secure the ship. Kala had to ask Inaya for a loan. Reluctantly, Kala retrieved the small purse of coin and thumped it into her palm.

Sabine looked inside and sneered. "That's it?"

"We're wealthy merchants, not royalty. Anything more would raise suspicion."

Sabine sighed but didn't argue, she simply tucked the purse into her belt next to her scythe blade and waved her hand at them to move. Kala stepped aside, letting her through, and Sabine crossed the street. Anxiety crawled up Kala's spine as she watched her disappear down a shadowed alleyway. It didn't feel right. Sabine could be leaving them stranded or alerting her family to their whereabouts, and they were expected to just wait there to be attacked. Her instincts screamed at her to run. Kala shifted her feet restlessly as her eyes searched the shadows.

"It's all right," Isa's voice was low and soothing, as if he were speaking to a spooked horse. "Whatever happens now, she won't win."

"Everything she said makes sense," Ele pointed out. "We wouldn't be able to just walk up to one of the ships at the dock and commandeer it."

Dema leaned against a wall, her bags dumped at her feet. "She hasn't betrayed you so far. She found the witch."

"Everything she's done has been to ensure her own survival," Kala said as she began to pace. If she couldn't run, she at least needed to keep moving. "Now that we're in her territory, the balance of power has shifted. There is nothing stopping her from killing us."

"She can try." Isa's tone was fatally calm.

"And if she does, she dies," Ele added.

As Kala continued to pace, her attention caught on a building that rose above the flat roofs of the city. It was framed by tall, round towers. Magnificent round domes featured on each corner, shimmering beneath the moonlight. She stopped and stared at it. A deep sadness settled into her weary bones. She had only lived in the palace for a few months before leaving Henri's kingdom. It had not been long enough to feel like home but it had been safe. The first safe place she had ever known. Within its magnificent walls, she'd learned how to trust. She'd chosen her family. People who cared for her and would risk their lives to protect her.

"You can see them if you want to," Isa said softly as he stood behind her. "I know you miss them."

She did. She hadn't realized just how much until this moment. The knowledge that she could walk over to the palace and demand to see the king pulled at the edges of her restraint. But it wasn't that simple. Kala wondered what Henri and Malik would say if they learned Tahlia had ascended to divinity but was about to stand trial for crimes that could end her immortal existence. It would rip open old wounds and shatter whatever peace they'd found over the past ten years.

Ever the strategist, Malik would think their current plan of confronting the gods in their own court foolish. He would quietly calculate every possible outcome before concluding that they were all doomed. Leading with his heart, Henri wouldn't even weigh the consequences. Grief and guilt would steer him like a broken compass. He would join their mission without a second thought for his own life and if he did, Malik would refuse to leave his side. Kala already felt the weight of everyone's lives on her shoulders. She could not bear to add two more. Besides, it would put Isa at risk and she refused to let her emotions put him in danger.

"I'll see them when we return," she replied and resumed pacing.

There was nothing else to do except wait. Minutes crawled into hours and Kala's patience frayed like her nerves. Dema had long since fallen asleep, slumped against the pavement with her back to the wall, but Isa and Ele remained alert, guarding their position. When something flickered in the shadow across the street, they both tensed, taking up a defensive stance.

Sabine appeared out of the darkness and hurried over to them. "It's done. Follow me."

Kala looked to Ele and Isa, a question in her eyes, but they had no choice. Kala gently shook Dema awake and helped her shoulder the rest of the saddle bags. They followed Sabine through the city until they arrived at the docks. The scent of brine filled Kala's nostrils and the hushed lapping of the tide met her ears. The port was quiet except for a few of the king's soldiers patrolling, but they were easy enough to evade.

Dozens of ships were moored along the coastline, mostly merchant vessels if she had to guess. Sabine led them to a medium sized cargo vessel with a long, narrow hull and two lateen sails. It looked fast and light, perfect for smuggling goods. A man was waiting for them at the bottom of the gangplank. Kala wondered if he was the captain. Sabine exchanged quiet words with him before waving at them to board the ship.

Kala's stomach clenched and her hands started to sweat but her feet propelled her forward. It wasn't just the prospect of betrayal that had her gut churning. The last time she was on a boat, she'd been kidnapped by slavers. She'd tried to fight them as they wrestled her up the plank onto the ship but as a child she was no match for their strength. They'd dragged her onboard and then shoved her below deck, down into a dark, damp hull filled with unwashed bodies. The floor had been slick with human waste, the smell almost unbearable. They'd secured an iron chain around her skinny neck, linking her to the other people they'd snatched from the streets, and fastened the end of the chain to the hull of the boat. The moment the men left, locking the hatch behind them, she knew there was no hope of escape.

Kala tripped on the lip of the ship as she stepped onboard but Ele grabbed her elbow, steadying her. Her hands were shaking. She tried to regain some composure as she glanced around the deck. A skeleton crew manned the ship, most of them curled up asleep beneath thin blankets. The few that were awake glanced at them with disinterest before returning to their duties.

"What's wrong?" Ele whispered in her ear.

Kala shook her head. She didn't trust herself to speak. It was taking everything she had just to keep breathing. Keep walking. Everything would be fine. She repeated it like a mantra. These people were smugglers, not slavers. Besides, she wasn't that helpless girl anymore, nor was she alone. Isa and Ele would keep her safe. *She* would keep herself safe.

The captain led them across the deck and stopped in front of a door. When he opened it and gestured for them to go inside, Kala could see stairs descending into the bowels of the ship. She went rigid. Sabine forged ahead of her and climbed down a couple of steps but then threw a look over her shoulder, her expression inquisitive.

"I—I can't," Kala stuttered.

"Move quickly now," the man urged gruffly. "You don't want to be spotted by the king's soldiers."

She didn't but she couldn't move.

"I can't," Kala panted, her breaths coming in short and sharp.

Sabine turned on her heel, climbing up a step. "It's fine. You don't have to."

The shriek of steel ripped through the air as hands suddenly seized Kala and flung her down the stairs. She slammed into Sabine, sending them both tumbling. Pain exploded everywhere as she crashed into the wall, cracked her head against the wooden steps, and slammed into the floor. She wasn't sure where Sabine had landed. Kala lay still for a moment, taking mental stock of her injuries, but she didn't feel like she'd broken anything. The sound of metal clashing up on deck sliced through her thoughts.

They'd been ambushed.

Betrayed.

Sabine.

CHAPTER TWENTY-FIVE

Kala opened her eyes in panic. The hull of the ship was bathed in darkness, but there was at least one torch lit because she could see the shadowy figures of the men who surrounded her. Before she could move, someone kicked her in the ribs. The force of it sent her sliding across the floor as the crack of bone vibrated in her ears.

"Don't!"

Another snap echoed in the space but Kala didn't feel the blow. Sabine. Adrenaline flooded her body, masking the pain and sharpening her mind. She covertly palmed a hidden dagger and tried to scramble to her feet but the men attacked, pushing her back to the floor. They punched her in the face with their fists and hit her body with blunt weapons she couldn't see. There were too many of them. Kala slashed out, her blade tearing skin, and the men cursed as they retreated a few steps.

Kala was on her feet in an instant but she was still surrounded. Sabine was sprawled on the floor ahead of her, blood dripping from her nose and temple. A man glared down at her, Sabine's twin scythe blades in his hands. There were at least a dozen of them cramped into the space but Kala only recognized two.

Her heart atrophied as her lungs screamed in silence.

In her nightmares, they were a decade younger but unbelievably strong. Now they had aged but it looked like time hadn't robbed them of their strength. Or their cruelty. She recognized the hatred in their faces. It had been burned into her memories. Their violence was a scar that would never truly heal. It still bled crimson tears just beneath the surface.

"Get up, traitor." Her father kicked Sabine in the stomach and she spat blood onto the floor. "Did you really think we wouldn't find out?"

It was happening again. Fear glazed over Kala, holding her limbs hostage. She suddenly felt incredibly small. She was strong but not strong enough. She was fast but she hadn't been able to escape them. The slavers. Her family. They would break every bone in her body, wash the floor with her blood, and discard her like she was worthless. She was Queen of the Black Sands but to them she would always be a traitor.

Despite the weeping slash across his abdomen, her uncle took a menacing step towards her. Kala knew she should move, defend herself, but she couldn't feel her body and there was nowhere to run.

"I knew you would." Sabine pushed up a little as her father reared his arm back to land a savage punch.

Kala's hand moved before she could think, her dagger soaring through the air to nail her father's palm. A scream of agony and rage tore from his lungs. Sabine used the moment to launch to her feet. She ripped the dagger out of her father's hand only to slash it across his throat. Blood sprayed as the other men charged at her, but Sabine fought like a wildcat, screaming a furious battle cry.

"You bitch!" Her uncle lunged for Kala, but she dodged his blow instinctively and palmed her second hidden blade.

It was a brawl, dirty and vicious. She had never fought in such a confined space before. Certainly not against multiple assailants. There was no room for strategy, only speed, and the desperate will to survive. Kala lashed out, kicking and stabbing, frantically trying to withstand every blow they rained down on her. She could not lose her footing. The moment she crumpled to the floor, she was dead.

Hands seized her wrist and twisted violently, wrenching a scream from her throat. The dagger fell from her broken wrist. Kala spun around, searching for anything she could use as a weapon. Crates were lined up behind her. She ripped off the lid to one and plunged her hand inside. Seeds. Her heart sunk but she grabbed a handful and threw it in the men's faces. They grasped at their eyes, momentarily blinded, and she seized the opportunity to barrel past them. Something heavy hit her in the back of the head, sending her slamming into the floor.

"Kala!"

She felt desperate hands grab her kaftan and roughly drag her back a short distance. Her vision swam when she tried to lift her head. Sabine was standing in front of her, a single scythe in her hand, ready to defend them both. But there were too many men and they had them surrounded, brandishing an array of weapons. Kala tried to rise but vertigo washed over her, anchoring her to the floor. She'd been hit hard, she was in no condition to fight.

Her sister was defending her. The thought stumbled into her mind. Her sister was going to die defending her.

Wood splintered. It sounded far away but then the pounding of feet downstairs filled the hull. A song of steel echoed off the walls as the fight erupted anew. Sabine held her ground, shielding Kala, ready to cut down anyone who dared to come close to them. Kala reached for Sabine's ankle. It was all she could manage, the only comfort she could give her.

"Hold on, your friends have come for you," Sabine said without tearing her watchful gaze from the brawl.

Consciousness kept slipping through Kala's fingers but she gripped it tight, holding on like Sabine told her to. Then came sudden silence. She looked around, her vision dazed as she took in the sight of utter carnage. Bodies lay torn and broken, strewn across the wooden floor. The stench of blood was thick in the air. Everyone had been slaughtered. The men who terrorized her dreams, whose violent hands were still imprinted beneath her skin, no longer drew breath in this world.

She couldn't believe it, despite seeing the evidence with her own eyes. Perhaps that's why she couldn't look away, not even when a tall figure casually strode over and crouched down a careful distance away from her.

"My queen." He held his hand out to her.

Kala's gaze drifted to the outstretched hand before lifting to him. She expected to see Ele but instead she gasped. Kala crawled across the blood-stained floor and flung herself into his arms. He caught her, pulling her into a fierce embrace, a safe harbor from the destruction around them.

"Henri," she whimpered into his shoulder as he caressed the back of her head tenderly.

"This is not how I pictured us meeting again," Henri said, his voice heavy with emotion.

"If we had visited her for her birthday like I suggested, all of this could have been avoided," came another voice.

"Malik!" Kala pulled away just enough to see Malik standing behind Henri, a warm smile on his face.

It faded to concern at the sight of her. "Henri, she needs a healer."

Henri's eyes swept over her, quietly assessing each wound, his expression growing more grim with each one. "We'll get you to the palace. You'll be safe there."

"Oh, another palace," Sabine chimed. "I always wondered what it looked like inside."

Malik cocked his head at Sabine as Henri helped Kala stand. "Who is this?"

Kala glanced over at Sabine and held her gaze for a moment. "My sister."

Malik's blade was at Sabine's throat before she could lift her scythe. "Seems we missed one. Shall I kill her for you?"

"Rude," Sabine spat.

"Not yet," Kala replied. "I want to hear what she has to say. Where's Ele?"

"Cleaning up his mess," Henri growled.

"Please don't be angry at him." Kala leaned heavily on Henri's arm as he helped her climb the stairs. "It was my fault."

"I'll determine whose fault it was," Henri replied sternly.

Malik escorted Sabine behind them, his shamshir never leaving her throat. When they stepped out onto the deck of the ship, Kala's lips parted in shock. It seemed like her father had brought all the men at his disposal to ensure that she wouldn't escape with her life. The battle had clearly been fierce, but Henri's soldiers were already gathering the bodies into piles, clearing away the massacre. Now she understood why Ele had not simply used his gift. There were too many witnesses. It would be impossible to explain to Henri and his soldiers why their enemies had suddenly dropped dead in front of them.

Kala's attention caught on a figure as she slowly came out from hiding behind a set of stairs leading up to the helm. Dema was visibly shaking.

"Dema, are you all right?" Kala would have run over to her except her head was still throbbing and her balance was not to be trusted.

Dema nodded and staggered over to them, making her way around the strewn bodies. Kala grabbed her hand and held it tight in reassurance.

Dema noticed Kala's other hand was hanging limp at her side. "Are you?"

"I'm fine. It's not my first broken bone."

"You're bleeding." Dema reached behind to touch her head.

Kala winced. "Or my first head wound."

"Kala." Ele rushed over to her, his eyes wide with fear as he assessed her for fatal wounds.

"Where were you, god-touched? We almost died!" Sabine spat, despite Malik's blade still at her throat.

Ele's eyes darkened with murderous intent. "You're the one who betrayed us!"

"Wrong. I didn't have to. You're all incredibly naïve. Nothing happens in Merovia that my family doesn't know about. When I didn't return weeks ago, they would have looked into it. And the moment we crossed the border back into the kingdom, they would have been alerted."

"You knew they would attack us," Kala deduced, even as her vision started to blur at the edges.

She leaned heavily against Henri, and he wrapped an arm around her waist, holding her upright.

"Of course. But I also knew that King Henri would be informed of his Captain's arrival and would send his soldiers to watch us."

"How did you know that?" Dema pressed.

"Because Inaya would have sent King Malik a pigeon the moment we left the Kingdom of the Salt Plains."

Kala, Ele, and Dema glanced over at Malik, who tilted his head in reluctant confirmation.

"Betrayed by one of your own." Sabine flashed a smug smile. "I knew that if my family made a move, King Henri's soldiers would retaliate."

Kala furrowed her eyebrows as the picture finally came together in her throbbing head. "You allowed your own family to be slaughtered?"

Sabine's features turned cold. "They tried to kill me. And you. Twice. They had it coming."

"I have to agree," Dema murmured.

Ele folded his arms across his chest as he stared at Sabine. "And it conveniently creates an opening for someone to take control of the family business."

Sabine shrugged. "Silver linings, Captain." She cast a look over her shoulder at Malik. "Still want to kill me?"

"More than ever."

"Malik." Kala reached out to place a gentle hand on his sword arm.

Malik lowered his shamshir and Sabine quickly stepped out of reach.

"We need to get Kala to the palace to see a healer," Henri said before turning to Ele. "You and I will have words later."

Ele's expression betrayed little but Kala could see the flicker of hurt behind his eyes. He'd let Henri down, perhaps for the first time in his life, and he would have to face the consequences.

"Wait." Kala surveyed the deck before exchanging a worried look with Ele. "Where's Isa?"

Sand suddenly lifted from the floorboards, swirling up into a tight whirlwind before materializing into a solid human form. Kala breathed a sigh of relief as Isa stood before them naked.

"I never tire of seeing that," Sabine purred.

Henri said nothing as he drew his sword.

CHAPTER TWENTY-SIX

ISA

They stared at each other, immovable forces locked in the promise of battle, neither of them willing to yield. Despite his stubbornness, Isa understood Henri's reasons for wanting to kill him. Henri would never forgive him for snatching Tahlia's lifeless body in the middle of the night and burning it in the hopes that the gods might allow her to ascend to divinity. But worse, Henri would never forgive *himself* for allowing it to happen.

Isa knew the guilt that hung around Henri's shoulders like a heavy cloak because he'd also worn it for a decade. They'd both failed Tahlia in their own ways and they would never find redemption. But it eased Henri's unbearable pain to focus his emotions on someone else, so he directed his anger at Isa. Isa deserved it. He would never claim otherwise. On any other day, he might have allowed Henri to take his revenge, knowing that it would feel justified in the moment but ultimately do nothing to heal the crippling wound they shared. Today was different, though. Tahlia needed him to live.

"I told you if I ever saw you again, I'd kill you," Henri seethed through clenched teeth.

Kala swiftly moved to stand between them, putting her arms out in appeal. "Henri, listen to what we have to say first."

"Tahlia ascended." Isa threw the words down between them like a gauntlet.

Henri flinched, as though the revelation had detonated inside him. His jaw slackened but he couldn't seem to form words.

"She's a goddess?" Malik breathed, stunned.

"Yes." Kala lowered her arms tentatively. "I'm sorry I didn't tell you. She didn't want anyone to know. She wanted you to move on with your lives. To remember her the way she was."

"You've spoken to her?" Henri asked.

Malik took a step closer to Henri and rested a hand on the small of his back, to steady him as much as comfort him.

"She has been with me since the beginning, watching over me and guiding me in my reign, but now she needs our help. She is being put on trial. For crimes she committed as a human and a divine."

"Trial?" Henri recoiled.

"What crimes?" Malik challenged.

"Rejecting her divination as a mortal. Hiding from the gods. Trapping a god and imprisoning him. Interfering with the realm of another divine by saving my life," Isa listed them coldly.

They were not crimes, they were choices. Choices she'd been forced to make as a consequence of the selfish actions of a god who worshiped his own ego.

Dema retrieved Isa's kurta from the deck and handed it to him. "We suspect there might be other lesser gods put on trial as well."

Isa took it, grateful, and put it on. "This is Dema, Shahri of the Naiab."

Henri cocked his head at Dema in contemplation of her words. "You think the Water Goddess will be put on trial?"

"She revealed the secrets of the divine realm to Tahlia and Isa. She helped Tahlia hide from the gods. She assisted in breaking the curse of the Black Sands," Dema replied.

Malik frowned. "The what?"

"It's not important." Kala waved a dismissive hand but the action made her sway on her feet.

Isa moved to help her but Ele was faster. He wrapped an arm around her shoulders and held her hand tightly in his, letting her lean against him. It was the instinct of a friend. Any one of them would have done the same for her. And yet there was something about the way they were standing together, something in the intensity of the fleeting look they shared. It set Isa's nerves on edge.

Kala's words broke through his thoughts. "If Tahlia is found guilty, the higher gods will enact justice. They will destroy her."

Henri looked to Malik. "Higher gods?"

"There are lesser gods and higher gods. I'll explain later."

Henri's tone was chilling as he turned back to Kala. "Destroy her how?"

"She will cease to exist," Kala said.

Henri froze as his face paled. He looked as if he were reliving the trauma of Tahlia's death. The raw, helpless agony. The splinter of disbelief. After a moment, his gaze moved to Malik, who held it tenderly. Unspoken thoughts and emotion passed between them. The silent language of an enduring love.

Around them, Henri's soldiers moved swiftly to clear the bodies. Isa had no doubt the corpses would be put on display within the city walls, a warning to those involved in the criminal underworld that no one was beyond the king's reach. They deserved a worse fate for what they had done, but now that it was over, Isa hoped it would bring Kala some peace. Perhaps her nightmares might finally lose their power.

"The trial is being held at the Divine Isle, a sacred place in the mortal world," Isa explained. "The Water Goddess is willing to guide us there but we need a ship. If you let us go, when we return, you can take your revenge. I won't stop you."

"Isa," Kala admonished.

Isa shook his head subtly, pleading with her to let it go. There was very little chance of any of them returning alive but it was the only thing he had left to bargain with. Henri's expression hardened as he considered it.

"You're all going to this Divine Isle?" Malik's tone was careful as he looked around at them.

"Fuck no. I'm not," Sabine said.

"The rest of us are." Though injured and unsteady, Kala lifted her chin in defiance, daring even the gods to challenge her.

Henri sheathed his sword. "So am I."

"Henri." Malik stepped in front of him, blocking everyone from view and forcing Henri to look at only him. Malik pitched his voice low but Isa could still make out the words as he said, "You can't leave your kingdoms ungoverned."

"They won't be, my love. I entrust them to you." Henri reached out to cradle Malik's cheek gently in his palm. "Wait for me to return."

Malik's posture tensed. Even with his back turned, Isa knew Malik did not like that answer one bit. It was an impossible situation. He would feel torn between his duty to his country and his loyalty to his lover. Despite Isa's fractured history with Henri and Malik, he had always respected them and admired their relationship. Their love had endured many trials and survived against insurmountable odds. It was clear that time had not eroded their love for each other, nor had it weakened their love for Tahlia if Henri was willing to risk his country to save her immortal existence.

They held each other's stare for a heartbeat longer before Malik turned to face everyone, his expression hard as stone. "I'm just going to say this once and be done with it. You do realize there is likely nothing that any of you can do to save Tahlia. Her destruction may be inevitable. And you will likely share in her demise for incurring the wrath of the gods."

While Isa's focus never strayed from Malik, in his peripheral vision he caught everyone exchanging looks, grave but resolute. Except for Sabine, who simply shook her head.

"Right then." Malik cleared his throat. "I will find a healer for Kala, organize supplies, commandeer a bigger ship, and appoint a regent to rule in our absence."

"Malik—" Henri's protest was cut off by Malik locking his hands on either side of his face and silencing his mouth with a fierce kiss.

When their lips parted, Malik said, "I told you years ago, no matter what decisions you make, I will stand by your side. I will fight against any enemy; mortals, or kings, or gods."

A smirk tugged at Henri's lips, the heat in his gaze unmistakable. "You did."

Malik released him and casually strode over to descend the gangplank. "We sail at dawn," he shouted over his shoulder.

Isa watched as Malik walked out onto the dock, issuing orders to Henri's soldiers before mounting his horse and riding off at speed.

"Henri, you don't have to do this." Kala's words brought Isa's attention back.

"Yes, I do." Henri offered her a small, reassuring smile. "If this is our end, then so be it. We will meet it together."

"You can ask the Goddess of Fate when you see her," Sabine suggested.

"She means Tahlia," Ele explained.

Henri tilted his head as if he hadn't heard correctly. "Tahlia is the Goddess of Fate?"

"The gods are cruel," Kala replied tightly.

CHAPTER TWENTY-SIX

"Even if Tahlia wanted to see the outcome of the trial, there are protections on the Divine Isle that make it difficult for her to see more than a fraction of the future," Dema reminded them.

Henri absorbed the information for a moment, his forehead lined in thought. "If anyone has a chance of outsmarting the gods, it's Tahlia."

"Speaking of outsmarting people, I have a family business to run. I would wish you all luck on your suicide mission, but no amount of luck is going to save you, so I'll just say goodbye."

Sabine turned toward the gangplank.

"Wait," Ele called to her, his arm still around Kala, who was now resting her head against his shoulder. "Is it safe for you to return to the Thaka?"

"Missing me already, Captain?"

Ele ignored the flirtation and persisted, "How are you going to explain the slaughter of your family?"

"Takeovers happen all the time. I simply used the king's army to ensure mine wouldn't fail. Don't worry about me. Murder and manipulation are admired where I come from."

"And how will you explain why you didn't kill me?" Kala's voice was weak, as if she were fighting the urge to pass out.

Sabine paused for thought. "You're worth far more to me alive, sister. You'll be looking for a new trade partner soon to sustain your kingdom. I'm sure we can come to some mutually beneficial arrangement."

It was a lie. Sabine knew the odds of them returning alive were slim at best. She would not have made her decision to spare Kala's life based on the hopes on a lucrative trade agreement. It was more likely that she knew she could not get away with killing Kala, and she knew she would be blamed if she let anyone else harm her. But there was also the remote possibility that she had protected her sister because of the bond they had once shared.

Kala didn't question her further. With no words left to say, Sabine's eyes lingered on her sister for a final moment before she made her way down the gangplank. It was only then that Kala collapsed in Ele's arms.

ELE

Ele watched dawn break over the horizon, spilling gold into the dark edge of the water and brushing the sky with hues of pink. It was a beautiful sight. Peaceful and hopeful, which was a stark contrast to everything that had happened in the past few hours. He wished Kala could see it but she was asleep in a hammock he'd strung up between two poles on deck. It looked ridiculous to have a hammock softly swinging in the middle of the ship, out in the open where she would be exposed to the elements, but Kala had refused to go below deck and the healer had been clear that she needed bedrest. Bringing the hammock up on deck was the only solution. Still, he would have to find a way to shade her so that the sun wouldn't blister her skin.

"That's it," Malik announced as the last of the soldiers departed the ship, having carried on board enough supplies to sustain them on a journey all the way to Sirasinda. "The anchor is raised, the sails are unfurled, and the rigging has been adjusted for the wind. All we're missing is the Water Goddess."

"Who knew you were such a sailor?" Henri smirked as his eyes roved over Malik in a new appreciation.

Malik winked. "I am a man of many mysteries."

Ele and Isa looked to Dema expectantly but she merely dropped her gaze to the wooden planks beneath her feet as if she were concentrating. Or waiting. Ele shifted his stance anxiously. If the Water Goddess didn't show herself to guide the ship, the mission would be over before it had a chance to begin.

The ship suddenly lurched ever so slightly, as if a large wave had hit it. Except the water was calm and still. Ele strode over to the port side, uncertain if what he felt had been real, but there was already a wide gap separating the ship and the dock. They were definitely moving. Ele rushed to the bow and stared down into the water to see the ship cutting through it with increasing speed.

"The Water Goddess, she's moving the ship," Ele called back to them as relief flooded his system.

"She won't inhabit me. She refuses to talk to me." Worry laced Dema's voice.

Ele returned to the group and Isa's expression hardened.

"Something's happened."

Ele was inclined to agree with Isa. It wasn't like the goddess to be silent or Tahlia to be absent when Kala's life was in danger.

Perhaps they were keeping a low profile, but to what end? Tahlia had already been summoned to stand trial.

"There is nothing else we can do for now," Henri said, though his tone betrayed his shared concern. "We've all had a long night. Everyone should get some rest while we can."

Dema reluctantly nodded and headed for the lower deck. Isa fell into step behind her. Ele made to follow them, hopeful of finding a tarp he could string above Kala to shade her from the sun, except Henri's words called him back.

"Not you."

Ele turned to see Henri's features had shifted to stone. Malik flanked him, his face carefully neutral, offering silent support to both of them. Ele inhaled a deep breath, allowing his shoulders to slump a little before bracing himself for what was to come. It wasn't the first time he had disappointed Henri. There were missions that had gone wrong. Late nights drinking and cavorting that had turned into lazy drills the next day. Secrets and information that he just couldn't get his hands on, no matter how many palms he greased or lives he threatened.

But this was different.

He had deliberately deceived his king. Any other soldier would be punished, perhaps even executed, but Ele knew Henri would never lay a hand on him. It made it worse. If he suffered a punishment, perhaps it would go a little way to making things right.

"Why didn't you tell me?" Henri's voice was fatally calm.

It was tempting to ask for clarification but Ele knew it didn't really matter what he was referring to. Tahlia's ascension, Isa crossing into his kingdom without permission, commandeering a ship without his knowledge, going to battle with the gods—it was all the same. He should have told Henri about all of it.

"I'm sorry."

"Not good enough," Henri shot back. "Do you honestly think that anything you've done, anything you are, or anything that's happened to you could make me turn my back on you?"

Ele blinked, confused, but he tried to plead his case anyway. "Kala asked me to keep it a secret. I would have confessed everything the moment we returned."

"I'm not talking about that." Henri's face wrinkled in irritated disgust.

"What are you talking about?"

"You are god-touched."

Ele's lips parted as the air was snatched from his lungs.

"Sabine called you god-touched after the fight," Malik explained gently.

Damn her.

"I," Ele began but he couldn't find the words.

"Why didn't you tell me?" Henri pressed, but the sting in his voice belied hurt, not betrayal.

"Why didn't you ask?" Ele countered. The truth felt fragile as it lingered between them. "You always suspected, right? They always said I'm too fast. Too strong. Too talented. My skills are a gift from the God of War and Valor. Except they're not. That's all me. I didn't want you to know because I didn't want it to change how you see me. And you didn't ask because you were afraid of the answer."

Malik watched carefully as Henri spoke. "Let me ask you now, then. What magic did the goddess give you?"

"She didn't give it to me, at least not knowingly. I have the ability to end lives. When things get intense in battle, I can sense it, like static in the air or the hum of a pulse. One touch and it's gone."

Henri's pupils widened but Malik's expression remained unreadable.

"I swear I've only used it on a few occasions when it was absolutely necessary."

"Does the Goddess of Endings and Beginnings know about this?" Malik asked.

"No."

"We need to keep it that way." Malik perched his hands on his hips as his eyes shifted in calculated thought. "You shouldn't be on this mission. What if the goddess takes one look at you and realizes you took something from her?"

"I know the risk. But wherever Kala goes, I go."

Malik lifted his gaze swiftly and Henri's focus sharpened on him. "Has something happened between the two of you?"

Ele sighed. He wanted to deny it just to avoid the inevitable interrogation, but he was not in the habit of lying to his king.

"Yes, but it's not what you're thinking."

"You have no idea what I'm thinking," Henri retorted.

"You know exactly what I'm thinking." Malik swatted Henri's shoulder. "I told you. Didn't I say this would happen?"

Ele ducked his head self-consciously. "It was just sex. Nothing more. We're still friends."

"But you want to be more than friends," Malik prompted.

"It doesn't matter what I want. It's up to her."

It was hard to admit it out loud. It made him feel powerless and cowardly, like he'd given up.

"You two have always shared a special bond," Henri said, measuring his words carefully. "If that bond were to turn into love, it would be the most powerful love you could ever know. But if one of you doesn't feel that way about the other, it could be the most devastating heartbreak you will ever suffer."

Ele knew Henri was talking from experience. The thought of Kala not feeling the same way as him was enough to bring Ele to his knees. But there was nothing he could do about that. He couldn't force her to love him, to want a life with him, to take a chance on what they could be to each other. Her reservations were valid and nothing he could say would ease them. She had to be willing to give him a chance, to prove himself. But Kala had been clear from the start that she wouldn't fall in love with him. Whether she wouldn't allow herself to or whether she genuinely could never feel that way about him, he couldn't hold it against her. At least she had kept her word.

"It's not important," Ele said dismissively, keen to change the subject. "We need to save Tahlia and survive the gods first, then we'll figure it out."

"Can I give you one piece of advice?" Malik asked.

"Can I stop you?"

"Be honest with her. Don't hide things from her. Don't love her in secret. There is never going to be a right time, there is only now. It's a short life, but it's your life, and love is all that matters in the end."

Ele absorbed the words, despite himself, because he recognized the wisdom in them. He had been honest with her. He'd told her how he felt about her. Now it was her turn. Except there was a high probability they would meet their end before she made up her mind.

Henri raised a single sardonic brow at Malik. "That's great advice. Pity you didn't know that a decade ago."

"No one's perfect." Malik flashed Henri a seductive smile. "But I have gotten better with age."

KALA

When Kala woke, she was being softly lulled by the sea breeze, her body cocooned in rough material. The immediate stab of panic was tempered by the fact that she could see stars shining above her through a thin piece of fabric that had been crudely fashioned into a shade cloth. She lifted her head cautiously to find that it no longer throbbed, though dried blood still streaked her hair. Her wrist had been bandaged and her other wounds had also been tended to.

As Kala tried to sit up, the hammock tilted dangerously, but steady hands caught her, before she fell out. Ele. He'd been sitting beside her, she realized, with his back turned to her but now they were face to face.

"You're awake," he blurted, the words sounding awkward somehow.

"How long was I asleep for?"

"All day." Ele righted the hammock and Kala relaxed her hold on the sides.

She craned her neck to look out beyond the ship. All she saw was the night sky.

"We've left Merovia," she murmured.

Part of her couldn't believe it. She had never left her country before. She knew there was a world beyond Merovia but she had never desired to see it. Now she was far away from her home, her country, sailing in foreign waters. It felt thrilling and terrifying at the same time.

"The Water Goddess is guiding the ship but she still hasn't shown herself," Ele explained. "Dema is worried."

Kala reclined back into the hammock. "Where is everyone?"

"Below deck."

Except for Ele. He had stayed by her side. He'd fashioned a bed on deck for her to rest in and she would bet anything he'd strung the shade cloth above her. The knowledge made her chest flood with warmth even as her heart twisted painfully. She could still feel the unease of their last conversation lingering between them in the silent moments. Unfinished.

"Are you hiding from Henri?" Kala teased, trying to lighten the mood.

"No. We talked. I lived." Ele revealed a cocky grin, seemingly happy to play along.

"I'm glad. I would hate to see you unemployed."

"I'd be alright." He turned his back on her but made no move to leave her side. "I'd return to the Citadel. Become a farmer. Scythe wheat."

"The Naiab women would love that."

Kala mentally kicked herself. Now she sounded jealous.

Ele didn't reply.

"You must be tired. You should go below deck and rest."

"I could." Ele lazily pulled himself to his feet and then turned to flash her a wicked smile. "Or I could get in the hammock with you."

Kala's eyes widened in alarm. "There's no room!"

Ele lunged, feigning to get in with her as Kala pushed her good hand against his chest whilst trying to guard her broken wrist.

"Move over!" He laughed as he leaned in close enough that his curls brushed her forehead.

"Eleuterio!"

He stilled, his mischievous smile softening as his eyes searched hers. For what, she didn't know. All she knew was that in that moment, beneath the moonlight, his blue eyes sparkled. Unbidden, her gaze roamed his face, taking in the shadow of stubble that lined his jaw and framed his beautiful lips, before returning to his eyes, which were staring at her so intensely that she couldn't look away if she tried.

"Say it again," he breathed, as if he were struggling to restrain himself.

It was a plea. And a command.

A tight curling sensation filled Kala's stomach. "Eleuterio."

She thought he might kiss her but he didn't, instead his hand slowly moved to slip under her kaftan. Kala's breath hitched in anticipation as his fingertips brushed against her leg. An aching pulse began in her core as he traced his way up her thigh to touch the nub at her entrance. She melted beneath him. He hadn't even caused any friction yet and she had to swallow a cry.

"Again," he said.

"Eleuterio."

She was going to combust. Every muscle in her body pulled taut as her nerve endings ignited and heat pooled in her center. He hadn't even started and she couldn't breathe.

"Take your hand off her or lose it."

Ele shot to his feet and Kala bolted upright in panic, bracing herself so that she didn't fall out of the hammock. Ele stood in front of her, protecting her dignity as much as possible, but there was no shred of it left because Isa was standing right there. He'd seen where Ele's hand had been. Knew what they were about to do. Kala felt herself wither like a seedling in the desert.

"Touch my son and I'll kill you," countered a deep voice.

Kala looked past Ele and Isa to see Henri striding towards them. For the briefest of moments, she wondered if that was the first time he'd called Ele his son, but she had no time to dwell on it because his lethal focus was fixed on the Naiab warrior, promising violence without mercy. Oh gods, had Henri seen them too? Her cheeks burned in mortification.

Isa didn't even turn around. He ignored Henri completely as he glared at Ele. "I warned you what would happen if you took advantage of her in my absence."

"Enough!" Kala moved, albeit not very gracefully, out of the hammock to stand beside Ele. "No one took advantage of me."

Ele sneered at Isa. "Stop acting as though you're protecting her honor. In case you haven't noticed, she's a grown woman."

"Oh I know. And she can sleep with whoever she wants to but you're different. You're going to break her heart and I can't stand by and let that happen."

Ele shook his head resolutely. "I won't break her heart."

"You will because your loyalty isn't to her." Isa turned to the side and pointed a finger at Henri. "It's to him."

Adrenaline and anger flooded Kala's veins, but she tried to keep her voice steady as she said, "Isa this is none of your business."

"You are my business. Your safety, your happiness is my business."

"Haven't you learned your lesson yet?" Henri's tone was a deadly warning as he drew closer. "Kala is free to make her own choice."

"Yes, but I'm responsible for her," Isa contended.

"No, you're not," Kala shot back. "I released you from your vow, remember? You are no longer my guardian. But I am still your queen. And I am ordering you to leave."

Isa locked his jaw as he stared back at her, his wild gaze furious and his chest heaving. She knew he was only trying to protect her but she didn't need him to. She was the custodian of her own heart. Whether she gave it to Ele or not, and if it broke, she would endure the pain and put it back together again.

Isa stalked away, his heavy footfalls loud against the creaking deck. Kala released a breath she didn't know she'd been holding.

"You, too." Henri directed the command to Ele.

Kala blinked, surprised, but Ele didn't hesitate. He offered a brief glance over his shoulder at her before striding off in the opposite direction of Isa. Kala's gaze drifted to Henri in silent question. He inclined his head to the side of the ship and casually walked over to it. Kala followed. They leaned their forearms against the railing as they both looked out across the midnight water.

"You should know that I'm always on deck. Perpetual sea sickness."

Fantastic. Kala pinched her eyes closed in humiliation. He had seen everything.

It felt strange to suddenly be alone with Henri. Kala had often wondered what it would be like when they reunited. Different scenarios had filled her head over the years, all of them joyful, but in the end, she knew that they were unlikely to come to pass. Now, in the most unlikely of scenarios, he was standing beside her. He didn't seem all that different to how she remembered him. He still had a calm, regal presence about him, juxtaposed by lethal authority and an impulsive nature. Henri ruled by his heart and his principles, he always had, and he made no effort to disguise that.

He looked for the good in people. He had seen it in her as a child, even when the world around her had tried to destroy it.

"How's your wrist?"

She followed Henri's gaze to her bandaged hand currently dangling over the side of the ship.

"Healing."

"Good."

She didn't know what else to say. There was so much to tell him and yet it felt odd to share anything about her life. He wasn't a stranger to her, but she also hadn't spoken to him in ten years.

"You finally managed to grow a beard," she observed.

Henri laughed as he stroked his beard affectionately. It was barely past his chin and peppered with gray hairs but it was considerably more impressive than when she had last seen him.

"It's my greatest achievement in life."

Kala smiled at the self-deprecation. "I'm sorry for crossing into your kingdom without permission."

"I understand why you did." Henri's expression turned thoughtful as he watched the rhythm of the dark waves. "And I owe you an apology for never coming to yours. To see you. I wanted to."

"I understand why you didn't."

"Ele kept us informed about you, how you were doing, but I have to say seeing you now ... grown ..." He was lost for words, the emotions on his face raw and unguarded.

It made Kala's throat swell.

"Tahlia would be proud of you. Proud of the woman you've become."

"She is."

Tahlia would be less than impressed with her mad plan to trespass into a divine court in an effort to save her from eternal destruction, but other than that, Kala knew Tahlia was proud of the life she'd built.

"And she would be happy that you and Ele still have each other. Whether that's as friends or something more, only you two can figure that out."

Kala let her eyes wander up to the night sky. "You don't have any opinions or advice on the matter?"

"No," he replied simply. "If you want opinions, ask Malik. He has plenty."

Kala laughed and Henri smiled. His face changed whenever he spoke of Malik. His features softened and the corners of his mouth lifted gently, almost wistfully. Kala knew he was thinking about him now. It was the look of a man very deeply in love. One day, she hoped she would look like that when thinking about someone. To love someone like that would be worth any price, even if it didn't last forever.

"But you should know that I won't stand between you two. Ele is free to live whatever life he wants with whoever he chooses."

It didn't surprise Kala that Henri was being selfless. He would always put those he loved first, ensuring their happiness before his own. But she knew it would devastate him if Ele left his side. They had been together since Ele was a child, surviving countless battles, risking their lives for each other. Whether he had said the words before or not, everyone could see that he treated Ele like his own son. And Ele felt the same way about Henri. Henri may believe that Ele owed him nothing, but Ele knew that he owed his king everything. And Ele had always been loyal to the core.

"I can't imagine him ever leaving you," Kala admitted sadly.

He cut her an earnest look as he said, "I can."

CHAPTER TWENTY-SEVEN

ELE

"Land!"

Dema's excited cries sent Ele racing across the deck until he was standing beside her at the bow of the ship, staring out at the thin stretch of land on the horizon. He blinked several times, trying to determine if it was a trick of the sun, but the land never disappeared. It only grew bigger as they drew closer. Ele was vaguely aware that Kala and the others had joined them but he didn't dare take his eyes off the island, afraid it would vanish if he did.

"The Divine Isle," Kala murmured in disbelief.

They had been at sea for days now. Without word from the Water Goddess, surrounded by an endless ocean, their hope had begun to sink. But now the grave reality of what they had come to do was staring them in the face, advancing steadily with each wave.

"Everyone, arm yourselves and get ready to go ashore," Henri commanded.

It was futile really. The hidden daggers, his sword made of Palescene steel, the finest in the country, were useless against the gods. But sharpening his blades and strapping them to his body was part of the ritual of preparing for battle. And this would either be his last battle or the most defining battle of his life.

When he was ready, Ele returned to the bow of the ship. The island loomed ahead of them now, close enough to make out some details. It rose out of the water like a mystical being, like a thought imagined. A sweet thin mist floated around it in ribbons. Through the mist, Ele could see a riot of vibrant vegetation covering every inch of land. Greenery blanketed the earth beyond the sand and flowers grew everywhere. Their colors were so bright it looked like someone had painted them. Behind the island's peaks, a rainbow tinted the sky. But there were no gray clouds or evidence of rain. It was as if the sky had produced a rainbow simply because it wanted to rival the beauty of the earth.

As the ship drew closer, the air changed from salty brine to fragrant florals and ripened fruit. The color of the sea transformed from a cold crystal blue to a sparkling jade. Peering down into the water, Ele could see all the way through to the vibrant coral and grains of sand. It was like looking through a glass mirror into a magical world.

"Ele."

At Henri's call, Ele cast a look over his shoulder to see that everyone had assembled near the port side. He made his way there as the ship moored softly in a bed of sand and Malik released the anchor.

Henri looked to each of them. "Is everyone ready?"

Heavy emotions were etched on their faces, the kind that came from knowing they were likely living the last day of their life. There was quiet fear but also brave determination. They would never be ready to challenge the gods, but they would also never back down when their loved ones were in danger.

"What's the plan?" Malik asked.

"Save Tahlia," Isa replied as he swung himself over the railing of the ship and deftly climbed the knotted rope down to the shallow waters.

"Try not to die," Ele suggested as he followed Isa's lead.

Malik shot them an unamused look. "So, there is no plan. Wonderful."

One after another, they made their way to the beach, fanning out to form a defensive line. Ele scanned the thick foliage for signs of life—animal, mortal, immortal—but there was nothing. It was as if the land had been created, not to be inhabited, but to be admired. Like art on a wall. Every element was perfect. Nothing was dying or decaying. It was immortality captured in a frame.

"I've never seen so much greenery in my life," Kala mused as she took in their surroundings.

"It's like being in a dream," Dema agreed.

Isa's frown was unimpressed. "It's the creation of the gods. They're showing off."

"I don't suppose anyone brought a map?" Malik asked, hopeful.

"Listen." The word fell from Ele's lips even as he strained his ears to hear.

The sound was faint. He wasn't sure what it was at first but then it came to him; the tinkle of tiny bells.

"Tahlia." In an instant, Isa crafted a double-tipped spear from the sand and charged into the undergrowth.

"Wait!" Ele called after him as they all gave chase.

A distant angelic voice joined the tinkle of the bells. It was beautiful but mournful. Like a heart breaking. The sound of grief. There was something else strange about it. It sounded like it was coming from inside his head rather than somewhere on the island, but that couldn't be right because clearly the others could hear it too. Isa was following it like a siren's call. It lured them, enthralling them to take a particular path where there was none.

"Isa, stop! It might be a trick!" Ele yelled as he tried to keep up with the warrior, batting away broad ferns and hanging vines as he dashed through the foliage.

Ele hoped it was Tahlia guiding them but he had a sinking feeling it wasn't. The gods loved to play games. Besides, it made little sense that Tahlia would help them now when she'd been silent ever since they'd lifted the curse of the Black Sands.

Suddenly, the dense canopy above them gave way, and the vegetation thinned to expose a large clearing ahead. Steep gray cliffs encircled it, white waterfalls cascading down their stony faces. Suspended in the sky above the waterfalls was a twin sun and moon, both of them full, glowing gold and silver. Ele slowed to a stop, mesmerized, but Isa simply crouched low at the edge of the glade.

CHAPTER TWENTY-SEVEN

A strong hand clasped Ele's shoulder and pulled him to the ground. "Get down before they see you!" Henri admonished.

It was only then that Ele noticed the beings gathered in the field. Divines. They were flawless. Breathtaking. Although they took human form, they did not appear to be solid, but rather looked translucent, like light trapped behind glass. Each radiated a warm ethereal glow. The power that pulsated from them was unmistakable. Ele could feel it in the air, raw and trembling. It sent his pulse racing.

The divines mingled amongst each other with cool indifference. Ele's jaw slackened when he noticed that some of them took the form of children, whilst others were elderly, though they all moved as if untouched by age. Their grace was unnatural. So was their beauty. The goddesses hair floated around their faces like strands of gold under water. The gods' physiques were impossibly strong as if chiseled from marble.

"Do they take the form of how they were when they died?" Kala speculated. The question was rhetorical as it was anyone's guess.

"I hope I look that good when I die," Malik muttered.

"Who are the faceless ones?" Henri's question was met with silence as everyone's attention locked onto three beings who stood apart from the rest, shadows in a field of light.

Though their forms were vaguely human, they had no faces, no features, barely even limbs. They radiated power, but it was not a warm ethereal glow, it was cold and cosmic. Their movements mimicked the human form but it was an illusion because they had never been alive or dead, they had simply always existed.

"The higher gods," Isa deduced.

Ele swallowed hard. In the midst of such great and terrible power, he felt like a speck of dust. Feeble. Inconsequential. Powerless. Any of the gods could end them with a single thought. How could they hope to stand against them?

The higher gods spoke in unison, a single word that sent shivers down Ele's spine. "Proceed."

The divines came together to form a circle in the field until one god broke formation, walking to the center in deliberate strides. He had a commanding presence, even amongst the divine, and they all appeared to respect his authority. If Ele had to guess, he would say it was the God of Justice and Kingship. He upheld the principles of fairness, righteousness, and cosmic order.

The god's voice carried across the glade as he proclaimed, "The gods summon the Goddess of Fate to stand before us and face divine judgment."

Ele's breath caught in his throat as a heavenly figure stepped forward. It was Tahlia, her body, her face, her mannerisms, exactly as he remembered her. Except divine. She was easily the most beautiful of them all. He understood now why the God of Beauty and Fertility had chosen her for divinity. It was as if she had always been one of them. And yet they all looked at her as if she were beneath them. Jealousy spoiled the goddesses flawless faces and petulant wrath twisted the god's expressions to hatred. Tahlia did not cower, though. She was poised beneath their collective judgment.

CHAPTER TWENTY-SEVEN

"Mistress of fate. Weaver of destiny," the God of Justice and Kingship began. "Your crimes are many and heinous. As a mortal, you rejected your divination. You were even so bold as to hide from us. Then, when we came to claim you, you trapped one of us and imprisoned him for vengeance."

Tahlia lifted her chin, meeting the god's gaze with fearless defiance. "Such accusations are baseless without evidence."

The god flung his arms wide to the assembled crowd. "We all witnessed it."

She lifted a delicate shoulder, unbothered. "You could all be lying. In fact, one would think that if I offended you all so greatly, I would never be permitted to ascend to divinity. Yet here I am."

"That was the decision of the God of Fire and Ash." The god's tone left no doubt of his disapproval.

"Someone pled for you," came a voice from the crowd, bored and unapologetic. "I was moved to show mercy."

Isa. The God of Fire and Ash had observed Isa burning Tahlia's body, heard his prayers, and decided to grant his appeal for her ascension.

"Your mercy is my eternal punishment."

"Insolence! Witness her ingratitude," the God of Justice and Kingship implored the crowd. "She was granted immortality, gifted a divine power, and yet she refuses to use it!"

"Instead, she dared to interfere with my realm!" A goddess called out in condemnation.

Tahlia remained composed as she slowly turned to regard her accuser. In one sweeping glance, she assessed her and then turned away again as if she found her lacking. "Even mortals spin lies better than that."

"It is no lie! You took a death that was rightfully mine."

"The Goddess of Endings and Beginnings," Dema whispered.

Henri instinctively looked to Ele, whose expression tightened in reply. He had no memory of the goddess or what she had done to save his life as a boy, but he knew it haunted Henri. He also knew what would happen if the goddess discovered what she had lost that day. It felt reckless to be so near to her. Like he was flirting with death.

"I altered a mortal's fate. That is my divine right. How is that interfering with your realm? First, you claim that I refuse to use my divine power and then you claim that I abuse it. Which is it?"

The goddess gaped at Tahlia in fury, but the God of Justice and Kingship merely warned, "Don't think you can talk your way out of this. Your tricks won't work here."

"Neither will your baseless accusations," Tahlia returned. "You are the God of Justice and Kingship. You uphold the law and ensure fairness. Surely you don't intend to convict me without evidence."

The god speared her with a searing stare of enmity, which Tahlia weathered with the composure of a supreme goddess.

"I have evidence."

A god approached them in the form of a child, a teardrop vial dangling from his hand.

Isa visibly tensed and Kala swore under her breath.

"The God of Earth and Salt," Ele muttered bitterly.

"Behold." The God of Earth and Salt wandered around the edge of the circle. "The God of Beauty and Fertility is trapped inside this vessel."

The gods murmured amongst each other, the prospect titillating yet frightening at the same time. To see one of their own brought so low, reduced to a prisoner, banished to existence in a small brass vial, by a human no less, was amusing. But if it happened to one of them, it could happen to any of them. They eyed the vial nervously. They weren't the only ones. Tahlia's stare clung to it as it was paraded around the circle, her composure finally faltering as if the vial held the one thing she feared above all else.

The God of Justice and Kingship must have seen it too because there was a hint of smug satisfaction in his voice as he challenged, "Do you deny it now?"

Tahlia schooled her features to a calm mask as she replied, "I see a vial. Not a god."

"Release him," the higher gods commanded as one.

"No," Kala gasped but it was too late.

The God of Earth and Salt opened the lid to the vial.

ISA

Isa wasn't sure what happened next. All he knew, all that mattered, was that Tahlia was in danger and he needed to get to her. Swiftly, he leapt into a sprint, twirling his spear in his hand until he was standing in front of her, one arm braced to shield her behind him while the other held the spear in a defensive stance. It was only then that he saw the God of Beauty and Fertility. He stood before them, gleaming with unfiltered ire and unchecked violence. He showed no signs of recognizing Isa or anyone else for that matter, his eyes were fixed solely on Tahlia as if she were the only thing in existence, and he wanted to destroy her.

But then the god laughed. It was a cruel hollow rattle that died in his throat. "After all your resistance, you still became one of us. I told you. You have always been mine. We are bound together. You will never be free of me."

Isa was going to kill him, god or not. Warm fingers brushed Isa's outstretched hand, lacing with his own until his arm was coaxed down to his side. Isa knew he shouldn't lose sight of his enemy, but he couldn't resist looking over his shoulder in disbelief. He could feel her. *Her.*

"Goddess," he breathed.

Tahlia's emerald gaze held him hostage as she offered the faintest of smiles.

"A mortal!" The God of Justice and Kingship's outrage echoed across the field like a battle cry. "Someone has betrayed the secrets of the Divine Isle!"

"I did."

Isa was vaguely aware that the Water Goddess had emerged from the crowd to stand by his side. Though he had never seen her true form or heard her real voice, he recognized her power. Still, he couldn't tear his eyes away from Tahlia. They were locked in a moment, savoring the miracle of each other's touch, and he swore he would never again let her go.

"Then you will answer for your crime!"

"Gladly. But I am not the only one who brought a mortal to the Divine Isle." The Water Goddess turned shrewd eyes on the God of Earth and Salt. "You would have had to use a mortal to transport the vial here. Where is he? Is he still alive?"

Isa's focus slipped for a moment; Samir.

The child god returned a derisive look. "I don't know, nor do I care. He served his purpose."

Which meant the god hadn't killed him but gave no guarantee that Samir was still alive. Either he was trapped on the island somewhere or he'd tried to escape back out to sea. Neither prospect was good. Isa could only imagine Kala's face right now, knowing that her friend might be somewhere on the island, either dead or dying.

"You betrayed the secrets of the divine realm in order to bring evidence to condemn a goddess, but you say nothing of the god who interfered with your realm," the Water Goddess pointed out.

Before the God of Earth and Salt could reply, the God of Beauty and Fertility spat back, "I cursed the land because you created them!"

Isa broke his stare from Tahlia to find that the God of Beauty and Fertility had switched his murderous gaze to him. It was all Isa could do not to smile wolfishly at the god. It emboldened him to be the target of the god's wrath, the thorn in his immortal side. The narcissism and entitlement of the god knew no bounds and yet the creation of the Naiab had gotten under his skin like a splinter.

"An army of god-touched. It's immoral."

"As is collecting beautiful women and sacrificing them to your altar," the Water Goddess retorted.

"Are you still jealous, wife? Is that why you interfered? For there is still one question unanswered by this court." The God of Beauty and Fertility spun around to address the crowd in dramatic prose. "How did a mortal woman evade our eyes for so long? Who was the informant who shared the secrets of the divine realm with her?"

The lesser gods murmured in agreement and the higher gods leaned forward intently.

Fuck.

Isa shifted his defensive stance slightly but Tahlia tightened her grip on his hand, silently ordering him to remain calm.

"What are you implying, husband? You forget, I was the one who uncovered her. She prayed and I answered."

"I do not forget," the Goddess of Endings and Beginnings interjected. "You interfered with my realm to save a king's life."

"You seem rather quick to claim interference with your realm," Tahlia said drily. "If your rule over it is so weak, perhaps you're not fit to hold it."

By all the gods, the woman was fearless and Isa loved her even more for it. The Goddess of Endings and Beginnings blazed at her as if she would turn Tahlia to ash.

CHAPTER TWENTY-SEVEN

"I did what was within my power to do," the Water Goddess countered. "You could have taken his life if you wanted to."

"The informant." The higher god's voices boomed, cutting through their bickering and startling the lesser gods.

"Yes. Tell us." The God of Justice and Kingship leveled Tahlia with a damning look. "It may lighten your sentence."

Isa tightened his grip on his spear because he already knew what Tahlia was going to say.

"I will take that secret to my immortal extinction."

In unison, the higher gods pitched their voices low as they held their fingers up to click them. "So be it."

"Stop!"

The higher gods halted at Kala's cry as she and the others rushed onto the field, weapons drawn. Dema hurried to the Water Goddess's side while Ele and Kala formed a defensive line in front of Tahlia. Tahlia immediately dropped Isa's hand as Henri and Malik ran to her, engulfing her in a tight embrace, one on either side. All composure lost, Tahlia whimpered into Henri's shoulder as Malik stroked her hair and murmured words of comfort in her ear. Years ago, seeing her in their arms would have stung Isa with bitter jealousy but now all he felt was an overwhelming sense of gratitude. Henri and Malik held on to her as if she made them whole.

They could feel her and she could feel them. Isa wasn't sure how that was possible, whether the Divine Isle held certain properties or whether the gods taking human form lessened the veil between the mortal and immortal world, but it didn't matter. This moment would mean everything to Tahlia. Though death had nipped at her heels her whole life, when it finally claimed her, it was sudden. Too sudden to say goodbye to the people she loved. This was the moment that had been robbed from her.

"Water Goddess! What is the meaning of this?" Thundered the God of Justice and Kingship as he surveyed them all with righteous indignation.

Releasing their hold on Tahlia, Henri and Malik moved into position on either side of her, blades raised and eyes sharp.

Kala stood in front of them, her voice unwavering as she announced, "We're here to challenge the court's verdict."

Isa's chest swelled with pride to watch her stand her ground, even against the highest of powers. She had been right to release him from his vow. She didn't need him anymore. She was a true queen in every sense of the word. Unyielding. Strong enough to defy any enemy.

"You cannot condemn a goddess for actions she committed as a mortal," Kala argued.

The God of Justice and Kingship returned a sour glare. "Are you claiming to know our laws better than us, mortal?"

Kala opened her mouth to respond but a trill of laughter erupted from the Goddess of Endings and Beginnings. "This is outrageous! The Water Goddess must have brought them here for entertainment."

The shrill laughter cut off abruptly and Dema collapsed to the ground like a puppet whose strings had been cut.

CHAPTER TWENTY-SEVEN

"Dema!" Kala cried in horror, letting her shamshir fall to the ground as she dropped to her knees to cradle Dema's face in her hands.

She frantically patted her cheeks trying to rouse her before her fingers scrambled along Dema's neck, searching for a pulse, but Isa already knew there wouldn't be one. The Water Goddess went stiff as she stared down at the Shahri's lifeless body. She would have witnessed countless Shahris die during her immortal existence, but all of them from old age after living a full life dedicated to their people and goddess. Dema had followed her goddess all the way to the ends of the earth, and now she was dead. The Water Goddess's eyes snapped to the Goddess of Endings and Beginnings with barely controlled anger.

The Goddess of Endings and Beginnings merely returned a sweet, satisfied smile. "You shouldn't have brought your toys if you didn't want us to play with them."

"We do like games," the God of Earth and Salt agreed. "I have one for you, Goddess of Endings and Beginnings. Are you missing something?"

Kala's face drained of color, and her gaze darted to Ele even as she sat with Dema's head in her lap. From the corner of his eye, Isa noticed Henri subtly move closer to Ele. Isa subsequently adjusted his position to close the gap, slipping into the space between Henri and Tahlia. The Goddess of Endings and Beginnings watched them carefully as she tilted her head in thought.

Isa silently cursed the God of Earth and Salt. None of this was a coincidence. It was the God of Earth and Salt who had bartered for the vial so that he could use it as evidence to condemn Tahlia, and now the God of Beauty and Fertility was free. It was the God of Earth and Salt who had let it slip about the trial, and now they were all here trying to save Tahlia's immortal existence. There was no doubt that the God of Earth and Salt had recognized Ele's power at the Salt Plains, and now he was using it to provoke a reaction from the Goddess of Endings and Beginnings. Clearly, the God of Earth and Salt had an agenda, but so did the Water Goddess, and so did Tahlia. It made Isa wonder who exactly was orchestrating all of this? Whose song were they all dancing to?

Suddenly, the Goddess of Endings and Beginnings locked her attention on Ele. "Thief."

CHAPTER TWENTY-EIGHT

KALA

"He's not a thief!" Henri stared the goddess down. "He was dead and you saved his life. How could a dead boy steal from you? Whatever transferred between you and him was not his fault."

Recognition flickered across her face but it was swiftly eclipsed by the furious tightening of her features. "He has the power to take life itself!"

"Because you gave it to him," Henri countered.

"Not knowingly."

"Our bargain still stands," Henri reminded her. "You cannot kill him."

Kala laid Dema's head gently on the ground, trying to leash her emotions as she retrieved her shamshir and stood up. Her legs felt unsteady beneath her, grief and fear threatening to pull her back down to her knees, but she couldn't afford to be weak. She had to be strong. The gods had already claimed Dema's life and Samir was likely dead too. She refused to let Ele be next.

He would not die. Not while she still breathed.

Ele stood silent, as if waiting for a verdict. He had known there was a risk of being discovered, what it could cost him, but he'd chosen to come anyway. For Tahlia. For Kala. She should have talked him out of it, but even as the thought entered her mind, she knew he never would have listened to her.

The goddess's lips twitched to a bitter grimace. "Fine. Then I will take what I am owed. An ending that was not fated. A beginning that will never come to pass. That was the agreement."

Adrenaline poured into Kala's bloodstream, pumping her heart wildly as cold unease crawled up her spine.

The goddess's fingertips drummed her lips in thought. "Perhaps I should take your first born."

The flex of his arm muscles was the only hint of Ele's distress. "That is your right."

No! Kala wanted to scream. *She has no right!* She couldn't do that.

The goddess surveyed each of them like prey. Mere chess pieces on a board, to be used or discarded at her will.

"Or perhaps I will take the life of someone you love."

No. No. *No.*

This couldn't be happening. Before today, there had been every possibility that Ele would never know who paid the price for the bargain Henri struck. But now the goddess wanted him to know. She wanted revenge. She wanted *entertainment*.

Desperate, Kala looked to Tahlia only to find that the goddess was eerily calm. There was no trace of fear on her face, only quiet acceptance. Had she known this would happen?

"But that's too easy." The Goddess of Endings and Beginnings pouted before her lips unfurled into a vicious smile. "I know. Because you have the power to take life, I will make you this generous offer; choose the life of someone here and take it. Your debt will be paid. If you refuse, I will choose for you, and take it myself."

Ele's mouth fell open in shock, and he looked like he was about to protest but Henri shook his head imperceptibly, the command silent but firm. Was it better to choose himself rather than let the goddess choose? Kala didn't know. Didn't want to find out. As if hearing her thoughts, Ele glanced over his shoulder at her. A thousand words he could not say passed between them and her heart listened to every one. Then he closed his mouth, resolute. He would choose, she realized. Her eyes widened, caught between pity and denial. She wanted to go to him, to hold his hand and comfort him, but dread rooted her to the spot.

"The balance of fates must be restored." The goddess's words cut like broken glass. "Choose, mortal."

Choose. How could he possibly choose?

Henri placed a gentle hand on Ele's sword arm, calling his attention back to him. "I was the one who made the deal that day. I alone should pay the price."

"Henri," Malik warned, his tone sharp with fear.

"No," Kala choked, the word repeating itself inside her head only to escape her lips.

Henri was his king. Ele could never kill him.

Henri walked over to Malik and cupped his cheek as he pressed his forehead to his. "It's all right. We shared the love of a thousand lifetimes together."

Malik's chest heaved rapidly as he forced himself to breathe through a storm of emotions. Kala knew he would be fighting his instinct to protect Henri at all costs, to pay the price for him, to convince him it wasn't his responsibility, whilst also knowing that he should respect Henri's right to choose.

Malik's voice was strained as he replied, "Forever would never be long enough."

Henri smiled sadly and then kissed him passionately. "I'll wait for you amongst the stars."

Kala clenched her fists, angry, rebellious tears welling in her eyes. "You can't."

The words were not directed at Ele but rather the Goddess of Endings and Beginnings. It wasn't right. It was cruel. Baseless. Spiteful. And the goddess didn't care. She *relished* in it. Ele looked past Malik and Henri to Tahlia whose expression remained calm and hollow, even as she watched her former lovers embrace for the last time. Why wasn't she doing anything? Saying anything? She was a goddess. She couldn't just let this happen! But she couldn't interfere either. If she interfered with the realm of another god, it would condemn her.

Ele's gaze flicked to Isa, who stared back at him with understanding and respect. "Do it."

CHAPTER TWENTY-EIGHT

Ele's forehead lined and his brows furrowed slightly as if he were concentrating. It was the only warning Kala had before Isa crumpled to the ground. His spear instantly dissolved into sand at his side. Someone screamed.

It was Kala.

Because Isa was dead.

Strong arms quickly wrapped around her, blocking her view of Isa's lifeless body and pulling her into a warm chest. She didn't know who it belonged to because she was still screaming, trying to understand what had just happened.

Isa couldn't be dead. He couldn't be.

"I'm so sorry," a voice repeated into her ear.

But it wasn't Ele because she could see Ele over a broad shoulder, watching her like his heart was being torn out of his chest. His face was drawn in agony at her anguish, his body caved inward beneath the weight of his choice.

"How boring," the Goddess of Endings and Beginnings lamented.

"Seems like you're losing your army," the God of Beauty and Fertility jibed at the Water Goddess.

Kala's scream morphed from shock to feral rage as she ripped herself out of Henri's arms and lunged for the Goddess of Endings and Beginnings. "I'm going to kill you!"

Ele darted into her path, deflecting her blade. She thrashed against him as he tried to say something to her, plead with her, restrain her, but she didn't hear a word over the rush of blood in her ears and the all-consuming desire for revenge.

"Kala, stop," Tahlia commanded.

"You did nothing!" Kala rounded on her. "You just stood there!"

"Enough!" The God of Justice and Kingship boomed, and the ground beneath their feet shook with unfiltered power. "This is a court of law. Two goddesses stand accused. The verdict is clear!"

Tahlia stepped forward over Isa's lifeless body as if he meant nothing more to her than the dust beneath her feet. Kala released a whimper at the sight, her body and soul suddenly drained and numb. Malik came to her side, not daring to touch her, but close enough so that she was aware of his presence.

"The Water Goddess's only crime was that she led mortals to the Divine Isle," Tahlia began. "As it was for entertainment purposes, and everyone here was thoroughly entertained, she should not be punished. If she were to be destroyed, the God of Earth and Salt would also be deserving of destruction, since he committed the same crime."

"The mortal is also correct in claiming that the Goddess of Fate should not be condemned for actions she committed as a human," the Water Goddess said. "One cannot commit a crime if one does not know the laws of the divine realm. And the Goddess of Fate has not rejected her divination. She altered the fate of a mortal, which is within her power to do, and she did not interfere with another goddess's realm. See for yourselves, the mortal is dead. What more proof do you want?"

"In fact, the only god here who interfered with the realm of another god is the God of Beauty and Fertility." Tahlia turned on

CHAPTER TWENTY-EIGHT

the god whose nostrils flared at her in indignation. "By casting the curse of the Black Sands."

"Silence! This court has heard enough evidence. The higher gods will cast their judgment."

Kala swayed on her feet, unable to take any more of this and yet helpless to stop it. Their blades would do nothing. Their words were irrelevant. Their lives inconsequential.

The Water Goddess stood firm and Tahlia braced herself, her eyes fixed on the higher gods.

As one, the higher gods held their fingers up to click them. "Guilty."

Click.

There was no explosion.

No shattering sound.

No remnants remained.

It was like a flame had been snuffed out by a silent breath. Here then gone. Erased forever.

Except Tahlia remained. So did the Water Goddess.

"But—" The God of Justice and Kingship spluttered, perplexed.

"A god allowed himself to be imprisoned by a mortal. Disgrace!" The higher gods bellowed in unison.

Where the God of Beauty and Fertility had stood mere seconds ago was now nothing but air. A hush fell over the divine court, the gods clearly shaken to witness the death of one of their own, and terrified by the realization that their immortality was not without its limits.

"And the goddesses?" The God of Justice and Kingship dared to probe.

"Justice is done." The higher gods vanished like light on the wind, leaving their audience staring after them.

Kala stood dazed, her thoughts struggling to make sense of it, her body heavy with grief. It was over. They'd won. But they'd also lost.

"Bravo!" The God of Earth and Salt clapped his hands as if a performance had ended. "I never liked the prick."

A quiet stir spread amongst the gods as they exchanged hushed words, but the God of Justice and Kingship only clenched his teeth as he announced, "Court is concluded."

"No, it's not." Tahlia pivoted to address the crowd, her power unfurling from her like silk caught in the breeze. The gods seemed to recoil from it. "There is one more matter to rule on."

"Are you holding court now, mistress of fate?"

Tahlia ignored the God of Justice and Kingship as she turned to Malik. "Burn the body."

Malik blinked, caught off guard, but followed her gaze to Isa's lifeless body. "With what?"

"What do you mean?" Kala's voice broke as she stared at Tahlia in alarm. "Is your hatred for him so strong that you feel nothing at his death? That you want to destroy what's left of him?"

Tahlia didn't reply as Ele moved to search Dema's body. He retrieved the parabolic mirror and handed it to Malik, who pulled a small vial of oil from his pocket.

"Don't do this," Kala begged as tears rolled down her cheeks. It was a broken plea because she had no fight left in her.

"Do it." Henri's face was calm and resolute, as if he knew something she didn't.

They watched as Malik poured the oil over Isa's body and positioned the mirror until it caught the rays of the sun. A spark ignited. Isa's body started to burn but Kala felt like it was her heart that was being reduced to ashes.

Satisfied, Tahlia announced, "I petition for this mortal to ascend to divinity."

Kala sucked in a sharp breath.

"I support it," the Water Goddess answered immediately.

Isa. A god. Was this Tahlia's plan all along? Had everything happened because she weaved it into being? There had been no escaping the divine court, and yet somehow Tahlia had managed to save herself and the Water Goddess whilst also destroying her enemy the God of Beauty and Fertility.

"It could be amusing," the God of Earth and Salt speculated with a wry grin. "I support it."

Even the God of Earth and Salt appeared to be in on it, which Kala supposed was unsurprising considering that he hated the God of Beauty and Fertility. Now Henri's bargain with the Goddess of Endings and Beginnings had been fulfilled, and Ele was no longer in danger of retribution for being god-touched. The only price paid was two lives: Dema and Isa.

"What has he done to earn such a privilege?" The God of Justice and Kingship challenged.

"Mortals do not earn divinity," Tahlia countered. "They are gifted it. Or cursed with it. It is within our power to grant."

"I do not," he bit the words out.

"We do." Two gods emerged from the circle holding hands. The way they glowed, one gold one silver, hinted that they were the Moon God and Sun God.

Their endorsement seemed to inspire others to give their support, however apathetic, but Kala knew that they needed the approval of at least one god in particular.

"God of Fire and Ash. You said you were once moved to show mercy because someone pled for me. Now I plead for him. What do you say?"

The God of Fire and Ash approached Isa's body, his finger tracing his chin in quiet contemplation. The flames licked the air greedily, the smoke coating Kala's lungs. The smell of burning flesh made her want to wretch but she couldn't leave. Not when there was still hope.

Isa had once watched Tahlia's body burn like this. He would have felt everything that she was feeling right now; the pain, the grief, the desperate hope. Was it wrong to want love to live on? She didn't think so. Isa had given his life to spare Henri, to spare them all. Perhaps he'd thought it was penance but Kala knew it was more than that. Isa had lived and died for those he loved. Now all she wanted was for him to exist for something else.

"Please," Kala's voice fell softly.

Decision made, the God of Fire and Ash folded his hands behind his back. Then he casually turned and walked away. Kala stared after him, unsure what that meant, before looking to Tahlia for an explanation. But Tahlia's expression was that of a person who had gambled and lost. The Water Goddess had told them that the island had protections on it and that was why Tahlia had only been able to see fragments of the future. Perhaps Isa's death had been a blind spot. An ending that was not fated.

The gods began to disperse. At least the Sun God and Moon God had the decency to spare glances of pity, the others didn't care at all. The entertainment was over, as far as they were concerned, and they could return to their immortal existence.

Henri came to stand by Malik but Ele didn't dare move closer to Kala. She was glad for it. She needed space and time to process all that had happened. All that she'd lost.

"Was this your strategy all along?" Ele directed the question to Tahlia. "Did you alter our fates?"

Tahlia sighed as she watched the flames dance. "Fate threads the tapestry, but choice is the knots you tie yourself."

She was right. Tahlia may have influenced a few things, but for the most part she had withdrawn herself, remaining silent as she watched events unfold, allowing each of them control over their own destiny. Looking back now Kala also could see every choice they'd made, like footprints in the sand. If given the chance, Kala knew she would make the same again. So would Isa.

"I'm sorry." Tahlia lifted her gaze to Kala but Kala was unable to meet it.

Her cheeks still stung with the trace of salty tears, a promise of grief yet to be unleashed. She shook her head softly. "Don't be. It's the death he would have wanted. His life in exchange for keeping you safe."

"And you," Tahlia reminded her gently.

The words unraveled Kala's heartstrings. It physically *hurt* to breathe.

"Did you forgive him in the end?" The question escaped Kala's lips before she could think better of it. She wasn't sure whether she wanted to know the answer.

But Tahlia replied without hesitation. "I loved him. Forgiveness is the final act of love."

"Goddess."

Kala's eyes widened at the familiar voice as they all whipped around to see Isa standing behind them, a divine being radiating luminous light. Kala's jaw dropped, unable to comprehend what she was seeing. The God of Fire and Ash had granted their wish. Isa was a god.

Kala ran to him, flinging her arms around his neck, and he caught her like he always did. He didn't feel the same, he was not as solid as he was in his human form, but she clung to him anyway. It was a miracle. Divine intervention. Or perhaps it was simply fate.

When Kala pulled away, she did so slowly, knowing it would be the last time. Because although Isa had been granted divinity, he'd still lost his humanity. He wouldn't be returning home with her. He would no longer be her guardian. Kala would have to rule her kingdom every day without his guidance and steady presence beside her. She knew she could do it but she didn't want to.

"You'll be fine," Isa said as if he could read her thoughts, which as a god, he probably could. "You're an indelible queen. You have friends who are worthy of you. And love, should you choose to accept it. You don't need me."

Kala knew the truth of his words but they still stung. Henri tilted his chin to Isa in respect and thanks. Ele, however, stood motionless, his expression haunted.

Isa noticed it too because he said, "Don't blame yourself. It had to be done."

Ele lowered his gaze slightly, accepting the sentiment but rejecting it at the same time.

The Water Goddess approached, a bittersweet smile on her face. "I was hoping you would get the chance to return to the Citadel."

"So was I," Isa confessed before his eyes slid to Tahlia. "But fate, it seems, had other plans."

He closed the distance between them until he was standing face to face with Tahlia, two radiant figures pulsing with divine power.

Tahlia's expression was carefully composed, but vulnerability laced her voice as she said, "I'm sorry. You didn't ask for this existence."

"Every breath I breathed was always yours to command, goddess. My mortal life. My eternal soul. All of it yours. Do with it what you will."

Tahlia lifted herself onto her toes and captured his mouth with hers. Kala's brows shot up in surprise but nothing could have made her happier in that moment. They deserved to find peace with each other, a love unbound by time and death. Kala quickly forced herself to look away, giving them what privacy she could. Henri and Ele did the same but Malik only smiled as he watched unapologetically.

After a moment, the Water Goddess cleared her throat. "You should go now. I will guide the ship safely back to Merovia."

"We need to bury Dema first," Henri said solemnly.

Dema would have likely preferred to be taken back to the Citadel and buried in the Idris Desert but her body would never last the journey.

"Give her to the sea," the Water Goddess replied. "I'll take care of her."

"Samir." Kala blurted out in sudden panic. "What about Samir?"

"He's alive," Tahlia answered. "The God of Earth and Salt left him on the beach near your ship, unconscious."

Kala felt relief flood her system. She couldn't bear to lose anyone else.

"I suppose this is goodbye, then," Henri said, his gaze lingering on Tahlia.

Malik reached for Henri's hand and squeezed it in silent comfort. "At least we get to say it this time."

Malik, Henri, and Tahlia moved toward each other, arms entangling until they held one another in a warm embrace.

"It will never be goodbye between us," Tahlia whispered. "I will always be with you both. In this life and every existence."

CHAPTER TWENTY-EIGHT

WEEKS LATER

ELE

"Are you sure you won't stay a few more days?" Henri asked, not for the first time.

As they gathered at the border between Henri's kingdom and the Idris Desert, Ele tried to ignore Henri's plea disguised as persistence. Of course, Henri and Malik wanted Kala to stay longer. They'd only just reunited with her, and surviving a divine court of judgment had brought them even closer together, but Ele knew what Henri was really asking. For Kala to reconsider her decision to leave *him*.

Kala returned an indulgent smile. "I would love to, but I have been away from my kingdom for far too long. I'll visit again soon, I promise."

Ele could feel Malik's stare burning into him in silent judgment, urging to do something. Say something.

There was no point.

Things had been strained between him and Kala since they'd left the Divine Isle. Kala had endured many things in her life but the loss of Dema and Isa had shaken something deep inside her. She'd spent the entire journey caring for Samir, rarely leaving his side. The experience of being a vessel to the God of Earth and Salt had left him traumatized. It was another reason why she was keen to return home as quickly as possible. Samir's recovery would be easier if he were surrounded by family.

In the current circumstances, it felt selfish to demand even a moment of Kala's attention. But he had been selfish. He'd tried. He'd managed to find a moment alone with her one night and broached the subject, but she'd shut him down before he had a chance to speak. She didn't hold it against him, she said. She understood why he chose to take Isa's life. She forgave him.

Yet she still kept her distance. Barely said a word to him.

Someone nudged his shoulder, interrupting his thoughts and causing him to stumble forward. He glared at Malik who inclined his head pointedly. The camel knelt dutifully as Samir mounted the back hump. This was Ele's last chance. In a moment, Kala would mount the beast and leave. Just like she had when they were children. There was no telling when he would see her again. A year. Five years. Never.

Still, he didn't move. She hadn't said goodbye, but then again, neither had he. Perhaps she didn't know how to because he certainly fucking didn't. Henri cast a glance over his shoulder at him but Ele pretended not to notice. He kept his expression stoic, clinging to his pride because it was all he had left. Beside him, Malik hung his head.

Kala mounted the first hump and ushered the camel to its feet, taking the lead at the front of the caravan. Henri had assigned a dozen soldiers to escort them back to their kingdom but the Captain of the Guard was not one of them. Ele could have volunteered, bought himself a few extra days in her company, but in the end, it wouldn't matter. Although Kala had said she'd forgiven him, it didn't change what he'd done. He'd killed Isa. And even though Isa was a god now, he was still gone.

As the caravan departed, Malik pivoted on his heel and whispered, "You're making a mistake, little shadow."

Henri didn't say a word but he squeezed his shoulder as he walked past Ele to join Malik. Ele knew he was making a mistake but he didn't know what else to do. Even before the Divine Isle, he'd laid his heart bare to her and Kala had hesitated. He couldn't force her to love him. Ele watched the caravan until it disappeared from sight, hoping she would look back even for the briefest of moments.

She didn't.

Perhaps they were never fated to be more than friends. They would return to the way things used to be, writing letters to each other and holding the memories of their friendship sacred. It would never be enough. Not for him. But he would rather have that small part of her than nothing at all.

EPILOGUE

MONTHS LATER

KALA

Kala stared down at a map of her kingdom spread across the table, lost in thought as Cemal slithered across its surface. Unfortunately, none of her thoughts featured the new trading routes she'd established, farm land she'd assigned, or textile techniques her people were endeavoring to learn so that they could trade rare items. These past few months, she'd devoted herself to finding a solution to financially support her kingdom in the absence of the black sand. It was still a work in progress, but it was also a welcome distraction, an excuse not to think about other things. Like the fact that Ele had not written to her since she'd left.

It was her fault. Despite being trapped on a ship together, she'd avoided him the entire journey back from the Divine Isle. She just couldn't think about the future or what they meant to each other until she returned home and pieced her life back together again. There'd been too much uncertainty, too many emotions, and grief that felt like a raw wound. It was not the right time to make life-changing decisions. But now that Samir had recovered and her kingdom had found a level of stability again, her thoughts drifted to Ele. Every night she considered writing to him, but what could she say? After everything they'd survived, everything they'd shared, could they go back to being just friends?

She didn't want to. But she would never ask him to leave Henri for her. Kala sighed at the circular debate that had repeated in her head a thousand times. They'd been doomed from the start. They both knew that. She'd promised not to fall in love with him and now she had to keep her word. Or at least pretend to.

Cemal stared at her, his tongue slipping out to taste the air.

Kala raised a brow at him. "I didn't ask for your opinion."

"Kafei!" Zaynab rushed into the study with Samir and Majid close on her heels. "Sabine has returned to the kingdom."

Kala's stomach plummeted. She knew it was only a matter of time before this day would come. Now that Sabine dominated one of the biggest cartels in Merovia, it was only natural that she would try to muscle her way into Kala's affairs for her own advantage. At best, Sabine would want a percentage of profits from her kingdom's trade. At worst, she would want her crown. Sabine was not to be underestimated. Kala had an army at her back but Sabine also had men under her command.

Kala tried to calm her rising emotions and think strategically. "Is she at the border?"

"She's at the fucking front door!" Majid exclaimed.

At Kala's bewildered look, Samir explained, "The guards escorted her to the throne room. She requested an audience with you."

"And they just let her in!?" Kala cried.

Majid, Samir, and Zaynab exchanged nervous looks before bowing their heads. Kala tried to remember to breathe. She took a moment to think before she began walking. Her friends fell into step beside her. She wasn't armed. She didn't even have daggers hidden on her. She was wearing a light kurta the shade of a pink lotus flower, and her hair was loosely tied into a single braid over her shoulder. Still, she refused to arm herself. If she walked into the throne room dressed for battle, Sabine would know that Kala feared her. It was better to confront Sabine as a minor inconvenience rather than a serious threat. It would throw her off guard, or at least piss her off enough that she might reveal her intentions. Besides, if Kala needed to defend herself, she could do so without a weapon.

"Have the guards secretly assemble. We don't know what she has planned."

"Yes, Kafei," Zaynab replied.

"How many men did she bring with her?"

"Just one."

Kala halted, furrowing her brows in confusion at her friends, before she resumed her pace. Anticipation crawled under her skin. Most likely, she was wrong but she didn't want to be. One man.

When Kala strode into the throne room, her attention immediately bypassed Sabine and went straight to the soldier standing at her side.

Ele.

"Sister!" Sabine flashed a mischievous grin. "I heard that even the gods couldn't kill you. Now that you've returned to your kingdom, you must be working hard to restore its prosperity. I have some ideas for how I can help you with that, but I also thought you might kill me on sight so I brought the Captain here to ensure my survival. They say he, too, is favored by the gods."

Kala barely heard her words because Ele was staring at her with his ocean eyes and it was all she could do to stare back. He was here. He'd come to her. She reined in her heart before it could bolt off into wild fantasies. Ele had accompanied Sabine in an official capacity, perhaps to ensure that they both didn't kill each other. That didn't mean he'd come for anything else.

"Wine!" Majid announced suddenly. "We can't start negotiations without wine. Sabine?"

Majid made a beeline for Sabine, hooking his arm into hers and practically dragging her backwards out the door.

"Do you have any balgarum?" Sabine asked.

"Of course I do," Majid whispered conspiratorially.

Zaynab and Samir followed them, casting a hopeful glance back at Kala before leaving her alone with Ele. The throne room suddenly felt too big, the space between them too wide, but she didn't try to close it. Her pulse was hammering in her ears, she swore it was echoing off the walls. Ele looked at her expectantly. Kala had thought she'd memorized how handsome he was, what it felt like to be under his gaze, but she hadn't. Her memory was a poor substitute for this moment. It didn't capture the warm flush that rose to her cheeks, the slight tremor in her hands that she tried to hide. Kala knew she should be the first to speak but she was at a loss for what to say.

"This is unexpected." Realizing that didn't sound welcoming at all, she rushed to add, "It's good to see you."

"You too. Samir looks better."

"He is. It's taken some time but we're all just trying to move forward with our lives."

Kala mentally chastised herself. It sounded like she was dismissing him, like she didn't want to talk about the past, but that wasn't true. She wanted to talk about what had happened between them. What they were to each other now.

"Are you?" she stammered, trying to recover. "Moving forward?"

Ele's steps were casual as he approached her. "I am."

What did he mean by that? Had he already moved on from what had happened between them? Had he moved on to someone else? If it was Sabine, Kala might actually scream.

"That's good." Kala forced the words out. "I was worried when I didn't receive a letter from you."

Ele stopped to stand in front of her, his nearness igniting every nerve ending in her body. "I told you I don't want to write you letters anymore."

Her heart sank. She knew things had become messy between them, but it had never entered her mind that he might want to end their friendship because of it.

"I see."

She didn't see at all. If she knew that falling in love with him would make her lose him then she never would have done it. Kala startled at the thought. It was the first time she'd allowed herself to name what she'd been feeling all this time. She'd avoided it because naming it somehow gave it the power to destroy her. She didn't want to get hurt or be let down but here she was anyway. Heartbroken.

Kala squared her shoulders, trying to collect herself. "So that's why you came? To tell me that in person?"

"Mmmm. And to ask you a question."

She searched his eyes for a hint of what more pain he could possibly inflict on her. "What's that?"

"Are you mine?"

Kala's breath stalled.

"I resigned as Captain of the Guard and left Henri's kingdom. All the things that I own are in two saddlebags waiting outside. I have no home. No king. No purpose. So I'm asking you, are you mine?"

Butterflies took flight in her stomach as tears sprung to her eyes. The answer was as instinctive as breathing, as unchangeable as the stars, as inevitable as fate.

"I am yours, Eleuterio. Only yours."

REVIEW REQUEST AND BONUS SCENES

Thank you so much for reading this book! I hope you enjoyed it. It would mean the world to me if you could leave a review on Amazon, Goodreads, or BookBub. One of the most important keys to an indie author's success is book reviews. Book reviews give social proof to potential readers that it is highly likely they will enjoy the book. With so many options for books out there, book reviews are a must! Especially at launch time. By leaving a review, you are helping other like-minded readers to find my book and therefore are greatly assisting me in building my career as an indie author. So thank you!

If you enjoyed this series, you'll love the FREE bonus scenes which you can get by signing up to my monthly newsletter. It's easy, just go to my website at www.clairebutlerauthor.com and sign up!

Find me at:
https://www.instagram.com/clairebutlerauthor/

Clairebutlerauthor | Facebook

Clairebutlerauthor (@clairebutlerauthor) | TikTok

Also by Claire Butler

THE RED WOOD SERIES
To Reclaim A Kingdom
To Reforge A Destiny

THE DIVINE TAPESTRY SERIES
Of Sand & Silk
Of Sky & Embers

ABOUT THE AUTHOR

Claire wrote her first book before she knew how to write the alphabet. It consisted of scribbling on a page and having her sister illustrate the page next to it. She has since refined her books to include actual words. Claire has a background in Psychology. She loves writing fantasy romance books because it allows her to explore social themes in new worlds, intense emotions, the formation and shifting of identities, the power of first love, and the enduring bonds of friendship. Claire lives in Australia with her husband and two children. She is obsessed with beaches, picnics, and sunshine. Often in combination with a good book. Her favorite authors include Sarah J Maas, Renee Ahdieh, Carissa Broadbent, and Tahereh Mafi.

If you enjoyed this book, please consider joining my monthly newsletter to receive information on future book releases and promotions.

It's easy, just go to my website at www.clairebutlerauthor.com and sign up!

ACKNOWLEDGMENTS

As always, the first acknowledgment goes to Menna my literary soul sister, work wife, soul mate, alpha reader and all-round hype woman. We fell in love years ago and even though it's not romantic love, it's the best kind of love.

To my beta readers Savannah, Teresa, and Sara – thank you!!! Your keen eyes, insightful reflections, amazing suggestions, and enthusiasm for this book made it so much better. I am so lucky to have you ladies.

Endless thanks goes to my editor Elyse at Phoenix Rising Literary Services for proofreading this book. You are so much more than an editor to me and I can't recommend your services highly enough.

To my ARC team and street team (aka Claire's Camels) thank you so much for championing this book.

Lastly, thank you to you, dear reader. I hope you loved this book and that we will meet again soon.

www.ingramcontent.com/pod-product-compliance
Lightning Source LLC
LaVergne TN
LVHW041616060526
838200LV00040B/1300